FOR THREE LINES

JEFF LEFKOWITZ

Mazo Publishers

For Three Lines

ISBN: 9781-956381-979

Contact The Author
jefflefkowitz6@gmail.com

Mazo Publishers
Website: www.mazopublishers.com
Email: mazopublishers@gmail.com

54321

This book is dedicated to

Blaine Bull,

one of the good guys.

FOREWORD

For Three Lines is a historically accurate novel. Most characters and the city "Krasau" are fictional, but the history is painfully accurate as detailed in the Historical Notes at the end of the book.

A primary purpose of this book is to honor the young men and women – in many cases boys and girls – who, with their elders, suffered to a degree unfathomable and yet persevered, including through resistance. Common to so many, and a driving force behind the original sources on which this novel is based, was the desire that they and their experiences be remembered. This book hopes to contribute toward that aim.

The title is based on the words of Aharon Liebeskind (1912-1942), the Krakow Akiva Zionist youth group's oldest leader, who said the young Jews' desperate fight against the Nazis was "for three lines in history."

Note. To avoid confusion for American readers, this novel does not use the metric system, though Poland used it during the 1930s and 1940s, or "military time" (a 24-hour clock).

"Palestine" has the meaning understood at the relevant times, as explained in the Historical Notes for the first chapter of Part One.

PROLOGUE

May 19, 1942
Krasau, Poland
Anna

Anna studied her reflection in the bathroom mirror.

She carefully applied light-lavender eyeshadow onto her eyelids and brushed it all the way from lash lines to eyebrows. Lighter shade on the lid and a deeper color on the creases to give her blue eyes a deep-set look. Like the Hollywood actresses.

She lined her eyelashes with a black pencil and applied mascara to both top and bottom. After packing a layer of foundation, she lightly brushed on powder to keep her skin soft and glowing.

Anna smiled. "Hi – been waiting long?" she muttered to herself. "No, I've done enough sitting today." She smiled again.

Her right hand shook slightly as she reached for the lipstick. The distant horn from a streetcar meant it was 4:00 p.m. Plenty of time. Deep breath.

She painted her lips red, and her eyes narrowed as she thought about the hours ahead. Outside the Pulaski Café, to the right of the door, he'll be holding a folded newspaper in his left hand. Tall, blonde and handsome.

Newspaper in the left hand, not the right. Approach him only if he is alone.

Anna didn't like the tint of her cheeks; she dabbed some lipstick and rubbed it in with her fingers. She shook her blondish-brown hair out of a bun and smiled wide to rehearse what she wanted the world to see. "Hi – been waiting long?" Pause. "No, I've done enough sitting today." Smile.

She put on her hat and coat, walked downstairs, and strolled from the apartment building down the sidewalk. She caught herself looking at her feet as she walked and immediately lifted her head and eyes. Don't ever look down, she reminded herself. Don't ever look down.

Be confident.

Stay focused.

Though barely past nineteen, the job was hers because she was the best.

•••

Anna walked down Maricka Boulevard. The trees flanking the street burst with spring's bright green leaves. To her right stood a huge Catholic church decorated by an expansive lawn and beautiful flowers. Two young nuns, in habits, sat on the grass enjoying the unusually mild weather; yellow daffodils and purple violets danced in the breeze.

As Anna passed the church, the aroma of kielbasa pork sausage greeted her from a sausage stand. Next to it along the sidewalk stood a street vendor hawking cheese, potato, and beef pierogis to two German soldiers on leave. Anna momentarily joined the sausage line but looked at her watch, frowned and hurried to the No. 6 trolley in front of Kunkel's department store.

She knew the No. 6 line well. It ran on tracks through the center of town, past the old police station and across the river. Anna had grown up in Krasau, a city of four hundred thousand people between Warsaw and Krakow.

She entered the crowded trolley car, which on the outside resembled a red passenger train car with large front and side windows but had a bus-like interior for passengers to sit or stand. A middle-aged man offered his seat, near a window, and Anna graciously accepted. A woman standing near her was reading a letter, others stared into space; two seated older men talked. A young mother across the aisle played little piggy with her toddler's fingers; he squealed adorably.

Anna paid close attention to her fellow passengers, more keenly than most. For self-preservation.

She caught eyes with the young mother and her little boy. "Meow," Anna purred at the child. "Meow."

"Is she a kitty cat?" the mother asked her son.

"No. She's a doggie!" he teased.

"Ruff ruff," Anna barked.

The boy giggled; his mother pulled a picture book from her bag, grabbing his attention.

One of the older men seated near Anna looked at her and smiled. Anna smiled back. The man enjoyed sitting near this cheerful girl, especially with all the gloom and doom around. Dressed nicely, he thought, she must be meeting friends at a café or going home from work at a fancy store. She reminded him of his niece, a typical Polish Catholic girl. He liked being around his own kind.

The man wouldn't have believed that Anna Allowitz was different. Fatally different.

She took a breath and began to relax. Her rendezvous was still an hour away. Always nervous when prepping, Anna usually calmed down after settling into a streetcar. Something about them. Warm feelings from when she was little? Whatever the reason, she'd take it.

Anna knew that most people judged others based on scanty bits of information. This included her fellow passengers. And undercover police. And Germans who might put a bullet in her head if they learned her true identity. She'd been trained to use her appearance, demeanor, and words to manipulate them to see what she pretended to be.

To survive, she lied. About everything. Not only for herself, but for her organization and those they hoped to save.

Softly smiling, Anna stretched and furtively glanced around the car. Everyone was self-absorbed. She thought of an old friend who once lived in this neighborhood. Her friend was gone, and most people she knew would also soon be gone. Years ago, friends were "gone" when off on vacation. Gone now meant something very different. Horribly permanent.

The trolley honked its horn and pulled up to the next stop, in a commercial area, and the man who had smiled at Anna exited. She gazed out the window. The sidewalk in front of the stores was full of people milling around or walking this way and that. Young women pushing baby carriages, men and women window shopping. People walking arm in arm, wearing fashionable hats and purses.

Anna noticed a young woman and her boyfriend holding hands. They looked so in love. A flower vendor offered the couple a bouquet of roses. The corners of Anna's lips curved into a sad smile, and she felt a familiar pang. She allowed the relaxed part of her mind to take her back to the night she'd met Mordecai. It was so long ago...

Anna had been in love. A love only poets and dreamers like Anna could imagine. A love that could not have been deeper or more real and would last forever. She had known it. So had he; she knew that too. But he and love were no longer here.

She sighed at what was lost but returned to the present and reminded herself to feel fortunate. With all that had changed, Anna would be selfish to ask for happiness now.

PART ONE

Closing the Trap

FOUR YEARS EARLIER, MAY 8, 1938
ANNA

After Passover, Anna's best friend, Estie, had dragged soon to be seventeen-year-old Anna to the Spring Celebration. Because "lots of Jewish boys will be there." Anna went because she wanted to help Estie land her first boyfriend, a noble but daunting task.

"Come with me!" Estie had said. "You're great at talking to boys."

Anna, who dated but never had a long-term boyfriend, said, "My specialty is drawing them in, not keeping them. Catch and release."

"Perfect. Line them up, and I'll choose. That's how it works, right?"

Anna thought it did seem true for the beautiful girls in their class. Boys hovered, making fools of themselves. Some people, like Mama and Bubbie, Anna's grandmother, said Anna was pretty. But she thought of herself as average looking, not pretty or unpretty. Average height, thin bordering on skinny. When Anna was little, people said she was so skinny she could hide by turning sideways.

It annoyed Anna that boys didn't notice smart, kindhearted, shy Estie, with her sleepy eyes and big nose. That Estie was the most clever, funny, creative person didn't seem to matter to boys who drooled over pretty girls. But as Bubbie would say, "Don't cry when your dog doesn't grow feathers."

Anna envied Estie. Because Estie never stopped trying. Anna was so afraid of failing – at everything – that she quit whenever she felt pressure. Fear, not laziness. Caring too much, not too little. The more important a project was to Anna, the less likely she'd finish it. Then came excuses, which were better than admitting she was afraid. A person should know her limitations. A turtle shouldn't expect to run fast or a cow to fly. Who needed the angst?

But Anna was happy to help Estie tonight at the Spring Celebration, a fancy name for a Zakkai Zionist youth group event in a huge party room at the Jewish Center. Feeble decorations but lots of music, desserts, at least a hundred teens aged fourteen to eighteen, energy and noise. Food and drink tables adorned with blue tablecloths anchored the middle of the room. Most of the girls huddled in scattered clumps, same with the boys. Some boys were playing an improvised soccer/football game, running around, cheering and yelling.

Anna had arrived late and found Estie at a pastry table, where Estie swallowed two apple strudels other than the powdered sugar that now topped her black sweater. Anna brushed it off, tidied up some wayward, brown curls on one side of Estie's face and said, "I love your sweater. You look so pretty!"

During the first few minutes, a tall boy scouted them and the desserts, ate a strudel and retreated with baked apple on his fingers. No one else approached. "We should have brought a ball for you to bounce," Anna said. "Boys love bouncing balls, like girls and chocolate."

They looked around, and Estie quickly calculated: about two boys their age per girl. Good odds. "OK, so what's the plan?" Estie asked.

"The plan?"

"Yeah. Your strategy on how you'll catch a boy for me."

Anna rubbed her chin. "Shouldn't you first tell me what you're looking for? I'd hate to go to a lot of trouble convincing a boy he's yours if his eyelashes are too long or his shoes the wrong size."

"Good point, and I've thought about it. I used to want a nice, handsome boy who is intelligent, athletic, popular and funny. But I've adjusted my goals."

"To what?"

"I'm now looking for three traits: alive, awake and likes pastries. In a pinch, I'd take a boy with two out of three."

"Estie," Anna laughed, "if you could relax and talk to boys like you talk to me, you'd–" Anna heard a deep, "Hi" from behind her left shoulder. She turned and saw a square face smiling at Estie. Straight nose, dark-brown hair curling over the tips of his ears, dimpled chin. The guy was wearing a stiff white shirt and dark slacks.

Cute! Anna knew Estie thought so because Estie's only words were "Hi... um... um."

"Welcome to Zakkai's Spring Celebration. I'm Mordecai. What's your name?"

"Esther," she giggled. Estie clutched Anna's arm. "And this is Anna."

He turned to Anna and saw a sincere smile and blondish hair that set her apart in a room full of dark-haired girls. Her hair was pulled back behind her ears and flowed onto her shoulders. He didn't notice the pink sweater because his eyes refused to leave her face.

"Hi Anna. I'm one of the Zakkai leaders. My job is to tell you about our group and answer q-q-q-questions," he stuttered. Mordecai gave them a short spiel about Zakkai and about himself. Eighteen, finished school, works at a butcher shop, avid Zionist, moving to Palestine at the end of the year.

"When we walked in," Anna said, "some Zakkai person told us about the group's leaders and said the one named Mordecai is really smart, an athlete, a member of an important Zionist–"

"You must have t-t-talked to my mother," he grinned.

"No, it was a guy..." He's modest, Anna thought. Could be a great catch for Estie.

Mordecai reached for a cinnamon cookie.

"You like cinnamon?" Anna asked. "Estie makes the BEST cinnamon desserts. And the best chocolate desserts, and the best everything."

Mordecai smiled at Estie. "The best everything?" She blushed and bit her lip.

"If you're lucky, Estie might tell you some of her secrets."

"Have you baked a long t-t-time, Estie?" Mordecai asked.

"Um, yeah, I guess," Estie said.

"Are you kidding?" Anna said. "Estie was a child prodigy – they called her the Chopin of babka."

Estie gave Anna a sideways glare.

"Do you work at a bakery?" Mordecai asked.

"No," Estie said, looking down.

"Estie is really talented." Anna smiled.

"Very cool," Mordecai said, his eyes locking onto Anna's smile. He paused but finally said, "What's your talent, Anna?"

"I'm talentless. But Estie isn't just a baker, she also–"

"Anna, I don't remember seeing you at other Zakkai programs," Mordecai said. He shifted away from Estie and faced Anna. "I don't know about baking, but that's OK because my job tonight is to t-t-talk to the talentless people." He smiled at Anna.

She saw the disappointment in Estie's face. "You must spend a lot of time talking to the mirror," Anna said.

Estie walked away, and Mordecai bristled. "What the–"

Anna crossed her arms. "If empathy is a talent, you don't have any."

A sad look spread across Mordecai's face, but he quickly recovered. "I was nice t-t-to her, but it's not right to lead people along if you're not interested."

"Good point," Anna said. She walked away.

• • •

Anna caught up to Estie at another dessert table. "That was a practice round," Anna said. "Don't worry–"

"That boy likes you!" Estie said.

"Nah–"

"And he's cute! Those big eyes with the wavy brown hair, and his smile. I'm the one who came here looking for a boy–"

"Yeah, his eyes were definitely burning in my direction. I thought my pimples would burst. But some guys are just born with those eyes. It doesn't mean a thing. See–" Anna pointed at Mordecai across the room laughing with other girls. "His eyes are probably smoldering at them."

"I go to a lot of picture shows. You wait. He'll be back – unless he's afraid. I think you made him nervous, the way he was talking."

"No, he wasn't nervous. He has a stutter, and people who stutter can't help it. I guess he deserves credit; he's not afraid to talk to people. But enough about him, let's scope out some boys with better taste."

Anna and Estie joined a group of girls they knew and talked about everything other than Zakkai or Zionism. After a while, Anna reminded Estie that she was there for boy hunting.

"I could use more strudel first," Estie said. They walked toward a dessert table, but Mordecai and two boys intercepted them.

"Estie," Mordecai said. "This is Avram and Tolek. They both love challah, and Avram's favorite dessert is babka. His father owns a bakery, and Tolek tries to be their best customer."

"My father made the strudel," Avram said, pointing at the dessert table. "Have you had any?"

"I'm on my way," Estie said. She and the two boys headed toward the desserts.

Anna smiled at Mordecai. "That was very sweet – if those boys are being sincere."

"They're good guys." He glanced at the boys and turned back to Anna. "I'm glad you came tonight to give Zakkai a try. Are you a Zionist or–"

"I'm a Zionist, my father is a Zionist. But I'm not much of a joiner. I'm here to keep Estie company."

"We have a lot planned tonight, and b-b-be sure to stay to the end for the folk dancing. Like our p-p-pioneers in the land of Israel who dance around bonfires. But we'll circle the punch bowl."

A ball from the boys' football game rolled near Anna's feet. She scooped it up and awkwardly tried to throw it back across the room, but the ball fell out of her hand, hit a chair near them and rolled to a stop a few feet away. A boy ran over and retrieved it. "When I said I'm not talented, I forgot about my throwing skills," Anna said.

"I see that. I know this is your first time to Zakkai, but if you'd like to get involved, Leah, one of the people in charge, is forming a group for new girls who'd come once a month and–"

"I'm not much into committing to that sort of thing."

"What sort of things d-d-do you commit to?"

"Nothing comes to mind."

"You're a noncommittal talentless non-joiner?"

"That about sums it up," Anna nodded. "Talentless is a little harsh because I am talented at not committing."

"You're only here to k-k-keep your friend company."

"Right."

Mordecai sighed and turned to leave. "Have fun tonight."

"You don't need to go."

"But–" A ball came flying and hit Mordecai in the face. He clenched his fists, looked around, saw the ball rolling a few steps away, picked it up and scowled. Two guys he didn't know, about his age, ran over to get it.

"Sorry," they said.

Mordecai relaxed and managed to smile, though his face still burned from getting smacked. "That's OK. But this is the second t-t-time. You should stop playing football in here. That ball could have hit this g-g-girl or–"

"Could have hit the g-g-girl?" one of the boys taunted.

Mordecai's face darkened. He threw the ball across the large room; it banged against the opposite wall. "Apologize now or I'll break you into t-t-two pieces."

"N-N-N-No," the boy said.

Mordecai stepped toward him, but both boys laughed and ran off.

"Are you OK?" Anna asked. "That must have hurt!"

"Yeah."

"Were you really going to hit him?"

"Yeah."

Anna frowned. "Isn't it childish to fight someone over–"

He shot her an annoyed look. "I didn't ask your opinion."

"I think–"

"I'm supposed to mingle and tell new people about Zakkai." He wanly smiled and walked away.

Anna spotted Estie, across the room, still talking to one of Mordecai's friends. Anna smiled to herself, returned to the group of girls she knew, and joined in their conversation about picture shows and Hollywood stars. She didn't bother trying to meet boys. She wasn't there for that. She did scan the crowd for signs of Mordecai but chided herself for doing it. She did it twice, OK, maybe three more times. All but once, he was talking to girls. If he was supposed to tell new people about Zakkai, why was he always talking to girls – especially pretty ones?

The one time she saw him spend more than a minute talking to boys was when he huddled with three other Zakkai leaders. They looked like nice guys, and Anna could tell they really liked Mordecai. One playfully threw his arm around Mordecai's neck, and another was laughing with him. Anna noticed that Mordecai was a lot shorter than the other three. He'd seemed tall when she was talking to him.

After a while, Zakkai leaders divided everyone into groups and led discussions about Zionism's goal of Jews returning to their ancient homeland. Then came folk dancing. Anna normally got nervous dancing – but this, with its loud, upbeat music, was different. They started with circle dances – grabbing each other's hands, tugging, weaving feet in and out. Then came the line dances, which Estie loved because girls could grab a boy's hand as easily as a boy might grab a girl's. Everyone was switching partners, laughing, and singing to the Hebrew words as best they could while music blared on the gramophone.

Mordecai didn't so much as glance at Anna the entire time. At least not while Anna spied on him.

They announced the final dance, a Jewish Mazurka, and Mordecai appeared from nowhere to ask Anna if she'd be his partner. She felt herself blush and said, "I'm sorry, but I don't know ho–"

"No p-p-problem." He took her hand and led her onto the floor with other dancers.

Terrified, she reflexively tried to pull away. "I'm a non-dancing, talentless–"

But he whispered, "Don't worry," and the music began. "I'll show you." He took her left hand, placed his on her back and guided her.

Through twirls and hops, he gave her tips and whispered, "You're doing great... You're doing great." He kept his eyes on her face; she looked at her feet, afraid she'd step on his. She felt incompetent, embarrassed and happy.

As the music stopped, he smiled into her eyes and whispered, "Thank you." She smiled back. Still holding her, he said, "That wasn't so bad, was it?"

"That was one of the not so baddest things I've done in a long time."

•••

Mordecai walked Anna and Estie home. Though Anna lived closer, he took a roundabout route to reach Estie's place first. "Like in a picture show," Estie muttered to Anna as she and Mordecai turned to walk away. At Anna's door, Mordecai said, "I could meet you tomorrow at 3:30 at the library n-n-n-near your school–"

"I won't be at the library tomorrow."

"You will if you come help me p-p-plan the next Zakkai event."

"I need to study. Why would I want to–"

"To be nice?"

"Why at the library?"

"Why not? And I've heard people study there."

Anna's instinct to flee was under attack by Mordecai's eyes. Nothing she couldn't handle, but she decided to meet him – just this once – because of how he'd redeemed himself with Estie. "OK, I'll see you tomorrow at 3:30."

•••

At the library, Mordecai led Anna into a crowded, quiet room, where they sat next to each other at an empty table. The only sounds in the place were of pages turning or an occasional cough. For about fifteen minutes, he whispered his plans for the next Zakkai event, and she said what she thought. She then laid her books on the table and began to study; he noticed her composition notebook and whispered, "Can I read this?" Anna nodded.

Flipping the pages, his mouth opened and stayed open. He laughed a couple times and whispered, "This is so incredibly good! You could be a professional writer."

An elderly couple walked into the room and sat at their table.

"You're very talented for a talentless person," Mordecai whispered.

Anna shrugged. "I think the man across from us is mad we're

talking." Mordecai glanced at the guy, who glared back.

"Should we go outside?" Anna asked.

"No. We were whispering when he sat down. He could have gone somewhere else."

Anna flushed red; she didn't like confrontation. "OK," she whispered as quietly as she could. "You said you're moving to Palestine this year?"

"Yeah – November, in six months."

"With your parents?"

"No, only me."

Anna made a worried face. "I'd be scared to move so far away by myself. Are you afraid? Do you have family there?"

"No, but I'll make friends. I've been dreaming of this my whole life." Mordecai's eyes lit up. "What an amazing time – our generation has the chance to reestablish our nation in Palestine after two thousand years, and I want to do my part."

"My father is a big Zionist and taught me some history. Masada, Bar Kokhba down to Herzl–"

Mordecai whispered, "Do your parents want to move there?"

"My father says maybe next year."

"The old 'Next year in Jerusalem' that people say but don't do?"

Anna shrugged. "Someday, I hope."

"Hmm... I have an idea. I could teach you Hebrew farming words that pioneers should know," Mordecai whispered, ignoring the "Shh!" from the man across the table. "So if you do go, you'll be ready."

Anna rested her chin in her hand, stared at Mordecai and furrowed her brow.

"What?" he asked.

"This isn't polite, but why – how are you talking so much without stuttering?"

"I don't stutter when I whisper."

A smile slowly crept across Anna's face, and she nodded. "Ah, that's why we're at the library." She was beginning to admire this guy.

Mordecai smiled back. "Do you want to come over tomorrow and learn some advanced Hebrew?"

"Tomorrow, at your home?"

"Yeah."

Anna felt her stomach tighten. The familiar feeling that meant she liked this boy. She put her hand in front of her face and blocked her view of his eyes.

"What are you doing?"

"Defending myself."

He tilted his head. "So, tomorrow?"

"I can't."

"Day after tomorrow?"

"Sorry, I can't." She dropped her hand and crossed her arms.

"I can't the rest of this week," Mordecai said. "What about a week from today?"

Anna sighed and again blocked his eyes with her hand. He's persistent. But he's too smart not to get the message. She slightly spread her fingers and squinted, through the gap, at his eyes. He's moving away. And maybe he's just a nice Zionist guy who wants to teach people Hebrew.

"OK."

•••

A week later, Anna walked from school to Mordecai's family's apartment in Krasau's old Jewish section. Mostly poor, Jews had lived there for generations, including Anna's family when she was little. Anna made her way down a long street filled with small tailor, shoemaker, bookbinding, hat making, and similar shops abutting the narrow sidewalk, their outside walls plastered with advertisements in Jewish script.

She walked past four little synagogues – out of the eighty dotting the Jewish area – politely ignored peddlers hawking their cheap goods, and turned onto a winding, cobblestone street lined with shabby three- and four-story apartment buildings, butted up against each other, all facing the street.

Mordecai was waiting on the sidewalk in front of his building. He led Anna into the run-down front entry and up three flights of creaking stairs to a small apartment. An aroma of baked cinnamon met them inside a tidy, little sitting room. The walls were decorated with old photos of grandparents, aunts, uncles and cousins, a large radio rested on a small table against one wall, and a dark-brown couch sat against the other. A floor lamp separated the couch from a light-brown, wooden chair. In front of the couch was a low, oak coffee table, and sitting on it was a warm cinnamon babka.

Mordecai sat on the couch, and Anna sat in the chair. "That smells so good!" Anna said.

"My m-m-mother baked it for you," he said, cutting them each a piece. Anna thought most boys would be embarrassed to say that.

For an hour, Mordecai taught her Hebrew agricultural terms, and he was impressed by how quickly Anna learned. She liked that he didn't let his stuttering stop him. "Repetition is important when studying a f-f-foreign language," he said at the end. "If you come back tomorrow–"

"Tomorrow?"

"To reinforce what you learned today."

Anna sighed. "Will the babka go stale if I'm not here tomorrow to help finish it?"

"Probably."

They met again the next day, Mordecai on the couch and Anna again in the chair. Lots of complicated agricultural terms.

"They have a lot of big words for such a small place," she said.

After an hour, Mordecai looked at his watch. "Time's up; I need to go to work." He walked her to the door. "You've learned a lot. But we should meet again to-m-m-morrow. For another session. Like I said, constant p-p-practice is very important, especially with so many tough words."

Anna stuck her hands on her hips. "I was here two days in a row. You expect me to come back again tomorrow?"

"Remember, you're a Zionist. All Jews, especially Zionists, should learn Hebrew. Come back tomorrow if you want to learn. I already know this stuff."

"Well, I AM a Zionist."

"Right."

"There's no other reason for me to come here."

"Correct."

She paused. "Alright. I want to learn, and to learn I need repetition... I'll be here tomorrow. To learn Hebrew. That's why I'm coming. To learn Hebrew. In case my family moves to Palestine."

"Exactly."

The next day, their Hebrew vocabulary expanded from farming to "Your eyes are so pretty." They walked to a park after studying in the apartment, and Mordecai picked her some "perachim" or, as Anna learned, "flowers" in Hebrew. She came over again the following day, took his hand when they walked upstairs, sat next to him on the couch, and he kissed her. Then she kissed him much longer.

"That was just part of learning Hebrew," Anna whispered.

Two days later, they went to the zoo. "You never know when you might need to say hippopotamus in Hebrew," Anna said. She packed a picnic lunch, and they spent the afternoon strolling along the river, holding hands. The next night, they went to a picture show and sat in the back row "so we can practice more Hebrew."

They saw each other or talked on the phone almost every day for the next three weeks.

•••

"What's it like to set a world record?" Estie asked Anna while they walked to a going away party for a friend moving to Warsaw.

"World record?"

"Yeah, your own personal one. You've been dating the same boy an entire month and have seen him, I think, between eight thousand and ten thousand times. I lost count. You were scheduled to break up with him three weeks ago and should have turned into a frog the third time he kissed you."

"I know..."

"So – what's it like?"

"It depends on who you ask. My heart would say it's wonderful, the greatest thing ever. But if you ask my stomach, you'll get moaning and groaning and stressing."

"At least you're the same Anna."

Anna loved talking to Estie. Not only because she was smart, nice, fun and said what she thought. But also because Anna knew that no secret entering Estie's ears exited her mouth.

"And your brain?" Estie asked. "That brilliant, wise mind of yours – the envy of me and everyone who knows you. What does it say?"

Anna sighed. "It's working overtime, trying to keep my heart and stomach from killing each other."

"I think a switch was installed in you backwards. You're supposed to fret when you can't catch a boy, not when you have one."

Anna shrugged, and they walked into their friend's house. The party was fun. Anna enjoyed talking to people, including a boy she had dated a few times but broke up with while she still had a crush on him. When she left the party, Anna was thinking about him, and about what Estie had said, and about Mordecai.

•••

Anna and Mordecai didn't see each other for several days because Anna was busy with exams, but her first free afternoon, Mordecai walked her from school to his family's apartment. Holding hands, he introduced her to an old man, a neighbor, standing outside. "I'd like you to m-m-meet Anna," he said, squeezing her hand very tight when he stuttered. She almost said something but kept quiet.

Upstairs, Anna laid her books on the coffee table, and they sat next to each other on the couch. She looked over a list of Hebrew terms, and Mordecai asked if he could read "her c-c-c-composition notebook."

"Sure," she said, noticing his clenched fist when he struggled to say "composition."

Mordecai leaned back and leafed through the notebook, occasionally muttering, "Wow, you're amazing!" Anna stopped studying and stared at him.

Turning the pages, he saw something Anna had written and dated two days earlier entitled "Ephraim." Mordecai knew of a popular boy named Ephraim but couldn't remember if he went to Anna's school. Mordecai glanced at Anna, whose eyes were on him; he looked back down at the notebook and read silently. "Ephraim, I love you so much. I can't explain all the reasons, but I'll start with your beautiful smile. You bring a glow to every room you enter. You are so naturally happy and kind. Each day, I love you more. It's hard to remember life without you..." She had drawn little hearts and flowers across the page.

Mordecai's face burned with anger and pain, and he looked again at the date. Two days ago. He scowled at her, sitting next to him on the couch. She was staring with a concerned look on her face.

"Can I ask you something?" she said.

"Yeah, but I need to ask you something f-f-f-first." His voice cracked with emotion. "Who is Ephraim?"

"Ephraim? Why–"

Mordecai dropped the open notebook onto her lap.

"He's my baby brother. Turning three. I write him each year on his birthday, and we're saving the letters for when he's older."

"Your brother?"

"Uh huh."

"I thought your brother's name is Frammy."

"Guess what Frammy is a nickname for."

Mordecai slapped his face and sighed deeply. "I knew that. I wasn't thinking."

"Guess not. My turn. When we were outside, you squeezed my hand tight when you stuttered, and you clenched your fist–"

"Yeah, so."

"It must be hard on you, to stutter."

"Not really, it's no b-b-b-big deal."

"Like the night we met, and you were going to beat up that guy–"

Mordecai raised his voice. "What's your p-p-point!"

"And the way you're mad now, ten seconds after you said it's no big deal."

He glowered at her but didn't say anything.

"I had thought you were amazing the way you just march forward and talk to people – you make it look simple. But now–"

"I'm no longer amazing?"

She threw her arm around his neck and whispered in his ear. "You're even MORE amazing because the secret truth is that it isn't easy at all. It's hard, but you do it anyway."

He removed her arm from his neck. "Can't you see I don't want to t-t-t-talk about this?"

Anna was silent.

"I know," she finally said, "but I do. I need to hear what you've gone through because – because the last time I cared even half this much for a guy without bailing on him was never. I need to know what it was like for you growing up with a stutter. Please?"

He frowned.

"I know it's hard, but... please."

Mordecai looked down at his hands and muttered softly, "OK. It wasn't easy, but I'm strong and I learned to fight." He shrugged.

Anna smiled. "The End? No, I want the whole story."

He sighed but told her how old he was when he first stuttered, and exactly what he was doing when a neighbor imitated him and made him cry. How he'd tried to hold his breath to make his stutter go away. That he'd prayed and promised to be a good boy. Did everything he could think of, but nothing worked.

"It got so bad, I was afraid to leave m-m-my house, I hated school. Always scared to open my mouth, and I didn't have any f-f-friends because I was afraid–" his voice cracked, and he turned away.

Anna took his hand and held it with both of hers; he looked at her with tears in his eyes. "A boy imitated me, and I hit him, and I sat on him and hit him again and again until the teacher pulled me off. My parents punished me. 'You must d-d-d-deal with this other ways,' they said. 'You need to learn that words can't hurt you.'"

Mordecai stood and started pacing. "For the first t-t-t-time in my life, I ignored my parents. I fought and became good at it. As I got older, I started lifting weights, became strong and learned wrestling and boxing. And when people made fun of me, I used what I'd learned. After a while, I didn't n-n-need to fight any more. But I was always ready.

"And I learned what it means to be a friend. Luckily, I have some very good friends – you know that. I'll miss them when I move away."

Anna clasped her hands between her knees. "If I were you, I'd have just hidden in a corner."

"No. You can't run from life."

"I guess you don't know me so well after all."

"What does that m-m-mean?" He walked toward her.

"That I'm a coward. A chicken. Every time I start something I care about, I quit so I don't mess it up. You say I'm a good writer? My teachers kept bugging me to write an essay for a national competition. Two years in a row, I started essays but didn't finish. Either one. Too scared I'd lose. I could give you a ton more examples, starting with why I keep thinking about running away from you instead of to you."

Mordecai furrowed his brow, and Anna rose from the couch, stood next to him and grasped his hand.

"You were the perfect guy for me. Because you're leaving. So you could be happy, I could be happy–"

"I could be happy that you're happy I'm leaving?"

"Just go with it. I thought I can't ruin anything with you because it will end on its own when you go. Perfect. Don't you see? You moving was my whisper. But it won't work anymore."

"What? I don't–"

"Because I have some news. My family is moving to Palestine. Next June. Seven months after you get there. My parents told us last night, and I don't know if I'm going to burst from happiness or stress."

"Oh my God!" Mordecai hugged Anna and lifted her off the ground. "This is so fantastic!"

Anna smiled wide. "But I needed to hear what you've been through. If you could deal with that, I can handle my stuff. Maybe. I hope. And besides, it shows you're not Mr. Perfect, and that you need me to teach you things, like not wanting to beat up people."

"I don't always–"

"Even sometimes is too often. You'll see. And since I'm for sure moving to Palestine, there's so much I need to learn from you. Like rhinoceros. How do you say rhinoceros in Hebrew? Or platypus? Who knows if someone from Australia might visit us – well, not us because we may not even see each other in Palestine. By the time I get there, you might have met some dark-haired beauty in short shorts who knows how to say rhinoceros in Hebrew – but I may meet the guy from Australia – and you could be the odd man out when you and I are both in Palestine. At the same time. To live there forever. Like we've dreamed. And until you teach me more fancy Hebrew words, I'll be lying awake every night worrying that I don't know how to say all these things. That's a lot of pressure. So, we need to work hard the next few months to accomplish it all. I hope your work schedule allows for that."

Anna gasped to catch her breath and continued. "If you–"

"Anna."

"Yeah?"

"Karnaf."

"Huh?"

"Rhinoceros in Hebrew is karnaf."

"Oh, good. All my stress is gone."

JULY 3, 1938
PETER WOJCIK

The boy in red shorts bolted across the field from inside his own half, passed the ball to a midfielder, received it back as he raced toward the goal, outran the defenders and calmly side-footed the ball past the diving goalie.

The boy's teammates roared, and middle-aged Peter, the only spectator at the practice game, banged his massive palms on the metal chain link fence separating him from the field. "Great play!" Wow! That kid is fast, Peter thought. And smart. He saw the shot, took charge and made it happen.

Peter Wojcik enjoyed an afternoon break to watch football practices at Pilsudski Park. He would leave the weary tension of life on the streets, cross a busy avenue, and step into the lush park, quiet and tranquil on weekdays. Then he'd amble past a fountain and granite statues of Poland's heroes and stroll down a long tree-lined path to the field. Tucked in pine-scented woods, the only sounds were of the young players kicking a ball, yelling and laughing.

The churches still fielded some very good teams, and watching these practices brought back happy memories. Of better times. When Peter was one of these kids. Young, agile, carefree. He reflexively massaged his bad left knee.

The red-shorts kid reminded Peter of himself – thirty years earlier, when he was thirteen or fourteen like these kids. Long before his marriage, wrecked legs, and an extra hundred pounds. Before he carried a gun, before he spent his waking hours with lowlifes and criminals.

Peter sighed, thinking back on the friends, the competition. He and his cousin had played on the same team and had dominated. "The Wojcik lightning bolts," they'd called themselves. "We were damn good," he muttered to himself. "I was damn good." And he wasn't the only one who said it. Lots of guys said Peter Wojcik had what it took. Even after his cousin moved to America, where they called football "soccer."

Peter watched the boys run some drills and finish their practice. As they walked off the field and toward an open gate, Peter hurried past empty bleachers and called over the red-shorts kid.

The boy, short and wiry with dark hair, shrugged at his friends and jogged to Peter. "You're quite a player," Peter said. "I've been watching you a few weeks. Excellent ball handler, smart. And I like how you take charge and accelerate for the kill. How old are you?"

The boy ran a hand through his hair. "Twelve, sir."

"Wow. What's your name?"

"Reuven."

Peter stifled a frown and eyed the kid's curly hair and Jewish nose. "How long you been on the church team? You go to the church?"

"No, sir. But Coach told me and my friend we could play. A few months ago. He says it's OK."

Peter nodded. This boy will sure as hell get knees in the teeth when he plays other teams. "Kid, I used to play against Jewish teams. Some decent players there. But not everyone is open-minded as me. Take some advice from someone who knows. On the football field, your name is Roman, not Reuven, got it?"

"Um–" the boy glanced at his friends heading away. "Yeah, OK," he shrugged.

"I'm telling you for your own good, boy." Peter's voice was deep and firm, but he flashed his handsome smile – this time sincere. "Roman, you're a great player for your age. I'm going to keep an eye on you, and in five or six years, when you play for Poland in the Olympics, I'll brag I knew you when you were a kid." Peter extended his right arm, and they shook hands.

"Thank you, sir," Reuven said before scampering off to catch his teammates.

Peter Wojcik was likable and good looking, tall and bulky with a round but not chubby face, bright blue eyes, and a friendly smile. And as Officer Peter Wojcik, he had used those attributes to great advantage during his twenty-year police career. The last twelve undercover. First, chasing down thieves, petty criminals, prostitutes, but as his reputation grew, he became THE GUY assigned to the impossible to solve murder cases. And he solved them. Not necessarily with the murderer, but always with someone Peter thought deserved punishment.

Some of his fellow undercover officers were good, but none had the intuition or came close to Peter's network of stooges and finks. No undercover cop could do his job without multiple sets of eyes in addition to the two in his head. And Peter was the best, with his mixture of looks, friendly nature, cash – and willingness to deliver a healthy beating when useful – at recruiting eyes. Criminals sweated when Peter was on their trail.

Of course, law abiding members of society had no reason to fear Officer Peter Wojcik. Why should they?

JULY 6, 1938
SZYMON

To honor the "momentous occasion," as Anna put it, of the almost second monthly anniversary of the night they'd met, Mordecai splurged by taking her to a picture show. "And if you're really nice," he said, "I'll b-b-buy you ice cream afterwards."

They watched a comedy called "Yidl with a Fiddle" about a Jewish father-daughter pair of traveling musicians; the daughter disguised herself as a boy for her safety, which led to all sorts of funny encounters. A big crowd, almost entirely Jewish, had gathered for the early evening show, and Anna and Mordecai were still laughing when it ended and the lights came on.

Holding hands, they walked toward the main theatre entrance. "Ice cream, anyone?" Mordecai whispered. The front door flew open, and a middle-aged woman, eyes wide with fear, ran past them frantically screaming. "I need towels! Wet towels, please! Outside – my husband!"

Mordecai dropped Anna's hand and they ran into the night. Lying face up on the sidewalk was a bearded Jewish-looking man, about forty, wincing and holding his head. Blood dripping down the side of his face. Leaning over him was a shirtless, blondish Pole, about eighteen, pressing his crumpled, white shirt above the man's eye to stanch the bleeding. The shirtless guy was also bleeding, but less so, from his mouth. A noisy throng, mostly Jewish people, were watching from a few yards away.

Mordecai and Anna rushed to the two guys. "What happened!"

"Antisemites," groaned the man on the ground, with his eyes squeezed shut. "Started yelling things and threw rocks – big rocks – at us. One got me. This boy," squinting and pointing up at the young guy, "helped fight them off."

The shirtless guy nodded. "This fellow took a good-sized rock square in the head. And they threw it hard. Probably should go to a hospital." Anna ran inside to ask them to call an ambulance, and the man's wife rushed outside with two wet towels. She knelt and lightly pressed one against her husband's head. The young Pole stood and put on his now red-splotched shirt. He was very tall, a head taller than Mordecai.

"What's your n-n-name – what happened to you?"

"I'm Szymon. I was on my way home – I live near here. Jewish people standing in line waiting for the show. Out of nowhere, three hoodlums started screaming, 'Go back to Palestine!' and other antisemitic things I won't repeat in front of a lady." He glanced at Anna, who had returned from inside.

"This guy," pointing at the man on the ground, "yelled back. The thugs ran at him, and from a few feet away – right on top of him – one heaved a big rock straight into the side of the guy's head, knocking him down. I ran over and grabbed the scummy looking boy who threw it – about sixteen or seventeen. Bigger than you but smaller than me. And then one of the others, almost my size, clocked me in the mouth, knocking me down."

Szymon wiped at blood dripping down his chin and frowned. "They ran away, and I called them cowards and every curse word I could think of to get them to come back." He paused and slyly grinned. "Lucky for me, they didn't. Then you came out."

Szymon seemed more mad than hurt; Mordecai could relate. "I wish I'd b-b-been here earlier so I could have helped you," Mordecai said.

"Oh, great," Anna said. "That's what we need – three good people bleeding instead of two."

"This is ridiculous," a woman in the crowd blurted. "I thought hoodlums had finally stopped attacking Jews in Krasau!"

Mordecai shook Szymon's hand. "You're a good guy. Thanks." Mordecai waved for Anna to go.

"I hope he'll be alright," Anna said as they left. "I just don't understand why some people hate like that."

"Yeah... Can't do much about it, but we can feel better by eating ice cream. Chocolate–"

"I don't really feel like it anymore. Not after–"

"Anna, let's get ice cream. We have something extra to celebrate. In four months for me and eleven for you, no more Jew hatred ever again."

JULY 7, 1938
IRINA

Mid-morning, Mordecai and Anna were sitting in Anna's house, a place Mordecai had set foot in twice for a total of three minutes. The night before, after ice cream, Anna had said, "Mama kvetches to me: 'We barely know this boy; he never visits. Is he afraid we'll bite him?'"

"What would I say to your mother?" Mordecai had asked.

"Isn't talking to her better than lugging around heavy, smelly beef carcasses at your job?"

"Do I have a choice?"

"No," Anna had said, and now here they were watching Anna's three-year-old brother, Frammy, pull himself up on the couch in the living room of Anna's family's home, climb onto the back behind the cushions, and teeter along the top edge. He balanced himself with a hand on the wall until he reached the tall cabinet that the couch butted against. Wrapping his little fingers around a decorative wood trim, he hoisted himself up halfway and then shimmied onto the cabinet top and stood. He reached overhead, almost touching the ceiling, yelled, "One, two, free, go!" and jumped through the air and into Mama's arms. She pretended to drop him onto the hard floor; he giggled, and she kissed his cheeks and tickled his tummy.

"Frammy was born laughing and hasn't stopped yet," Anna said. "Don't you love his dark-brown curls? He got them from my Papa."

"Um, yeah," Mordecai said.

"Frammy was named after Mama's father, Ephraim, who I never met," Anna said.

"Oh," Mordecai said. "Um..." He looked at Anna's mother, who was sitting on the floor holding Frammy on her lap and waiting for Mordecai to say something.

"Mama," Anna said. "Tell Mordecai about your father. He'd–"

"He doesn't want to hear–"

"Yes, I do," Mordecai said. Anything to fill the silence would be good.

"Well, OK," Mama said. "My father was a wonderful man. He lived his entire life in a little town in what is now eastern Poland but had been part of the Russian Empire. My parents were Hasids; my mother still is."

"Do you know the history of the Hasids, how they originated?" Anna asked.

"T-T-Tell me," Mordecai said.

"Eastern Europe is so full of Hasids that everyone thinks they've been here since Moses," Anna said. "But it's only been two hundred years. The Hasidic movement brought joy, song and laughter into Jews' lives. Remember, most Jews were very poor, worse than now. The Hasids said that God didn't want dull, mechanical prayer, and his Jews had enough Torah scholars. God wanted cheerful, sincere prayer and lots of singing. Ya da da da and na na na na did just fine."

"It fit my father perfectly," Mama said, her eyes brightening. "At home and synagogue, he sang and danced. Dressed in his black hat and long dark coat, his bearded face was always smiling."

Mordecai smiled at how upbeat Anna's mother had become, and for the first time, he noticed that Anna looked like her mother. Same eyes, light hair, thin faces. But her mother wore a drab, gray dress very unlike Anna's crisp white skirt, colorful blouse and white scarf.

"Unfortunately," Mama said, "eastern Europe saw much bloodshed after the World War – am I boring you?"

"Not at all." Mordecai meant it.

"Russian communists fought anti-communists, Poles against Russians, Ukrainians against Poles. In March 1919, when I was seventeen and my father was forty, Polish soldiers marched into our town. The Poles had heard Jews there were communists, and they were fighting communists.

"About fifty of the two thousand Jews in our town were communists. The other 1,950 were Hasids like us, or Zionists, or just people wanting to be left alone. But to the Polish soldiers, if some Jews there were godless communists, they all were – what else could the Poles expect of people they believed killed Christ? So, the Polish soldiers did their own killing."

Mama's voice cracked, and she looked down. "Papa and I were in the town square during market day. I watched them murder him."

"I'm s-s-so sorry!" Mordecai said.

"Thank you, and I'm sorry too – I didn't mean to get upset... But three years ago, God brought me Frammy. He couldn't be more like his grandfather. Enjoying life and bringing happiness to everyone. Unlike my papa, Frammy will live a full, long life! We try not to spoil him, but how could he not get special treatment? Especially with Anna all grown up. It's hard to believe Anna was born almost seventeen years ago – she was such an easy child that I once believed I was a great parent."

Mama shook her head. "But then came Irina."

"Where is Irina?" Anna asked.

"In the bedroom, doing who knows what."

"Mama and Irina sometimes fight," Anna said.

"Sometimes? Irina has battled me for eleven years, since the moment she was born. She pished on me the first time I held her and has been pishing on me ever since."

"Mama," Anna said. "Irina also has a big heart and would risk her neck to save not only a cute kitten but also an ugly frog. And Irina is great with Frammy. I wish I could be more like her: independent and feisty."

"Please!"

Irina erupted from the bedroom she shared with Anna. Light haired, she looked to Mordecai like a younger version of Anna, but with a scowl instead of a smile. "I'm not deaf, you know!"

"From the way you ignore what I say, I thought you were," Mama said.

Irina headed to the door.

"Where you going?" Mama demanded.

"I'm meeting Roza."

Mama frowned. "Why not visit with one of your nice friends?"

Irina stopped, turned and crossed her arms. "Roza IS one of my nice friends."

Mama shook her head. "Oh, really?"

"Yeah, REALLY." Irina considered leaving, but she was sick of Mama criticizing everything she did. Now, her friends weren't good enough! "Hey, what's wrong with Roza?"

Mama held her chin in feigned concentration. "I'll think hard to answer... Where should I start? She's wild. She's rude. She's disrespectful. She doesn't say hello or goodbye, she wears heavy lipstick and makeup at twelve years old as if she belongs under a lamppost–"

Irina pivoted and headed for the door.

"Where are you and Roza going?"

"We're – we're going to stand under a lamppost."

Irina slammed the door.

•••

On the other side of Krasau, a young, brown-haired woman sat alone in an outdoor café on Kopernika Street, one block from the heart of the commercial district. Across Kopernika was the grandiose Saint Michael's Church, bordered by Mickiewicz Avenue on the left and an alley on the right. Saint Michaels was famous for its two magnificent bells that rang death knells to welcome parishioners, deserving or not, into heaven.

The young woman, perhaps early twenties, had an oval face, long nose and full lips. Wearing an expensive, fashionable violet dress with a low-cut V-neck, she dined leisurely with a cigarette in one hand and a drink in the other, striking a picture of carefree wealth. A café regular, the waiters knew how to avoid the woman's ire: seat her at a table facing the church and move fast when her fingers snapped.

As usual, the café was crowded and noisy with the clanking of dishes and diners' conversations. Full of customers taking a break from frittering away their money at one of the upscale galleries, stores and boutiques that lined this side of the street.

The young woman had been sitting for an hour when her eyes began to follow a man across the street, wearing a casual blue shirt, walking from her right toward the church. When he reached the alley that abutted it, the man stopped and stood with his hands in his pockets. The woman saw that he was thin and average height but couldn't see his face because his gray fedora hat was pulled down.

After a short time, two young guys approached the blue-shirted man, and they briefly talked. The woman wasn't sure, but she thought one of the guys handed the man something as they ducked into the alley. Soon, all three reappeared; two left and the man in blue remained.

Her eyes glued on the man in blue, the young woman puffed on her cigarette and dropped ashes into the ashtray and onto her round iron table. Soon, another guy approached the man, they briefly spoke, walked a few steps into the alley and handed each other something. This time she was sure. And she got a good look at the man in blue. About thirty years old, long face, light-brown mustache but no beard.

The woman retrieved a pen and paper from her purse, wrote a note and neatly folded it several times. She finished her cigarette, snapped her fingers for another drink and pushed the folded paper, scented by her perfumed hands and cigarette smoke, to the other side of the round table. She returned to watching strollers go by, occasionally glancing at the blue-shirted guy and sipping her drink.

She looked at her watch. Sitting for almost two hours in the afternoon sun, it was now 3:00. She lit another cigarette, looked to her right down the crowded sidewalk, and saw a well-dressed man in his forties, tall and heavy set, walking her direction. When he reached the café, he breezed by the young woman's table without a nod, casually picked up the folded paper and kept going. The young woman blew smoke into the air, opened a newspaper and began to read.

"Regina, we're here!"

The young woman looked up at two young girls and smiled. "Thanks, Roza," she said. "I wouldn't have guessed that."

"OK, whatever," Roza said. "But this is my friend, Irina Allowitz. Irina, this is my oldest sister, Regina."

"Hi," smiled Irina.

"Sit down. I've been saving these chairs for you."

"I told you my sister's rich," Roza bragged. "Do you know ANYONE who can afford a café in this neighborhood?"

Irina shrugged.

"Are you just sitting and watching other rich people walk by?" Roza asked her sister.

Regina grunted. "Is anyone else worth looking at?"

•••

Officer Peter Wojcik, undercover cop, had read the folded paper he scooped from Regina's table, walked two blocks past Mickiewicz Avenue, turned right, and circled back to the opposite end of the alley bordering the church. He was heading up the alley, which smelled of urine, toward his target. The blue-shirted man's back was to him, hands stuffed in his pockets, facing Kopernika Street.

Officer Wojcik was sick of drug dealers selling in nice parts of Krasau.

The man didn't hear him approach until he heard Wojcik's deep voice from behind his back. "Hey – can we do business?"

The drug dealer turned and narrowed his eyes at the big man wearing a coat and tie. "I don't know you, and I don't know what you're talking about."

Officer Wojcik took a step back, smiled wide and raised his open palms. "Didn't mean to spook you. But I hear this is the place to get the best stuff. I've brought a lot of cash. You sure you can't help?"

The dealer sized him up quickly; even the guy's shoes looked rich.

Nicely dressed customers meant wads of money. "What are you looking for?"

"Cocaine."

"How much cash you got?"

"As much as I need."

The dealer smiled, showing two missing teeth. "You came to the right place." He stepped past Wojcik, gestured for him to come deeper into the alley, lifted his shirt and pulled a small paper bag from inside his pants. "This bit here will cost you–"

Wojcik grabbed the drug dealer's shoulders, spun and shoved him face first against the alley's brick wall, knocking off the man's hat. "You're under arrest!"

The drug dealer jerked his head backwards and shrieked, "You broke my nose!" He moaned as blood oozed down his chin. "At least let go of my hand so I can wipe my nose!" He dropped the cocaine bag onto the pavement.

Wojcik loosened his grip and bent to pick up the bag. The man whipped out a knife and stabbed at Wojcik's neck. Wojcik raised his arm in time to block it, grabbed the knife hand, yanked it behind the man's back, and growled, "Big mistake, asshole!"

With one huge, rough hand jerking the guy's arm behind his back and the other clutching a fistful of hair, Wojcik repeatedly smashed the criminal's face against the brick wall. Holding the man upright with one hand, Wojcik then pounded his unconscious face with the other, threw him on the pavement and stomped on his neck.

Panting and purple faced, Wojcik slowly calmed down, looked at his handiwork, wiped sweat off his face, knelt and checked for a pulse. None.

"Oh, what the hell," he muttered, stripping the body of the remaining cocaine bags and emptying the pockets of cash. He'd dispose of the cocaine; the cash was now his.

He wrapped the gash on his arm, cleaned his hands of blood, and snatched an envelope from his coat pocket. He placed a hundred zlotys in it, dropped the envelope back in his pocket and left the alley the direction he'd entered.

•••

Regina snapped her fingers to summon a waiter and ordered her sister and Irina drinks. "How old are you, Irina?"

"I'll be twelve next week."

"Holy Jesus, I thought you were at least sixteen. You're well-developed for your age. I was going to ask if you wanted to meet any boyfriends. But you're a little young for that."

"Thanks, I think," Irina said.

"What about me?" Roza asked. "Do I look sixteen?"

Regina smirked. "About ten. Even with your five coats of makeup."

Roza frowned. "Can I take a few drags on your cigarette?"

"Yeah, but you need to start buying your own."

Roza took some puffs. "I love the feeling of smoke in my lungs. Here–" She blew smoke into Irina's face and jabbed the cigarette toward her, but Irina didn't take it.

"Hey, no thanks. I tried once. Cigarettes and me don't get along."

Regina threw her head back and laughed. "Sometimes you need to try things more than once. Go ahead – you may like it this time."

"Do it," Roza said.

"You'll be sorry," Irina said to Roza. She took the cigarette, placed it between her lips, inhaled, exhaled smoke and coughed. Irina's eyes flicked up at Roza and down at the cigarette. She took two more quick puffs, exhaled and coughed into her hand.

Roza fake coughed and laughed. "You're a baby!"

Irina took another puff and coughed again.

Regina glanced to her left and saw Officer Wojcik walking toward them. She pointed excitedly to the right, said, "What's that!?" and dropped her open left hand onto the table.

Roza and Irina turned to the right; Officer Wojcik slipped an envelope into Regina's left hand and walked by, unnoticed.

Roza and Irina turned back toward Regina, and Irina vomited on Roza.

THE SAME DAY
ANNA

Anna flipped the pages of a Hollywood glamour magazine until her eyes latched onto a picture of the gorgeous actress Norma Shearer wearing a sparkling, black evening gown with a bare shoulder. The dazzling elegance of Hollywood!

Anna loved fashion. She liked colorful clothes and did her best to dress nicely and wear her hair stylishly. She knew she'd never wear stunning clothes like in the magazine. You needed money for that. But she imagined Mordecai decked out in a tuxedo and her in a beautiful white dress under a chuppah in Palestine. He hadn't exactly proposed and there was nothing official, or even unofficial, but there were no rules against dreaming...

Irina burst into the bedroom, where Anna was sitting on the bed the two of them shared.

"Hi, Irina! Did you have fun with Roza?"

"It was OK," Irina muttered.

"What did you do?"

"Nothing much." Irina walked into the room, and a dense odor of cigarette smoke came with her. She trudged to the bed and looked down at Anna. "Mama asked me to help make dinner. Could you PLEASE do it instead? I'm not feeling so great."

"Yeah, sure... Been smoking?"

"Hey, how could you tell?"

"You reek."

Irina sniffed her shoulder and shrugged.

"I thought you tried smoking and didn't like it."

"Whatever. Mama's waiting, and if you're gonna help–"

"OK." Anna could see that Irina was unhappy with herself and didn't need her big sister to pile on. She got enough of that from Mama. But Mama was right about Roza. Irina was a good soul but should spend time with better friends. Roza wasn't leading her anywhere good. "I have an idea for something fun. Tomorrow night there's a Zakkai Shabbos dinner. My friend, Estie, will talk about when she lived in Germany–"

"Sounds boring, like school," Irina said.

"A boy your age will be there. My friend Benec's brother, Reuven–"

Irina's eyes brightened. "Reuven Katzman? Always playing football?"

"I don't know about the football, but yeah, Katzman is their last name."

That boy is so cool, Irina thought. "Isn't Zakkai for older kids, like at least thirteen- or fourteen-year-olds?"

"Yeah, usually. But I told Benec what Estie will talk about, and he said he'll bring Reuven. If you wash the cigarette odor off between now and then, you can come too."

Irina bristled but thought about the chance to meet Reuven. "Hey, I guess I'll go. Whatever."

JULY 8, 1938
ESTIE

The next night, Anna, Estie and Irina walked together to the Zakkai Shabbos dinner. "I thought Zionists don't do religious stuff," Estie said.

"You're thinking of the left-wing Zionists," Anna said. "Zakkai is a middle Zionist group. Like us, they keep kosher and celebrate Jewish holidays and Shabbos."

"Then why did Bubbie kvetch that Zakkai is a bunch of atheists?" Irina asked.

"Because very devout Jews, like Bubbie, are waiting for God to bring us back to Israel, and they get mad at Zionists, who say people must do it."

Estie rolled her eyes. "The people tonight–"

"They're like us," Anna said. "We all go to Polish schools, have Polish and Jewish friends. The really religious, who go to Jewish schools, don't belong to Zakkai and neither do the really unreligious. You'll love our leaders, Jozef and Leah! He's about twenty-seven and she's twenty-four, but they joined Zakkai in high school, got married, he became a lawyer, they moved to Palestine and came back to train teens to emigrate. Leah is a tiny, really nice bundle of energy. And Jozef, when he's not inventing or fixing something–"

"Hey Estie," Irina interrupted. "Anna says you'll talk about when you lived in Germany. Are you going to tell us fun stuff–"

"When I'm done," Estie said, "tell me if 'fun' is the word for it."

•••

Before sunset, about twenty-five teens stuffed themselves into Jozef's and Leah's apartment; after dinner, Leah led everyone to the living room, where they sat on the floor. The room was too small for one circle, so they made a circle within a circle and leaned against each other.

Anna sat next to Estie and introduced her to the group. Estie hadn't attended a Zakkai event since the Spring Celebration two months earlier. Anna could see that Estie was nervous; she was silently opening and closing her mouth and biting the side of her finger. She'd never talked about her life in Germany even though Anna had asked.

"Hi," Estie began with a shaky voice, looking at Jozef. "I was born in Poland, but we moved to Nuremberg in Germany when I was a year old. I'm sixteen now, so that was in... um..."

"About 1923?" Anna helped.

"Uh huh. Anyway, I don't remember much from when I was very little, but I grew up like any other German child, I thought. Yeah, my parents were immigrants and didn't really speak good German, but I did. I went to kindergarten there, primary school, and made friends. I spoke Polish at home and German outside. Um..." Estie fidgeted with her necklace.

"The Nazis took over five years ago, in 1933," Jozef said. "How were you treated before that?"

"Like everybody else, I think. I mean plenty of Germans don't like Jews, I know that since I'm older, but I was a little girl and didn't know the difference until sixth grade, after the Nazis came. Before, things were great. My best friends were Hilda and Ingrid from my apartment building. We were such best friends, always together. We were in the same class through fourth grade. And then we were separated at school but still best friends at home." Estie smiled wistfully.

Estie started feeling more comfortable and glanced around as she talked. "In sixth grade, Hilda joined a girl's group called German League of Girls. It was Hitler Youth for girls. They met twice a week, and I went with Hilda to her first meeting. The leaders talked over and over about how Germans are superior and Jews are inferior, and I remember Hilda looking at me funny. But we laughed about it afterwards.

"Hitler Youth became very popular. I'm sure it's even more popular now. Boys dress as Nazis – even to school – in brown uniforms, they march and carry flags. They're told what to believe. They are the master race and will conquer the world. Anyone with different beliefs is inferior. Poles are stupid but Jews are the worst. One of their songs went something like: 'We'll hold our flag high until Jewish blood spurts from our knives.'" Estie paused, nodded as she looked around and said in a hushed voice, "And they mean it."

Anna's eyes widened.

"Anyway... sorry, I went out of order. Before seventh grade we saw a list that said Hilda, Ingrid and I would be in the same class, and we were so excited! We held hands and jumped up and down.

"When seventh grade started, Hitler had been in power a long time. Maybe six months or a year. I don't remember. We were at school, and I was late to the lunchroom because I had to go to the bathroom." Estie blushed. "Um, so when I got to the cafeteria,

Hilda and Ingrid were eating with other girls, like normal. And then something happened that I won't forget as long as I live. I walked over and Hilda said, 'Get out of here, dirty Jew!'

"And I remember looking at her, not comprehending. I thought, What? I'm not dirty. I took a bath last night like I always do. I stood there trying to make sense of it, and Ingrid stuck her mouth right in my face. Ingrid was my best friend and so was Hilda. And Ingrid screamed at the top of her lungs, 'We said go away, dirty Jew!'

"I went to the other side of the room and ate by myself.

"After school, I told my mother what happened, and I cried and cried. She hugged me and said, 'You'll need to get used to it.' I said, 'But they're my best friends. How could they hate me?'

"My mother repeated herself. 'You're Jewish and need to get used to it.'

"Not a single student said a nice thing to me the entire year. They would write me notes like 'Jews out!' Or 'Jews perish!'

"The teacher, Miss Schultz, was nice though. She was strict with everyone but nice to me. I know she felt sorry for me. One day, she told the class that some Jewish German soldiers were killed in the World War, and a member of the Hitler Youth shouted, 'They died of fright. Jews don't have a fatherland.'"

"Estie," Anna asked. "Do you think many kids secretly felt sorry for you, but they were afraid? I think most people want to be nice, and–"

"I don't know. But it's a lot easier to be nice when you're supposed to be nice, and easy to be mean when you're supposed to be mean. Eighth grade taught me that. In seventh grade, I had Miss Schultz on my side. In eighth grade, there was me and a Jewish boy, Walter. Poor Walter..." Estie took a deep breath and forced a smile in Anna's direction.

"In eighth grade, the teacher was a Nazi, Mr. Schickel. He had a mustache like Hitler and wore his Nazi uniform to school. He told the class to give Walter a nice hello whenever they passed his bench. Mr. Schickel said, 'You should give him a nice hello on his arm, like this!' and he slammed his fist on his desk. The message was clear. Hit Walter. Whenever you walk by him.

"And they did. Girls too, not only boys. Maybe not every student, but for sure most of them. I'd cringe when I heard the thud of a boy socking Walter's arm."

Estie shook her head. "Poor Walter, a nice, average-sized boy with a pointy face and wavy brown hair. He'd sit there like a sack of wet flour and take it."

"Did he ever fight back?" Benec asked.

"No. There was nothing he could do. You can't understand unless you're in that situation."

"But," Benec began, "when you let someone bully you, you encourage more bullying. You need to stand up for yourself. Usually, the bullies will respect you and–"

"That's stupid," a boy named Itzhak interrupted. "Lunatics are not mollified by futile attempts at bravery. It's childish to think otherwise."

Anna liked most of the Zakkai regulars. But not Itzhak. He was arrogant and abrasive, a short, squat, old-looking guy about Mordecai's age. With an owlish face and big nose. An old rabbi's face, without the beard.

"Since when do we call people stupid for what they say?" Leah asked.

"When what they say is stupid!" Itzhak replied.

Leah locked eyes with Anna, who frowned and shook her head.

"Um," Estie said. "Mr. Schickel lectured on race. He said Jews kill babies. We're dishonest. We conspired to destroy Germany and rule the world. The Jews are a lower form of human being."

Estie's voice turned dark. "Everything was upside down because you're supposed to go to your teacher for help. But Mr. Schickel scared me the most. We watched a film that showed the typical Jew as an obese man with bulging eyes clutching giant moneybags. We saw it at least five times. The narrator, with hatred in his voice, said 'The Jews are boils on the back of the German people, a subhuman species comparable only to rats. The Jews must be eradicated!' Mr. Schickel made us memorize those words."

Anna grew pale as she imagined being forced to listen to that vile hatred – directed at her and those she loved. She glanced at Irina and saw her wipe away a tear.

"Walter got pounded hardest after Mr. Schickel's racial lectures." Estie looked down and sighed.

"My last day at that school was in the middle of eighth grade after a lesson on Jewish faces. Mr. Schickel ordered Walter and me to stand in front of the class, and with a long stick he pointed to our noses, mouths and eyes, and compared them to the ideal Germans in the textbook. Like we were animals.

"We were standing up there and everyone was laughing and calling us monkeys, and I looked out and saw that half the class also had dark hair or other features they were making fun of. I–" Estie whimpered and covered her face with her hands. Anna reached for Mordecai's hand and, like everyone else, quietly waited until Estie gained her composure.

"I'm sorry. I pointed at Gerta, a girl with black hair whose nose was at least as big as mine. She was in the German League of Girls and loved calling Walter and me Jewish pigs. I yelled, 'Gerta should be up here. Her hair is darker than mine!' The class got totally quiet, and Mr. Schickel grabbed my hand. With spit spewing from his mouth, he screamed in my face, 'Don't you ever point at a German!' He made me hold out my hand, and he whacked it with his ruler so hard that I couldn't bend two of my fingers for weeks.

"When I got home from school and told my mother, we cried together. That night, my father said I was done at that school. Lots of Jewish schools were opening, and they were full of teachers because the Germans had fired all Jewish teachers from state schools. I started going to one of them, and later we moved back to Poland where I finished up eighth grade. My father has had a hard time getting a decent job here, but at least we're safe." Estie rested her chin in her hand.

"Thank you, Estie," Leah said. "We know how hard it was to tell us your story."

"I'm not done," Estie said, and everyone laughed. "I'm sorry," she squeaked, hunching her shoulders.

"No, no, go ahead."

"There's one more important thing. It wasn't only in school. It was everywhere. Signs on Jewish stores. Don't shop here. Signs on so many places. Jews not allowed. No Jews on park benches. No Jews can swim. No Jews or dogs welcome. No Jews can buy at this store.

"Even worse were the pictures and lies about us. The Nazi newspaper showing ugly caricatures of Jews with huge noses and rotten teeth eating German babies or cheating Germans. You couldn't get away from it. Jews are inferior. Jews are ugly and evil. And it was so hard. It was so hard, hearing it all the time, not to believe it. I started believing I was inferior, and I started believing – my mother told me 'You're not ugly.'"

Estie stared down at the floor. "My mother said, 'You're not ugly Estie, you're beautiful' – but I knew it wasn't true. Because I was a Jew, I was ugly. I knew I was ugly, and–"

"Wow," Anna interrupted. "That was an incredible story." Anna put her arm around Estie's shoulders. "Very sad, but I do have a favorite part – when you moved here in eighth grade because that's when we became friends!"

Some people started to stand, but Jozef said, "Wait, let's have a group discussion – after I give Estie a giant Zakkai hug." He climbed over Mordecai and Anna and hugged Estie.

A girl said, "What I learned from Estie is the idiot Germans have bad eyesight!"

"Estie, the Germans are a horrible memory, but that's all they are," Benec said. "They can't hurt you ever again. You're safe here."

Itzhak slapped his head. "Safe in Poland! Do you live under a rock? Do–"

"Itzhak, we've heard enough from you!" Leah said. "Is it so hard to be nice?"

Itzhak ignored Leah and brusquely said to Estie, "I have a question. Did you hear much in school that Germany must expand to the east – to Poland, Ukraine, Russia, and take land from the inferior Slavs and Jews and give it to German people?"

Estie paused, deciding if she should hit back at Itzhak for being so rude. "Yeah, I heard that a lot. The Hitler Youth, other Nazis say it's Germany's right to conquer Poland, and Russia too."

Anna shuddered and felt a rising terror. Will the Nazis come here? Could they conquer Poland?

"We have France on our side," Benec began. "The Germans–"

"The Germans will conquer Poland if that is what they want," Itzhak said. "Hopefully, they'll set their sights elsewhere."

Anna squeezed Mordecai's hand. She disliked Itzhak, but he was smart. She'll be gone from here, off to Palestine, in less than a year. But her friends and cousins?

"Enough talk!" Mordecai said. "Act with your f-f-f-feet. Everyone. Move to Palestine. Talk to your parents and get it done."

Mordecai's words silenced the group. They respected him and knew he was right. Anna again squeezed his hand, and Leah started singing. This was Anna's favorite part of a Zakkai Shabbos, when they sang Shabbos and Zionist songs as the Shabbos candles flickered, boys and girls together, late into the night. Always ending with Hatikvah, the Jewish Zionist anthem that Anna's father loved to sing: *"So long as the Jewish spirit is yearning deep in the heart, with eyes turned toward the east, looking toward Zion, then our hope – the two-thousand-year-old hope – will not be lost. To be a free people in our land, the land of Zion and Jerusalem."*

•••

As they were about to leave, Leah asked Anna to stay a few minutes. Mordecai walked Irina home.

"Can we talk about Itzhak?" Leah asked. "I saw the look on your face when he spoke."

"Oh, I'm sorry–"

"Don't be, Annaleh." Leah reached for Anna's hand. "I know he can offend people. Itzhak is my cousin – please tell me what you think of him. You're a lovely person, Annaleh. Be honest with me."

Anna frowned. "We don't go to the same school, so I know him only from Zakkai. He seems very smart. But also negative and unhappy. He's not friendly – at least not to me. And he seems like an old man." She shrugged.

"Have you tried to get to know him?"

"Honestly, not so much. He was arrogant, dismissive. So – that's it."

Leah sighed. "Itzhak is his own worst enemy. We go through life surrounded by people we know so little about. Even our friends. We often see only what they want us to know. And then we have people like Itzhak who allow us to know nothing."

Leah looked down and back at Anna. "I'll tell you about him, for your ears only." She paused. "And for your friend, Estie – I see you're close; if she starts coming to Zakkai events, please share this with her too."

Anna nodded.

"Itzhak is a genius," Leah said. "A genius with a huge, wonderful heart. A heart that has developed a thick barrier preventing it from reaching out or being touched.

"When Itzhak was born, his umbilical cord was wrapped around his neck, and there was something else that, well, the doctor said Itzhak wouldn't live through the night. And if he did, his mind wouldn't develop properly. Miraculously, the doctor was wrong. Not only did his mind develop; by two years old, everyone could see that little Itzhak would be brilliant. At six, he was reading and writing like a twelve-year-old. By twelve, he was doing university-level math calculations.

"Now he's seventeen. He long ago stopped paying attention

in school. You could find him most afternoons in the library where he studies things professors don't understand. If Itzhak can get into university despite the Jewish quota, he'll someday make great discoveries to benefit the world. I'm sure of that."

Anna saw tears well in Leah's eyes as her voice softened. "But the cord around his neck was far from harmless. He walks but can't run. His legs won't allow it. Watch him on stairs. He readies himself and then slowly makes his way with the aid of the guard rail. He has no athletic ability of any sort. That is very hard on a little boy, especially one like Itzhak who loved sports and imagined himself a footballer. And it can be even more difficult for an older boy. In sports, Itzhak wasn't picked last – he couldn't even play.

"But you'll never hear him moan about his maladies. I've never heard a complaint, and we've had many talks. But he's seen his circle of friends shrink. That's natural; he doesn't participate in most activities. He's still friendly with one or two boys not intimidated by his genius. He'd love to have a girlfriend, but as you can imagine that hasn't happened."

Anna thought of Estie but said nothing.

"From these burdens he's developed a bitterness, a thick callus around his heart. I'm not asking you to try to break through it. Just be sympathetic and open – you and your friend, Estie – like only a girl can be, knowing that a beautiful soul is on the inside, wishing it could get out."

THE SAME NIGHT
IRINA

Eleven-year-old Irina and eighteen-year-old Mordecai were walking home from the Zakkai program. At first, Irina was annoyed – she was old enough to go home alone! But the twenty-minute walk would be twenty times longer than she'd ever talked to Mordecai, or maybe forty times longer. Whatever. And it was the first time without Anna.

They were making their way silently on the sidewalk in front of gray, four-story apartment buildings. Other people were walking about, but no one near them.

"Did you have f-f-f-fun tonight?" Mordecai finally asked.

Irina shrugged. "Parts were good. No girls my age."

"I saw you talking to a boy for a little bit. Did you already know him?"

"Um, sort of. That's Reuven."

"What did you think of what Estie said about Germany?"

Irina shook her head. "Bad. Really bad. If people hate you like that... It's good she left."

"Did you–"

"You already asked three questions."

"Huh?"

"One of my friends, me and her say that more than three questions in a row and you're acting like a mother."

Mordecai laughed. "Your t-t-turn."

Irina wanted to ask something but kept quiet. They crossed a street, entered an industrial area, and walked on a dark road past huge, unlit warehouses.

Irina said, "If you..." but she stopped, they walked further in the dark, and after a few moments of silence, she said, "What if..." but stopped again.

"Are you having trouble g-g-g-getting your words out?" Mordecai asked.

She frowned.

"Try again."

"Hey, I guess I kinda don't want to hurt your feelings but OK, whatever. If you try really hard, can you talk without stuttering?"

"No."

"Even really, really, really hard?"

"No."

"That stinks."

Silence.

"Have you stuttered your whole life?"

"Almost as long as I can remember. My mother says I started when I was four."

"It seems like people stutter if they're nervous, but why would you be nervous talking to me? I'm eleven! And you're old and handsome, and you have a girlfriend, and Anna says you're so cool! I don't get it."

"I don't either. It's not b-b-b-because I'm nervous with you. It's something my brain makes me do."

Another long silence as they left the warehouses and reached a residential area.

"Do you get teased a lot?" Irina asked.

"I used to, when I was little."

"That must have been really hard."

"Yeah. But not by my f-f-friends, and I'm lucky that I have a lot of friends." He smiled his handsome smile.

"I have a friend who used to be nice," Irina said, "but half of a sudden, she started doing mean things to me."

"Half of a sudden?"

"Uh huh. Sort of slowly, not suddenly."

Mordecai nodded. "Have you wondered if you should stay friends with someone who is mean to you?"

"A little."

Silence.

"Do you want to be my friend?" Mordecai asked. "You're already my m-m-mother because you asked me more than three questions in a row."

"I'm sorry! I didn't mean to!" Irina paused. "But yeah, I want to be your friend. I'd really like that. And if I ever hear anyone making fun of you, they'll be in big trouble!"

September 30, 1938
Itzhak and Szymon

Tall, athletic, eighteen-year-old Szymon casually strolled down the tree-lined walkway bordering his school. A satchel full of books held by a muscular arm, his bright eyes and blondish hair glinted in the sun. A girl chatting on the walk with her friend stopped mid-sentence; both girls turned their heads and watched Szymon walk by. He didn't notice.

The Curie-Skłodowska Gymnasium students hailed from a mixture of middle- and upper-middle-class families. Szymon's was upper-middle-class; both his parents were lawyers. Active in his church, Szymon hoped to attend prestigious Jagiellonian University, study philosophy and become a priest.

He passed a small fountain and tossed his satchel onto a hard wooden bench where the smartest person at Curie-Skłodowska was sitting: short, dumpy, unathletic Itzhak. Szymon, who innately understood people and the world around him, and Itzhak, the analytical genius, had been friends since fifth grade. Back then, they met at the library to discuss books on history or science. Szymon would ride his bike; Itzhak walked because his legs couldn't peddle.

They'd grown apart in recent years as Szymon shifted toward sports and became popular as a very competitive, modest teammate. Hot tempered and friendly, lighthearted but serious when needed. But a good friend to Szymon at age eleven was a friend for life, and he'd occasionally meet Itzhak to debate current events or other interesting topics. Did Szymon's friends wonder why he spent time with Itzhak? A Jew, no less? Szymon didn't know and couldn't have cared less.

Today, their history teacher gave them a reason to meet often, almost like the old days. He instructed them to work together and turn in a written report at year's end evaluating the risk of war with Germany.

Szymon plopped next to Itzhak on the bench, which faced the school. "I might ask Ruthie on a date," Szymon said. "What do you think?" Ruthie, a Jewish beauty with long black hair, was Itzhak's cousin. She was an actress, active in theater, bubbly and flamboyant.

"I think I have a question," Itzhak said. "Future philosophy student, explain the logic behind the infatuation of a nice Catholic boy with a Jewish girl."

"She's so pretty, I can't keep my eyes off her."

Itzhak nodded. "Why are you focused on Ruthie, an observant Jewish girl who would never date a Catholic, instead of one of the freethinking Jewish girls who might even convert for you?"

"She's so pretty, I can't keep my eyes off her."

"And why would a future priest be infatuated with this Jewish girl?"

"Same answer."

"You get credit for consistency, but what happens after you become a priest?"

"I'll be like you. Forever celibate."

Itzhak smirked and blushed. "Thanks a lot. But I did deserve that."

Szymon tossed a book onto Itzhak's lap. "Let's get to work. How's your German?"

Itzhak grunted. "Mein Kampf? You want me to read Hitler's book?"

"What better way to learn what the Germans will do?"

"Hitler has said when the Czechoslovakia problem is solved, Germany won't claim anywhere else in Europe – which means Poland is safe if we believe–"

Szymon pointed across the tree-lined walk toward the school. "Class is out. Let's finish dividing up responsibilities."

"No, first look at the microcosm of Poland."

Szymon raised his eyebrows as they watched students leave the building.

Itzhak shook his head. "We're seeing Polish Catholics walk with Polish Catholics, Jews with Jews, some Ukrainians with Ukrainians, and a few small clumps – Hooray for Poland! – of both Poles and Jews."

"You realize that when you say 'Poles and Jews,' you're excluding Jew from the definition of Pole."

"That's been rammed down my throat by Polish society," Itzhak said. "'You're not a Pole – you're a Jew!'"

Szymon gestured toward the school building. "How do they fit in your categories?" Benec Katzman, whom Itzhak had argued with at the recent Zakkai meeting, was walking arm in arm with his Polish Catholic girlfriend. "That guy is single-handedly making Poles – at least Polish girls – love Jews."

"Yeah... maybe there's an exception for Jews who look like Hollywood stars," Itzhak said. "But–"

Szymon held up a hand. "Back to what you said a minute ago.

How would you respond to people who say it's natural for Poles to view Jews as non-Polish because that's how Jews forever viewed themselves? Polish Catholics hear Jews speak Jewish, or Polish with a Jewish accent, huge numbers of them dress as if they live in the 18th century and socialize only with each other – are you shocked Poles think they're aliens?"

"Let's paint the whole picture," Itzhak said. "The nation of 'Poland,' destroyed in the late eighteenth century by Russia and other empires, didn't exist again until twenty years ago. In those empires, Poles spoke Polish, Ukrainians spoke Ukrainian, and Jews spoke Jewish, sometimes called Yiddish – 'Yid' meaning Jew. You can't expect millions of people who speak Jewish as their first language to suddenly speak Polish with no accent."

"As more Jews, like you, go to Polish schools and acculturate into society, the average Pole will view you and other Jews as Polish citizens just like them."

"Pffft – Just like them?" Itzhak scoffed. "Me, the Christ killer? They won't think I'm a communist or a rich capitalist trying to control the world?"

"OK, we still have many bigots. But you can't expect change all at once."

"Almost three and a half million Jews live in Poland, more Jews than any country in the world except America. If Poland were a free society, Polish Jews would succeed as Jews do there. Instead, the government supports boycotts of Jewish businesses and limits the number of Jews in university and trade schools. Do you know that although about half the lawyers and doctors in Poland are Jews, 80% – eight out of every ten Jews in Poland – receive charity to make ends meet? Charity from Jews in America."

"Even big problems finally have solutions. Our generation will see change–"

"This government encourages Jews to leave, not to succeed," Itzhak said. "If they had somewhere to go, we wouldn't still have millions of Jews in Poland."

"What about Palestine?"

"Can't trust the British. Too willing to appease the Arabs."

"The Arabs?"

"Yeah. The Arabs are being given vast portions of the old Ottoman Empire to create multiple Arab kingdoms, but they rampage and murder to prevent the Jews from having our tiny ancient homeland.

The British have been limiting Jewish entry to Palestine, and I fear they'll cave in to the Arabs and shut it down. If so, Jews suffering under the Nazis will be trapped."

Szymon grunted. "The British are good at appeasing."

"Yeah – but back to Poland. The Polish Catholic Church isn't helping. How many churchmen and newspapers say 'the Jews' are communists and pornographers, and good Poles should boycott Jewish businesses?"

Szymon gave him an angry look. "You're attacking the Church? You forget that I plan to become a priest?"

"My father, a tailor, should be boycotted?" Itzhak paused, knowing that fiery but open-minded Szymon would cool down.

Szymon opened his mouth, said nothing and sighed. "It annoys me when you're right, which does happen occasionally. Many church leaders have forgotten the Bible says to love their neighbors as themselves. A lot of young Jews are patriots; I want them to help build the new Poland. And I want you to stay and find a cure for polio or cancer so the world's newspapers will blast the headline: 'Pole cures polio and cancer.'"

Itzhak laughed. "I hate to steal from Einstein, but only if I succeeded would Poles call me a Pole. If I failed, I'd be a Jew."

"Be patient," Szymon said. "Within our lifetime, Poland – especially the Jewish community – will change so much as to be unrecognizable."

"We can only hope."

•••

Szymon and Itzhak didn't notice a man in a dark suit sitting at a table about twenty yards further down the walkway. No reason they should have noticed; teachers and others seeking a place to work outside frequently sat there.

If they'd seen him, they might have described the man as in his forties, below average height, with brown hair and a brown mustache. A Polish citizen of German descent writing names, descriptions and addresses in a notebook. Not of students. But teachers' names, including their history teacher and the head of the school.

The man's notebook was thick and full of information gathered throughout Krasau, including the names of lawyers, some of whom had children at the Curie-Skłodowska Gymnasium.

If they'd asked the man his name, and if he'd been honest, he would have said "Heinrich Schmidt."

NOVEMBER 16, 1938
ANNA

Anna ran her finger through Mordecai's wavy hair and along his ear. Wearing long, dark coats and hats, they were sitting next to each other on a bench between two tracks at the bustling train station. Mordecai's right foot rested on a suitcase, and a map spread across his lap. He was showing Anna his route by train across Poland and down to Konstanta, Romania, where a passenger ship would take him across the Black Sea, past Istanbul and on to Haifa in Palestine. He occasionally glanced down the rail line, eagerly awaiting his train.

Anna was working hard to seem excited, but mostly not to cry.

"Look at this map," Mordecai said. "It shows the network of t-t-t-train tracks across Poland and the major lines across Germany and half of Europe. So m-m-many places, and we've never been to any of them."

Anna noticed two folded maps under the one open on Mordecai's lap. "How many maps are you bringing? You afraid the conductor might get lost?" She forced a smile.

They'd been talking about this day for weeks. That Mordecai would leave in mid-November for Palestine, to be followed by Anna and her family in June after she graduates. Anna had ached to go with him, but her parents said no. "You'd leave our family, unmarried – and before finishing school?" Mama asked. "What is a seven-month delay over an entire life?" Papa had said. She'd considered going anyway but stayed out of respect for her parents.

Mordecai planned to join a Galilee kibbutz where other Zakkai members from Poland lived. He'd then scout around for where Anna's family could stay, and when she comes in June he'll ask her to marry him and begin their life together.

So why was she so sad? She battled it and squeezed his arm, bulky from years of weightlifting. "Should I carry your bags onto the train? I don't want you to hurt yourself so early in your trip."

"Maybe you should, for the practice. Before long, you and your family will leave on a train out of here." He smiled. "But thanks, I'll manage."

Mordecai looked down again at his map, and she twirled a finger in his hair. She was going to miss him so much, but that wasn't why she felt overwhelmed by sadness, why she fought to hold back tears.

Anna was terrified – illogical she told herself – that she wouldn't see him in seven months. Or ever again.

Not because of anything Mordecai had done. No love could be stronger. Her nightmare stemmed from something too enormous to comprehend – Nazi Germany. A week earlier, the Germans had rampaged against their Jewish neighbors in what they were calling "Kristallnacht," Night of Broken Glass. Estie's story about Germany had been scary, but Kristallnacht was horrifying. The Germans murdered almost a hundred German Jewish men, arrested thirty thousand more and threw them in "concentration camps" – simply because they were Jews. The Nazis smashed Jewish homes, businesses, schools, and more than a thousand synagogues.

Located right next to Poland, Germany had become a barbaric, Jew-hating nation of horrors ready to ransack Europe. Anna was terror-stricken they would invade Poland, prevent her family from getting to Palestine, and unleash their evil on Polish Jews.

Mordecai lifted his brown eyes from the map. "I almost forgot to tell you. Since I'll be gone, you need to get vegetables for the Zakkai Shabbos d-d-dinner this week."

Anna stopped twirling his hair and angrily stared at him. "You're leaving me to travel a continent away, and you talk about vegetables?"

"Well, they need–"

She pulled her hand away. "Why don't you say you'll miss me and hate leaving me?" She was suddenly annoyed in addition to being upset.

He rested his hand on her thigh. "You know I'll miss you terribly." He paused as a loud train left the station. "But Friday night, they'll m-m-miss ME if you don't bring vegetables."

"Why don't–" she stopped, sighed and thought: What are you doing Anna, squabbling when he'll be gone in a few minutes? "I'll get the vegetables."

Mordecai wrapped an arm around her shoulder and whispered, "Separating is hard, even when it's temporary, and I really will miss you terribly. You know that. But I have a simple antidote. I think about June. In Palestine, in each other's arms. I think that and smile. Do it – think about next June."

"But what if we never see each other again?" Anna blurted. "What if the Germans attack Poland?"

"Never see each other again!" Mordecai laughed. "I promise. We'll see each other again." In a consoling voice, he said, "Of all the things t-t-t-to worry about, that the Germans will stop us–"

"I'm terrified," Anna managed, choking back the tears. "I overheard my father, always the optimist, say we should have left this year."

"Anna, we can't control what the crazy Germans might do, but I'm not worried." He cupped her face in his hands and said with a voice of absolute certainty, "In seven months, you and your whole family will be far away from here. Picking oranges in Palestine. And swimming in the Mediterranean with m-m-me."

They heard the rumble of his train in the distance and craned their necks to watch it approach. Mordecai stood, as did Anna, who grabbed his hand. He kissed her forehead, and she hugged him tight as the train slowly and noisily pulled into the station and rolled to a stop.

"It will be OK," he whispered. "You'll see."

"I know," she lied in a half sob followed by a quick smile.

He wiped a tear from her eye and gazed at her with the same intensity as the night they'd met. "I p-p-promise. You have nothing to worry about." He gathered her into another hug.

Mordecai kissed her deeply, said goodbye "for now," grabbed his bags and carried them onto the train. Anna pushed her face against a window and stood on her toes, straining to catch sight of him one more time. She saw him walking down the aisle, and she hurried alongside the train until he sat near a window and looked out for her.

When the train began to move, he smiled broadly and blew her a kiss. She blew one in return.

The train left the station, and the tears Anna had been holding back poured out. She prayed this wasn't their last goodbye.

NOVEMBER 24, 1938

The German Armed Forces High Command, per Adolph Hitler's orders, secretly instructed the German military to prepare for an attack on Poland. No decision yet made to carry it out.

•••

JANUARY 10, 1939
PAPA

At 3:00 p.m., Alexander Allowitz, Anna's father, was sitting in a small lobby outside the office of Stanislaw Nowak, head of the local passport office. Alexander had been at that office since 9:00 in the morning. He'd waited an hour to talk with a clerk, got nowhere, had a fruitless discussion with a supervisor at about 11:30, and had been waiting ever since on the building's fifth – top – floor to see Mr. Nowak.

"Will he be available soon?" Alexander again asked Mr. Nowak's pretty secretary, whose desk sat nearby.

She looked at him and saw a Jew of average height and build, with dark, curly hair and mustache but no beard. "Mr. Nowak should be with you in a few minutes," she repeated from an hour earlier.

"Thank you," he sighed.

Alexander paced, found a window at the end of a hall and peered out. He'd never been so high inside a building and wistfully gazed toward where he was born, a few miles away. Back in 1897, his birthplace was a small village; it now belonged to a sprawling city.

He'd lived his whole life here except during the World War. Now he was leaving. With mixed emotions. To leave your friends and everything familiar at age forty-one wasn't easy. He'd built his bicycle shop and a reputation for honesty, lived in his own two-bedroom house and earned enough to support his family, which was more than most Polish citizens, Pole or Jew, could say. A decent life, all things considered, despite Poland's problems and its antisemitism.

Alexander's uncle had moved to America twenty years before and still sent money to help the family. America was closed to Alexander; immigration laws had changed. But that was OK. He wasn't religious, but his passion was Zionism – the Jews' right to rebuild their nation in the Land of Israel. Alexander had wanted to move there when he married, but his wife, Chana, had yearned for safety after her father's murder. He and Chana sent their daughters to public schools so they'd speak Polish with no accent, like real Poles. Unlike Alexander, who was embarrassed by his thick Jewish accent.

Helping create a new country was nothing new to him, but this time it would be his own. He had fought for Poland, and the same victorious nations that re-created Poland after more than a century also laid the groundwork for a re-created Jewish country after two thousand years. Britain was given a "mandate" to rule Palestine until the Jewish national home would be established. Alexander was eager to help make it happen.

"Mr. Nowak is ready for you."

Stanislaw Nowak, sitting behind a massive oak desk in his spacious office, didn't bother to rise when Alexander entered, hat in hand. A stiff nod sufficed. Dark-haired Alexander stood and awaited permission to sit from the nicely dressed, middle-aged bureaucrat. Alexander noticed the neatly trimmed mustache on Nowak's broad face, the perfectly combed brown hair, and the spotless desk. A man who never met an i that didn't need dotting. A portrait of General Pilsudski, war hero and deceased former leader of Poland, hung on the wall behind Nowak.

A flick of Nowak's wrist permitted Alexander to sit in a small chair opposite the desk.

"Good afternoon, Mr. ... Allowitz. I understand you insisted on talking to me. Please explain what is so important that my attention is required."

Alexander nervously began. "My family, we going to Palestine. Six months ago, I begin paperwork process. We all have passports except my wife. We applied for hers. Your men said she would have it in three months. We need all passports to apply for transit visas from other countries and to get British permission to enter Palestine. It has been six months and still no passport for my wife. Three months ago, I come here, a gentleman say to come back in thirty days. I come back. No passport. I come again after another thirty days. They again say come back after thirty more days. I do that. Still nothing. Today I come and they tell me same thing. I ask who I could talk to, and they give me your name. I respectfully ask your help. I'm waiting outside your office more than three hours."

Nowak yawned. "I'm sorry you had to sit outside my office while I attended to my duties."

"It's fine. Do you have information about the delay? Can you issue the passport today, yourself?"

Nowak grunted. "No, I cannot issue the passport. Only the Warsaw office does that. They will forward it here when ready." Nowak opened a file resting on his desk and pulled out some papers, which he quickly perused. "Your wife was born in eastern Poland, in what was Russia. Endless numbers of Jews say they were born there but have no papers to prove it. Your wife is lucky that the Polish government recognizes her as a citizen... But she has no passport. You people think we can ignore all regulations and simply snap our fingers to suit you. We are a country of laws, Mr. Allowitz. Laws, rules, and regulations are essential to effective governance and the well-being of our citizenry."

Alexander stared at the antisemite, disgusted at himself for putting up with the condescension. But he needed the passport. He nodded.

Nowak glanced down at his file and furrowed his brow. "What my subordinates told you is accurate. The passport ordinarily would have been received in this office by now. Perhaps the Warsaw office sees a problem with your wife's citizenship or with her paperwork. Or with something else. I cannot guess the issue."

Nowak folded his hands on the desk. "So, the delay is not at this office. It's in Warsaw. Is there anything else I may assist you with today?"

Alexander was dumbfounded. "You haven't helped me! I come here for help. What must I do to get my wife's passport?"

"Mr. Allowitz, do you even read Polish?"

Alexander gritted his teeth and felt his head throbbing with anger. "Yes, I read Polish. Pretty good."

"Then when you applied for your wife's passport, you read what I have stated. The passport is not issued by this office. It comes from Warsaw. You and your nice family are not the only Jews who want to leave Poland. And as you should know, the Polish government wants as many of you as possible to go. There are too many Jews in this country, Mr. Allowitz, and we would love to help you depart. This afternoon, you have provided a nice example of why that is. You take up my time as if you're entitled to do so. You, who cannot even speak proper Polish, want me to jump over hurdles–"

"Enough!" Alexander slammed his hands on the oak desk and stood. "I am not a real Pole? Where were YOU during the World War!" Alexander pointed at the portrait on the wall. "I served mit General Pilsudski in the Polish Legions. Jews and Poles. We shed our blood. Don't you–"

Nowak smirked at Alexander's Jewish "mit" instead of "with" but motioned for him to sit. "Please, Mr. Allowitz. I didn't notice your war service..." He calmly reopened his file and ran a finger down a page. "Yes, I see you did serve in the Legions. You volunteered?"

"Yes." Alexander strained to calm down.

"Very commendable. I've never met a Jew who fought in Pilsudski's Legions."

"We had many Jews, officers and men, fighting mit Poles."

Nowak stifled a grin but again reviewed his papers, this time more carefully. "It says here you plan to leave in June, only a few months from now. Have you applied to the British for entry to Palestine?"

"No. As I said, we waiting on the passport–"

"Mr. Allowitz, I strongly recommend that you apply for entry with the passports you do have. I've heard rumblings about the British. You don't know if they'll let you in."

"The British? Why–"

"You understand that you can't go to Palestine unless the British permit you to enter. Poland saying au revoir does you no good if the British don't say hello, Mr. Allowitz."

"Why wouldn't the British let us in?" Alexander heard his voice rise with fear.

Nowak sighed and looked at his watch. "I'm not saying the British won't let you in. I'm not saying the British will let you in. I'm simply trying to recommend that you move forward on that front before too much time elapses, while we see what can be done about your wife's passport. I could help on that."

Alexander's eyes widened. "So you can help us?"

Nowak leaned forward. "Let me see what I can do. I'll check with Warsaw, get to the bottom of the holdup and have the passport issued expeditiously."

"I would greatly appreciate that, sir." Alexander suddenly felt better. Serving in the army may finally have benefited him.

Nowak's chair creaked as he leaned back. "But Mr. Allowitz, this will take considerable effort on my part, requiring time outside normal working hours. My salary covers only my usual workload. Not extra favors I perform, however deserving the recipients may be."

"OK..."

"It would only be fair that I receive compensation for the time I spend, after hours, learning of your situation, expediting matters, and remedying it on a rush basis so that we get your family to Palestine as they deserve."

Realizing that Nowak was demanding a bribe, Alexander again

became incensed; his hands clenched into fists and his face flushed red. But this time, he controlled it. "How much you talk about? I'm not a wealthy man."

"No, I'm sure you're not. I'm sure you're not. I believe 900 zlotys would be fair."

"900 zlotys!"

"Yes. Anything less would be inappropriate. If this matter is important to you, bring an envelope containing 900 zlotys to this office. Put my name on the envelope and mark it confidential. Next week, I begin time-consuming projects, so you should bring the payment to me within the next two days if you want my assistance."

Nowak stood and pointed to the door with his open hand. "I don't expect any difficulties. I'm well connected with our Warsaw office."

After Alexander left, Nowak picked up his telephone receiver and dialed his secretary. "You can send in the next person."

FEBRUARY 4, 1939
ANNA

"I love Errol Flynn!" Estie raved. "This will be my second time to see him in a motion picture, not just in magazines. He's so handsome!"

Anna, Estie and two girlfriends from school were sitting in a cinema waiting for their picture show, *The Adventures of Robin Hood,* to begin.

Between munches of popcorn, Estie leaned toward Anna and whispered, "I heard this show might win the Oscar, and that Olivia de Havilland is great!" She handed Anna the popcorn bag.

"Can you imagine actually being at the Academy Awards?" Anna said. "It's so glamorous! Like a ball from a fairytale."

The girls and crowd quieted as the pre-show newsreel began to play. Its light reflected off the girls' suddenly forlorn faces as they watched Adolf Hitler, dictator of Germany, strut across the screen and deliver a speech commemorating the sixth anniversary of his Nazi party taking power. Hitler's devoted followers thrust their hands forward in stiff-armed salute and wildly cheered.

Estie quietly translated parts of Hitler's speech. Germans needed living space, but wanted "peace and quiet," and "the friendship between Germany and Poland" was "reassuring."

But Hitler attacked all Jews as parasites and mocked the western democracies for criticizing Germany's treatment of Jews but refusing to let those same Jews immigrate. He accused "the Jews" of lying about Germany and being "warmongers." He passionately declared, "I want once again to be a prophet. If ... the Jews ... succeed in plunging the peoples of the Earth once again into a world war, the result will be ... THE ANNIHILATION OF THE JEWISH RACE IN EUROPE." The on-screen thunderous applause and beaming German faces sent an icy chill down Anna's back.

"I can't watch this," Estie finally said. She left for the restroom and didn't return until after *Robin Hood* had started. But the girls loved the show, and no one talked afterwards about the newsreel.

•••

At 2:00 in the morning, Anna awoke with a start. Though the night hung quiet and dark around her, Anna's heart and mind were racing. How could so many Germans believe the garbage that spewed from

Hitler's mouth? Not just believe, but relish and worship it. And their insanity targeted Anna, her family and friends. She felt helpless, as if they were all dangling by a wire over the abyss. Her worst fears were coming true. Please God, let us get out of Poland while we still can!

Anna fought to control feelings of panic. She sat up in bed and took deep breaths. We must get Mama's passport so we can go to Palestine. She felt a flicker of gratitude that Mordecai was gone. At least he was safe. Why won't other countries let Jews in?

What will the Nazis do if they come here? Humiliate and abuse Irina and little Frammy in school, like with Estie? Or worse? Her mind ran wild. What do evil people do when they hate you?

Anna felt a helpless dread of the future and couldn't shake it. Weeks before, she'd believed her fear was irrational. She no longer did.

FEBRUARY 6, 1939
RABBI LEIBMAN

Seventy-year-old, gray-bearded Rabbi Shlomo Leibman of Krasau, son of Rabbi Avraham Yisroel of Warsaw, son of Rabbi Shlomo Meir of Bobruisk, son of Rabbi Reuven Tzvi of Biecz, son of Rabbi Binyamin Yaakov of Bircza stumbled early afternoon from his cluttered desk to the bed. Holding his searing, throbbing head, he lay still with eyes pressed shut as bolts of light flared across what should have been quiet blackness behind his eyelids. A newspaper report of Hitler's speech lay open on his desk. For his readers and his congregation, he must write and warn of the inescapable cataclysm.

His head pounded and the flames flashed for a length of time immeasurable due to their intensity, and when Rabbi Leibman opened his eyes the room began to spin. He closed them and the words arrived. "Woe unto us, for the evil nations will torture and burn the Jewish people of Europe in an unimaginable hell. We have fled from God and forgotten the purpose for which God made us his messenger. But a remnant, a remnant shall survive. For they shall have a mission."

A mission? To do what? Rabbi Leibman sighed. He knew he had only a few minutes to write these words down before they vanished from his mind. He sat up against the headboard, but the room spun with such force that he collapsed back onto the mattress. He must get to his desk! He tried a second time to sit and again failed. "Only a remnant shall survive..."

He lay on his pillow with eyes closed and tried to contain the growing nausea. The bolts continued to flash.

His nightstand. His nightstand drawer should contain a pen and paper. He twisted his old body toward the side of the bed, moaned in pain as his head pulsated, and opened the top drawer of his nightstand with such force that it fell to the floor.

Rabbi Leibman lay back on his pillow, took three deep breaths, painfully scooted to the edge of the bed, rolled himself onto his side, opened his eyes, looked down and saw a pen and paper spinning with the floor. He extended an arm but couldn't reach them. With colossal effort he tumbled face first from his bed to the hard wooden floor, bracing the fall with his hands. His throat burned, and with eyes closed he shifted his face to the side and threw up.

Turning onto his back, Rabbi Leibman again opened his eyes, turned his head, grasped the pen and paper laying near his vomit, and shut his eyes. The final words came to him. "The remnant shall serve God by feeding the hungry, clothing the naked and caring for the homeless. They shall pursue right and justice and teach all peoples the path to goodness."

He scrawled the entire message; the flashing lights subsided, and he fell asleep on the floor.

THE SAME DAY
ANNA

Late afternoon, Anna was peeling potatoes in her family's small kitchen while helping Irina study for a history test. Frammy played on the floor with the shreds of potato skins that flew off Anna's knife and missed the garbage can. Mama, stirring fried onions on the stove, checking the meat, and boiling water, was maneuvering between them.

The front door slammed, and Papa rushed in waving a little booklet in his right hand and shouting, "Mama's passport! Mama's passport! I got it today!" A huge smile across his face, he grabbed Mama around the waist, lifted her in the air and spun around. "This week, I'll go to the British Embassy in Warsaw and get our permits to Palestine!"

Mama's face lit up; Anna screamed with joy and burst out crying. Papa set Mama down and lifted Anna high into the air. One, two, three times he raised her up and then dropped her into his arms for a big hug. Anna looked so happy that Papa's eyes filled with tears. Even Irina, who fretted about missing her friends when they moved, joined in the excitement and hugged Mama, leaving her a little stunned.

Frammy ran to Papa, who had started singing the Zionist anthem Hatikvah, and squealed, "Me too, me too!" Papa lifted him and announced, "Let this prove that you should never give up! Always have hope and try to make your dreams come true!"

Anna rushed to the bedroom and dove onto the bed to tell Mordecai. The potatoes could wait.

She wrote him almost every day, and Mordecai did the same. But to save postage, they usually mailed their letters – consisting of multiple pages – every two weeks. In his most recent letter, Mordecai had enclosed a picture he drew of a couple dancing on a hilltop under a starlit sky. In return, Anna wrote a poem that she mailed a few days ago entitled "The Dancer" about a boy who danced his way up a hill with one partner after another until, at the crest, he found the girl he'd dance with the rest of his life.

Her letters sometimes flowed with sappy romance, like "When I lay in bed last night, I heard a soft breeze rustle the leaves of our oak tree, and I imagined floating on it into your arms." But not this time.

The entire letter, which she immediately thrust into an envelope, read: "We have Mama's passport!!!!"

April 3, 1939

The German Armed Forces High Command secretly issued a revised directive to the German military leadership: prepare for a German invasion of Poland to occur at any time from September 1, 1939.

•••

April 28, 1939

Hitler stated in a speech that he did not understand why Poland was acting as if Germany wanted war. Germany had "not thought of proceeding in any way against Poland..." The notion "was merely invented by the international press."

MAY 3, 1939
ITZHAK AND SZYMON

Szymon and Itzhak met in a small room at the library to work on their school project entitled "Will Germany invade Poland?" Itzhak wore old gray slacks and a baggy white shirt. Szymon, straight from a football game, was dressed in shorts and his team jersey. The boys hadn't talked about their paper in a month, and it was due in two weeks.

"Before we depress ourselves with Germany, what's the latest on your love affair with Ruthie?" Itzhak asked.

"She recently started sitting at a table near mine during lunch."

"So, your relationship is progressing."

"Exactly."

"Have you again considered asking her on a date?"

"Two hundred times. But since she wouldn't date a Catholic boy, I decided Plan B is more suitable."

"Plan B?"

"Looking at her."

"Not very proactive."

"Inaction is sometimes the best choice."

"Nice transition to our paper. Your strategy is reminiscent of Poland's regarding Germany. Have you summarized why you think war is inevitable?"

"Yeah," Szymon said. "The democracies were so hesitant to fight when the Germans were weak that they did nothing as Germany built the strongest army in Europe. They then gave the Germans whatever they demanded because Germany had become too powerful. Germany now wants Poland."

"Details?"

"After the World War, to ensure that Germany would never again threaten Europe, the Versailles Treaty prohibited Germany from maintaining a large military and from expanding their territory. The treaty restricted Germany to one hundred thousand soldiers; they now have more than two million. The treaty said no air force. They now have thousands of warplanes.

"Hitler wants to expand Germany's borders to include where ethnic Germans live. He took over Austria, did the same to Czechoslovakia even though England and France were obligated by treaty to stop him, and last week, Hitler said he wants the part of Poland where many Germans live. France and England have promised to defend Poland, but I have no faith in them."

"If only they'd stopped Hitler years ago," Itzhak said, "when he started violating the treaty by building his war machine–"

"It's human nature," Szymon said. "When bad guys threaten good guys, the good guys do whatever they can to avoid war even though inaction makes the ultimate conflict so much worse. Only a very rare and wise statesman has the guts to begin a war to avoid a worse one later."

Itzhak sighed. "My job is to say who would likely win the war, and the answer is equally pessimistic."

"Have you factored in the bravery of the average Polish soldier fighting for the nation we've yearned for the past hundred years?"

"The problem is that German forces are so much better trained, organized and equipped."

"What about the British and French armies?"

"Before they fire a shot, Germany will conquer Poland."

Szymon massaged his temples and rubbed his face. "I wish I disagreed with you." He sighed. "What do you think will happen after Germany conquers us?"

"It depends on what century the Germans live in. The Nazis say Poles are inferior. Will they enslave the Polish people as if this were the tenth century? And Hitler says war would bring the extermination of the Jews. Would civilized Germans even contemplate something so absurdly horrible? My mind says no.

"But when I lay in bed at night, I remember what I heard from a Jewish girl who lived in Germany: German youth sing about Jewish blood dripping from their knives."

"What kind of people teach children to sing about murder?"

MAY 16, 1939
PAPA

Alexander turned his wrench, loosening a rusty nut that held the bicycle seat in place. He removed the worn seat, installed a new one, tightened two new nuts and looked at the rusty chain. A reliable customer had asked him to spruce up an old bicycle. Easy work that allowed Alexander to daydream.

Anna recently said Mordecai had found a place for them to live and may even have found a job for Alexander as a machinist. At a place called Migdal, near the Sea of Galilee. Near hills, a forest, the lake. Alexander smiled. His day would come soon – at last – a pioneer in the Land of Israel.

He pictured Frammy and Irina growing up in the Jewish homeland; Frammy won't remember he was anything but a Jew in his own country. Anna marrying Mordecai under the stars. Jewish grandchildren in their own nation. He heaved a happy sigh.

Alexander wasn't a fool; it wouldn't be easy. New climate, new culture, hard work, leaving old friends, maybe trouble with Arabs... But how many pioneers had it easy? When you pursue your life's dream, your passion, you put up with things and work toward your goal. Like a man, not a nothing. With pride. And with hope. Far, far away from Polish antisemitism and German Nazis.

He hadn't yet received the British entry permits into Palestine, but he wasn't worried. He'd learned a lesson from the delays getting Chana's passport. Bureaucrats were bureaucrats. Alexander told his family they'll go in August instead of June to allow the British time to get their act together. To be extra careful, he'd arranged to meet tomorrow with a man who had great contacts at the British Embassy. For a steep fee, Alexander would have the entry permits in ten days. He was glad he'd bribed the Polish bureaucrat and was willing to do it again for the British.

He smiled, remembering his family's jubilation when he brought home Chana's passport. Peace of mind was worth the money.

MAY 18, 1939
STANISLAW NOWAK

Stanislaw Nowak, head of the local passport office, reclined in his office chair and sipped a cup of steaming, bitter coffee. Well-polished shoes on desk and newspaper on lap – his favorite position. His eyes scanned the headlines but stopped when they reached an article entitled "Goodbye Jerusalem." He frowned as he read it.

The British are shutting the doors to Palestine. Yesterday, May 17, 1939, the British government issued a White Paper modifying British policy. The British government no longer supports establishing an independent Jewish nation in Palestine and has severely limited Jewish immigration.

The news is especially harsh for the approximately 200,000 Jews clamoring to exit Germany and the more than 400,000 Jews in Nazi occupied Austria and Czechoslovakia. The new British policy restricts Jewish immigration to a maximum of 10,000 individuals per year for five years, and up to an additional 25,000 refugees. After five years, immigration will totally cease...

Cynics have lambasted British Prime Minister Chamberlain for once again rewarding aggression. His move benefits Arab terrorists in Palestine and those Chamberlain fears elsewhere in the Arab world in the event of war between Britain and Germany.

The British move renders it essentially impossible for Polish Jews to emigrate to Palestine because the more than 600,000 Jews under Nazi rule should have priority, reports an anonymous government official in London.

Nowak sighed. Dammit! Poland is stuck with our 3.3 million Jews.

May 23, 1939

In a secret meeting with the heads of the German armed forces, Hitler announced his decision to "attack Poland at the first suitable opportunity" to enlarge Germany's living space and secure ample food supplies.

•••

August 15, 1939 Berlin, Germany
Karl Beck

"If it's your job, do it," Karl Beck said.

"Pardon me?" said Franz Sauer.

"That's what my grandfather would say when I griped about my chores. 'If it's your job, do it.'"

"And why are you blurting this while I'm trying to work?" Franz asked Karl, with whom he shared an office on the first floor of a busy government building in Berlin.

"Because I'm glad my job won't include, um, disposal," Karl said.

Franz's eyes narrowed. "And if it did?"

Karl shrugged but then remembered who Franz was and what he wanted to hear. "That's my point. I wouldn't like it, but I'd do it. Simple rule – if it's your job, do it."

Another day at the office for Karl and Franz. Each had his own desk in the small room; the secretaries worked in the hall. When Karl wasn't initiating a conversation, the clatter of typewriters and shuffling of papers provided the only sound in the quiet office.

Thirty-two-year-old Karl Beck was born and raised in Berlin, one of three children from a wealthy family. The youngest of the bunch, Karl was a first-rate swimmer as a teenager, fun-loving and popular. Unsure what to do with his life, he studied philosophy for two years, went into business with a family friend, joined the Nazi party because it seemed a prudent career move, and landed a government job. He was a bachelor: above average height, solidly built with high cheekbones, a strong jaw and short brown hair that he liked to comb back. His round-framed glasses gave him a scholarly look, which tickled his old friends.

Franz Sauer, devoted Nazi, was also in his thirties. Receding hairline and a little heavy at the waist, Franz was average looking and not much of an athlete. Unlike Karl, he was quiet and serious by nature. Franz had friends but was never the life of the party. Married with two kids, he liked spending time with his family or listening to classical music when he wasn't working to improve Germany.

Today they were proofreading the documents for their soon-to-be operational euthanasia program. They'd been working for months and enjoyed a strong sense of pride; it's good when your work has value. The feeling ran especially deep for Franz. For years, he'd been interested in eugenics – the "science" seeking to improve a society's "genetic quality" – which lay at the heart of their project and of the Nazi party.

Everyone knew that German society included undesirables. Not only the racially inferior, like the Jews. Plenty of Aryans – Germans and related Europeans – were mentally or physically defective. The defects were often hereditary, passed from one generation to the next. Any nation had the right to improve itself, and one obvious way was to sterilize undesirables. Doing so was good for society, logical and reasonable.

In 1933, the Nazis passed a law requiring the sterilization of severe alcoholics and of people whose mental or physical defects were hereditary. The law identified specific defects such as inherited blindness, deafness, severe physical deformities, epilepsy, feeblemindedness and schizophrenia. By this year, 1939, more than three hundred thousand of these "lives not worth living" had been sterilized.

Franz was proud that Germany had acted so forthrightly, and he was thrilled that the government was taking the next logical step: disposing of undesirables living among us, taking up space, time and resources that should instead be available to healthy people. Germany would be better off without them.

In May, Karl and Franz finished the forms that physicians and midwives will submit to the government regarding the condition of newborn babies, and the forms for all children up to three years old. The procedures for evaluating the child, deciding if it should be disposed of, and rights of appeal had been finalized and approved.

Today, Karl and Franz were proofing the forms and protocols for undesirable German adults. Disposal of children would be via medication. But they would need a way to handle multiple adults simultaneously if, as expected, the volume of adult undesirables far exceeded the number of handicapped children. Of course, no one would be disposed of until evaluated and all forms filled out by the appropriate government personnel. For efficiency, final disposal decisions would be based solely on paperwork. Only the initial evaluator needs to personally see the undesirable.

"Hey, look at this," Karl said.

"What now?" Franz, annoyed, looked up from his notepad.

Karl walked a file to Franz's desk. "I was curious what types of people get sterilized as feebleminded since, under our program, they could get disposed of. Flipping through files, I came across a boy named Erwin, twenty-one years old. He was deemed feebleminded and got sterilized.

"On the 'acquired knowledge' section of his intelligence test, he knew his hometown, province, the capitals of Germany and France, that Columbus discovered America, Martin Luther was the founder of Protestantism, who Bismarck was, our current form of government, the dates and meanings of Christmas and Easter, and most other questions. The examiner noted that Erwin's school knowledge was 'surprisingly good' and that he gave prompt answers, but nevertheless concluded that Erwin was feebleminded because of his appearance and behavior."

"So?"

"Under our program, this guy could get killed for being feebleminded. Seems a little rough."

Franz looked over the forms. "You see there was an appeal, and the appeal confirmed the sterilization decision. Obviously, the evaluator saw the big picture and didn't get stuck on whether the imbecile scored well on a particular test. National Socialism will make Germany great by rewarding the valuable and eliminating the valueless. Only someone able to contribute to society is valuable. That is just plain logic."

"But–"

"The process worked." Franz handed the file back to Karl.

Karl thought that to kill a guy for being dumb didn't seem right, but if Franz questioned his devotion and reported him, Karl could be back on the streets looking for a job. "I agree, but what's funny is that I'd answer the same as him on those questions, and so would–"

Franz laughed. "You afraid of getting classified as feebleminded and then snuffed out? Don't worry. We're too busy, and I need your help. Especially if the Poland war rumors are true."

"Huh?"

"Imagine if Germany occupies Poland, and you and I bring our program there. The place is full of defectives of all varieties; we'd never sleep." He paused, rested his chin in his hands and added, "But think of all the good we could do."

"Um–"

"And remember. If it's your job, do it."

THAT NIGHT – 8:00 P.M.
FRAMMY

When Mommy tucked four-year-old Frammy in his cot in Mommy's and Daddy's bedroom, she reminded him that tomorrow is Wednesday. Frammy especially loved Wednesday afternoons! That is when Mommy and Bubbie took him to Mr. Kowalski's candy stand.

Twinkly eyed Frammy always wore his sailor suit on those special days, the one with short pants and a giant Navy bow in front. Like what the brave sailors wear on ships out on the humongous ocean, which he has never seen but knows holds more water than a hundred bathtubs. And he always brought his stuffed bear, "Beary." No candy until Mr. Kowalski got to hear what Beary had been up to since the last time he and Frammy visited.

Out of all the candies at Mr. Kowalski's candy stand, Frammy loved the lollipops best. Red, orange, yellow, green and the special red and white ones like the Polish flag. It had circles, though of course the Polish flag didn't have circles. But Mr. Kowalski called it his Polish flag anyway.

On the way to the candy shop, Mommy, Bubbie, Frammy and Beary would walk past stores with fancy dresses that Mommy looked at through windows but never went in, and the shoe store, hat store, and every other kind of store that Bubbie always wanted to see. Mommy always said, "We don't have time because we need to do our food shopping," and Bubbie always looked anyway and said not to worry, they had time.

Frammy would try to rush them along because he fretted, "What if Mr. Kowalski runs out of lollipops!"

But luckily, Mr. Kowalski never did. He always managed to save his last Polish flag lollipop for Frammy. He'd stand there in his long white apron, and Frammy would tell him about Beary's week. Beary and Frammy always had lots of adventures. In exchange, Mr. Kowalski gave Frammy the candy, which Frammy would lick while Mommy and Bubbie shopped and when they sat on the bench under giant trees and listened to the birds chirp. And sometimes, Frammy was still licking his lollipop when he fell asleep on the trolley ride home.

The best thing about those Wednesday afternoons, even better than the Polish flag lollipop – if that was possible – was that Frammy had Mommy and Bubbie all to himself. No cousins! Frammy liked his cousins, all five of them, though Sonia could be a little bossy and Isaac was sometimes mean. But it seemed like whenever Frammy saw Bubbie, at least three or four cousins were climbing all over her. Always. And on Shabbos, the closest Frammy got was a big hug and kiss when he came and another when they went home.

But not Wednesday afternoons. Mommy and Bubbie each held one of his hands when they walked, and it was not possible to feel happier. Bubbie would moo and squawk like her pet cows and chickens from when she lived on a farm, and she'd describe some of the millions of cakes and cookies she'd made in her life.

Frammy licked his lips, yawned, and quickly fell asleep.

Soon, he was dreaming of a cake made of lollipops.

•••

2:00 A.M.

IRINA

Irina stirred in the bed she shared with Anna; she loved waking up in the middle of the night. The still darkness, as if everyone in the world except her was sound asleep, and you had lots of time left in bed.

Irina snuggled with her extra pillow and wondered about the new school year, set to begin in two weeks. She was so looking forward to the first day. Not because school was fun. Parts were good and others lame. But the first day, you got to see who's in your class. Last year, she met Roza on the first day. That turned out to be the best! Roza taught her how to get away with things she never would have imagined. Why do what the teacher says if you can just ignore her?

Irina yawned and squeezed her pillow. Which of her old friends might be in her class? Or people she barely knew. She wouldn't complain if Reuven were there! She hadn't seen him since the Zakkai event when Anna's friend spoke about Germany. He talked to her for at least ten minutes, and they laughed. He was so cool!

Would he remember her?

Why not? She remembered him.

Roza said she was friends with Reuven. Does Reuven think girls look glamorous when they smoke? Irina could practice so she wouldn't throw up like last time. Roza sure didn't help any. Roza sometimes didn't seem like such a nice person. But no one is perfect.

Better to think about Reuven. It would be fun to get to know him. Did he think she was pretty? Some people say she's pretty... Irina began to drift off to sleep. Maybe she'd watch him play football. What if he asked her to watch him play? What would she wear if he asked her? ...

•••

3:00 A.M.

ANNA

Anna heard Irina's even breathing; she was asleep. Irina was a good kid, looking forward to school and the months ahead.

Anna envied her. She ached to be happy again but felt so terribly, terribly sad over losing Mordecai and couldn't shake it. She'd never see him again. The doors to Palestine were shut, and she may not be allowed in for ten, fifteen years, or never. Was Mordecai supposed to grow old waiting for her? Give up his life's dream of rebuilding the Jewish homeland?

She wrote him two months ago that she understood he couldn't wait forever. That they must accept the truth. She would love him always, but he was free to find someone new. She'd composed the letter through a flood of tears.

When she finally received his response, she stared at the unopened envelope. Unsure, hoping – but at the same time fearing – that he'd refuse to let her go, that he'd promise to swim across the sea with her on his back, that he'd do anything to be together always.

But he didn't say any of that. He wrote that he loved Anna and always would. He wrote how sad and anguished he was... Sometimes ties are unwillingly broken. His grandmother was always sad because she'd never again see her children in America. And that Anna was so pretty and kind and smart and must look forward, not back. Unless the British suddenly changed their policy, she must put him behind her, find someone new in Poland and lead a beautiful and meaningful life there as she deserved.

All logical and clear and true and heart-wrenching. Ever since she'd received his letter, she knew they were finished. But everywhere she went, she saw his shadow, heard his laugh. Felt his absent strength. When she sat in her house and when she walked outside, when she lay down and when she got up. He was there, and yet he wasn't.

And she was terrified the Nazis would conquer Poland. Her family must leave. Go anywhere, she told her Papa. But all doors were closed. The western countries had just met in Evian, France to discuss the plight of Jews under Nazi control. They all said nice things, but none would allow in more Jews – even Jews already in the Nazis' clutches.

Palestine, the Jewish homeland, was the obvious haven, but the British had given in to Arab pressure. How could the Arabs be so cruel? They were receiving vast amounts of land but refused to let the Jews return to their tiny homeland. If the Germans do horrible things to millions of innocent Jewish people trapped in Europe, what will the Arabs do? Apologize?

Anna tossed and turned, unable to sleep. She tried to think about Irina and how happy Irina seemed. Happy things. Anna thought of when she was Irina's age. Laughing with friends. Her old classmates. Her thoughts ebbed and flowed, and she finally drifted to sleep.

But her subconscious showed no mercy and put her on a boat. Elation! She has received special permission to go to Palestine! She's standing at the railing as the boat approaches the Holy Land. All along the beach are trees full of bright, lush oranges. And someone is standing on the beach waving to her. It's Mordecai!

He's walking toward her. Anna is wading in the water, fast as she can. Estie is suddenly next to Anna pulling her along and onto the beach. The two of them walk to Mordecai, but he's not alone. He's holding hands with a dark-haired girl Anna doesn't recognize. The girl screams: "Dirty Jew, get out of here! Dirty Jew, go away!"

Anna and Estie are back on the boat, and the passengers and crew are German. The captain is Mr. Schickel, Estie's teacher. In his Nazi uniform. He orders Anna and Estie to stand in front of the class, which is full of men in Nazi uniforms sharpening their knives and yelling, "Jewish blood will soon spurt from our knives!" One of them grabs Anna's arm, and she screams, "Oh my God!"

"Anna! Anna!"

She opened her eyes. Irina was shaking her. "Wake up, wake up! You're having a nightmare. Are you OK?"

Anna stared with wide eyes, sat up, looked around the room and covered her face with both hands. She dropped them and took a deep breath. "Yeah, it was a bad dream. Oh my God, it was bad."

Irina was squeezing Anna's arm. "Are you better now?"

Anna rubbed her face and sighed. "I'm fine... Thanks."

"Good," Irina mumbled, turning over. "I was having a great dream. I'm going back to sleep to finish it."

AUGUST 20, 1939
PALESTINE
MORDECAI

The citrus grove was nestled between the bananas and the avocado orchard on a small plot of kibbutz land in the Galilee, near the blue Mediterranean Sea. Mordecai worked at the kibbutz with old-timers and twenty recent Jewish immigrants, boys and girls in their late teens or early twenties. A few from Poland but most from Germany, Mordecai fit in perfectly.

Fluent in Hebrew, Mordecai's enthusiasm made him popular with everyone. He helped his new friends learn Hebrew at night and enjoyed hiking or visiting other communities with them on days off. He loved the sounds and smells of this land; the sweet pine forest, the crashing sea, the cry of the hawk. The chatter of Hebrew and mix of native born and immigrant, he felt welcomed. And at home.

He and his kibbutz friends spent most days tending the crops, now under the raging August sun or in the even hotter sheds. Young Jews working to recreate a Jewish country in this land after two thousand years.

Today, Mordecai had been sweating in the citrus grove since six in the morning. Dressed in tan shorts, sandals, and a wide-brimmed beige hat, he left the grove two hours later. Carrying a sealed envelope in his hand, he walked a mile along a dusty road to the nearest post office. He should have written the letter a month earlier.

Twice a month, Mordecai would receive a letter from Anna. Surrounded by his bunkmates but oblivious to them, he'd disappear into Anna's voice, savoring every word. And then he'd read the letter again and again. His new friends would tease that her letters transformed him from happy to happiest.

In July, after a longer delay than normal, Mordecai had received one of Anna's treasures. As usual, he didn't open it until he'd worked all day and completed his after-dinner chores. When he walked into the bedroom he shared with several guys, one of them announced: "Mordecai received an Anna letter. Line starts here to borrow money or get help on chores." Mordecai had laughed, pulled off his shirt and shoes and climbed into his upper bunk bed. Reclining against his pillow, he opened the letter.

This one he didn't savor. She wrote that they must accept reality: they'll never see each other again. She didn't expect him to wait forever, and he was free to find another girl. His mouth opened, and blood drained from his face. He reread the heartbreaking words and felt like he'd been stabbed. Life stopped. He held his face in his hands and cried; his roommates glanced at each other and left the room.

He'd known she was worried, but how could Anna think they were finished? She knew he loved her and wanted to marry her. He repeatedly reread her words while wiping the tears from his eyes. That night and the next days and nights. He tortured himself trying to understand. She said she knew he couldn't wait forever. But she knew he WOULD wait forever and would use that forever getting back to her. She wrote that he was free to find someone else. But she knew he didn't want to find someone else. Her meaning must be different from her words.

There was only one explanation. Anna wanted to be free. She believed the British White Paper was a huge problem, as he did, and she loved him. But to wait years was unfair to both of them, and she needed to be set free. She couldn't bring herself to hurt Mordecai by saying it, so she wrote that she knew he couldn't wait forever as a gentle way to say she can't wait forever, and that she should be free to find someone new. Anna was asking Mordecai's permission.

Nothing else made sense.

Mordecai had decided that he must be strong and pretend he agreed. She had asked his permission, and he wrote back and gave it. They must look forward, not back. She was free to find someone new. It broke his heart to put that letter in the mail, but he did it. For her. About a month ago.

He'd suffered ever since.

This morning, well before the sun rose, he wrote what he really felt. That he had not given up. He would never give up. He would find a way to get them together. In Palestine. He explained why he had sent the other letter. He said that if she really wanted to move on, she was free to do so, but he was not moving on. He'd find a way. He had placed the letter in an envelope, carefully addressed and sealed it, and licked on extra stamps to be sure. He'd double-checked the address and carefully put the letter in his backpack.

He arrived at the post office, walked past the bin for letters and directly to the clerk. He again checked to make sure he'd addressed the letter correctly and asked the clerk if he had enough postage. "Twice as much as you need," the clerk said. "Must be to your girl. Don't worry, she'll have this in her hands in two weeks."

Instead of going straight back to work, Mordecai walked west about a quarter mile under the summer's deep-blue sky and climbed a small hill overlooking the Mediterranean. He sat against a tree, rested his elbows on his crossed legs and held his face in his hands. He heard the boom of the waves hitting the shore.

They had two choices. To live in Poland or get Anna illegally into Palestine. Which meant they had no choice. He must get her illegally into Palestine. But how? He looked out over the vast sea that once had seemed so beautiful but now represented an insurmountable barrier. He pondered and changed his mind. The Mediterranean wasn't the obstacle; the British were the obstacle. He had been focused on getting acclimated in his new home, but it was time to check out the Jewish underground groups.

With that decision, invigorated by the notion that he might be able to do something other than mope, Mordecai made his way back to the citrus grove.

Meanwhile, his letter to Anna began its journey. It was properly sorted and handled by the post office, bundled with other letters, and sent on its way to Europe.

On September 1, 1939, Germany invaded Poland. Mordecai's letter was never delivered.

PART TWO

The Trap

SEPTEMBER 7, 1939
THE ALLOWITZS

The Poles surrendered Krasau on September 6, 1939 to spare it certain devastation, but continued to battle across Poland to the north and east. Anna, Estie, and hundreds of others lined the streets the following day to watch the conquering Germans march through the city. Thousands of them, in perfect order. Fierce and determined, as if Satan's warriors had marched up from hell.

Anna wondered, how can you wake up one day and your world has vanished and been replaced by a dark unknown? For so long, the Nazis had tormented Jews – but that was far away, in the newspapers, in Germany, not here. Not in Krasau.

This couldn't be real, but it was.

•••

Late that afternoon, Papa hung up the phone and, hands trembling, quickly talked to Mama and summoned Anna and Irina to the living room. Papa and Mama sat on the couch and the girls on chairs; Frammy was napping.

Papa spoke fast. "I've learned the Valoskys are leaving Krasau early tomorrow morning. They'd wanted to go last week but got delayed. They'll hide in a horse-drawn wagon under hay – Mr. Valosky is paying a farmer – and get to Mr. Valosky's cousin's village, where they have a truck." He took a breath. "They'll head to eastern Poland, where the Germans haven't conquered, and stay there or go to Lithuania or Russia. Should take two or three days depending on many things. They have room if we want to join them."

Mama and the girls stared at him with silent, open-mouthed, wide-eyed fear.

"I know it's hard." Papa clenched and opened his fists. "But we have only a few minutes to decide." He said softly to Mama, "You'll see why I've included the girls."

Silence.

Irina broke it. "Hey, what if we sneeze from the hay or Frammy makes noise, or whatever – and the Germans catch us?"

Papa nervously ran a hand through his hair. "I don't know. The Germans have ordered everyone except some farmers to stay home. It could be very bad. Or the soldiers might just tell us to turn back."

Mama, pale, stared vacantly; her initial shock was slowly replaced by anxious dread as haunted memories of her father's murder flooded her mind. The despair from that horrible time ripped at her. "Will the soldiers be cruel?" she mumbled quietly, as if asking herself. Her father's smiling face as the soldiers approached. His hand on her shoulder. "Everything will be fine, Chani," he'd said.

Only one thing mattered to Mama. She must protect her children, her family. "No! We should risk our children's lives on the whims of soldiers with guns? Tell the Valoskys no."

Silence.

"Papa," Anna said, "what do you think? Is it smart?"

Papa grimaced. He wished he knew. Should he take his family from where it still seemed safe? And violate the German order? "It's hard to avoid battles in a war zone. But Mr. Valosky is smart, he has maps and believes he knows where the fighting is. First, we'd need to make it out of town in the hay wagon. Will Frammy stay quiet? Will the Germans inspect the wagon? Do they care about refugees? And if we succeed, how could we pay for food and a place to stay after our money runs out? There might be Jewish organizations to help. Here we have a home, I have the bike shop."

Papa shook his head. "But if we hope to go, now is the time, with the chaos of war."

Mama slapped her hands to her face. "Do you think it will get so bad here that we should risk our lives?"

"Mama," Anna said. "The Nazis hate Jews. The humiliations–"

"No!" Mama cried. "They can humiliate me! They can hate! But don't give them an excuse to murder us." The terror had overwhelmed her. She could see her family hiding under the hay. A soldier randomly decides to check, or Frammy whines. The soldiers order them out and take Papa, like they took her father. "No. Frammy is a little boy. He won't understand."

"Chana." Alexander reached for her hand. "I talked with Mr. Valosky about Frammy. You, Frammy and I could stay, and the girls go."

"What!" Mama shrieked. "Divide our family?" Had Alexander lost his mind? Send her daughters away and not know for days or weeks or months if they're safe? "No, we'll stay together!"

"It might be best," Papa said softly. He looked at Anna. "That's why I called you in here. If you want to go without us, alone or with Irina, you can do it."

"If soldiers find you in a wagon," Irina said, "you can't run away. But at home you can hide, like under the bed or in the attic. I'd go with Anna if we weren't stuffed in a wagon–"

"We don't get to choose," Papa said. "It's hay wagon or stay."

"Then I want to stay," Irina said.

Papa nodded, paused and looked at Anna. "You can still go. But I don't know what's best, so I won't insist–"

"She's not going!" Mama commanded. Mama walked to Anna, still sitting, and caressed her neck. "Stay with us, Anna, we're a family. Please stay with us," she whimpered.

Anna looked at her anguished Mama and her uncertain Papa. Her two choices – stay or leave – were both awful.

"I'm worried about the Germans," Papa said, "but we should be OK if we obey them and don't make trouble. They were fine when they occupied us during the World War. Some were antisemites and brutes, but plenty were good men. Underneath the uniforms are people. Like you and me. People are people."

"Like the people who murdered my daddy?" Mama coldly asked.

Anna thoughtfully rubbed her chin. "The German soldiers in Krasau are ruled by Nazis who hate Jews. Your men were ruled by the Kaiser – the Kaiser who met with Herzl."

Papa sighed. He thought Anna should go but wasn't sure enough to say she must. What if he was wrong and something terrible happened? "If you want to go, Mr. Valosky is a good man. He'll look after you as best he can. And we'll give you money. In Lithuania, if you go there, will be Jewish organizations, probably many refugees, maybe trying to go to Palestine. The British might have sympathy–"

"Palestine?" Anna mouthed. Mordecai's image flashed in her mind.

"Maybe it's possible, that's all," Papa said softly. "I don't know."

"Anna, DON'T GO!" Irina cried.

"When do I need to decide?" Anna asked.

Papa looked at his watch. "In five minutes."

Anna stared down at the floor. Voluntarily leave home and risk getting killed in a war zone? But the Nazis terrified her; she should do whatever possible to escape. But what if the Valoskys ask her to do something important, and she messes up? What if she gets nervous and endangers all of them?

Anna rubbed her forehead with a sweaty hand; her heart raced as she imagined hiding in a wagon, petrified the Germans would catch them. She then pictured herself lying peacefully in the bed she shared with Irina.

"I'll stay."

•••

Anna called Estie later that night and told her she'd passed on a chance to leave Krasau. Estie answered with a somber, "You should have gone."

"Well, I didn't," Anna said. "You lived in Germany. Do you think they'll–"

"The Nazis say Poles are subhuman and Jews are even lower."

"You think they'll make special laws for Jews, like in Germany?"

"Yeah."

"What will they do – will they be cruel to regular people?"

"We're all about to learn what 'cruel' means."

September 14, 1939
Itzhak

The nicely dressed congregation rose from their seats on this first day of Rosh Hashanah, the Jewish New Year, as gray-bearded Rabbi Leibman marched a Torah scroll down the small synagogue's center aisle, as customary after reading the Torah.

Families who hadn't seen each other in months used the break to talk. "Where are the Zubelskys?" a man asked a guy standing near him.

"Not sure. We heard they fled east. Any news from your son?"

"Thanks for asking," the worried father replied, nervously twirling the strings of the tallis, or prayer shawl, draped over his shoulders. "He's with an artillery company, and his last letter said he was near Warsaw. And your boys?"

"One is in the infantry and the other is a medic. We haven't heard anything and are praying for their safety and for the army to push the Germans out of Poland."

And so the conversations went.

The synagogue held two hundred people. The wooden pews on the right extended from the back of the synagogue to the front. On the left, the benches went only three-quarters of the way; on the front left was a large, raised lectern where the rabbi stood and led the service. At the front, center, were three steps leading to a raised cabinet, inset into the wall, containing the Torah scrolls. Columns in the classical style bordered the cabinet, as if the Torah were encased in Jerusalem's ancient Temple.

Itzhak sat with his father near the raised lectern. Throughout the year and on holidays, Itzhak's job was to help Rabbi Leibman with whatever he needed. Find a missing book, set up for the service, shush noisy children. He received no pay but spent a lot of time with Rabbi Leibman. Itzhak treasured those moments; in his eyes, Rabbi Leibman was a compassionate genius. A gentle man who enjoyed poking fun at himself. The man who, months before, had written that an unimaginable hell was about to descend upon the Jewish people.

Like his friend, Szymon, Itzhak had once considered a life of piety. But as he'd grown older, his religious doubts had increased. Itzhak still volunteered because of Rabbi Leibman, but religious services usually bored him.

Not today. Itzhak wanted to be here, in synagogue, with his parents and the families he'd known for so long. The words of wisdom, the familiar customs and tunes provided a needed anchor. Itzhak sensed warmth. A feeling that together, everything might be OK.

The congregation rose and recited the Rosh Hashana prayer that life is fleeting and fragile; all mankind passes before God like a flock of sheep as God determines their destiny. "Who shall live, and who shall die; who shall pass after a long life, and who before his time; who by sword... who by famine and who by thirst... who will live in peace, and who will be tormented..." The prayer struck closer to home this year.

As the service neared its end, Itzhak stood in the center aisle next to the raised lectern, and Rabbi Leibman read the 27th Psalm. "The Lord is my light and salvation; whom shall I fear?... Though an army should encamp against me, my heart shall not be afraid... One thing I ask of the Lord: that I shall dwell in the House of the Lord all the days of my life... You have been my help, do not cast me off or forsake me, oh God of–"

Women suddenly screamed in back as German soldiers burst into the sanctuary. "Shut up! Everyone shut up!" they shouted. The Germans overturned a bookcase of prayer books onto the floor, smashed two large, ornate vases – the glass shattering into a thousand pieces – and marched up the center aisle toward Itzhak. An officer in front followed by several soldiers in dark uniforms. The officer yelled in broken Polish, "I need to piss! Where's your Torah!"

Itzhak froze. The officer, a head taller than Itzhak with a chiseled face and venomous eyes, marched toward him. Itzhak's father cried from his nearby pew, "Itzhak! Come here, sit down!"

"You!" the officer barked, pointing at Itzhak, "Where is the Torah! I need to piss!"

Itzhak's pulse pounded in his head, and he stood mutely as the German approached.

The officer loomed over him. "Get it!" he sneered.

Itzhak smelled alcohol on the German's breath. Knees shaking, Itzhak didn't budge; he stared defiantly into the seething blue eyes and said nothing.

Congregants of all ages stumbled over each other and out the back door. The officer pulled a pistol from his holster; Rabbi Leibman, who had rushed from the lectern, pushed Itzhak away, and Itzhak's father pulled him to a pew. Rabbi Leibman pointed to the cabinet at the front of the synagogue.

The German smirked, shoved the rabbi aside, climbed the steps, jerked open the cabinet and saw three upright Torah scrolls, each covered in velvet and ornamented with silver crowns on top and a silver breast plate. "Aha! We found them!" One at a time, he heaved the Torah scrolls down the steps; they crashed against the front pew and onto the floor.

Itzhak watched the soldiers rip off the Torah coverings and strew the sheepskin scrolls across the floor. The officer berated Rabbi Leibman in German, "On your knees! Read! I want to hear what garbage you pray." Soldiers wiped their feet and stomped on two open scrolls, and Rabbi Leibman, red-faced, knelt next to the third one, pulled his glasses from his pocket and read the Hebrew words. Itzhak recognized them, from when the children of Israel wandered in the desert.

"No, idiot! Translate it!"

Rabbi Leibman recited in German as if he were reading: "You shall love the Lord your God with all your heart, with all–"

The officer unzipped his pants and pissed on the scroll, creating a small puddle on the holy words near Rabbi Leibman's face. He stopped reading and stared at the German in wide-eyed horror. The officer jammed the barrel of his pistol against Rabbi Leibman's head. "Read!"

Rabbi Leibman shook his head no, squeezed his eyes shut, and awaited the bullet.

Itzhak ran as quickly as his feeble legs would take him, fell to the floor next to Rabbi Leibman, and "translated" into German. "You shall love the Lord your God with all your heart"; two other Germans laughed, unzipped their pants and pissed on the other scrolls. Itzhak heard the splatter.

"With all your soul and with all your might. Take to heart what I teach you today." A soldier kicked Rabbi Leibman's back, sending him sprawling face down onto a scroll. Other soldiers peed onto Rabbi Leibman's head and on Itzhak; it slowly dripped down their faces. Itzhak tasted the urine, wiped his lips, and with clenched fists kept reciting, but the soldiers' laughter drowned out Itzhak's words in the almost empty sanctuary.

"And teach them to your children..."

OCTOBER 8, 1939
SZYMON

Szymon's housekeeper showed Itzhak into the palatial home and escorted him to the large parlor, where Szymon sat waiting with his parents near floor to ceiling windows overlooking their garden.

"Itzhak Scheinman," Szymon said, "please meet my parents, Andrzej and Maria Bartosz." Szymon's tall, blonde mother hugged short, chubby, dark-haired Itzhak, and Szymon's handsome father welcomed him with a warm handshake. "So, this is the famous Itzhak!" Mr. Bartosz said.

Itzhak blushed. "I'm Itzhak, but I'm not famous."

"Ah, but you're famous here. Szymon describes you as a cross between Einstein and Copernicus."

"Thank you, sir."

Mr. Bartosz's voice darkened; still clenching Itzhak's hand: "We also heard about your very frightening experience on the Jewish holiday. We're glad you're OK."

Itzhak nodded.

Mrs. Bartosz smiled. "To what do we owe this visit?"

"Itzhak and I are going to Filip's house," Szymon said.

Mr. Bartosz heaved an irritated sigh. "Itzhak, I'll expect you to advise Szymon to avoid whatever dangerous schemes Filip might suggest. And Szymon – come home before curfew."

"Not a problem," Szymon said, waving Itzhak with him to the door.

Szymon's father sternly repeated, "Szymon, make sure you're back before curfew. Don't test the Germans."

"I agree, sir," Itzhak said, and they left.

•••

"Andrzej."

A groan.

Maria's voice. "Wake up!"

Andrzej's sleepy eyes opened briefly but closed again. Why is she waking me? It can't already be time for work. "What time is it?" Andrzej mumbled.

She shook him. The only sound in their dark bedroom was her distraught voice. "It's 3:00. Get up! Now!"

Maria sounds worried. Must have had a nightmare. God knows

there is plenty of reason for that. Partially awake, but with his eyes still closed, Andrzej reached his hand across the bed to draw her close – but she wasn't there. He opened his eyes, turned his head and saw her standing next to the bed, leaning over him. He shut his eyes and reached for her hand, but she jerked away; in her panic she slapped his face and screamed, "You need to go!"

He opened his eyes. She slapped me? She's never hit anyone in her life. He looked at her for the first time. Her eyes were huge, and her left hand yanked furiously at her hair.

"Andrzej, please!" she shrieked.

He looked up again at her eyes.

Terror.

Szymon. Something happened to Szymon! Andrzej bolted upright.

"Was Szymon caught violating the curfew!" Images of German soldiers beating Szymon, taking him to jail. Or shooting him in the forest. Andrzej's arms and legs started to shake uncontrollably. "Where did they take him! I told Szymon not to stay out late. What happened, where is he!" He swung his legs off the bed and stood next to Maria. "We need to–"

"No, Andrzej, it's not Szymon. It's you!"

"What–"

"Jan just called. The Germans are arresting people. Tonight. In their homes! They're piling people into trucks. They've arrested Stefan Adamczyk and Jakub Kaminski." She spoke rapidly. "They have a list. You're on it," she gasped. "You need to go. Now!"

"Szymon's OK? He's here? He–" Andrzej put a hand on the back of his head and took a deep breath, finally beginning to think straight. "They're coming for me? Why–" He paused. "Because I'm a lawyer? But – but so are you. We both need to go. Get dressed, I'll wake up Szymon–" Andrzej pulled off his tan pajama shirt. "Who says I'm on the list?" Maria sometimes gets carried away. Before violating the German curfew, he should understand what was happening.

Maria tugged at her nightgown. "Andrzej, please!" The rumors they'd been hearing terrified her. That special German units had arrested Polish civilians, shot them in the woods–

"I want to make sure we're not being foolish. Quickly – tell me what you know."

"Jan called a few minutes ago. You were sound asleep." Her dread increased as she re-lived the conversation. "He said the Germans are arresting people. They have a list. Right now, that you need to hide–"

"Did he see the list?"

"I don't–"

"Did Jan see a list with my name on it, or say I'm probably on a list, or I may be on a list?"

"I don't–"

Andrzej began to calm down; it sounded like Jan was guessing. He grasped Maria's hand. "The Germans may or may not want to arrest me." His tone was soft and comforting. "I agree it's smart for us to leave, to be careful. But we shouldn't panic." He paused and calmly said, "We'll need money, IDs, clothes... like for a long vacation."

Andrzej's relaxed voice somewhat calmed Maria. She sighed. "I'll get money and jewelry from the safe and then start packing. Afterwards, we'll wake Szymon."

"OK. I could call Leon. They live close enough that we shouldn't run into any Germans. And they have an empty bedroom. But I'd hate to call in the middle of the night–"

"I think we have a good reason–"

They heard scraping on the side of the house, and Maria's eyes bulged. The Germans must be breaking in the windows!

"Probably the tree," Andrzej said. He peeked outside and saw windblown branches brushing against their house.

"Please call Leon now," Maria pleaded. "What if he doesn't answer?"

Andrzej nodded. "OK, I will. But first, come here." In the darkness, they hugged each other tight. "We may want to bring some food with us," he said.

Maria shook her head, but the ridiculous comment further calmed her. "Only you would think of food when we're traveling less than five blocks."

Maria watched Andrzej yawn and stretch; she might have overreacted. Of the two men Jan said were arrested, one was a socialist and the other was Jewish. She and Andrzej were neither. It was nice of Jan to call – he was being careful. But the Germans obviously didn't share their secret arrest lists with him. He's just speculating that Andrzej is on it.

"Thanks for calming me down." She kissed Andrzej's cheek.

A truck's engine rumbled outside. Andrzej rushed bare-chested to the window without flicking on the light and peeked through the shutters. An army truck stopping in front of their house. "They're here! Szymon needs to hide!" Andrzej barked, running in the dark toward Szymon's bedroom. "I'll help him hide. You fix his bed so they think no one slept in it. No lights!"

Andrzej rushed to their beloved son's bedroom and frantically whispered, "Szymon!" Andrzej yanked off the covers and forcefully twisted Szymon's legs off the bed.

"What–" Still asleep in his underwear, Szymon flailed his arms in self-defense.

Andrzej slapped Szymon's face. "No time. Germans here. Need to HIDE NOW!"

Szymon's Papa dragged him to the bedroom closet. Szymon turned his head and saw his Mama hurriedly fixing his bed, and he heard loud pounding on the front door. From across the room, Mama reached a hand toward him, painfully smiled, and fled. Papa pointed at the closet floor. "Crouch on the floor, here. Then don't move. No noise. It shouldn't be too long."

Heart pounding, Szymon obeyed and felt a blanket thrown over him and something heavy on top of it. The banging at the door grew louder. Mama hollered from another room, "Coming!"

Papa whispered, "Szymon, live your life with honor."

Szymon tried to answer, but no sound left his open mouth.

October 10, 1939
Jozef

They crouched, all fourteen of them, waiting for the target to arrive. Their leader communicated via hand signals, reinforcing the need for silence. At exactly 4:50 p.m., as prearranged, the door opened and he entered the apartment to a loud burst.

"Surprise!" the teens yelled. "Happy birthday, Jozef!"

The shocked Zakkai leader hovered in the doorway and smiled at his wife, Leah, whose eyes beamed at him. He gave her a hug, followed by fourteen bear hugs, one for each Zakkai kid from the cheerful, round-faced giant. As more teens trickled in, for each a gargantuan hug.

Leah took Jozef's hand and led him into the living room, where she shoved a small kremowka, a cream-filled puff pastry, into his mouth, and everyone sang Sto lat, the traditional Polish song wishing him a hundred years of good health. Jozef gobbled another kremowka, decorating the tip of his nose with cream.

"That's a nice look," a teen teased, and Jozef tried – to the delight and rowdy encouragement of the crowd – licking it off with his tongue until he admitted defeat, and Leah – to enthusiastic cheers – licked it for him. Jozef then thanked everyone for coming, chatted with the teens for a while, and let them separate into groups.

Though still standing in the crowded room, within moments Jozef's mind had returned to where it was before he'd opened the door. To a secret conversation with old friends who, like him, were very worried about the Germans and not inclined to stay passive. What that meant exactly and where it might lead, none of them knew.

Jozef thoughtfully shook his head. He should be celebrating his twenty-ninth birthday in Palestine; he and Leah had moved there years ago, but she missed her family. Or he might have grown up in America, like his cousins. Jozef's uncle emigrated in 1920, worked hard in New York and sent money for Jozef's family to follow. But his grandfather objected. "In America, Jews work on Shabbos!" he warned Jozef's father. "Would he raise his children in a God-less place?" A few years later, Jozef's father decided to move, but America had shut her doors to eastern Europe, partially to keep out "God-less communists" – like Jozef's family?

Instead, Jozef lived in Poland, now under German occupation.

"Happy birthday!" someone said.

"Thank you," Jozef replied absently, locked in his thoughts. What lay in store for these kids? For any Jew or Pole? If only the British would let these kids into Palestine.

Jozef sighed, finally forced his mind to re-join the party, and listened to the teens talk. "I heard German soldiers beat up two Jews just minding their own business," a boy said. "Broke a guy's arm."

"Did the Jewish men disobey them?" a girl asked. "No one gets beat up if they didn't–"

"No, I'm telling you – they were just standing there–"

"Did you see Mr. Yergen?" someone else said. "Soldiers cut off his beard in the middle of the street with a knife! Left him all bloody."

"That's nothing, what about–"

"Hey!" Leah hollered. "This is a Zakkai event. Here, we talk about happy things – about Zionism, becoming pioneers, creating a just society. And it's a birthday party! Worry about the Germans outside our doors."

Eighteen-year-old Anna and thirteen-year-old Irina walked into the living room. "Happy birthday, Jozef! Sorry we're late."

"Thanks!" Jozef grinned at Irina in her long, braided pigtails. "It's nice to see you again, Irina; I think this makes three weeks in a row. I noticed Reuven in the other room."

Irina blushed. "Hey, thanks." She headed toward Reuven, missing Jozef's wink to Anna.

Jozef gestured for Anna to follow him to a quiet corner. She was one of Jozef's favorites. Smart, honest, friendly and a lot of depth. Leah had done a great job keeping Anna involved after Mordecai left. Anna didn't want to become an official leader – she must have obligations at home – but she sometimes wrote articles for their newsletter and had become a role model for younger girls. Anna spoke her mind to Jozef, and he knew he could trust her.

"I liked your article, especially the bits on Zionism." He began to speak softly. "Leah said you asked if Zakkai might do little things to resist the Germans. I'm afraid that would be too dangerous and has nothing to do with settling the Land."

Anna looked puzzled. "Leah misunderstood. I was just wondering–"

"Don't get me wrong. I appreciate the sentiment, but not for Zakkai. You're talented. Preparing leaflets – or other things – may become very important as time passes."

"Other things?"

"We don't know how the Germans will treat us next week, next month, next year."

"My father – he's knowledgeable – he says the Germans are on edge and if we, Poles and Jews, obey them, they'll see we're not a threat and will relax. And things should be fine. The Nazi leaders are terrible, but the average German isn't."

"Many people agree with your father."

"You don't?"

"I think the Nazi leaders make the rules, and the rest follow."

"Either way, what could ordinary people do about it?"

"Anna, don't ever believe that an ordinary person can't do extraordinary things. Some people say we shouldn't simply sit back and watch." He moved closer, looked at her with a serious intensity she wasn't used to seeing in him, and whispered, "I agree with them."

Anna's eyes narrowed. "What are some people doing?"

"At this moment, I'm talking to you. Finding smart people who can keep secrets is a good first step."

Anna flushed red. She didn't agree with Jozef; what Papa said made sense. And even if she did agree, wishing others did something – especially something dangerous – was very different from doing it yourself. She silently shook her head.

"Saying 'no' brings no shame. I'll never mention it again. Contact me if you change your mind and say nothing to others about our conversation. That is very important."

Anna nodded.

"Come on." Jozef waved for her to follow. "It's time for more kremowkas."

FEBRUARY 20, 1940
ITZHAK AND SZYMON

Szymon devoured the bowl of steaming broth, carrots, onions and bits of chicken. "Thank you," he said, wiping his mouth with a napkin. "That was delicious!"

Itzhak's round, apron-decked mother smiled. She loved Szymon. Not because she knew him well, which she didn't, or because she'd seen him often, which she hadn't. But she'd learned from Itzhak that Szymon was a true friend to him. His only friend, it seemed. A boy his own age.

Szymon and Itzhak were sitting across from each other in Itzhak's family's kitchen, and Itzhak's mother hovered nearby. "How is your niece, Ruthie, doing?" Szymon asked.

"How do you know Ruthie?"

"From school."

"Mama, he is quite an admirer of Ruthie," said Itzhak, who somehow managed to remain stone-faced when Szymon kicked his shin under the table.

"Ruthie is a talented actress," Szymon said. He lay down his napkin. "So how is she doing?"

"Well," Mama frowned, "days before the Germans came, my sister's family, including Ruthie of course, left to a small town where we have relatives. But the Germans have resettled all Jews from there to Krakow. Then we heard they'll be resettled to Warsaw, with nowhere to stay. The Germans are forcing Jews from one place to another. From villages to towns, from towns to cities. And poor Ruthie and her sisters. What could be worse–" Mama suddenly remembered Szymon's parents and felt like a fool. "I'm sorry, we don't need to talk about that. I'll bring you more food. We have potatoes–"

Itzhak caught Szymon's quick glance. "Mama, Szymon and I have work to do but little time, so..."

Still blushing from her comment, Mama hesitated, said, "Szymon, tell me if you want anything else," and she left the room.

"Any news on your parents?" Itzhak asked softly.

Szymon lowered his eyes. "Life is strange. We know it will include pain, loss, tragedy; but we're shocked when it strikes us. But no, no news. Only hope. Diminishing hope," he said under his breath.

Itzhak nodded.

"Time for work," Szymon said, opening his notebook. "I'll read you my notes on treatment of Poles, Polish Catholics. And you'll read your notes on Jews. We'll continue to jot down important events as they occur, meet every few weeks, and hopefully someday publish them as a historical document on the German occupation."

"The title can be 'Life under the Bastards.'"

"Hopefully, they'll be gone within a few months," Szymon said, "and our book will be thin. Surely France and England will attack soon from Germany's west and, hopefully, from the north. You'd think Norway would allow the British to attack from their territory. But here's my quick summary.

"The Germans invaded Poland September 1, the Russians invaded from the east in mid-September, and Poland surrendered before the end of the month. Russia conquered eastern Poland, and the Germans have occupied the rest for almost five months. We address the German occupation.

"The Germans have arrested, and perhaps executed" – Szymon took a breath – "many of Poland's intelligentsia and other leadership.

"The Germans have shut down all newspapers and radio stations.

"All schools, except for little kids, closed because the Germans believe Poles are imbeciles.

"At least tens of thousands of Polish men and women, and older boys and girls have been abducted from their families and sent to Germany to work in factories.

"Hundreds of thousands of Poles are being evicted from their homes to make room for Germans.

"It's tough to know whom to trust. A Polish policeman informed on seven former university students who had installed an illegal radio receiver. The Germans arrested and shot them.

"The Germans constantly work to increase the hatred of Pole against Jew through German-controlled radio, leaflets, newspapers encouraging Poles to attack and steal from Jews."

Szymon looked up from his notes. "Your turn."

Itzhak opened his notebook.

"All Jews older than ten must wear a Star of David armband.

"It's against the law for Jews to travel by train.

"Jews must fill out a form listing all their possessions.

"All Jews must take off their hats when passing a German.

"The Germans have forced hundreds of thousands of Jews to leave their homes and resettle in large cities.

"The Germans enjoy humiliating Jews. They forced a rabbi to

defecate in his pants. A man defended his father from attack by soldiers, and they beat him so badly he's now brain damaged.

"Jews are allotted smaller rations than Christians. The bread ration for Jews has been cut to 200 grams; Christians get 570. Christians get sugar, Jews don't.

"The Germans seize men and women for forced labor, such as scrubbing military barracks, clearing rubble. Some German overseers beat people.

"The Germans ordered Krasau's Jews to create a leadership group, called the Jewish Council, and an unarmed Jewish police force to enforce their rules. The Germans require the Jewish Council to provide Jews for forced labor and gave the labor administrator twenty lashes for not meeting his quota.

"Polish hoodlums attack Jews in the street, knowing the police won't interfere. Between that and forced labor, many Jews are afraid to leave their homes.

"The courage of some religious Jews, those bearded men dressed in all black, has been inspiring. They know they'll suffer abuse, but many still follow their traditions at great peril.

"That is my summary, for now," Itzhak said.

Szymon rested his hands on the table and leaned forward. "So, what are we going to do about it?"

"Do?"

"The Polish government in exile in London is urging Poles to resist. Resistance groups are being formed, orders come from England. And people – they're creating small cells."

"And you've joined one."

"Thinking about it."

"Thinking?"

Szymon sighed. "I've promised – myself and God – that if my parents are alive, I'll devote my life to the priesthood." He looked down and then back up. "If they're not, I'll join the resistance."

Itzhak paused, carefully choosing his words. "You may not know for a long time."

Szymon nodded.

"Let's hope–"

"I have a friend in a resistance group," Szymon said. "They have one radio. If I join them, they'll want me to get my hands on others. I could get some nonworking, incomplete, and bits and pieces of radios – you're a genius. Can you build radios?"

Itzhak frowned. "No, but I know someone. He could turn a broomstick into a radio. His name–"

"Don't tell me his name! If I join the group and the Germans arrest me, I'd rather not know. You sure he'd help?"

"Definitely."

"Tell your friend if he's caught, his best future will be execution, and his worst will be torture and execution."

"Not an issue."

"Same for you."

"Understood." Itzhak twirled the dark, curly hair above his ear. "Why don't you put me in touch with your friend, and you stay out of it? Become a priest, as you've always dreamt. I'll join–"

"No. Won't work–"

"Because my friend and I are Jews?"

Szymon shrugged.

"You should keep better company."

"I'll think about that too."

•••

Gloved hands in his pockets and a brown, wool scarf wrapped around his neck, Szymon walked the mile or so from Itzhak's house through the winding, impoverished, icy streets of Krasau's old Jewish section. Some peddlers roamed the area, hawking their wares in Jewish or Jewish-accented Polish. But far fewer than before the occupation. And Jewish script still advertised the names of shops above their doors and windows – but the Germans had forced most to close.

After about twenty minutes, Szymon entered the neighborhood where he shared a room with his cousin, Filip. Deep in thought and oblivious to the noise and exhaust fumes of passing cars, Szymon made his way uphill several more blocks, his breath steaming in the frigid air. He reached his family's church, an old, thick-walled, red-brick building with a tall, cylindrical bell tower topped by a giant cross. But he didn't enter. Instead, he continued on the sidewalk next to the ice-coated, black-iron fence bordering a small cemetery.

Szymon reached an open gate, sighed deeply and stepped inside. Alone and heavy-hearted, he followed the slick, narrow cobblestone walkway that wound along the graves, each headed by a gray tombstone, some more than a hundred years old. Gnarled trees and plants filled the open spaces; flowers, crucifixes and candle-holding lanterns of red or clear glass decorated the tombs per Polish custom.

Szymon walked to the resting places of his mother's great-grandparents, grandparents, and parents, one next to the other. Arranged neatly in front of each tombstone were lanterns and potted plants his mother had respectfully placed there months earlier. Szymon bowed his head and silently prayed.

The wind picked up, shaking the smaller branches and rustling the leaves of a short, ancient tree standing next to his grandparents' headstone, its limbs sheltering the grave from snow and rain. Eyeing its twisted, knotted roots and thick trunk, Szymon pulled the scarf tighter around his neck, sat on the cold ground and stared at the tree for a long time.

Remembering good days from when he was young, his mind reached back to a different tree, in their yard, that his mother had climbed to rescue a scared kitten. Szymon's father had laughed so hard at his mother's shocked face when the poor creature's claws suddenly latched onto her. And then she and Szymon had howled when the cat leapt from her hands onto his father's head.

Szymon smiled.

Finally, he rummaged through his coat pocket, removed a knife, knelt, and slowly and carefully carved into the trunk about three feet off the ground. Two sets of initials – "AB" for his father, Andrzej Bartosz and "MWB" for his mother, Maria Wisniewski Bartosz. He dug a rectangular hole next to the tree, removed two lanterns from his grandparents' headstones, and gently inserted the lanterns into the hole.

Kneeling before his parents' symbolic graves, Szymon closed his eyes and recited, "Eternal rest grant unto them, O Lord. Let perpetual light shine upon them, and may they rest in peace." And then he cried.

For the loss of his parents, and also of his future.

When he could cry no more, Szymon returned to his cousin's home and called his friend. "I'm ready."

THE SAME DAY
IRINA

Bundled up against the Polish winter and wearing Star of David armbands – white cloth with a blue star – on their right coat sleeves, Anna and Irina were walking home late afternoon from Irina's friend's apartment. Irina had stuffed her light-brown braids inside her hood and tied it tight to defend against the bitter wind cutting into her face. They had walked half a mile, past where Mordecai's parents had lived – they disappeared weeks ago, someone said to Warsaw – and were almost home. Bare trees lined the sidewalk, their dead leaves driven by the wind.

Irina had said almost nothing the entire way, and Anna was worried about her. The last few months had been tough on Irina. School never started, and after the Nazis ordered all Jews over age ten to wear Jew armbands, Papa said Irina couldn't go anywhere without permission. Too many rumors about hoodlums beating up Jews and doing who knew what to Jewish girls.

"You're awfully quiet," Anna finally said. "You OK?"

"Yeah."

They kept walking. Irina kicked a stick off the sidewalk, cupped her hands over her mouth, blew warm air and quickly stuffed her hands back into her pockets. She'd forgotten her gloves again. "I have a question and don't know who else to ask," she muttered.

"OK." Anna struggled with so many questions of her own; how could she answer Irina's? Why must Jews wear armbands? When would things calm down? Every few days brought a new Nazi law. They forced Papa to give away his bike shop; how will they earn money? She hadn't talked with Jozef about the Germans since his birthday party. Should she ask what he had in mind? "What's your question?"

Irina looked down at her shuffling feet. "Hey, how do I get Reuven to kiss me?"

Anna tried to stifle a laugh but failed. "I thought you had a question about the Germans."

"The Germans? If you can make them disappear, do it. But to just moan – I'd rather talk about something else."

"Like kissing Reuven?"

"Yeah."

"You think he likes you that way?"

"I think so. But I'm not sure."

"What have you done to find out?"

Irina's voice energized, and she started walking faster. "We laugh all the time, and I love talking to him, and he's really funny when he sees me, and – wait – what do you mean what have I done?"

"Have you tried holding his hand?"

"Uh huh. Twice."

"And?"

"Both times, we were walking, and I kinda just took his hand. He kept holding mine for a long time. I know he liked it. But all he did afterwards was act like nothing happened. He's never grabbed my hand, and" – Irina slapped her legs – "he hasn't kissed me!"

They reached their house and walked inside and into the warm kitchen. No one was home. "Were you alone when you held hands?"

"One time."

"Maybe he's shy."

"No way, he's the coolest guy!"

Anna smiled and draped her coat on the back of a chair. "He could be really cool but not know how to show a girl he likes her. How old is he?"

"Thirteen, a few months older than me. He'll turn fourteen in April."

"If I were to guess, even though he's so cool, it sounds like he could use some help."

"Huh?"

"I mean you start the kiss, and he'll finish it."

Irina shook her head. "No way! I don't want to kiss him. I want HIM to kiss ME."

"What I mean is you'll move towards his face – I'll tell you how – and then he'll kiss you."

"Is that what you did with Mordecai?"

Anna felt a jolt. "Um, sort of... I don't kiss and tell. But here's what you need to do. First, find a quiet place where it's just the two of you."

"Duh."

"Then, you'll need to move close, smile and look into his eyes. That may do the trick, and he'll take it from there. If not, rub imaginary lint off his collar, next to his neck. Then, looking in his eyes, slowly lean your face towards his. If he backs away, stop, but if he doesn't, angle your face like this" – Anna placed her palms on each side of her own face and tilted her head – "so you don't bump noses, and lean your face towards his with your mouth aiming for his mouth. As you move closer, pucker your lips a little to get ready for the kiss."

Irina tilted her face and puckered her lips. "I feel like a fish."

"Yeah. Don't swim your face all the way to his. Instead, one of two things will happen. He'll kiss you – and I think that's what he'll do. Or he'll back away, which probably means he's not interested. That doesn't feel good. But it could be he doesn't know how to react. It's hard to know because most boys are clueless."

"Not Reuven. He's so smart. I watched him play a football game. He tells everyone what to do–"

"Boys' brains are divided into compartments. Reuven's football compartment may be full, but that doesn't mean his girl compartment contains any more than Frammy's. Because unless a girl has taught him, it's empty."

"Hmmm...."

"So don't expect boys to act how they should. Especially since, like bears, most boys are more afraid of you than you are of them. And one more thing, I almost forgot. Close your eyes when you kiss him."

"Why?"

"You don't look at each other. That would be awkward."

Irina shrugged. "OK... but what if I forget to close my eyes?"

"I don't know. I've never kissed a bear with my eyes open."

APRIL 10, 1940
KARL BECK

Karl Beck was sitting at his desk, wearing a white shirt and black tie, daydreaming. Both the euthanasia project and his career were progressing quite nicely. As expected, many more handicapped German adults required special handling than children. To meet demand, the German government had established disposal centers at two German hospitals, with more to come. Adults were handled with gas rather than medication.

Setting up the disposal centers wasn't complicated. Maintenance men took an existing room near a hospital reception area, sealed it off, and laid pipes. An attendant would pump in gas by turning a valve outside the room. So far, everything had worked smoothly: evaluations, forms, and disposal. Karl's boss was so happy with his performance that he recommended Karl to the Gestapo, the German secret police. The Gestapo guys sent Karl to Krasau, where he now officed with Gestapo employees.

Franz Sauer had been right about war affecting their work. Wow! Not only because of the volume. Working with the SS allowed for so much improvising. Karl recently had to dispose of a thousand German and Polish handicapped undesirables. A practical-minded SS officer arranged to drive them to a forest, where Polish prisoners dug long pits, the SS shot the undesirables at the pits' edge, they fell in, and the SS then killed the Polish prisoners. Poland was full of huge, dense forests where things could be done away from prying eyes.

Karl was happy he didn't witness any of it; he read a report. Too much gore for him.

Recently, someone dreamed up the clever idea of mobile disposal centers – gas trucks. This allowed for special handling of the handicapped where there was no nearby disposal center and eliminated the shootings, which were loud and messy and required more personnel. The gas trucks – which looked like big moving vans – were a blessing. All they needed was a driver and to put the handicapped into the back of the truck. The medical staff simply told the patients they were going on a trip.

Karl watched one mobile disposal at a mental institution to gain firsthand knowledge. The nursing staff had helped six men into the back of the truck, the driver locked the door from the outside and drove with Karl to the forest. Once they were on the highway, the driver turned a valve to open the flow of carbon monoxide through a pipe running from near his seat to the back of the van. Soon, Karl heard muffled screaming and banging on the walls; he and the driver had talked louder to each other until the noise ceased.

After about forty minutes, they arrived at the dump site, off the road in a quiet forest. There, the driver emptied the van. The driver said he typically arranged for two helpers to meet him at the forest when he hauled more than ten undesirables.

Hearing the noise and seeing the bodies was very unpleasant to Karl. But it was better than shootings, especially if they disposed of thirty or forty at once. He was glad he was on the administrative end.

Krasau had been a good career move. Along with his euthanasia job, Karl worked as the Gestapo liaison with the Krasau Jewish Council, ensuring Jewish compliance with German regulations. The "Jewish question" was a popular topic at Krasau Gestapo headquarters. Everyone wanted to get rid of the Jews. Some Gestapo men said Jews should be expelled from all German territory, including Poland. Many thought they should be worked to death. Others wanted to use Jews as labor for the German war effort.

But they all thought Jews were subhuman and must be separated from society. Thus, the Jew armbands, so everyone would know when they were dealing with a subhuman. One of Karl's coworkers asked if he might borrow Karl's van and "give some Jews a ride home from synagogue." His remark had led to good chuckles.

Although Karl wouldn't tell anyone, he didn't believe that nonsense. Sure, he'd seen bearded, dark-clothed Jews who looked like they were from another planet. He didn't know about them. But the Jews who dressed like everyone else... When Karl was young, one of his friends, Hans Kernmann, was Jewish. Hans' father had been decorated for bravery in the World War, and Hans was a nice guy. They lost touch, and Karl later heard that Hans had left for Palestine in 1937. A smart move by a smart guy. Was Karl now supposed to believe Hans was subhuman?

Karl wasn't falling for it and had no problem trying to ease things for Jews, within the rules. It made them less likely to create problems.

But if one of his bosses instructed him to be firm or harsh?

If it's your job, you do it.

APRIL 18, 1940
BUBBIE

"I hate being a burden," Bubbie sighed to her daughter Chana. "But these days, I don't seem to have much choice."

This morning, Bubbie's tooth – one of the few remaining in her head – was hurting like the dickens, and her thin face had swollen and bulged out. A Jewish dentist worked not far from Chana's house; it was illegal for Christian doctors and dentists to treat Jews, and Bubbie had planned to go there on her own. She was proud she could walk long distances. Not so fast but still steady on her feet.

But the dental office was at a corner where German soldiers with bad reputations stood guard. Why do soldiers guard near a dental office? Bubbie wondered. So Chana said she would take Bubbie, and then Chana's husband, Alexander, said he'd go too. Alexander was a good man, for a non-believer.

Bubbie lived with Chana's family. Luckily, they were able to squeeze her mattress into the girls' room, which she shared with Anna and Irina. Bubbie had been staying with her oldest daughter's family, but they fled to Russia with Bubbie's other grandkids. Bubbie couldn't make the trip, so... that's the way it goes. God's plans you could never guess.

She'd had many roles in her life: daughter, sister, wife, mama and Bubbie. She felt sorry for her grandchildren. Life was simpler before cars, noise, the big city. Now, with the Nazi monsters, what did God have in mind? Her years were coming to an end, and her final role was as Bubbie for her daughter's children.

Right now, her tooth was killing her.

They were walking near the curb on a busy street – Jews weren't allowed on sidewalks – in front of drab, pastel buildings housing one business after another; the dentist's office was at the end of the block. Bubbie and Chana wore dresses, with coats and hats to protect against the wind and occasional rain on this chilly spring morning. They also wore Star of David armbands on their right sleeves, as did Alexander.

It was normal to see German soldiers walking about. Soldiers in different styles and colors of uniforms, who knew what all that meant? They usually ignored you. This morning, two sets of soldiers had walked by in their shiny boots. No problem, but Chana reminded Bubbie that the soldiers who sometimes stood near the dental office were bad.

"Uh oh," Alexander said, pointing, when they neared the corner. Two Jewish men were doing jumping jacks in the street in front of the dentist's office. Looming over them were two tall German soldiers, their backs to the building, wearing long gray coats, greenish-gray helmets, long black boots and gray gloves. Rifles slung over their shoulders and pistols holstered on their belts, the soldiers were yelling at the Jewish men. Walking in the street two buildings away, Bubbie couldn't hear what they were saying.

"Maybe we should go home and come later," Chana worried.

"Oh, Chana," Bubbie moaned. "My face hurts so much. They won't bother with me. I'm an old woman. You stay here, and I'll walk behind them and go right inside. It'll be fine."

Chana looked at Alexander, who shrugged. "She may be right. Let's watch, and we'll help her if she needs it."

Bubbie stepped over the curb and onto the forbidden sidewalk, hesitated, and with a confident stride walked toward the corner building. With luck (for her), the soldiers would focus on mistreating the two men and not notice her.

When she reached the dental building, Bubbie froze against the front facade about thirty feet from the door. The soldiers were standing about fifteen feet in front of the entrance, with their backs to it. The two harassed Jews were in front of them, in the street. A Polish mother and young boy passed by on the sidewalk. The child pointed at Bubbie and muttered something in Polish that Bubbie didn't understand. The mother shushed him, and they kept walking.

Bubbie watched the Germans harass the Jews. One Jew was young, had a beard and looked religious. The other was at least fifty, clean-shaven. They were now doing push-ups with heavy tiles on their backs. The older man was struggling, and his face was very red. Bubbie heard the soldiers' hearty laughter, like at a carnival. How could they be so cruel?

Heart thumping, Bubbie gathered her courage, set her eyes on the door and headed behind the soldiers as quickly as she could. As she grasped the door handle, a soldier happened to glance over his shoulder.

"Stop!" he barked in German. "Come here!" He pointed at the pavement in front of his feet.

Bubbie shuddered and submissively obeyed.

"You were sneaking by? These Jews!" he hollered to the other soldier, "even the old women are sly!" He viciously clutched Bubbie's arm and threw her toward the curb. She wailed, lost her balance and fell face-first into the street. The other soldier grinned. The younger Jewish man stood and rushed to help Bubbie, but the soldiers yelled, "Go!"; the two terrified men scampered away, leaving Bubbie alone.

"Get a rag and clean the street mud from the curb!" one soldier roared.

Dazed, ears ringing, and sprawled in the street, Bubbie raised herself to her knees and looked absently up at the soldiers, standing on the sidewalk next to the curb. They had such young faces, these hateful boys. Who raised them to act like this?

"I said get a rag and clean the mud!"

Bubbie began to feel sharp pain in her scraped hands and blood dripping down her face and, slowly coming to her senses, realized she was sitting in mud. She understood some German because of similarities to Jewish. "I don't have a rag," she apologized.

"You ARE a rag!" the soldier on her left thundered. "Clean the mud with your underwear! Then put it back on, Jew bitch!"

"Leave her alone!" yelled Alexander in German. He had rushed to the soldier, a head taller than him, on Bubbie's left. "She's an old–"

A German fist smashed Alexander's jaw, knocking him flat. As he started to rise, the German kicked him in the stomach, pounding the air out of him. Alexander covered his head with his arms, partially deflecting the German's boot aimed at his face. Next came a kick in the ribs that turned him onto his side. Cringing for the next blow, Alexander hoped Chana and her mother were escaping while the soldiers worked on him.

"Please! Please stop!" screamed Chana in Jewish to the soldier whose boot now rested on Alexander's neck.

The other soldier growled, "Another cleaning woman!" He grabbed Chana's arm, twisted it behind her back, and threw her to the sidewalk. Pointing at Alexander, he raged, eyes bulging and spit flying from his mouth. "You two bitches clean the mud with your underwear, or we'll kill this sack of garbage!" Chana, breathless and reliving the terror of her father's murder, crawled to the soldier's feet and looked up at his face. "Please!" she shrieked. His boot knocked her backwards; she tumbled off the curb and into the street.

The soldier who had beaten Alexander now rested a foot on his chest. He removed his pistol from its holster and pointed it at Alexander's head. "Bang!" he said, pretending to shoot, and both soldiers chuckled. Horrified, Chana reached under her dress, yanked down her underwear and helped Bubbie pull off hers. Chana took Bubbie's hand, they knelt in the street next to the curb and furiously started pushing mud into the gutter.

"Don't clog the drain!" the soldiers snarled.

One soldier stood at the curb, close to Chana and Bubbie. The other was standing on Alexander, lying on the sidewalk. Polish shoppers hurried by, veering around them. Alexander heard one Pole say to his friends, "They're getting what they deserve."

A middle-aged Polish couple stopped to watch; the woman looked very upset. The soldier near Chana glared and shouted, "We have two Polish volunteers to clean the street!" The husband clutched his wife's arm, and they rushed away.

Coated with mud, Chana stared blankly at the soldier near her. What did he want her to do? He said not to push mud in the drain, and she knew not to put it on the sidewalk. Unable to speak, she slapped her filthy hand to the side of her face and managed only "What– where–"

With a savage expression, the soldier pointed at Alexander. "He'll eat it." The other soldier removed his boot from Alexander's chest and jerked him to his feet. Alexander glanced at the rifle slung over the soldier's shoulder. If only I had a gun, Alexander thought, I'd shoot down both these beasts.

"Sir," Alexander bowed his head and meekly said in Jewish-accented German, "I fought mit the Germans in the World War. I–"

The German slapped his face. "No Jew ever fought with Germans!" The soldier threw Alexander into the street. He stumbled, fell, quickly stood, and looked into the barrel of the soldier's pistol pointed between his eyes. "Eat the mud!"

"Please," Alexander cowered with a hand in front of his face. "We're people, like you."

The Germans, standing next to each other, smirked. "You're not people. You're not even animals. You're Jews. Eat!"

Alexander knelt in the mud next to Chana and Bubbie; he and Chana looked at each other. Blood oozed from Alexander's nose, down his face, collected at the point of his chin and dripped onto the street. "It will be OK," he sighed. Pedestrians on the sidewalk continued to walk quickly past, and cars drove by.

Alexander scooped a slimy handful of mud and brought it toward his mouth as a shiny black Mercedes pulled up next to them and stopped. Everyone turned and looked. The driver remained seated, but the passenger opened his door and exited a couple yards from Alexander. The man wore a black uniform, black hat, and a red-cloth armband displaying a black swastika in a white circle.

This new German asked the soldiers, "What have we here? Troublemakers, I assume?"

The soldier pointing his pistol at Alexander's head lowered it. "Yes sir. These Jews tried to sneak by us, and we're teaching them a lesson. The bitches are cleaning the street, and the kosher pig is about to eat some mud." He cackled.

The Gestapo man walked around Alexander to avoid getting mud on his well-shined shoes, and he waved for the soldiers to follow him toward the building. "I understand what you're doing," Karl Beck smiled, "and normally wouldn't interfere. But today, for reasons I won't get into, I'll ask you to stop. I'll tell the Jews to go on their way."

"Yes sir," the soldiers answered.

"You can stay here. I'll talk to them."

Beck walked to the edge of the sidewalk and, snapping his fingers, said, "All three of you, get up! Do you understand German?"

Alexander bowed his head. Mud oozing off his fingers, he said, "Yes sir, from when I fought with Germans in the World War."

"Against who?"

"Against the Russians, for two years."

Beck nodded. "Where were you going before you ran into these gentlemen?"

"My mother-in-law," nodding at Bubbie, "has a bad toothache, and we were going to a dentist right here–"

"Go to the dentist and then go home."

"Thank you, sir–" Alexander started.

Beck pointed to the door. "Go." They walked straight to it without looking at the soldiers and stepped inside.

"Finally," Alexander whispered. "A human being."

"A miracle," Bubbie said.

They stood in the lobby, Chana and Bubbie both holding their filthy underwear, and looked at each other. Alexander tasted blood in his mouth, his ribs and jaw ached, and he winced when he tried to turn his head. Chana took a deep breath and, with a shaking hand, wiped blood off Alexander's face. For the first time, her mind registered that they all were covered in mud, and she saw blood trickling down her mother's face. She dabbed it with her sleeve.

Somehow, Chana forced herself to seem calm. "We need to go to the dentist. Are you OK, Mama?"

"I can't walk in dirty–"

"We'll explain. The dentist will understand," Chana said.

Alexander nodded. "I'll wait in the hall. These Germans–"

The door opened; the Polish couple that had briefly stopped and watched walked inside. The husband stayed at the entrance, and the wife hurried to Chana with a bag in her hands. "Take these. Towels and two of my underwear–"

"We couldn't," Chana began.

"Take it," the woman repeated and thrust the bag into Chana's hand. The woman's husband furiously waved for her to hurry, and they rushed out the door.

Chana wiped Alexander's face with a towel and, carrying the bag, helped Bubbie limp to the dental office. Alexander leaned against the wall, near the building's entrance, and slowly shook his head. He had seen a soldier yelling at Bubbie, ran over, tried to help, and was suddenly knocked to the pavement and kicked. He lay there like a pathetic, helpless child, unable to defend himself... His purpose in life was to protect his family. But he had become a groveling beggar, pleading and moaning.

His heart raced, and he began to sweat. He hadn't even seen the German swing his fist. It happened too fast, and he had reacted like an old man. How could he protect his children? He had no guns, little money, barely a job. He trembled.

The building's front door opened, and Alexander cringed, terrified that the soldiers were hunting them.

A child's voice and laughter. No soldiers – only a mother and her little girl. They walked by.

Alexander held his face in his hands. His ribs ached, and he took only short breaths, unable to breathe normally. Dejection and despair overcame him. The soldier was right. Alexander was no longer human. Humans protect their families. He was useless as a cockroach, scurrying madly to delay getting stomped.

He worked harder to breathe but felt as if he were suffocating. Lightheaded, Alexander staggered down the hall a few steps and clutched the handle of a closet door. He managed to stay upright by hanging onto it.

He'd become a nothing. Even worse, he was to blame; his own hand had thrust the knife wedged in his heart. Anna could have escaped to Palestine when Mordecai left, or they all could have fled the Germans and gone to Russia. Because of his bad decisions, they'd stayed. Because of him. He leaned his head against the door and cried.

•••

That afternoon, Alexander told his daughters what happened. They'd never seen him so down. "Papa," Irina said, "you told us some Germans are good, and others are bad. You ran into very bad ones, but that doesn't mean–"

"No." He shook his head. "No. If we get a chance to leave Krasau – things must be better somewhere else." His voice sounded hollow, and Anna and Irina exchanged worried glances.

Papa looked down and sighed. "But we'll figure it out. Life has never thrown a problem we couldn't handle, and we don't give up hope," he muttered dully, as if trying to convince himself.

"The British and French will probably attack soon," Anna said.

"Hey, yeah, the French will blast the Germans so hard they'll run away like little babies!" thirteen-year-old Irina said, and they hugged each other tight. "We love you so much, Papa."

•••

Anna, who still occasionally wrote Mordecai but never mailed the undeliverable letters, carefully composed a letter to him about what had happened to her family and what she must do. She then tore it up and dropped the shreds into a trash can.

She walked into the living room, picked up the telephone receiver and called Jozef. "I'm ready to hear what you want me to do."

Silence.

"I'll get back to you," Jozef said. "Could be a while. Don't tell anyone."

The line clicked.

APRIL 25, 1940
ZAKKAI

Pitchfork and rake slung over his shoulder, Jozef walked in late to the Zakkai planning meeting. Anna, Benec, Leah, Itzhak, and three other seated Zakkai teens gaped at him with puzzled faces.

"Who's ready to work on a farm?" Jozef asked.

"Since Krasau has no farms, and Jews are banned from leaving here, I'd say it's someone other than present company," Itzhak said.

"You're smart, Itzhak. And wrong. I just met with a Gestapo official and asked him to let Zakkai create a Zionist farm to train our kids. I told him about the abandoned Kriegsberg farm twenty miles north of here. I said farmwork would keep our young people out of trouble.

"The German's name is Karl Beck. A friend on the Jewish Council told me Beck is reasonable. He's right; Beck approved my request. We can go in two weeks, stay the summer and again next year if he doesn't hear of problems. Beck also said no mandatory armbands at the farm, and that we'll have the place to ourselves."

"This is amazing!" Leah said. "For our kids to get away from the madness, breathe fresh air – it sounds wonderful!" She hugged Jozef.

Jozef said, "The place is old but not dilapidated. It has water, and we can make a sleeping cabin for twenty boys and another for twenty girls. Anna can teach the girls Jewish history and Zionism, Benec and Itzhak can teach the boys, and everyone will work with their hands, study Hebrew, learn to farm for when we get to Palestine."

"How will we get everyone to a farm twenty miles away?" Itzhak asked.

"Ah, the icing on the cake. I'll give Beck the date, and his people will take us. It will be tight, but Beck will furnish a truck big enough for forty people, and he'll let Leah and me drive my old car – that I 'sold' to a Polish friend – with two of you."

Itzhak frowned. "Germans making Jews happy? I don't like it."

"Itzhak asks a good question," Anna said. "Why would the Germans do this? They make us wear armbands, we walk in the gutter, they abuse us. Now they'll chauffeur a youth group?"

Jozef nodded. "Yeah – and I have an odd answer. The Gestapo man, Beck, wants to be accommodating. I know it's hard to believe, but we had what felt like an honest conversation, and I didn't discern an ulterior motive. I respectfully asked him why he would do this for us. He said teenagers get in trouble, part of his job is maintaining order, and he likes the idea.

"Anna will make a leaflet about the program, and we'll talk to the kids. If they're interested, I'll tell Beck, give him a list, and set a date."

•••

Two weeks later, a loud, large truck – looked like a moving van – rolled slowly to a stop at Jozef's and Leah's apartment building. Although only 7:30 in the morning, forty girls and boys between the ages of thirteen and seventeen cheered its arrival. All wearing Star of David armbands. The younger kids included Irina and Reuven. Their leaders were Jozef, Leah, Anna, Benec, Estie and Itzhak.

As Jozef had expected, Zakkai kids had jumped at the chance to escape Krasau for four months on a Zionist farm, and few parents balked at the German offer to transport the kids. If a kind German wants to aid us, we should welcome the help. When German officials – not vile Nazis, but regular men – get to know us, they'll see we're just people, no matter what propaganda they've been fed. And besides, the Germans had no reason to hurt teenagers – innocent children.

Eighteen-year-olds Estie and Benec would ride with the kids; nineteen-year-old Itzhak and eighteen-year-old Anna would go with Jozef and Leah in their car.

The truck driver, a tall, heavy-set German with a round, pink face and big neck, opened the truck's back door. Kids piled in, starting with two young boys who raced to claim the best spot. The interior looked like a long, rectangular, gray box. Benec told everyone to put their packs in the middle and form two concentric circles around them, one against the sides of the rectangle and the other inside of it.

One young boy was claustrophobic, and Estie asked the driver in German if the boy could sit with him up front. The driver said, "My instructions are everyone sits in back."

Anna offered to switch places with the boy. "You go in the car, and I'll ride in the truck. We're going to the same place."

Worried what his friends might think, he mumbled, "No thanks." He and Estie climbed into the back. "If you get nervous," Estie said, "close your eyes and take slow, deep breaths. That should help calm you."

Irina watched Reuven and his friends trading snacks their mothers had packed for them: a bagel for half an apple, a chicken leg for a slice of poppy-seed cake. They then hopped in. Irina didn't bother sitting with Reuven; she'd practiced Anna's kissing lesson on her pillow, and thought four months at the farm should give her plenty of time to apply her skills. She got in with two friends.

"Hey, smells kinda funny in here," Irina said. "Like puke and bleach," her friend, Rivka, said. Irina nodded. "Bleach, that's it, that's what I smell. The last kids in here must have made a mess, and they bleached it up."

Jozef, Leah, Anna, and Itzhak waved goodbye and drove off in the car.

Once everyone was seated in back, the driver shut the door and locked it from the outside. The kids suddenly sat in total darkness; many screamed. The driver heard them, sniggered, and walked toward the front of the truck. Benec and Estie each turned on a flashlight. "Daylight again!" Benec said. He'd anticipated the darkness and brought flashlights for the trip.

The driver took his seat behind the wheel. To his right was a pipe that fed into the back of the truck. On it was a valve.

The driver turned the ignition, placed his right foot on the accelerator and drove away. With his left foot on the clutch, he changed gears from first to second, and the truck roared. It did the same when he moved from second gear to third. The kids in back didn't hear the noise, or if they did, paid no attention because they were too busy talking and yelling and laughing.

As lively kids tend to do.

•••

Two guys stood waiting at the forest when the truck rumbled down the empty road. Right on time, forty minutes had passed since the last teen had settled in the back, and the driver had shut the door. The truck pulled off the road and slowly backed into a small clearing. The driver turned off the engine, exited the vehicle, walked to the back and nodded at the two men. He spat on the ground.

A beautiful spring day, the sun was shining brightly, warming the cool, pine-scented, morning air. Killing the truck's engine had restored the forest's sounds: leaves rustling in the light breeze and birds chirping, as if to announce, "What a beautiful world it is up here in these tall trees."

The driver unlocked and opened the truck's back door.

"Welcome Zakkai!" Jozef and Itzhak hollered; the kids stepped out, blinded by the light. "This is as close to the farm as the road goes," Jozef said. "We'll walk the rest of the way."

Jozef thanked the driver, who nodded and left.

JULY 14, 1940
IRINA

Nine tired girls aged thirteen to fifteen sat slumped, faces in hands, at two rickety wooden tables outside their cabin. Most wearing dark shorts and brightly colored blouses, they looked dutifully at Anna standing in front of them with sunlit hair. Behind her, about twenty yards away, sagged a dilapidated barn that made their shack-like cabin seem deluxe by comparison.

Anna gazed past the girls. The farm buildings were encircled by fields, and past them a dense forest so large that it reached the mountains in the distant horizon. All quiet and peaceful. An hour earlier, all forty Zakkai kids *had returned from the fields and the forest, walking in rows with sickles and axes on their shoulders, their faces glowing with smiles. The picture of health and youthful vigor.** Now they struggled to stay awake for Zionism and Jewish history classes. Estie taught the older girls, and Anna the ten younger ones. Itzhak and Benec instructed the boys at night.

Anna's class met outside, and this afternoon's weather was perfect: cloudy and breezy. She quickly counted the girls. "Where's Irina? Does anyone know where she is?"

No one answered, but two girls shot each other glances.

"Miriam, Rivka, you seem to know something." At Anna's upturned eyebrow, they both blurted, "I don't know."

Anna sighed. "Let's continue with Im tirtzu. What did Herzl mean by 'If you will it, it is not a fable?'"

"If you want something badly enough, it will come true?" someone said.

"Maybe – but does that make sense?" Anna asked. She noticed the girls' eyes drift to her right as shirtless, muscular, eighteen-year-old Benec walked by. He stopped a few feet behind the group and flipped his notebook to a drawing he was working on of Anna teaching her class. Never shy, Benec had tried unsuccessfully to earn Anna's attention other ways. He was a talented artist; maybe a personalized gift would help.

Anna continued. "If I badly want the Germans to leave, will they

---

* Everything in italics in this and the following chapters are quotes (some slightly revised for context) by people during the Holocaust, many of whom perished. See the Historical Notes.

go? If I want my Bubbie healthy again, will she be cured? Is that what Herzl meant?"

"No," the girls responded in monotone.

"Then what did Herzl mean?"

The girls answered with bored faces; Benec sauntered closer to them and raised a hand. His eyes locked on Anna, in her black shorts and white blouse. He wished Herzl's words meant just wishing for something made it happen. Anna smiled and pointed to him.

"Herzl was talking about Zionism, creating a Jewish nation," Benec said. "He meant if you simply dream, but do nothing, it will never come true, but if we the Jewish people work hard, very hard, we can make it happen."

"Did everyone hear that? And how do we make it into a peaceful and just society?" Anna asked. Benec noticed his younger brother, Reuven, glide out the barn and head the other direction, past the shack only Jozef and Itzhak were allowed in, and out of sight.

"Girls," Anna said, "How do we–"

The girls were tracking something behind her. Anna turned and saw Irina walking toward them from the barn. Everyone silently watched as Irina smiled at no one in particular, nonchalantly squeezed between two girls and sat.

"Hi Irina," Anna said. "We're talking about Herzl–"

Two girls at Irina's table giggled, and another pointed at her. Benec glanced twice at Irina and headed off to find Reuven. Puzzled, Anna looked closer at Irina, frowned, and said, "Everyone seems tired today – class is over early." Suddenly energized, the girls quickly stood and headed toward their cabin.

"But Irina!" Anna called. "Please stay here. I'd like to talk to you."

Irina shrugged. "OK."

Anna sat next to her. "What have you been doing? Why were you late?"

"Nothing... I was with Reuven. Just taking a break and lost track of time."

"I saw you this morning and thought you looked cute, as usual, with your braided pigtails and favorite light-red blouse. Your favorite, properly buttoned, light-red blouse."

Irina looked down and saw that the top slit of her blouse was unbuttoned, and the other buttons were fastened in the wrong slits.

Her face turned redder than the buttons.

"Why is your blouse messed up?"

"Um..." Irina fixed the buttons and crossed her arms. "I thought you're my sister, not my mother!"

"It depends on what you did."

"Nothing! Reuven gave me a back rub. There's nothing wrong with that. He didn't see anything he's not supposed to. I just kinda pulled my blouse up when I was lying flat on my stomach. I must not have buttoned it back right because I was in a rush to get here."

Anna shook her head and sighed. Did Irina have any idea what trouble this boy could get her into? "We've been at the farm for two months, and you've spent a lot of time with Reuven. I don't want to be a busy body, but what else were you doing?"

"I don't kiss and tell," Irina smirked.

"Look, it's fine to kiss him and get a back rub, but you're thirteen – that's way too young for some other stuff, and when one thing leads to another–"

"I'm mature. Everyone says I've developed early–"

"That doesn't mean your brain is mature."

"My brain's part of my body. And besides, I didn't do anything wrong. I didn't take off my blouse, I only unbuttoned it for the back rub. And I'm not stupid. I know you shouldn't do some things, no matter what. Don't worry. And I'm almost fourteen."

Anna shook her head.

"And hey," Irina said, raising her voice, "the person you should worry about is yourself!"

"What does that mean?"

"It means stop mourning over Mordecai and return to the world."

Anna glared at her.

"I'm just being honest."

"I don't want to hear it."

"I'm telling you anyway. You said you and Mordecai are finished, not me. You're eighteen-years-old and have the cutest boy your own age right here who likes you, and you don't pay attention–"

"Cutest boy?"

"Hey, you're right. Second cutest. Cutest is Reuven. But his brother Benec is SO handsome, and if he wasn't too old, he'd be the cutest. He's smart, he's a Zionist, he draws, he's funny. He's perfect."

This is ridiculous, Anna thought. Her little sister giving her boy advice? "Nice try changing the subject, but we're talking about you, not me."

Irina leaned forward. "That's up to you, but I won't do anything stupid."

Anna sighed. There was nothing more she could say, and Irina seemed to get it. Anna stood and gestured for Irina to follow her to the cabin. "I think you understand how important this is. I'll talk to the girls before the hundred rumors about you become a thousand."

"Nah, I don't care. Everyone's been gossiping about Rivka for sneaking out at night to neck with her boyfriend. Now she has competition."

"Well, I am curious – what did Reuven say to convince you to unbutton your blouse? You don't need to do that to get a back rub."

"I know, he didn't say anything. It was my idea."

Anna grinned. "Have I created a monster?"

"Maybe." Irina smiled back.

•••

Late that night, Anna crept quietly out of the girls' cabin. She walked along the gravel path connecting the scattered farm buildings, gazed up at the moon and, as she often did, wondered if Mordecai, so impossibly far away, might be looking at the same moon right then.

She sighed deeply. Could she finally put Mordecai behind her? Escape the memories of her head resting on his shoulder? Holding hands, laughing, teasing him, planning their wedding, their lives together.

Tears clouded Anna's eyes. She knew Irina was right – she should accept reality, as Mordecai had written, and move forward. But sometimes you're stuck, even when your mind says to get moving.

Anna found herself wandering near the small, wooden, flat-roofed shed that only Jozef and Itzhak were allowed to enter. A quiet night other than the distant chirping of crickets, Anna thought she heard noise from inside and stuck her ear against one of the windowless walls. Someone talking.

She knocked on the door, waited, and knocked again. Itzhak, his dark, curly hair a mess and his shirt half untucked, partially opened the door, stepped outside and closed it.

"Something wrong?" he asked.

"I heard people talking, and I wanted to know–"

"I'm the only one here. Go away."

"Go away?! Itzhak, will you ever learn to speak politely?"

"Sorry – go away, please."

Anna shook her head. "No. What are you doing in here?"

"Why are you outside in the middle of the night? You should–"

"Are you letting me in?" Anna interrupted, annoyance in her voice.

"No."

"Why not?"

"You know why. It's off-limits."

"I'm as much a leader of this group as you... No, I'm more of a leader–"

"This has nothing to do with Zakkai. It's our project, Jozef's and mine, and we're keeping it to ourselves."

"Why–"

"Anna." Itzhak put his hand on her shoulder, but quickly withdrew it. "For you, this is Pandora's box. Don't open it."

Anna hesitated while her sleepy mind registered the reference. "Pandora's box? Isn't the world already filled with pain and trouble?"

"Entering would increase yours. Please stay out." Itzhak's voice was soft, almost pleading.

This was a side of him that Anna had never seen. Itzhak seemed concerned about her. She was still irritated, but it wasn't only Itzhak; Jozef had instructed everyone to stay away.

"OK, fine."

Anna returned to the girls' cabin and lay down to sleep. Itzhak obviously was involved in Jozef's resistance activity but didn't know she and Jozef had talked. Why hadn't Jozef gotten back to her? Should she ask him? What would Mordecai say she should do? Papa would kill her.

Pandora's box? She could wait to hear from Jozef.

JULY 15, 1940
SZYMON'S JOURNAL

From April through June 1940:

The Germans conquered Denmark.

The Germans conquered Norway.

The Germans conquered Belgium.

The Germans conquered Luxembourg.

The Germans conquered Holland.

The Germans conquered France.

France, our savior, is no more.

England remains free, but for how long? Whatever the answer, they cannot help us. Hopefully, they can defend themselves.

Despair in Poland.

•••

NOVEMBER 12, 1940
ITZHAK'S JOURNAL

Two months have passed since Zakkai returned from the farm. Seems like an eternity.

We were back a week when the Germans ordered every one of the seventy thousand Jews in Krasau to move into a newly formed "Jewish Quarter," an area that had housed twenty thousand, and to bring no more than sixty-five pounds of possessions. The Germans would get the rest. Many Jews ignored the weight limitation and lugged mattresses, furniture, as much as they could drag or carry.

*Try to picture one-*fifth *of a large city's population moving through the streets in an endless stream, pushing, wheeling, dragging all their belongings from every part of the city to one small section, crowding one another more and more as they converged. No cars, no horses, no help of any sort was available to us by order of the occupying authorities. Pushcarts were about the only method of conveyance...*

In the ghetto, as some of us had begun to call it, half ironically and in jest, there was appalling chaos. Thousands of people were rushing around at the last minute trying to find a place to stay... Children wandered, lost and crying, parents ran hither and yon seeking them, their cries drowned in the tremendous hubbub of the uprooted people.

Some Jews had been living in what became the "ghetto," but most were Poles. The Germans evicted them, just as they did to us. Some

Jews and Poles swapped homes.

As devastating as this was, the most frightening aspect occurred a month later when the Germans locked us in. The ghetto is now surrounded by walls topped with barbed wire. Guards man three gates through which everyone must enter and exit. Jews can leave only with a special permit.

Despondent people ask, "Why? – why have they done this?" A popular answer is that the Germans plan to invade Russia and have locked us up fearing we'd act as a fifth column. "Then why only the Jews?" is a question unanswerable.

The barely paid, unarmed Jewish police roam the ghetto directing traffic, helping guard against smuggling, checking building codes, and that sort of thing. Some think this means the ghetto is a blessing and that the Germans will leave us alone. Like when European Christians locked Jews in ghettos in the 16th and 17th centuries. But the Jewish police are subservient to their Polish and German masters; more importantly, Germans patrol the ghetto's streets and abuse Jews at their leisure.

The day the ghetto walls were finished, several Poles threw sacks of food over the walls to their Jewish friends. They stopped when the Germans shot one of them. Through loudspeakers and leaflets, the Germans have warned Poles that they will be severely punished if they give food or any help to us.

JANUARY 7, 1941
PETER

The meeting took place, as usual, in a small, windowless room on the second floor of the Ossolinski district police station. Peter Wojcik's seven-man undercover unit filled the two rows of tightly jammed chairs. Three men wearing civilian clothes in the second row and four, including Peter, in the first. Tall and bulky Peter was average size for the unit.

Behind a lectern at the front stood fat, bald, stupid but blue-uniformed Captain Stanislaw Anderjevski – "Fat Stan" Peter called him. Although the men looked to Peter for practical leadership, all orders came from the captain. These weekly meetings offered Fat Stan the chance to exercise his authority for about an hour.

But not today. Two special guests were in attendance: Officers Schmidt and Beck from the Gestapo. They stood at the front; Beck off to the left and Schmidt, smoking a cigarette, front and center next to Fat Stan. When the Germans conquered most of Poland in September 1939, they abolished the Polish police. But the arrogant supermen soon realized that was a mistake if they wanted to control society's lowlifes. So they brought the police back, minus Jews, of course, under strict German control.

Fat Stan reported directly to Schmidt.

"Gentlemen," Captain Anderjevski read from behind the wooden lectern, "we're honored to have Officers Schmidt and Beck with us today. I've had the pleasure of working closely with them. Under their supervision, we're operating with renewed efficiency..."

Peter looked the Germans over as Fat Stan ran his mouth. Beck was nondescript with a phony "I want to be your friend" look on his face, but not Schmidt. With the derisive lips common to Germans, Schmidt was a flashing sign that read, "I'm a member of the superior race." He appeared to be in his forties, below average height, wore a nicely pressed navy suit, perfectly knotted tie and neatly combed hair. His brown Hitler mustache was smartly trimmed.

Peter took pride in his ability to read people, and Schmidt struck him as one of those guys – like Peter – who inhaled all data around him, always processing. Peter watched Schmidt size up the room and each man in it while pretending to listen to Fat Stan.

Peter guessed Schmidt had been an experienced police officer before joining the Gestapo. Maybe undercover. Topflight undercover cops were very high on Peter's hierarchy of quality human beings, next to savvy football players with breakaway speed. Peter would do well to stay on Schmidt's good side even if Schmidt was a Nazi pig.

Fat Stan rearranged his papers on the lectern. "I'll now get to the subject of today's meeting." He handed out a city map with the Jewish Quarter borders marked in red. At the top were two lines of German that Peter didn't understand, other than the word "Juden" for Jews. Juden, as well as the Polish counterpart, "Zydzi," had become quite common under the German occupation. Usually paired with "Verboten!"

"We have a growing threat in our city," Fat Stan announced. "Jews outside the Jewish Quarter without Jew armbands or work permits. Moving about during the day, some at night, and some even living on the Aryan side. We don't have reliable numbers, but the problem seems to be growing."

Schmidt studied each man as Fat Stan talked about the Jews.

"I'm sure everyone knows the Quarter's boundaries, but we thought it couldn't hurt to pass out a reminder. Our German friends take this threat very seriously, as do we." He nodded respectfully toward the Gestapo men. "In a moment, Officer Schmidt will summarize some important regulations."

"Are we worried about young Jewish men, Captain?" asked Officer Jowak from the front row to the left of Peter. "Are they robbing people? Burglarizing? Stealing – all of that or what exactly?"

"No," Gestapo agent Schmidt answered. "These Jews are of all ages, male and female. We refuse to wait until they form violent criminal gangs that harass good Polish citizens. All Jews belong in their Quarter. It's forbidden for them to exist outside it without a permit and a Jew armband. These are crimes. Serious crimes."

Schmidt speaks very good Polish, Peter thought. Probably a Polish citizen of German heritage who rooted for his compatriot thugs to take over our country.

Officer Jowak, who once had a Jewish girlfriend, wouldn't let it go. He sipped his coffee, looked at Fat Stan, and with feigned excitement said, "So Captain, we proud Polish policemen now protect our citizens from old Jewish ladies who visit their Catholic neighbors they've known for fifty years ... because they might accidentally tap someone's toe with their canes?" He paused. "And we need to stop little Jewish kids from dropping candy on the sidewalk?"

Gestapo agent Beck's face flushed red, Fat Stan clenched his hands and Peter grimaced. Jowak, you idiot, Peter thought. Your love of Jews will screw all of us. The Gestapo torture and execute on a whim.

The officer sitting behind Jowak kicked him and muttered, "Hang yourself on your own time!"

But Officer Schmidt showed no emotion. He looked directly into Jowak's eyes, calmly walked a few steps, and stood in front of him. Schmidt slowly brought his cigarette to his mouth, placed it between his lips and took a long, slow drag, never moving his gaze off Jowak's eyes. He took the cigarette out of his mouth and blew the smoke above Jowak's head, still focused on Jowak's eyes, which were locked on Schmidt.

No one moved. The only sounds were the faint click, click, clack of a typewriter across the hall.

Long puff, exhale.

Long puff, exhale.

All eyes except Peter's were on Schmidt and Jowak. Peter watched Beck's eyes narrow.

Long puff, exhale.

To Jowak's credit, his eyes never left Schmidt, though beads of sweat gathered on Jowak's forehead, and his face began to pale.

Peter wanted to help Jowak but didn't know how without putting himself at risk. Schmidt continued to stand over Jowak, who still looked up at him.

Schmidt reached into his coat's inside pocket and pulled out a small notepad and pen.

"What is your name?"

"My name is Officer Jowak," he mumbled.

"I didn't hear you."

"Officer Jowak," this time louder but with a shaky voice. He looked down at his feet, furtively glanced at the men to his right and left and back up at Schmidt.

"How do you spell Jowak?"

Jowak quietly answered him. The coffee cup in his hand was shaking.

"First name?"

Officer Schmidt wrote in his notepad and returned it and the pen to his coat pocket. Still standing over Jowak, Schmidt turned toward the captain and said, "Is Jowak a good example of your men? Will he – and they – follow simple orders?"

"My men follow orders," the captain managed. "Um, we–"

"I'd be happy to track down old Jews with canes," one officer called out. "Less running."

A couple men nervously laughed. "You don't need to worry about me–" another man started.

"Officer Schmidt." Peter stood, only a few feet from Schmidt, spread his hands, and smiled. "I've worked with Officer Jowak for ten years. Not only is he a great policeman; he's also a comedian. Sometimes it takes a while to appreciate his sense of humor. If you'd said to look out for bank robbers, he'd have said, 'Why? The Jews own all the banks.' The Jew jokes he told a few minutes ago weren't so funny, but that's all they were. Jew jokes."

Fat Stan nodded, and one of the men said, "Yeah. That's true."

Peter continued. "We may not be the smartest or best-looking police unit, but we know how to follow orders. All of us would be happy to round up Jews for you."

Schmidt looked down at Jowak. "Is that true, Officer Jowak? You were trying to be funny?"

"Yes sir," Jowak shrugged.

"Good," Officer Schmidt said. "I also can be a comedian." Smiling, he dipped his cigarette butt in Jowak's coffee.

Peter sat down in his chair. Jowak didn't move. Stay calm, Jowak, Peter thought. Stay calm.

"I expect you didn't like my joke any more than I liked yours, Mr. Jowak," Schmidt said. "But that is human nature. We laugh loudest at our own jokes."

Schmidt lit another cigarette, returned to the front, and stood next to Fat Stan.

"I see that most of you don't like me." Schmidt turned his head slightly and blew his smoke at Fat Stan. "That couldn't be less important. Only one thing matters. You follow orders, or you're gone. Very simple." He again exhaled toward Fat Stan.

The man knows how to get his point across, Peter thought.

"No questions?

"Good. Let's talk about the Jews – the smelly subject that won't go away. Yet.

"No Jew, of any age, at any time, is permitted outside their Quarter unless the Jew has both a permit and a Jew armband on their sleeve. If they lack either, immediately arrest them. No warnings, no fines. Straight to jail. Second, any Pole who helps a Jew by giving them food, a ride, anything – arrest them. No fines or warnings. Straight to jail.

"We're relying on you, the uniformed Polish police and other fine

Polish citizens to help us find every Jew illegally on the Aryan side. There may only be a few now, but like rats their numbers will explode if we don't act decisively. We'll pay a nice cash reward to every Pole who turns in a Jew. This is very important because Poles are better than Germans at sniffing them out. Remember that some Jews have permits to work outside their Quarter. If they have permits and wear armbands, they're not breaking the law.

"Jews fall into three categories. First are the religious with their beards and black hats or long sleeves and dresses. Any idiot can recognize them. Then there are Jews who dress like Poles but talk Polish with a Jewish accent. Most Germans can't tell regular Polish from Polish with a Jewish accent; we need your help identifying those Jews, who comprise the largest group, especially if the religious ones wise up and start dressing like everyone else.

"Then there's the third category, which is the toughest. Jews who speak Polish with no accent. Luckily, more than half have curly dark hair, big noses or other easily identifiable characteristics. But a fair number talk like Poles and look like Poles. Especially since half of Christian Poles have dark hair. Any questions?"

"Yeah," Peter said. "You're right about Poles pegging Jews by how they talk. But you skipped the best people at snooping out Jews–"

"Educate me."

"Other Jews. No one knows a Jew like a Jew. I've used a couple as snitches in my undercover work. Can I get permission for one or two Jews to live on the Aryan side without armbands and act as eyes and ears for me – to help hunt down other Jews? And will you pay them cash rewards?"

A sick smile flashed across Schmidt's face. "Excellent idea. I can see each Jew trying to out-swindle the next one for the reward." He laughed. "Your name again?"

"Officer Wojcik. My Jews will need paperwork to protect them from getting picked up."

"Get me their names, and I'll take care of it." Schmidt turned to the captain. "My presentation is concluded, but I'll expect you to handle two things. First" – he pointed at Jowak – "fire him from the police force, effective immediately. Second, rearrange Officer Wojcik's assignments to prioritize catching Jews."

Peter felt bad for Jowak but stifled a smile at his own success wooing Schmidt. That is one man you don't want against you.

And Peter was sure as hell glad he wasn't a Jew.

MARCH 25, 1941
ANNA

They formed a tight circle, the Zakkai group, arms wrapped around each other and singing songs. They might have been disheartened in Jozef's and Leah's cramped ghetto apartment if not for their leaders' contagious enthusiasm. When they'd left for the farm in May 1940, escaping to Palestine seemed possible, though unlikely, because the Germans had still allowed Jews to emigrate. If only the British had let them in. But those days were long gone. The Germans now locked all Polish Jews inside Poland and confined Krasau's Jews in the ghetto.

After most teens had left, Jozef led Anna into the "dining room" where Leah and Itzhak sat waiting at a small, square folding table. Anna sat next to Leah and Itzhak and across from Jozef.

With a look of severe seriousness, Jozef began. He spoke slowly. "Anna, we need your help. We wouldn't ask if this weren't important because what we have in mind is against the law and very dangerous. If caught, you'll be sent to prison. Or worse."

Leah interrupted and put her hand on Anna's, which was resting on the table. "Before anyone says another word, think carefully about what Jozef just said. If you don't want to take that kind of risk, we'll wish you a good week, you'll go home. End of story."

Anna shrugged. "Jozef hasn't said enough for me to decide anything. I break the law when I go outside after curfew; they might arrest me for working on Zakkai newsletters." She nervously smiled. "But it seems you want me to do something very different – so I'm listening."

"Itzhak and I are involved with others in unlawful activities," Jozef said, sounding like the lawyer he once was. "I mention this only because you know we did something secret at the farm. We're not asking you to join us in that and won't say what we did. Our request tonight is unrelated."

"OK."

The wail of a neighbor's violin penetrated the walls.

Jozef continued. "The three of us are very concerned about what the Germans have in store for the Krasau Jewish community. If it's bad, we want to know in advance. We weren't surprised when the Germans forced us into the ghetto because we knew they'd established ghettos elsewhere. But now, we're shut off from the Jewish world.

People tell us what they or someone else heard. Rumors of horrible places where prisoners are worked to death. We can't act based on rumors.

"We need reliable information. We need someone to contact Zakkai leaders in other cities. Exchange messages with them. Maybe other things. A courier. We'd like you to be that person."

Anna didn't react.

Itzhak raised his eyebrows at her poker face.

"You would pose as a young Christian woman," Jozef continued. "We'd give you a fake identity card and other documents with a Christian name to use outside the ghetto, and money to buy food, train tickets, and lodging. Itzhak would teach you everything we anticipate. How to respond if questioned. Where to sleep and eat."

"Will the fake documents look real? The ID–"

"Yeah," Itzhak replied. "Our artistic friend, Benec, is an excellent forger."

Jozef continued. "It's illegal for a Jew to leave the ghetto without permission. It's illegal for a Jew to go without an armband. It's illegal for a Jew to ride a train. It's illegal for a Jew to pretend to be a Christian. It's illegal for a Jew to do everything we're asking you to do."

"Why me?"

"Other than your sister – who we think would be great if she were older – you're the least Jewish-looking girl we know well and trust, and you speak Polish without a Jewish accent. Estie would be identified as a Jew at a hundred yards. Two other girls we considered are blonde, Aryan looking, outgoing and confident, but they speak Polish with a Jewish accent."

"What about boys? At least three or four Zakkai boys don't look Jewish at all–"

"They do if the police pull down their pants," Itzhak said.

Anna blushed.

"I go outside the ghetto if needed," Jozef said. "Smugglers and others do it often. But a girl would be safer, not only because boys are circumcised, though that is the main danger. Also, it's normal for a young woman to shop or walk about during the day. A man walking around raises suspicions."

Anna took a deep breath, rested her elbows on the table, and clasped her hands under her chin. This was much more dangerous than she'd expected. But she thought about Papa's hope to move somewhere safer. "Are other places in Poland better for Jews?"

"We don't know," Jozef said. "That's why we need reliable information."

"How would I get out of the ghetto and back in? And how would I get into the ghettos in Warsaw or other cities?"

"I'll explain the options in detail later if you say yes," Itzhak said. "The possibilities range from sneaking under, over, or through walls or bribing guards. It's possible to knock holes in walls and enter and exit the ghetto by squeezing through the holes. But you don't know who might be waiting on the other side. Or one could jump from the rooftop of a building inside the ghetto to the roof of a building it butts against outside the ghetto. I don't recommend either of those except in an emergency.

"The best way would be bribing guards at the gates. We know bribery often works; smugglers and others do it all the time. Sometimes they get arrested. We'll need to know which guards to bribe. That's my job.

"Of course, you'd wear an armband inside the ghetto and dispose of it outside the ghetto. To enter ghettos in other cities, you may pretend to be a Christian selling something inside the ghetto. You and I would discuss that."

Anna nodded but felt overwhelmed. One of her legs began to shake under the table.

Itzhak leaned forward with his shoulders hunched. "You must honestly ask yourself if you can do this. If they interrogate you and you crack, we're all in danger. Can you constantly pretend to be someone you're not? Can you bribe a guard, knowing he may turn on you? Can you confidently respond to a Polish policeman or Gestapo agent who suspects you're a Jew?"

"Are you trying to convince me not to do it?"

"No. But say yes only if you can handle the pressure. We wish you could do a trial run, but it would be foolish to risk arrest practicing to sneak out of the ghetto. Your first mission will be to Warsaw – you'll leave the ghetto, take local transportation, a train to Warsaw, local transportation there, sneak into the ghetto, sneak out and return trip."

"Anna," Leah said, "Itzhak believes – and we agree – that you are very smart and capable. His question is whether you're fearless. Because that's what you'll need to be."

"I'd like to amend that," Itzhak said. "I think you're perfect for the job IF you can hide your fear and control it enough to think clearly.

That is what you must decide."

Leah stood and rested her hand on Anna's shoulder. "You don't need to tell us tonight, Annaleh. Take a few days, search your heart. And, of course, please don't tell anyone."

Anna looked at her watch. "We have an hour before curfew. It takes me fifteen minutes to get home. I'll return within forty-five minutes with my answer. Since I can't talk to anyone, I don't need more time than that."

Leah and Jozef glanced at each other. "We'll be here," Leah said.

Anna left and meandered the darkening ghetto streets with people going home before curfew and past emaciated beggars. She imagined herself pretending to be a Christian on the Aryan side and immediately felt fear rising within her. She realized how secure she felt in the ghetto. As difficult as life had become, Anna believed she was being asked to leave relative safety for a black unknown.

She remembered when her family had turned down the chance to flee with the Valoskys. Papa had fretted that they might run out of money; here he had his bike shop, and Anna had wanted to stay in the warmth of her bed. She'd learned later that the Valoskys made it to eastern Russia, very far from the Nazis. Papa no longer had his bike shop nor Anna her bed.

If she became a courier, she could be arrested at any moment. But Mama and Papa had followed the rules and were almost murdered walking to the dentist. She could control not looking scared, but could she handle BEING scared, living with terror hours or days at a time? Was that the life she wanted? She imagined trying to bribe a guard and felt almost nauseous.

She'd always run from pressure. Why change now?

She thought about Mordecai and about what she'd learned through Zakkai. This wasn't only about her. Jozef, Leah, and Itzhak needed information. Not for themselves. For us. The Jewish people were in danger, and Anna could help.

She walked near a ghetto gate and saw stern-looking Polish police and German soldiers along with unarmed Jewish police. She must decide wisely. This wasn't a kids' game where winners and losers all get to play again.

She headed toward her home. If she could ask, what would Mama and Papa advise her to do?

Mama might say, "Risk your life for what? For news? Don't do it."

Papa would say, "This sounds very dangerous. Why you? Can they find someone else?"

Anna stopped walking. What would Papa say if he had the chance to do it himself?

She thoughtfully nodded, walked back to Jozef's and Leah's apartment, tapped on the door, and without stepping inside said to Jozef: "I'm in."

APRIL 20, 1941
ANNA

Itzhak sat with his arms crossed at the table in Jozef's and Leah's apartment. As usual, his dark, curly hair was uncombed and his shirt untucked. Anna sat across from him, as she had done, morning and afternoon, every third day since the meeting a month earlier. Itzhak refused to allow Anna to go on a mission before she was ready.

During the past three sessions, Itzhak had quizzed her, insisting that she recite what he'd taught her. His manner had been stern and brusque; this was not a time for games. Today was more of the same. Anna wore a dark skirt and colorful, patterned blouse, and her light hair was brushed behind her ears. The window shades were closed. The room was dim and quiet other than their voices.

"What is your name on the Aryan side?" Itzhak asked.

"Helena Kowalska."

"Describe yourself."

"I'm a Polish Catholic girl. My parents were Zygmunt and Wanda. My father died when I was three, and my mother died two years ago. My best friend was Maria Jankowski. She was killed in the German invasion, trapped in Warsaw visiting relatives." Anna's voice saddened, as if she still mourned her lost friend.

"What seat do you choose when riding a trolley or train?"

"I always choose a seat in crowded cars, near people with whom I strike up friendly conversations. I never sit far from other travelers. When I ride a trolley divided into a section for Germans up front and Poles in the rear, I sit at the front of the Polish section, near the Germans, because no Jew would do that."

"Who can you trust on the Aryan side?"

"I must be wary of everyone. Not only uniformed police and soldiers. Also undercover police and civilians who hunt Jews for cash rewards or to extort money. They don't wear uniforms, and I won't know who they are. A friendly woman who thinks I'm a Jew might be a wonderful person wanting to help Jews, or she could trick me as a first step to arrest."

"Who can you go to for help on the Aryan side?"

"No one. I'll be totally alone."

"What about inside the ghettos?"

"There, I'll have Zionist groups and many others to help me. But even in ghettos, I might run into a Jewish informer for the Gestapo or police. And I must avoid the Jewish police."

"Recite the Apostles' Creed."

"I believe in God, the Father Almighty, creator of heaven and earth, and in Jesus Christ, his only son, our Lord, who was conceived by the Holy Spirit and born of the Virgin Mary, suffered under Pontius Pilate, was crucified, died, and was buried. He descended into hell; on the third day, he rose again. He ascended into heaven and is seated at the right hand of God the Father Almighty. He will come again to judge the living and the dead. I believe in the Holy Spirit, the Holy Catholic Church, the communion of saints, the forgiveness of sins, the resurrection of the body, and life everlasting. Amen."

"The sign of the cross."

Anna crossed herself and said, "In the name of the Father, and of the Son and of the Holy Spirit. Amen."

"Hail Mary."

"Hail Mary, full of grace, the Lord is with thee. Blessed art thou amongst women, and blessed is the fruit of thy womb, Jesus. Holy Mary, mother of God, pray for us sinners, now and in the hour of our death. Amen."

Itzhak smiled. "You make a nice Catholic."

"Thank you."

"Where are your eyes when you're on the Aryan side?"

"Always up. Never down. Looking down indicates concern or fright. I'm always fully confident because I have nothing to worry about. But I'm vigilant, aware of my surroundings."

Itzhak stood. "No reason to recite everything else. You're ready. Any questions?"

Anna stayed seated. "When we met a month ago, you said I'm perfect for this job. Did you mean it – and why?"

"Ah, yeah..." Itzhak sighed. "You may not like the answer."

"And, the answer is?"

"I carefully checked you out, talked to people from your past. They said you're a quitter. That you start and don't finish. You have talent, but you're too lazy to use it. Very uncomplimentary, and they gave me examples."

Itzhak put his hands on the table and leaned forward. "I've watched you. I saw you prepare for the classes you taught. Other things. I've thought about it – about you – and concluded they're wrong. Very wrong. You're not lazy. You're scared. Scared of failing. And that's what makes you perfect for this job."

"Being scared makes me perfect for a job where I need to not be scared?"

"Yeah. Because you've spent your whole life pretending not to be scared. You're what's called an experienced employee." He chuckled. "You should relate."

Itzhak furrowed his brow. "How is that?"

"You're also perpetually scared. Not of failure. Of getting close."

Itzhak blushed. "We're not talking about me."

"I am. I may leave tomorrow and never return. We met more than fifteen times the past month, and you didn't smile at me once. Because you're afraid. You laugh at your own jokes, but that's it. You're formal and curt. I know you have a good heart – share it."

"When – not if, but when – you return from this mission, you can psychoanalyze me. But for now, we'll remain focused. Tomorrow morning, you'll join the women's labor battalion leaving at 7:00 out the west gate, as we discussed. I'll bribe the foreman and he'll bribe the guards. From there, you're off to Warsaw. I'll see you in about a week, and I look forward to hearing how noneventful your experience was."

Anna took a deep breath, exhaled, walked around the small table and hugged Itzhak. He awkwardly hugged her at arm's length. She kissed his cheek as a friend might do, said, "Thanks Professor," and left.

APRIL 21, 1941
ANNA

At 6:30 the next morning, Anna left her family's apartment for the ghetto's west gate. With Jozef's permission, she'd told Mama, Papa and Irina the night before that she was traveling illegally to Warsaw. She couldn't simply disappear for a week and didn't want to lie. What if she were arrested, and they had no idea where she was?

Mama, though upset, was surprisingly quiet, Papa asked questions, and Irina said she wished she could go. They promised to tell no one, not even Bubbie. Papa said to get to bed early, but Anna slept little and was very tired when they hugged each other tight this morning.

By 6:45, Anna was walking on the street that led to the gate. The weather was windy but unusually warm and humid. Anna was mentally prepared, merely one of many Jewish women leaving the ghetto for work. No reason to worry.

Unless something went wrong. Budding fear had begun to mount.

She kept walking. The gate, manned by police and soldiers, was about fifty yards ahead. To her left stood the ghetto's brick wall, topped with barbed wire. Next to the wall stretched a long line of Jewish men awaiting permission to leave the ghetto for work. To her right, a sidewalk ran in front of several buildings; about twenty yards in front of her a line of women stood on the sidewalk. Anna stopped and looked at the line and at the guards stationed at the gate.

Itzhak had said that the foreman had a list of thirty-one women authorized to exit the ghetto with this work group. The guards wouldn't check names against the list; they'd simply make sure each woman had an exit permit and, ordinarily, that thirty-one women were exiting. But the foreman and two guards had been bribed to allow thirty-two women – including Anna – to leave this morning instead of thirty-one. Anna's name wasn't on the list, but that didn't matter because the guards wouldn't look at it. They'll simply count thirty-two women, each of whom will show her exit permit, and out they'll go.

Easy.

Anna glanced at the men's line. Itzhak said the guards followed the same process for them. Her trembling hand reached into her small purse and pulled out a forged exit permit. What if a guard who wasn't bribed looks at the list of names and discovers that Anna isn't on it? Or what if they search her?

Anna was wearing three pairs of underwear and two dresses. An empty backpack was wrapped and tied around her thigh. She would have worn the same dress every day for the week and not carried the pack, but Itzhak said traveling on a train to Warsaw without luggage might arouse suspicion. And because a Jew couldn't march out to work carrying a backpack, she hid the pack and extra clothes on her body. Her outer dress was big and hid everything underneath – if no one searched her.

Anna's fake documents, identifying her as Helena Kowalska, were stuffed inside her underwear along with cash and a letter from Jozef to Zakkai leaders in Warsaw. A Star of David armband was wrapped around her upper arm; her hand now held the forged permit authorizing Anna Allowitz to exit the ghetto for work.

She again eyed the soldiers and police. Which of them was bribed? Who wasn't? Anna's mouth dried, and her pulse raced as her fear increased. It wasn't too late to change her mind. She could leave. Just turn and walk home. No one would notice.

She took two good breaths, as Itzhak had taught her to control fear, moved forward and joined the line.

Her job now was to blend in as a young woman among many going to work. Some women chatted, but most stood silently. With a facial expression of tired indifference, Anna dropped her arms to her sides, and her eyes seemed drawn to bits of windblown trash tumbling along the pavement. But her heart pounded.

The women walked single file down the sidewalk and stopped about ten yards from the gate. The guards waved forward the line of men across the street, to Anna's left. About twenty-five women stood in front of her and five behind.

A policeman slowly ambled down the line of women, checking them out. Anna's eyes and face looked up, as she'd been taught. The other women paid little attention to the policeman; Anna mimicked them. But she felt him drawing close. Heart thumping, she blew her nose into a handkerchief as the policeman approached. He stopped, looked at her face, and continued past. Why did he stop? Was he now standing behind her, staring at her clothes to see if she was hiding something underneath?

Calm down, Anna scolded herself. You're imagining things. She recited Itzhak's lessons. "When in line, I'm off to work, off to work. Same as everyone else. Small talk is good. New people are in this line every day, and no one will wonder why I'm here. I'm off to work, off to–"

"Are you feeling alright?" asked a disheveled, middle-aged woman in front of her. The woman had wild, uncombed, dark hair, oddly bulging eyes, and a worried look on her face.

"Yeah, fine," Anna smiled. "Why'd you ask?"

"Your face and neck are drenched in sweat. Do you have a fever?"

"No, I told you–"

"Are you sure?" The woman bit her lip. "You don't look good at all... Do you have typhus!?" the woman shrieked and stepped back. "I've heard typhus is spreading. The last thing I need is typhus!" The woman looked toward the police at the front of the line, and two other women moved away from Anna. "They shouldn't let you go with us if you're–"

Anna laughed. "I've heard this my whole life. I have a condition that makes me sweat. My mama used to say I could water her flowers by sniffing them."

The woman's bulging eyes narrowed. "I've never heard of that." But another woman said, "I think I have."

"It's rare," Anna said. "Some people have strange conditions. When I was little, one of my classmates would randomly laugh for no reason. Another broke out in a rash when she played outside." Anna smiled wide. "Don't worry, sweating isn't contagious."

The women nodded skeptically but stepped back in line. Anna wiped her face with her used handkerchief.

"Halt! The numbers don't match! Show your papers," a policeman ordered in Polish. The voice came from Anna's left, where the men were exiting the gate.

"Those are Gestapo men," a woman near Anna fearfully whispered.

Two Germans in dark uniforms hovered near the police and soldiers slowly walking down the men's line, checking names against a list. "Since when does the Gestapo monitor who goes to work?" the same woman muttered.

A policeman dragged a young man from the line. "I'm just–" the Jew started to say. A German guard slammed his rifle butt into the Jew's head, knocking him down. Terrified, Anna wondered if the Jew had bribed that guard, and if the same guard had been bribed for her. The Jew struggled to stand, took a wobbly step and collapsed. "Send the rest through!" yelled a German guard to the police. The men filed out the gate, past the unlucky man sprawled on the pavement. The

Gestapo officers and guards made their way toward the women.

Itzhak hadn't anticipated the Gestapo. Anna was still near the back of the line; she should leave and come back next week.

Yeah. Definitely. The increased risk was unexpected. She should go. She turned and saw a woman behind her flee the line – making fewer women. Anna took a few steps to the side and hurriedly counted. Thirty-one women, including Anna. She didn't know why the woman fled, but there were thirty-one women on the list. No reason for the Germans to check names. Sweating, she moved back in line.

A guard waved the women forward. As their line snaked, Anna noticed a very short woman, perhaps a dwarf, toward the front. Had she included her when she counted? She couldn't remember. She must have.

The Gestapo men stood at the front of the line, just as they had with the men.

Anna would have remembered someone so short if she'd seen her when she counted. She must not have seen her. Which meant thirty-two women were in line but only thirty-one names on the list.

The Gestapo will tell the guards to check names against the list, as they did with the men.

Panic.

She must leave! No choice. Anna quickly glanced at the guards. None looking her way.

Still walking forward, she turned to go. Four women behind her. Next to them walked a policeman.

Too late.

She moved forward with the others, and the police counted. Thirty-one.

The women exited the ghetto.

THE SAME DAY
PALESTINE
MORDECAI

"Slow fire at 200 yards, standing!" yelled British Sergeant Roger Smithson. "Followed by 200 yards kneeling, 500 yards prone, and rapid fire at 300 yards, prone from standing, ten shots in 70 seconds!"

Mordecai took careful aim.

"Commence firing!"

A torrent of shots rang out, echoing off the hills. Followed by "Cease firing!"

Mordecai, with seventy other Jewish recruits, had been receiving rifle training from the British for a month to augment what they'd learned from the Jewish Haganah underground. Mordecai had joined the Haganah a year earlier. Now, the Haganah provided the men, and the British furnished the weapons and instruction.

Today, they were practicing in groups of fifteen at a range near Kibbutz Mishmar Ha'Emek in northern Palestine, founded twenty years earlier by Polish Zionists. Nestled in the Jezreel Valley, where the ancient Israelites fought several battles, the kibbutz was about four miles from Megiddo, known as Armageddon in the New Testament – the site of the final battle at the end of time. The smell of gunpowder overwhelmed the pine scent from the nearby forest planted by Zionist pioneers.

The sergeant wiped sweat off his face and checked the targets. "Good show, lads," he said. "You're getting quite the hang of it."

After they finished and the other trainees had left, Mordecai stayed to help the sergeant set up targets for the next group. Mordecai had become proficient in English, having worked hard for more than a year. He'd heard that this Englishman was friendly to Jews. "Any news on when we'll see f-f-f-fighting?" Mordecai asked.

"No, but that's the way the British army works, you see. One moment tea and crumpets, then without warning, off to a trench."

Sergeant Smithson was a veteran of the Great War. He'd fought at Gallipoli in Turkey, career army, and spent much of the '20s and '30s in Palestine with the British Mandatory administration. Mid-forties, a tad heavy around the waist and barely taller than Mordecai, Sergeant Smithson sported the erect bearing of a British soldier and the customary well-cropped mustache. "You'll get your chance soon enough, young man, and then you'll wish you hadn't."

"Not me," Mordecai said. "I'm eager to fight, and I'm waiting to hear the British are f-f-f-finally forming a parachutist's group and will drop me into Poland. I want to find my family, my girlfriend–"

"Yes, indeed, I've heard the same from a few of you Jewish buggers. Drop from the sky and save your people. It's a nice wish but don't hold your breath. You'll go where the British army sends you. Right now, with the Luftwaffe using air bases in Syria, and the German army knocking on Egypt's door and salivating at the entire Near East, you can expect the British army to keep you here. We British need to protect our oil, but you Jews also shouldn't want Jerry marching into Tel Aviv."

"I'm g-g-g-glad–"

"If you ever lack ammunition, you should scream at the enemy, and they'll think you're a machine gun."

Mordecai scowled.

"Sorry, lad, couldn't help myself. You were saying?"

"I'm g-g-glad you're allowing Jews to fight instead of acting like we're the enemy."

"By jove, you're right there. Today, I'm training you to shoot. Tomorrow, I might arrest you when you practice. Strange irony. For years, we British helped you people build this place to become the Jewish homeland, and when the Arabs in 1936 again started massacring Jews and threatening our oil pipeline, we trained thousands of young Jewish chaps to help teach the Arabs a lesson. After three years of fighting, we did an about-face, clamped down on Jewish immigration to make the Arabs happy – stranding millions of your fellow countrymen to Nazi abuse – and arrested some of the same Jews who'd fought with us."

"Exactly."

"Today, we need you – rumors say we'll soon attack in Lebanon and Syria. If true, off you boys will go, perhaps led by that odd-looking chap, Moshe Dayan, and attached to an Australian or Indian brigade. We love giving our colonials the chance to sacrifice themselves for the Union Jack. My advice is to enjoy life before then."

"You're the first British soldier who's been friendly to me. Most don't seem to like Jews."

"I won't pretend you're wrong. Most British officers and soldiers do favor the Arabs. But it's quite understandable. Many of you Jews are too annoying. We British are tasked with keeping order. Some

Arab peasants can be excitable, but except for fellows like the Mufti, who cozies up to Hitler, the wealthy Arabs are polite and welcoming. People to have tea with. You Jews, on the other hand, don't know your place. 'Give me this, give me that. Now isn't soon enough.' Can be quite irritating, you see."

"Well–"

"No need to explain. I was raised in a Restorationist church and know your history–you've wandered for two thousand years dreaming of returning here; Britain promised they'd help but then swept the magic carpet from under your feet. You're justifiably unhappy with the turn of events, but the average British soldier doesn't know your story. To him, you're just another whiny Yid."

"You're different because–"

"For me, it's simple. *When I was at school, I was looked down on and made to feel that I was a failure and not wanted in the world. When I came to Palestine, I found a whole people who had been treated like that for scores of generations, and yet they were undefeated, building their country anew.*"

Smithson paused and quietly said, "I belong with that people."

•••

That night Mordecai sat against his pillow, beneath Anna's photo nailed to the wall, and wrote her. He did so twice each month and saved the letters; they'll enjoy reading them after the war.

Dearest Anna,

I scored second highest at the shooting range. I think I'm learning fairly well. Hopefully, life is close to normal for you since Poland is so far from the fighting. With Germany rampaging across the world, they shouldn't be concerned with Jews in Poland. Are you helping your papa in his bike shop? Trying to help your mother not pull her hair out over Irina? She must be fourteen now and a terror to her teachers.

I hope you still see Jozef, Leah and some Zakkai kids. On a subject I'll save for another time: in faraway Poland it's easy to imagine Jews and Arabs getting along and building a peaceful society. Things here are more complicated.

I'll end with a subject close to my heart. We had the best food at the kibbutz seder two weeks ago.

Nothing like the chicken soup, brisket, potato kugel, and everything else we used to have in Poland, and that you hopefully ate at your seders unless you're badly affected by wartime rationing. Here, only one seder rather than two; takes getting used to. But the food doesn't.

I'm past ready to share it all with you.

With all my love,

Mordecai.

MAY 3, 1941
ANNA

At noon, Itzhak was nodding off at a table in his parents' apartment. He'd barely slept the past two nights worrying about Anna; she should have returned three days earlier. He would have been concerned about anyone but had grown especially fond of her. Smart, kind, thoughtful, perceptive. And such a pretty smile.

So when he opened the door to knocking and she stepped inside, he reflexively spread his arms and screamed, "Anna!"

She rushed to him; they embraced, looked into each other's eyes and smiled, but as if a switch were pulled, Itzhak withdrew his arms, pointed at a chair, and they sat across the table from each other.

"I'm very happy to see you," Itzhak said. "No one else is here; tell me – did you learn much in Warsaw? Have you reported to Jozef?"

"No. Well, yeah, I learned a lot. But no, I'm exhausted. I just entered the ghetto and came straight to you."

Itzhak raised his eyebrows.

"Your training saved my life. More than once."

"Good. After you've rested, tell me everything and we can plan accordingly for next time."

"I'm so tired, I'm almost delirious. Yeah, let's talk later. We spent so much time together, I've missed you."

Itzhak blushed a deep red and looked down at the table.

"Never look down. It shows lack of confidence."

Itzhak looked up at Anna.

"Better."

"I know you're exhausted, but please give me a quick summary."

She sighed. "I learned nothing good. Four hundred thousand Jews are crammed into the Warsaw ghetto. Four hundred thousand! Like here but on a massive scale. Nowhere in Poland is safe for Jews. We've been shut into ghettos everywhere.

"I was told each ghetto is different, depending on the Jewish leadership, the Germans in charge, random bad luck, but conditions are miserable everywhere. Germans humiliate and kill and abuse whoever they want whenever they want." She shook her head. "And starvation, disease. You wouldn't believe the dead bodies on the streets in the Warsaw ghetto. Some Jews try to live on the Aryan side, but it's extremely difficult even for assimilated Jews unless they have Christian friends risking their lives for them. And it's almost impossible for Jews who speak Polish with a Jewish accent.

"Everyone I talked to believes the Germans will lose the war. The question is how long it will take. But if smugglers keep bringing food into the ghettos, most Polish Jews should scratch through and pick up the pieces when the war ends."

"Did–"

"I'm sorry, I need to talk to Jozef before I collapse." She stood and headed to the door.

"Anna."

She turned. "Yeah?"

"I was worried about you, and I'm very glad you're back." Itzhak smiled.

Anna grinned. "I'm very glad to see you too, and it's nice to see you smile."

JULY 15, 1941
SZYMON'S JOURNAL

From April through June 1941:

Germany conquered Yugoslavia.
Germany conquered Greece.
Germany invaded Russia.
Germans roam North Africa and have attacked Egypt.

The Germans have forced hundreds of thousands of Polish teens and adults, of both sexes, to work in Germany. They treat the Poles there as inferior beings, decreeing that all Poles in Germany must wear a letter "P" badge on their clothing. Poles there are banned from attending church, cinema and the like with Germans or engaging in sexual relations with them. For the latter, the penalty is death for Polish men.

In Poland, the Germans are attacking the Catholic Church. Many priests have been executed or sent to forced labor or concentration camps where they work prisoners to death. Parishes have been closed. Thankfully, most churches remain open in Krasau.

In response to the Germans closing schools in Poland, some underground schools are operating. Many resistance cells have been established for a future revolt, but attacks on German soldiers have been minimal.

NOVEMBER 4, 1941
FRAMMY

"And they dug and dug and dug and found a giant treasure chest!" Mrs. Kornbluth said. "It was SO HEAVY that it took both boys, hrrumphing and grrrumphing, to lift it from its hole. The boys pried off the lid, looked inside and saw" – Frammy's and little Janek's mouths opened, and their eyes grew wide in anticipation – "that the chest was full of pastries and cakes for them and all their friends!"

For almost an hour, six-year-old Frammy and five-year-old Janek had sat on a narrow bench shoved next to a small wooden table, and on the other side sat fifteen-year-old Irina on her bench. It was Tuesday morning, and they were attending school in the cramped attic above Mr. Kornbluth's shoe repair shop. The table and two benches were lodged between wooden joists, beams, and piles of dusty equipment and tools.

Mrs. Kornbluth was the teacher. As usual, the students were Frammy, Irina, and their classmate, Janek. Schools in the ghetto were illegal, but Mama had learned that Mrs. Kornbluth secretly taught in her husband's shop's attic.

Frammy loved Mrs. "Corn blewit." She had once taught in a really big school, back before the "awkya payshun." She was gentle and kind and told the best stories about wizards and lions and boys searching for treasure. Irina didn't get to listen to those stories because Mrs. Corn blewit almost always made Irina do math or history or things like that, and Irina had to write really tiny so she didn't waste paper. Frammy felt sorry for Irina because she spent most of her time holding a pencil, scratching her head and moaning about something called "gee I'm a tree." Frammy couldn't understand what triangles and circles had to do with trees.

"I have some very exciting news for you, Frammy and Janek," Mrs. Kornbluth said. "Next Tuesday, you'll get to read out of a REAL book, with pictures and everything. And–"

Clang-clang-clang. Mrs. Kornbluth suddenly put her finger to her now very serious face, reminding everyone to keep perfectly still and quiet. That was Mr. Kornbluth's warning hammer from downstairs. Three quick clangs on his metal anvil meant a Jewish or Polish policeman was in the shop to get shoes repaired. Frammy knew that if a policeman heard them in the attic, they would be in very, very big trouble.

After a few minutes of quiet and then the all-clear signal, Mrs. Kornbluth finished her lesson and went downstairs to make sure it was safe for everyone to leave. She called up, and her class of three climbed down the narrow, wooden attic steps, returned Mr. Kornbluth's wave and said goodbye to each other.

Frammy and Irina headed home, walking along the curb on a winding road, near the ghetto wall, filled with pedestrians and a few cars. Lying in front of them was the corpse of an old man. They stepped around him and kept going.

"Why do dead people sometimes have their eyes open?" Frammy asked. "Can they still see you?"

"No, when you're dead, you can't see anymore."

"That man looked really sad," Frammy said. "Do you think it's because he couldn't see his friends outside the walls? Bubbie says we live in a box, and Mama says I had friends on the other side, but I barely remember them. Do you remember?"

"Uh huh, I remember, and it's sad to think how we're locked in here, and so we should just, um..." Irina paused, and with feigned excitement said, "Mrs. Kornbluth said you'll get to read from a real book next week."

"I hope it doesn't have circles and triangles, and–"

"Halt! Stop!" boomed a deep voice somewhere up ahead. A very thin boy about ten, barefoot and wearing raggedy clothes, ran toward them in the street and darted past. He was followed a few moments later by what looked to be his younger brother, maybe five or six, scampering as fast as he could. A police whistle shrieked, and then a red-faced policeman came running and grabbed the smaller boy from behind. The boy, thin with wavy brown hair and worn clothes, tried unsuccessfully to wriggle away.

"What are you doing!" the policeman hollered. "I told you yesterday – no more smuggling!"

"I didn't smoggle!" the boy whined, rapidly blinking his eyes.

"Liar!" The policeman slapped the boy's face with a loud whack, knocking him backwards; his little head smacked the pavement. "I just saw you crawl through a hole in the wall!" The policeman emptied the boy's baggy pants of two potatoes. "It's time you learned your lesson!"

"Come on Frammy, let's get out of here," Irina said. She tugged Frammy's hand, but he resisted; his eyes were frozen on the policeman, who looked like a regular man but acted like a monster.

The policeman flipped the boy – now screaming, crying and thrashing his arms – onto his stomach. The policeman knelt on the boy's back and pounded his thigh three times with his fist.

"This is better than a German bullet in the head, which you'll get when they catch you on the other side," the policeman said. His knee still pressing down onto the boy's back, the policeman examined each potato, put them in his own pockets, and walked away.

The little boy stopped howling and lay motionless for an agonizingly long moment. Frammy worried he was dead. But he finally sat up, wiped at the blood oozing from his nose, and relocated a potato, which the policeman hadn't seen, from inside his underwear to a pocket. He struggled to stand, winced, and hobbled after his older brother.

NOVEMBER 5, 1941
ITZHAK'S JOURNAL

The Germans have decreed the **DEATH PENALTY** for Jews who leave the ghetto without permission and for Poles who help them. Yesterday, the Germans executed six Jewish women and two men for violating this order, including a young woman unable to pay a policeman the bribe he demanded and a father working on the Aryan side to feed his young children. Several hundred Jews are in jail, in line for execution.

The executions have set us all trembling. Everyone is shocked the Germans would kill people simply for stepping outside the walls.

With that demoralizing backdrop, I'll recap major milestones and address some important aspects of ghetto life. The Germans occupied Krasau September 1939. They locked us in the ghetto October 1940. For more than a year, thousands of people have never set foot outside the ghetto.

On a happier subject, our Zakkai youth group spent two summers at the farm, with Gestapo permission, in 1940 and again in 1941. Vacations to heaven. Zakkai has added members, and we've grown very tight. Amidst all the fear and uncertainty, Zakkai provides a magical escape. We still talk of becoming pioneers in Palestine. Is that hope or delusion? Herzl said if you will it, it is not a fable, and we could not "will it" any stronger.

With that detour, I now turn to ghetto life.

Smuggling is a key to survival. Without it, everyone would starve. Smuggling takes several forms. Could be children sneaking outside the wall, begging on the Aryan side and returning with food for themselves and their families. Or it may be large scale between Jewish businessmen inside the ghetto and Christian businessmen outside it. Typically, Jews bribe the guards to permit them to leave the ghetto. The Jews make deals on the Aryan side to buy potatoes, flour, and other food, which the Christians may deliver by heaving sacks over the wall at predesignated locations and times. That is simply one example.

Although Germans and Polish police arrest and now will execute smugglers caught outside the ghetto, some guards manning the ghetto gates see the opportunity to make money and let smugglers pass upon paying a bribe. A ghetto riddle: what three things are unstoppable? The German army, the British navy and Jewish smuggling.

Starvation is a terrible concern. Smuggled food does no good without money to pay for it. The Jewish Council runs soup kitchens but lacks sufficient food. Every day, more corpses dot the streets.

Parents without money give the food they gain from begging to their children, the parents die because they don't eat, and the children are left to beg. In the cold, frozen children lie dead in the streets. But as of now, most people work or possess some savings and therefore have food (smuggled in) to eat.

Typhus This disease spreads through lice, bad sanitation (a problem due to inadequate sewage facilities), and too many people in closed spaces – the perfect description of the ghetto. The symptoms are horrible, and many die from it.

Not knowing whom you can trust is another issue. Some people, including the smugglers, say we must break the law to survive, and a few are active in Jewish or Polish resistance groups. But other Jews believe the Germans would be more lenient if everyone obeyed them. They might point to the Gestapo man, Beck, who allowed Zakkai to run our Zionist camp again. German kindness amid depravity punctuates the absurdity of our situation.

A few Jews, hopefully not too many, are paid informers for the Gestapo. They are the lowest of the low, deserving of divine justice. Human hands may accelerate the process.

Culture and war news offer some hope. Underground schools exist, mostly taught by rabbis for religious students. Writers and professors present lectures for the public to maintain a semblance of intellectual life.

In June, the Germans made what optimists say was a fatal mistake: they invaded Russia. Napoleon's undoing. Many people believe Germany will lose the war within a year. The question is if we'll be dead from sickness or starvation by then.

NOVEMBER 7, 1941
REUVEN AND BENEC

Reuven kicked the ball from the goal area high into the air, where it caught the gusting wind, flew over his opponents' heads, bounced on the hard dirt and rolled off the field to the side of a building.

"What are you doing!" yelled Benjamin, standing at midfield as the ball sailed past. "You expect us to run the whole way down there?"

"That's how the game is played," Benec hollered. Benec, nineteen, and his brother Reuven, fifteen, were playing a two-on-two football game on this freezing, gray, windy afternoon against two other Zakkai boys, Benjamin, seventeen, and Levi, sixteen. All four boys wore dark pants and layers of shirts and jackets. The small field, carved with German permission from a lot stuck between four warehouses, consisted mostly of dirt with a few patches of grass.

Benjamin and Levi turned and walked toward the ball. "These teams stink," Benjamin said. "I thought I was a good player, but then I met Reuven and learned what good looks like."

"At least you're tall and quick," griped short, chunky Levi.

Reuven, laughing, sped toward them. "Whoever gets the ball earns last kick!" he yelled. Benjamin and Levi started racing Reuven to the ball. Reuven quickly passed Levi; the only question was if he'd also overtake Benjamin, who had a several-yard head start.

"Show some respect!" barked two men in Jewish police uniforms standing on the sideline. "Come here!"

The boys stopped and trotted to the policemen; Benec ran to them from the other direction. Both policemen were wearing blue police hats and dark clothes. One looked to be in his forties; Benec knew the other guy, named Henryk. He was a year or two older than Benec. Some Jewish police, Benec thought, tried to maintain order and help their fellow Jews, but many, like Henryk, were weasels who took the police job because they wanted to boss people around.

Both policemen were blowing into their hands and stomping their feet to try to stay warm. "Show some respect," Henryk repeated. "Three days ago, the Germans executed Jews, and you're out here laughing and playing!" He pointed an accusing finger at Benec. "Do you even care?"

Benec, fighting to control his temper, stared silently at Henryk before finally saying, "Anything else?"

"You didn't answer me."

"Don't lecture us," Benec said.

Henryk stepped toward Benec. "What the hell are you doing out here?"

"Who are you to ask?" Benec calmly replied. "The Germans murder Jews, and you still play policeman for them? You're not fooling us. You do whatever they tell you. When the Germans need Jews for their work camps, it's you, the Jewish police, who drag people from their families. Unless, of course" – Benec rubbed his fingers together – "they pay you a nice little bribe."

Henryk slapped Benec's face; Benec clenched his fists, but Benjamin threw his arms around Benec and yanked him backward with Levi's help. "If you hit him," Benjamin whispered, "they might give you to the Polish police. And from there to the Germans."

Reuven stepped in front of his brother, who still had Benjamin's arms wrapped around his chest. "Hey, we're out here having fun. We're not hurting anybody–"

"Everyone relax," the older policeman said. "We're on the same side. But listen. We know at least two of you are with Zakkai, and that YOU" – he pointed at Benec – "are one of their leaders. I always thought of Zakkai as the harmless Zionist group that sits around holding hands, singing songs and talking about how nice life will be in Eretz Israel. But lately, we've heard some things I don't like."

Benec broke free of Benjamin but stayed still. "I don't know what you're talking about," he said.

"Don't lie to me!" the older policeman shouted. "I'm sure you heard a couple boys from the Beitar youth group were arrested for what the Germans call subversive activity." He stepped forward and poked his finger hard into Benec's chest. "No one returns from where those boys were sent. Stick to eating challah and saying your Shabbos prayers. Because if Zakkai makes the same mistake as the Beitar boys, you'll suffer the same fate."

Benec glared at him. "You threatening to murder us?"

"It's not what I want. It's what the GERMANS will do – and they don't ask my opinion."

The boys silently glanced at each other. Finally, Reuven grabbed Benjamin's arm. "I came to play football. Race you to the ball!" He took off running and pulled Benjamin with him. Benec and Levi turned and walked after them.

"Show some respect!" Henryk yelled.

"Yeah, Yeah!" Benec hollered but kept walking with Levi toward the ball, their brown wavy hair blowing in the wind.

"Those guys are such losers," Benec said.

"Yeah, they're clowns," Levi said. "They should wear clown suits with big red balls for noses."

Benec smirked.

"But what was he talking about – what does he think Zakkai is doing?"

"Nothing. Don't worry about it," Benec said, stuffing his hands in his pockets. He couldn't tell Levi about the resistance work, but he thought of Levi as a deep-thinking, smart guy. "Do you think it's disrespectful for us to be out here?"

"We're living in a graveyard," Levi said. "But that doesn't mean we should make our insides, our selves, into graveyards. They allow us to have this tiny field, so let's enjoy it. They allow me to play my harmonica, I play it. If I could find a girl who'd let me, I'd kiss her."

"Yep," Benec said. "I walked past two dead bodies on my way here and barely noticed. We're caged behind barbed wire, any minute they could send us to a labor camp where the Germans might beat us to death, or a German patrolling the ghetto might shoot me for fun. I could give up like so many older people who've lost the light in their eyes. But that's not for me. If we might die tomorrow, we'd better live fast as we can – now. Until the end, I plan on laughing, playing, and finding a girl to chase. Much as I can."

"You still chasing Anna?"

"Yeah, right," Benec said sarcastically. "I've tried – I was even alone with her a couple times. Like what a normal human would think of as dates, if there's anything normal in this putrid place. She laughs, I think we're having a good time, but no romance. Zilch. No matter what I tried."

Levi chuckled. "So, your little brother gets pretty Irina, and you strike out with her big sister?"

"Yeah," Benec laughed. "And it pisses me off!" He shivered in the cold wind. "I'm kidding. I once heard good advice about girls: be yourself. Some will like you and some won't. If you give it a shot with a girl and it doesn't work, don't moan. Just move on and look for one who likes you."

"How is it possible that thirty seconds after talking about murder and death, we laugh and talk about girls? Could anyone outside this hell understand?"

Benec opened his mouth to reply, but then closed it, looked down and shook his head.

JANUARY 20, 1942

In the Wannsee suburb of Berlin, German government officials met to coordinate the "Final Solution to the Jewish Problem" - the murder of every Jew in Europe.

•••

APRIL 7, 1942
PAPA

The sun barely awake, Alexander trudged off to work at a factory inside the ghetto. Thank goodness for that job. His days marching under police eyes to work on the Aryan side, fighting to get his exit permit renewed, suffering random humiliations along the way. All in the past, hopefully forever.

They'd lived in the ghetto a year and a half, and life had gotten tough. Bubbie was sick, their apartment often lacked electricity or water, and an annoying family had moved in with them. Their two-room apartment now held eleven people. The Germans had forced all Jews in surrounding villages to resettle in Krasau, and the Jewish Council ordered Alexander to take in a family. Too many Jews and too little space in the ghetto. Frammy learned to turn his head when Mama or Bubbie changed clothes, and Anna and Irina spent many nights sleeping at their Zakkai leaders' apartment.

Lurking always was typhus; Alexander worried it may strike his family any day. And then there was the impact of ghetto life on his kids. Little Frammy thinks it's normal for swarms of gaunt boys to steal food and for him to walk past dead bodies. For so long, Alexander had ached to get his family away from this nightmare, and he still clung to that hope. But his rational mind said escape was impossible. His one goal was to keep his family healthy and alive.

Thankfully, starvation was not a problem for his family. The earnings from his factory job and the part-time jobs he found for Chana, Anna and Irina sewing torn German army uniforms put smuggled food on the table and allowed him to give a bit of bread each day to one beggar. By helping beggars, Alexander felt he was still human, and for that he credited Bubbie, his religious mother-in-law. She insisted that it was easy to follow God's laws when times were good, but that sharing your meager possessions with the stranger and orphan, as God commands, was even more important now.

Choosing which beggar wasn't easy. He often walked past at least thirty, of all ages, on his way to work. His heart bled mostly for the children, but he occasionally gave a morsel to older beggars as well. Alexander chastised himself for thinking of them as "beggars," not people. But it wasn't easy. Their emaciated faces, filthy, lice-ridden bodies in smelly, tattered clothes, incessant pleading, hands out – in your face – their disregard for your own troubles. Some adults held photographs of themselves from better days, as if to prove they too were once people.

Several weeks ago, one boy caught Alexander's attention; ever since, he was the most frequent recipient of Alexander's bounty. The boy looked about ten, but it was hard to tell with the hollow eyes, bony face and bloated stomach. He wore the same clothes every day; his pants were in tatters, a loop of string served as a belt, and his filthy, oversized shirt was pocked with holes.

The boy never stood or spoke when Alexander walked by. Instead, he would sit against a building, pen in hand, and write in a notebook. Some days, the boy lifted his eyes and hand toward Alexander. Others, he rested his head against the wall with eyes closed or wrote in his book, head down.

Today, as Alexander approached the boy's usual spot, which smelled of urine, a dagger pierced Alexander's heart. A man was lifting the boy's lifeless body and placing it in a wheeled cart that two men dragged through the streets, collecting corpses for burial.

The boy's notebook lay next to the wall, where he had sat. Alexander picked it up – a school workbook; the boy had written in the margins. Page after page of poetry. The boy had dated his entries, beginning in 1940 when he was eleven. So, he was thirteen, not ten. Alexander flipped to the back and read the boy's last poem, from two days ago – two days before the boy died.

One day, I shall fly
With the wind at my back, over the clouds I will sail.
Into space, with Mars on my left and Venus to the right;
Through the galaxy, I will go.
With no one to hold me back
I will explore and search and search
Until I reach the face of God.
And ask him Why.

Alexander sighed, wiped tears from his eyes, gave bread to the next boy he saw, and made his way to work.

•••

Alexander was standing with hundreds of Jewish men in the factory warehouse. The foreman had announced that a German official was on his way to speak to them. Men from nearby factories came and stood behind Alexander's group. "He must be giving us a raise," Alexander said. "No," someone replied. "They'll make us honorary Germans and increase our rations."

The workers quieted when Germans, none in uniform, entered and mounted a small platform. The German factory owner introduced a smartly dressed German as Karl Beck, "Gestapo Jewish liaison." Alexander recognized Beck – how could he forget the man who had saved his life? Alexander anxiously listened.

"Hello everyone." Beck spoke in German and a translator shouted in Polish. "I'm sorry to interrupt your workday, but I have some news I think you'll enjoy hearing. Life has been difficult. The Jewish Quarter is overcrowded, not enough food, too much illness, inadequate facilities. I'm aware of the problems and want to solve them.

"The main issue is overcrowding. I know it's worse with the influx of ten thousand people from outside Krasau, but it's been a problem from the beginning."

"Since when do Germans give a damn about Jews?" whispered a man next to Alexander.

"I've met this one. I believe him," Alexander replied quietly.

"I'm here today," Beck smiled, "to announce the beginning of the solution. Resettlement. This won't solve the problem, but it will help. We'll begin with the most vulnerable: the elderly and families with young children. They, most of all, should live in less uncomfortable surroundings.

"A resettlement area is being established near the town of Belzec. It's in the country, with fresh air, grass and trees, the opposite of a dense city. We'll ensure the new place will not be overcrowded. Therefore, the number of people to go is limited to five thousand: two thousand five hundred elderly and two thousand five hundred parents and young children. The elderly will be allowed in two weeks from Tuesday, and the young children and their parents the following day."

Beck paused as comments and conversations rippled through the crowd.

"Workshops will be set up in the very near future, and there is already work, for the able-bodied, repairing roads and in agriculture. Also, we are arranging transportation. I've taken care of it myself. I can't promise first-class accommodations" – Beck smiled again – "but the journey won't be too long. Passengers will come to the train plaza on Grozner Street and from there, we'll take you."

Beck looked out over the crowd. "You're not elderly and may not have young children, so I don't know how many here will take advantage of this opportunity, but please spread the word. Does anyone have questions?"

Several hands cautiously rose. "Should we sign up in advance? Do we buy tickets for the train?"

"Good questions, and the answers are no and no. This will be first come, first served. The train will leave at 9:00 a.m., and we'll take up to two thousand five hundred people, but no more, each day. You should arrive early to guarantee a spot."

"Is there an age limit for the children?"

"Yes. Under age ten. And for the elderly, only those above sixty."

Alexander almost screamed with joy. Finally! A way out of the Krasau nightmare. He raised a hand, and Beck called on him. "My mother-in-law, an old woman, lives with us, but I also have a young boy. Should we go in the first group or the second?"

"It d–" Beck paused and started again. "Go with the second group, so that your little boy will have other children to play with."

Makes sense, Alexander thought.

Someone asked, "We have little kids but also an older child. Can we all go with the group for young children?"

A Jewish Council member, standing near Beck, interjected. "Mr. Beck is doing us a great favor. He's told us the rules. Only children under age ten. If you have older children, your family won't come."

Beck added, "Remember that we're striving to avoid overcrowding. Over time, the facilities will expand, allowing for more people. If only some members of your family fit our requirements, you could wait until later. Or part of your family could go now and the remainder will join them soon, after we increase capacity. You decide what works best for your family."

When Beck finished speaking, the Jews applauded, and Alexander could hardly control his excitement. Today had proven that his hope to leave the ghetto wasn't irrational. He was upset that Anna and Irina would need to wait, but Bubbie had emergency money to sustain the girls for a long time. And it should only be a few months. Alexander would talk with their Zakkai leader about stepping up if something unexpected happened in the meantime. He's a good man. This time, Chana must agree to temporarily split the family.

Plenty of Alexander's coworkers said they planned to go, which made Alexander nervous. He'd better get to the train plaza very early two weeks from Wednesday.

•••

That night, Papa told Anna the wonderful news. He hugged her and hugged her again. Almost giddy, he said, "I know it's not perfect. Perfect would be you and Irina coming with us. For Frammy, for all of us, to be in the open country air! And you should join us in a few months at the latest."

"It seems so strange, Papa, the Germans doing this for us. Everywhere–"

"It's Beck. Karl Beck. You said that how Jews are treated may depend on which German is in charge. We're lucky – we're blessed – to have Beck here. It's the same as when he let you go to your farm!"

Anna's eyes watered seeing her Papa so happy. He'd been down for so long. "I hope you're right, Papa. I'm going to Warsaw soon. On the way back, I'll see what I can learn about the Belzec resettlement area."

"OK. And when Irina gets here, don't tell her. Just say she needs to talk to me about great news."

PART THREE

The Cauldron

APRIL 8, 1942
ANNA

Itzhak's mother welcomed Anna with a friendly hug into her rundown apartment. "You look so pretty, as usual!"

"Thank you, Mrs. Scheinman," Anna smiled.

"I'd offer you a drink, but our water has been off the past few days–"

"Oh no! Hopefully, it will be fixed soon."

Itzhak's mother adored Anna. So sweet and polite. Neither Itzhak nor Anna ever said they were a couple, and Itzhak rolled his eyes when his mother referred to Anna as his girlfriend, but why else would a twenty-year-old girl visit a twenty-one-year-old boy so often? Anna sometimes came three times in a week and at least once every two weeks. They'd stay in the back room and talk so quietly that no one in the apartment could hear a thing. Even with an ear to the wall. And Anna always looked nice for him. Today, she was wearing a tan skirt, blue and white polka-dotted blouse and a blue bow in her hair.

"Itzhak is in back," his mother said.

Anna knocked and entered the back room, where Itzhak was reclining at the end of a small, dark couch; his painful legs lay lengthwise, leaving no room for anyone else. He had just pulled off the shirt he'd worn the day before and slept in, and he replaced it with a clean white shirt. He'd even combed his hair after hobbling to the bathroom mirror on swollen feet.

"Sorry," Itzhak said, "my foot is acting up, so it's best if I stay here."

Anna enjoyed her meetings with Itzhak. She'd been working as a courier for a year, and before every mission he'd help plan, anticipate issues, and build her confidence, whether she was delivering messages to or from a big city, or to a small town where the Jews eagerly welcomed news from the outside world. Itzhak was still Itzhak – serious, but also intensely smart, decisive and caring in his own way. She'd grown very fond of him.

She pulled a small wooden chair next to him, leaned over, kissed his cheek, and sat.

"I talked to Jozef," Itzhak said. "He agrees that the German offer to transport people to a supposedly better place is quite suspicious. But Beck's involvement gives it credibility, and worst case, why would the Germans harm five thousand old people, families with little children? Bottom line is we can't advise your parents to go or not go. You might learn something on your next mission."

"Thanks. That's what I thought. Today, are we–"

"I've invited a girl named Miri to join us. She's about to become a courier for the left-wing Zionists, Hashomer Hatzair. I think she'd benefit if you told her your mindset and thoughts when you're on the Aryan side. To prepare her in ways I can't."

Anna heard knocking on the apartment door; she left the room and returned with a tall girl of about sixteen or seventeen with dark brown hair pulled into two braided pigtails. Dark eyes and a straight nose, Anna thought she would easily pass for Jewish in a crowd of Jews. Whether Christians would spot her as Jewish on the Aryan side, Anna wasn't sure.

"Hi! I'm Miri." She flashed a warm smile. Looking at Itzhak, Miri said, "Are we lying on the couch together?"

"No," Anna started. "Itzhak is–"

Miri laughed. "I'm teasing."

Anna liked the girl's outgoing personality. It might help her survive. Anna brought over another chair, and they all sat.

"Sprechen sie Deutsch?" – "Do you speak German?" – Anna asked her.

"No, is that bad?"

"One of the thousand bits of helpful advice Itzhak gave me is that it's good to know what Germans are saying, especially if they think you don't. I'm lucky because I have a good friend who lived in Germany. She's teaching me, and Itzhak helps."

"But like you," Itzhak said, "Anna didn't speak German when she started. Anna, please tell Miri what goes through your mind when you're on the Aryan side."

"OK," Anna said, taking a deep breath. "You're CONSTANTLY pretending, and you know that if you drop your guard–" Anna paused; her voice darkened, and her eyes narrowed. "I've been on twelve missions. Sweaty palms and a pounding heart are still my companions. Itzhak can teach you to hide your fear, not kill it.

"On the Aryan side, you're *at risk of revealing your Jewishness in a thousand small ways: every anxiety-filled move; every glance that bespeaks the terror of a hunted animal; the face on which the ghetto has left its mark. The Jew hunters know you're nothing more than a Jew, not only because of the color of your eyes, hair, skin, the shape of your nose, the many signs of your race.*

"But because of your lack of self-assurance, your way of expressing yourself, your behavior and God knows what else. At every step, the Jew hunters look into your eyes suspiciously, challengingly, until you become confused, turn beet red, lower your eyes and show yourself to be undeniably a Jew."

Miri's face worried. "That sounds terrifying."

"By the time you make it to the railroad station, you'll already have absorbed a series of beatings, administered by prying eyes, wordless questions inflicted by the enemy lurking in every passerby, chance encounters with hoodlums. Drained from your emotional reserves you'll barely have enough left to get to the next town, where you find yourself scrutinized by organized terror.

"All sorts of police milling around with the sole purpose of ferreting out disguised Jews. Secret police, Germans, Ukrainians. You have to be very cold-blooded to get yourself to walk through the station with your head held high, to flash back the impertinent stares of the secret police, and then to step calmly onto the railroad car."

"How is it on the trains?"

"After expending so much nervous energy to deceive your would-be tormentors, you then eavesdrop on conversations about Jews. 'They're getting what's coming to them. The Jews tried to hoard all the gold, but it was taken from them just in the nick of time.'

"And you sit there, listening, not daring to let a single muscle on your face so much as twitch, for if you betray any excitement or pain – aha! – surely you must be a Jew!

"Every step outside the barbed wire is like passing through a hail of bullets. You know that the only thing that can save you is chance. Chance and inner strength."

Shaken, Miri silently stared at Anna. "A lot to think about. Thank you."

Itzhak had planned for Miri to stay and ask questions, but he was worried about Anna. "Miri, we'll talk tomorrow," he said. "I'm sure you won't leave the ghetto before you're ready."

Miri nodded and left, and Itzhak moved his legs off the couch, sat up straight, and gestured for Anna to sit on the couch. She sat next to him, and he softly said, "You never told me any of that."

Anna shrugged.

"You can quit – we'll find someone else. I'll talk to Jozef–"

"No." She shook her head. "It's fine." She paused, reached for her purse and cheerfully said, "I have something for you." She pulled out a sheet of paper and handed it to him. "It's been a year since my first mission, and you've been such an enormous help – so I made you a gift. Read it out loud."

Itzhak looked at the paper, filled with beautiful calligraphy, up at her smiling face, back at the page, and began to read:

Certificate of Professorship. Know all men that in the fourth month of the year 1942, this Certificate of Professorship has been bestowed with admiration and respect upon Itzhak Scheinman for his knowledge and wisdom, as exemplified by his caring and detailed instruction to his loyal and devoted student and friend, Anna Allowitz. Signed this–

"Oh, I forgot to sign it!" Anna grabbed the paper from Itzhak's hands, took a pen from her purse and added her signature – this 8th day of April 1942, Anna Allowitz.

Stunned, Itzhak gaped at Anna. No one but his parents had ever given him a gift. Certainly not one so personal. Courageous, intelligent, beguiling Anna, whom he admired and adored, cared about HIM – Itzhak – whose life had been almost friendless. "It's beautiful, Anna. It's truly beautiful! I didn't realize you're so artistic – with the elegant curving lines outlining the page and the amazing calligraphy. And the–"

Anna laughed. "Benec did the outline and calligraphy. I scribbled the words, and he put them on the paper in his beautiful handwriting. But I did go through about six drafts before settling on the language. I made it all one sentence to represent your endless effort."

Itzhak felt a little stab when she mentioned Benec. He knew that Benec liked Anna; they might now be boyfriend and girlfriend... But that's OK; Itzhak's desires should be realistic.

He looked again at the paper and at her, sitting close to him on the couch. "What you wrote is perfect. Absolutely perfect."

"Thanks," she smiled and held her eyes on his.

He slapped his thighs. "We finished early today."

Anna looked at her watch. "OK, I should go anyway." She kissed his cheek and left.

Itzhak remained seated on the couch, his eyes staring down at Anna's gift.

APRIL 9, 1942
ANNA

Anna marched out the ghetto's west gate at 7:40 a.m. as a member of a women's labor group. Fifty tired, bedraggled women trudging in two lines off to a factory on the Aryan side, to return twelve hours later.

She noticed two young Jewish boys, couldn't be more than ten years old, run down the street and turn into an alley. Anna had become accustomed to seeing ghetto children, often emaciated, on the Aryan side. They escape the ghetto through holes in or under the wall, beg for food and return – if they survive the day – with some crusts for their families.

Anna's group halted at the first intersection, waiting to cross. *At the corner, a Jewish child sat, a little skeleton, four or five years old, as in India. A Polish passerby put a bun in his hand. An elegant German came by, opened a sewer-grating, took the child, and threw him into the sewer.*

Anna's group crossed the street.

•••

REGINA

Twenty-five-year-old Regina stood in the doorway of a building on Bogadowa Street, two blocks outside the ghetto's west gate. She liked the location because Jewish labor battalions plodded by, and occasionally she'd notice people drop out of line. She sometimes followed them and found that they were desperate. She'd befriend and turn them over to Officer Peter for a nice reward.

Did Regina feel guilty that she, a Jew, helped catch Jews outside the ghetto? Not really. Why should she? For years, she'd helped Peter arrest lawbreakers. Weren't these Jews lawbreakers? Why should it bother her more to catch a Jew without an armband than a Polish drug dealer? And when Peter takes money off Jews, he splits it with her. The Germans will catch them anyway – why shouldn't Peter and Regina get their money instead of the Germans?

She looked at her watch and frowned. 7:40 a.m. Peter was late again. Regina was annoyed but couldn't stay mad at him for long. Peter was good to her. He'd given her official documents permitting her to live on the Aryan side, without wearing a Jew armband, and had found her an apartment. No way would she wear an armband!

Regina knew she led a strange life. Her family had left for Warsaw two years earlier; she hadn't heard from them since. Though her papers kept her safe, she was somewhat Jewish looking and always felt eyes on her. Idiot policemen had arrested her twice because they thought her papers were forged.

All she did, one day after the next, was work the streets for Peter, get food, and sit in her apartment. Thank goodness for Peter. Not just for the apartment and the official documents, but he was her only friend. Some nights, Peter visited her apartment.

But waiting for him was annoying. He said he'd be here at 7:30, and it was now 7:50. He may not show up until 8:30 or later! But if he comes and she isn't here – that happened once; never again would she be on the receiving end of his temper.

Regina noticed a women's work group heading her way from the ghetto. She'd been watching these groups for so long that she recognized some faces, including a young woman with light-colored hair walking toward the back. Regina was fairly sure she'd seen that woman ditch the line. Regina looked at her watch, frowned, and decided she could risk five minutes following them. She was curious about that blondish one.

Regina trailed them for a block and after they turned at the next corner. Moments later, the light-haired woman ducked out of line and went the opposite direction. Regina followed her, and the woman entered a building. Regina again looked at her watch; ten minutes had passed since she'd left her meeting spot. She really didn't want to risk a beating. But she waited a few moments, and the young woman reappeared, no longer wearing a Star of David armband.

The young woman intrigued Regina. While in line, she'd walked with her head down, degraded like the rest of them. But now she strolled with an air of confidence, as if she had transformed *from a Jew into a human being.*

Regina was very familiar with Jews who pretended to be Aryan. Spotting them had become a sport. She prided herself that she once identified (and turned over to Peter) a young woman from Warsaw who worked as a courier for a Jewish group there. Like the girl Regina followed now, that one seemed self-assured.

Regina looked at her watch again. If only Peter had come on time, he could have arrested this woman, and Regina would have received a reward with little effort. She rushed back to her meeting place.

Regina made mental notes of the young woman's appearance. Next time, she'll get her.

MONDAY APRIL 13, 1942
FRAMMY

"I'm going on a train!" six-year-old Frammy grinned. "With a real engine in front pulling lots of cars!"

"You'll have so much fun!" Irina said.

"I know; I can't wait!"

Bubbie smiled.

Irina was sitting on the floor in the middle of their "bedroom," helping Frammy and Bubbie pack. Bubbie sat in a chair giving thumbs up or down as Frammy tossed things into the pile that Irina stuffed into a gigantic burlap sack. Mr. and Mrs. Polnick, who lived with them, were sitting in the same room, and their friend, Mr. Grynstein, hovered above Frammy and Irina.

"I'm afraid this bag will be too heavy for me," Bubbie said.

Irina laughed. "Don't worry, Bubbie, I'll help carry it to the train."

"We're leaving Wednesday, right?" Bubbie asked. "And today is Monday?" Bubbie had asked the same questions twice in the past hour.

"Oh Lord," Mr. Polnick snorted. "If she again asks–"

Irina shot him a look that said, "If you finish the sentence, I'll rip out your tonsils." Irina couldn't stand the Polnicks, though Mr. Grynstein seemed nice enough. "Bubbie, you're leaving tomorrow early in the morning. You were going to leave Wednesday, but they changed it to Tuesday. And yeah, today is Monday – 2:10 in the afternoon to be exact."

"I wanna bring my boat!" Frammy said. He was holding a small piece of scrap wood; Papa had cut it into the shape of a boat and added a nail with an attached piece of cloth as the sail. "Maybe in the country we'll have a river to float it on. But don't pack it. I'll carry it on the train."

"You're going to the country?" Mr. Grynstein asked.

"Yeah. Papa said our new home will be near lots of grass and fields, and maybe a farm," Frammy said. "And I might see dragonflies. How hard is it to catch a dragonfly? I think I saw dragonflies when I was little, but I can't remember."

Bubbie smiled. "In the country, you'll see butterflies and dragonflies and fireflies. But they're for looking at, not catching. You don't want to hurt them." Bubbie wistfully remembered her time on the farm. To be in fresh air again... A good place for her final years, and the country will be great for Frammy if what the Germans are saying is true.

"Will there be animals to play with?" Frammy asked.

"You'll have lots of animals on a farm!" Mr. Grynstein said. "Make friends with a cow, and she might lick you with her big, long tongue. Does that sound fun?"

"Yeah," Frammy shyly grinned.

"And if you and the cow become best friends, she'll let you ride her like a horse!" Mr. Grynstein tapped Frammy's head with his fingers.

Frammy giggled. "Are you teasing me?"

"Maybe a little," Mr. Grynstein said.

Bubbie smiled. "Talking about animals reminded me of my dream last night. The same dream I used to have when I was little. That two boys, one of them holding a sword, and a girl dressed in funny clothes were playing and laughing with a goat! I don't know anyone in the dream, but one of the boys made me think of my grandson, Shlomo, your cousin. I wonder what it means?"

"I don't get the sword part, but maybe because you're returning to the countryside," Irina said.

"Why don't you come with us?" Bubbie asked Irina. "Afraid you'll miss your boyfriend?"

"I'm too old, but Papa thinks Anna and I can come in a few months. But yeah, when we go, I want Reuven and his family with us."

"How old is Reuven?" Bubbie asked.

"He just turned sixteen, and I'll be sixteen in a few months."

"Enjoy your time with him, every minute," Bubbie said. "You never know what can happen from one day to the next, especially now. Your Zaida was in his forties when they killed him – I'd thought we'd be together forever. Do you understand me, Irina?"

Irina hesitated. "I think so."

"Your Zaida was eighteen, and I was sixteen when we married," Bubbie said.

"Young lady," Mr. Grynstein said in mock formality, "I think your Bubbie is planning a wedding."

Irina blushed though she knew he was kidding.

"I've never been to a wedding," Frammy said.

Mr. Grynstein slapped his knee. "You can ride your pet cow there, Frammy."

"Yeah!" Frammy giggled.

"No, no, no," Bubbie said. "Anna gets married first. Where is Anna? I want to give her a big hug and kiss goodbye before we go."

"Of course," Irina said. Irina knew that Anna was away on one of her trips. Anna had said she should return by Monday – today – or certainly by Tuesday. But Anna already told everyone goodbye in case she'd get delayed. Mama wasn't too happy, but Papa said it didn't matter if she said goodbye a week early – they'd all be together again soon. Now that they're leaving Tuesday instead of Wednesday, Anna may miss them.

"Anna is out looking for a cow to ride to Irina's wedding," Frammy teased.

"Perfect!" Mr. Grynstein said. "Two cows are always better than one at a wedding. Frammy, do you know what to tell the cows if they get in the way?"

Frammy smiled and shook his head.

"Tell them to steak out a different place."

"Or," Bubbie said, "tell them to mooove."

Frammy giggled. "We're going to mooove on the train tomorrow."

THE SAME DAY
ZAMOSC, POLAND
ANNA

The half-empty passenger train pulled an hour late into the station at Zamosc, a city of thirty thousand people. Anna stood and grabbed her pack; out the window she saw the slender green dome of a clock tower looming over the old town. In the past five days, she had traveled by train to Krakow, to Warsaw, and now Zamosc.

Jozef had asked Anna to go to Krakow and Warsaw. She added Zamosc because of the upcoming resettlement of her family and five thousand other Krasau Jews to Belzec. Weeks earlier, a courier from Warsaw had reported that the Germans massacred at least tens of thousands of Jews when they invaded Russia in mid-1941. But what did those wartime massacres mean for Polish Jews, locked in ghettos far from the fighting?

Warsaw was rife with rumors; Anna's job was to ferret out the truth. Warsaw Zakkai leaders said the Germans had started sending Polish Jews to extermination centers and murdering them. How could they believe something so insanely impossible! A European country would transport and murder millions of innocent people, children, families? Absurd.

But the story struck horribly close to home: one of the supposed extermination centers was at Belzec.

Belzec.

Belzec was where her family was headed this Wednesday. Today was Monday. Anna wanted – wanted desperately – to believe the rumors were false. But she needed reliable information and, if the insanity was real, to return tonight or definitely by Tuesday to warn everyone.

Belzec was a tiny town 150 miles from Krasau, east of the north-south rail line between Warsaw and Krasau. The train schedules showed that she could detour to Belzec and return to Krasau by Tuesday. But what if Germans or Polish police questioned her? Why would a young Polish woman who knew no one in Belzec travel there? Zamosc, less than thirty miles from Belzec, was much bigger, gave rise to less suspicion, and had a Jewish community of several thousand. Anna remembered that Mordecai had a good Zakkai friend in Zamosc. She decided to come here and sneak into the ghetto; if something horrible was going on in Belzec, he should know. She would return to Krasau tonight.

Anna exited the train with a large pack, filled with clothes and knitted scarves, slung over her shoulder. She wore a colorful peasant scarf and dress.

Two middle-aged women were sitting outside the station at a table, selling socks, belts, and knickknacks.

"Hi, my name is Helena Kowalska," Anna said. "I sell scarves. I've been to Warsaw, and I'm on my way back home to Krasau. I won't compete with you at the train station – where else in town is good to make some sales today?"

The women looked her over. One said, "You could try the Square – it's about half a mile from here. Walk down Szczebrzeska Street toward the tall clock tower. You can't miss it."

"Is there a Jewish Quarter? I've had luck with them when they let me in."

"There is, but not today," the woman smirked. "Two days ago, the Germans went wild, shot oh, I don't know how many Jews – and forced half of 'em onto a train to Belzec."

Anna suddenly felt lightheaded as blood drained from her face. "What's in Belzec?"

"For Jews – death! At least, that's what people say."

"What? Why would–" Anna started.

"Not my problem," the woman shrugged dismissively.

"Hello ladies! How's business?"

"Bad as usual, Dr. Klukowski."

An old man with a thick, gray mustache and gray hair combed back, amplifying his receding hairline, had appeared out of nowhere. He wore a light-colored shirt tucked into his high-waisted pants. Over the shirt was a white medical jacket. Offering his hand to Anna, he said, "I don't believe we've met. My name is Zygmunt Klukowski."

Anna smiled. "I'm Helena Kowalska. Nice to meet you."

"Likewise. I apologize, but I eavesdropped. I'm going to the Square and would be happy to escort you."

"Thank you," Anna smiled again. They turned from the women and headed down Szczebrzeska Street. "They called you 'doctor.' Are you a physician?"

"I am. I live in Szczebrzeszyn, about twelve miles from here."

"Ah, but you have patients here and–"

"Yes, I do. I heard you say you sold scarves in Warsaw and are returning to Krasau. Why did you detour so far to the east, if I may ask?"

Anna's stomach tensed; she chuckled. "Because I'm being a bad girl. I don't want to go home yet, I've never been here and thought I'd take some time and explore."

The man nodded, expressionless. "Explore by selling scarves?"

"OK, I'm not so adventurous. But I enjoy talking to people, and I have scarves left to sell, so why not?"

The man offered a brief, courteous smile, and Anna felt a jolt of fear – he's suspicious, and it was her fault. They walked another two blocks without saying a word. "Let's turn here," the man said.

"Huh? The women said the Square is next to the tower – straight ahead."

"It is. But I'd like to show you the Jewish Quarter. It's this way." The man pointed.

Anna's heart began to race, and she stopped walking. "The women said not to try selling there today, and that I should go to the Square."

"That is true. But you said you want to explore. Indulge me." He waved for Anna to follow.

Anna felt the sweat on her palms. She needed to get away from him, and it would be normal to call out his pushiness. "You're very ... persistent, Dr. Klukowski." She put her hands on her hips. "What is so important at the Jewish Quarter?"

"I'll show you. Follow me." He smiled and started walking again.

"Wait – is it far?"

"Ten minutes."

"Will I have time to make sales at the Square?"

"Yes."

Anna hesitated. She did want to get into the ghetto, and going with this guy would be less strange than circling back later and possibly running into him. Unless he suspected her and was heading to the police.

She followed him.

About fifteen minutes later, they turned a corner and saw two Polish policemen and a German soldier standing less than twenty yards away, in the middle of the street. Her heart pounding, she had no choice but to walk with Dr. Klukowski as he headed toward them. She was carrying nothing illegal, and simply needed to remain calm.

"This young lady is selling scarves," Dr. Klukowski said to a policeman. "Will she find many Jewish customers today?"

"No. They were cleaning up earlier, but not many on the streets now."

"Oh, bad luck for Helena then. Do you mind if I show her what the place looks like? We'll be out in a few minutes."

"Suit yourself." A policeman pointed at Anna's pack and gestured for her to bring it to him. He opened it, saw scarves, closed and returned it to her. Anna and Dr. Klukowski stepped inside the ghetto.

They walked two blocks and turned onto a narrow street leading to a small Square. It was empty and quiet; the only sounds were of birds chirping. The stench of rotting garbage followed the breeze. "I brought you inside to tell you what happened here two days ago. I was standing up there." He pointed to an area overlooking the ghetto.

Across the street, a Jewish man stood in his doorway watching them.

"This Square was crowded." Dr. Klukowski looked at Anna with mournful eyes. "It was the Jewish Sabbath, and in the afternoon many people were walking about, talking. *The Germans fell on them like a pack of savages. It was a complete surprise. The brutes on horseback created a panic, slashing out on all sides with their whips. Bodies everywhere, in the streets, in the courtyards, inside the houses; babies thrown from the third or fourth floors lay crushed on the pavement. Three thousand men, women and children were driven to the train station and deported."*

"Deported to-to where?" Anna stammered, fighting to remain calm.

"Belzec. I've watched from my home for more than a week. *I know for certain that every day at least two trains have passed through my town, with about twenty wagons each, crammed with Jews going to Belzec. There, they are taking the Jews out of the trains, pushing them behind barbed wire fences and killing them either by electrocution or poisoning with gas, and after that they burn the remains.* I've talked to railway men, and others."

Anna felt dizzy; the impossible was real. Everything in her field of vision became white, and Dr. Klukowski grabbed her so that she wouldn't fall. "That is so terrible," she sobbed. Anna allowed herself to cry. Anyone with a heart, Catholic or Jew, would have done so. "But I can't believe it. Why kill innocent people!"

"Everything I said is true. I'm certain," Dr. Klukowski said. "About seven thousand Jews lived here last week, three thousand were sent away and murdered; four thousand remain." He caught the attention of the Jewish man across the street and waved him over.

"Do you know him?" Anna asked, sniffling.

"No, but I don't want you to rely only on my word." The Jewish man, tall, balding, about fifty, walked to them.

"Hello, sir. My name is Zygmunt Klukowski, and this is Helena. Would you please tell her what happened Saturday?"

"Who are you?"

"No one important," Anna said. "But I'd like to know what happened."

"There was a massacre here Saturday. A massacre!"

"Did they take people away?" Anna asked.

"Thousands."

"Is your family still here?"

"Yeah."

"Thank you, sir." Anna looked at Dr. Klukowski. "I want to go."

They walked away, and she felt Dr. Klukowski's eyes on her. "Hail Mary, full of grace, the Lord is with thee," she whispered loud enough for Dr. Klukowski to hear. "Blessed art thou amongst women, and blessed is the fruit of thy womb, Jesus. Holy Mary, mother of God, pray for us sinners, now and in the hour of our death. Amen."

She stopped walking. "Why did you bring me here?"

"The look on your face when the women at the station talked about the Jews. I saw you're a caring person. I want you to tell people in Krasau what you've learned. You're returning tomorrow?"

"Tonight, on the 6:30 train."

"There is no 6:30 train. You somehow must have seen an old schedule."

Anna frowned and bit her lip.

"If it's urgent for you to go this evening, I could drive you in my car, but we'd need to leave soon."

She now desperately wanted to get home tonight and was almost certain Dr. Klukowski was a good man. But almost certain wasn't the same as certain. If he was very cleverly trying to trap her, she'd have no explanation for suddenly wanting to return home. And the police might hold her for days, even if they let her go. If she declines his offer, she'll still arrive tomorrow morning, in time to warn her family, leaving Wednesday.

"Thank you, but I want to sell scarves today. I'll catch the nine o'clock train tomorrow morning."

They retraced their steps to leave the ghetto, and Dr. Klukowski waved at someone looking out a window.

"You have friends in the ghetto?" Anna asked.

"A few, and many in Szczebrzeszyn, where I live."

"Do you think the Germans will murder all the Jews here?"

"There was nothing special about those taken Saturday."

"I didn't see a wall around this ghetto, at least not where we've walked."

"There is no wall."

"Won't the remaining Jews run away?"

"They'll try, but the Germans will execute every Pole who helps them. Some would quickly give water or food to Jews, but only a saint would hide them. Others, many more than I like to admit, will help the Germans murder Jews and look forward to stealing their property. Including the two women at the station."

"How can Jews save themselves?"

"What can old people or families with little children do? Perhaps someone young and strong could hide in the forest, but that would prove very difficult in winter. They would need shelter, food with no ration cards while hiding – both from Germans and Poles."

"What about your friends? How will they survive?"

Dr. Klukowski sighed deeply, and his eyes filled with tears.

TUESDAY APRIL 14, 1942
KARL BECK
7:00 A.M.

The Germans, using Jewish forced labor, had built a railway siding off the main rail line, extending along the northern edge of the Krasau ghetto to a train "collection point plaza" just inside the ghetto. This allowed a train to exit the main line, enter the ghetto, collect cargo at the collection point, and return to the main line. The plaza was simply a large, open concrete pad adjacent to the tracks. It sat between warehouse buildings to the south and the railroad tracks on the north. North of the railroad tracks and running parallel to it stood the ghetto wall.

At 7:00 a.m., when Karl Beck arrived in his dark Gestapo uniform, at least fifteen hundred Jews were already there. Moms, dads, kids – over a thousand little children – with their luggage, sacks, bags, toys, food, and blankets were milling around. Satisfied, Karl smiled to himself.

More than a hundred soldiers and police lined the plaza. Karl met with their officers at 7:15. "Gentlemen, every family here this morning has come voluntarily. Soon, we'll seek more volunteers to resettle. Therefore, no beatings, no shootings. Yesterday, we had two episodes that, if repeated by anyone, will result in severe punishment. You're here to maintain order, not compel submission."

•••

8:00 A.M.

Karl spoke to the Jews, now more than two thousand five hundred people. A Polish policeman translated with a megaphone.

"Welcome everyone! The train will be here soon, and after a journey of several hours, you'll arrive at your new homes." Karl paused while people applauded. "I want to remind you that the train passage will not be comfortable. It may even be uncomfortable because I couldn't arrange a passenger train. Instead, you will sit or stand, as you like, in a freight car. Not the best, I know, but an acceptable annoyance in exchange for what lies at the end of your trip.

"Best wishes to all of you!"

FRAMMY
8:30 A.M.

The Allowitzs waited in line near the tracks. Papa had awoken everyone very early; they'd pried off the mezuzah to take to their new home, gathered the bags and luggage, and walked in darkness until soldiers yelled where to go. That was hours earlier, when the wind howled, and Mama seemed scared but Papa said not to worry. Six-year-old Frammy, clutching his toy boat, hoped their new home would have fewer soldiers.

Mama was wearing her nice dress, the one with big pink buttons, and Bubbie had asked if Mama thought she was going to a dance. Irina had apologized to Bubbie for not packing Bubbie's tutu, and everyone laughed. Even Frammy, though he didn't know what a tutu was.

After the sun rose, Frammy had played tag near the train tracks with other little boys, but now he sat half asleep on a blanket, waiting with his family for the train.

"Listen, Frammy! What's that noise?" fifteen-year-old Irina asked.

Frammy stretched and strained to hear, squinching his eyes. "I just hear people talking and babies crying."

"No, listen harder. You hear rumbling?"

Frammy tried again, and his face suddenly brightened. "The train?"

"Yeah," Papa said. "I'll show you." Papa lifted Frammy and plopped him onto his shoulders. "You're getting heavy!" He pointed to the left. "Do you see it?" The rumbling had grown louder, and its shrill whistle pierced the air.

"The engine is so gigantic! I can't believe we're going on a train!"

The bellowing engine, pulling twenty-three cars and with steam pouring out both sides, slowly approached from their left and came to a stop; the engine and some cars to their right and the rest extending to the left. The Germans had divided the Jews into twenty-three groups, one for each car, lined up perpendicular to the tracks. The Allowitzs were slotted to enter the sixth car; about thirty people waited in line in front of them and seventy behind.

Mama looked around and muttered, mostly to herself, "Everyone in this line stuffing into one freight car?" A dark disquiet settled over her. Why so many soldiers with guns? She hadn't liked the idea since she first heard it. But guilt from blocking their chance to leave years ago had kept her quiet. And Alexander was so happy again, so optimistic. She looked at him, ruffling Frammy's hair and patiently explaining something to their little boy. She loved Alexander and Frammy – her whole family – so much. Hopefully, this move would bring better times.

A boy bounced a ball to Frammy; giggling, Frammy kicked it back. Mama managed a smile.

"Stand up!" a policeman commanded. "When the doors open, quickly board the train!"

Papa lifted a huge pack, put it on his back, and grabbed a suitcase. Mama also held a suitcase. Irina, who had come only to help carry luggage, stood near Bubbie, who still sat on the large bag that Irina had filled with Bubbie's and Frammy's things. Frammy cradled his boat.

"Shouldn't you go home, Irina?" Bubbie asked.

"No, Bubbie. I'll help carry the bag to the train. Then I'll go."

"I think Bubbie's right," Mama said. "These policemen are in a hurry. At least let's hug goodbye now."

Irina gave them each a big hug and kiss, and Mama cried, "I love you, Irina."

"I love you too, Mama. But why are you crying? I'll see you soon!"

Mama shrugged, wiped tears from her eyes and brushed Irina's hair with her hand. "Don't let the Polnicks push you and Anna around. It's still our apartment until you join us in Belzec."

The Germans slid open the freight car doors with a crashing sound. "Everyone get on!" policemen yelled. "Now! Move!"

Their line inched forward. When the Allowitzs reached the train, they saw that the freight car's floor was three feet above the ground, and that the narrow wooden ramp leaning against it was too wobbly for Bubbie to walk on. Papa hurriedly tossed the suitcase inside the car and put his pack next to it.

"Move it!" hollered a huge policeman standing at the open car door. "Get on now!"

"We're helping our Bubbie," Irina said.

The policeman scowled at Irina, raised a hand to hit her, paused and dropped it to his side. "Hurry up!"

Papa helped Bubbie up the ramp and into the freight car, and then Frammy scampered inside. Papa grabbed Mama's suitcase and Irina's large sack. Mama quickly hugged Irina once more and stepped into the car. Irina turned to go.

"Where you going!" growled the policeman. He grabbed Irina and threw her onto the train as if she were a sack of potatoes. Irina's knees and hands hit the hard, wooden floor; Papa's quick hands saved her face from smacking onto it.

"She's not coming!" Papa yelled. The policeman ignored him or didn't hear above the din of children laughing, screaming, and crying. Mama and Frammy checked to see if Irina was OK, and another family entered the car with their things, forcing the Allowitzs from the entrance. The policeman raged at a man and clubbed him, creating panic. The man's children screamed and rushed onto the train. The next family quickly followed with their packs, bundles, and suitcases, pressing against the people in front of them and driving the Allowitzs deeper inside. Parents dragged luggage and pushed with their children to find places to sit along the wooden walls.

The crowd separated Irina from her family and pinned her against a wall. People and things crammed in, and a big man and his kids accidentally knocked Irina onto the wood floor. A child fell on top of her; Irina managed to get to her knees, but more people shoved toward the back of the car, butting against each other and pressing down on her. Still on her knees, Irina pushed at everyone around her but couldn't stand. Suddenly terrified that she'd suffocate, Irina panicked; with her pulse pounding in her ears, she clawed furiously and screamed, "Help me!!" The man who had knocked her down lifted her to her feet.

Papa suddenly appeared and clutched Irina's arm. He momentarily thought she should go with them to Belzec; but she didn't want to, and Anna shouldn't stay in the ghetto without family. He dragged Irina over kids and bags, and they moved closer to the door but from deeper inside the freight car, Mama shrieked, "Alexander, help! Bubbie fell!" Papa and Irina looked at each other; though Irina was scared, she nodded and they turned back toward Mama. The crowd slightly parted, allowing them through. Sprawled motionless on the floor, amid a horde of people, Bubbie stared blankly at the ceiling. Irina and Mama knelt and held her hands.

Slowly, Bubbie began to feel better. "I'm OK," she said. By then, more than seventy people had stuffed into the car, forty of them between the Allowitzs and the car's open door. More were entering, prodded by policemen and soldiers.

Lying on the floor, Bubbie cried as loud as she could, "Go, Irina! Before it's too late! Go!"

Papa helped Bubbie stand, clutched Irina's hand, and yelled,

"Move!" at everyone near them. He and Irina fought their way toward the door, shoving and stepping past one family and then another. They squirmed close to the opening and heard a policeman holler, "Shut the door!"

Papa frantically thrust a man aside and threw Irina past the man's family and to the open door. She leapt from the car and started to run; a policeman grabbed a fistful of her hair and dragged her back. Irina screamed and helplessly slapped the air. "I'll throw this one in," the policeman hollered. "Then shut the door!"

"Stop!" boomed a German voice from behind the policeman.

Karl Beck.

"Mr. Beck," Papa yelled in German. "My daughter came only to carry luggage. She must go home. Please allow her to leave!"

Mr. Beck scolded the policeman, nodded to Irina, and pointed with his open hand away from the train. Irina hurried away.

"That Mr. Beck is such a mensch," Papa said.

•••

ANNA

1:30 P.M.

Anna rushed upstairs to her family's apartment. Her train had arrived early, but she was delayed entering the ghetto. Thankfully, she had plenty of time. Papa and Mama might be at work, but Bubbie and Frammy would be here; Anna ached to hug them both. She hurried down the hall and opened their door. Mrs. Polnick gave her an annoyed look.

"Hello," Anna said. She hurried past Mrs. Polnick into the other room and returned to the front. "Where's my Bubbie, and where is Frammy?"

"They all left this morning on the train. Woke us up early, they made so much noise! They–"

"No!" Anna said. "They're not going until tomorrow." Anna felt her knees wobble, and the blood draining from her head.

"Where is Irina?" she managed.

"Irina went with them."

Anna fainted.

THE SAME DAY
BELZEC
FRAMMY

"Frammy, wake up. We're here."

Mama's voice. Frammy yawned and opened his eyes. "We're here?"

"Yeah," Papa said.

Frammy stretched, lifted his head off Mama's lap, and looked into the darkness with the hundred others stuffed inside the freight car. Many, like his family, sitting on top of each other; others standing, and a few lying. The car smelled of excrement. The bucket everyone used had tipped over.

The train slowly came to a halt, and the door to their car slid open. The flash of sunlight blinded them. "Everyone out! Hurry!" yelled men's voices. Mama clasped Frammy's hand and reached for a suitcase.

"No luggage! You'll get it later! Come on! Get out!"

Parents, holding hands with little kids, climbed down from the freight car. A man hopped down, and his wife handed him, one at a time, three little girls and a bag with bottles and baby food. Mama and Frammy scampered down, and Papa helped Bubbie. Some children cried, but most were happy to stretch their legs after the cramped four-hour journey.

"This way! This way!" voices hollered. Mama took Bubbie's hand, and the four of them walked with the throng exiting the train. Soldiers holding rifles walked alongside and led them toward two men in an open area, away from the tracks.

"Do you see cows, Papa?"

"No, Frammy, I don't. But I see a forest. And–"

"I wanna see!"

"It's on the other side of the fence," Papa said. He noticed that they were walking in a large, maybe a half-mile, square area enclosed by a fence. Papa pointed.

"I see the forest! Wow! Look at all the trees!" Frammy said. "And I see giant fields of grass everywhere!"

"Take a deep breath," Bubbie said. "That's the sweet smell of pine trees."

The Allowitzs kept walking. Four out of two thousand five hundred people under a partly cloudy sky on a cool, spring day. The group reached the open area where the two men stood, one in uniform. He spoke, as did the man next to him. But Frammy missed it. Too busy watching a giggling, little girl in a pink dress sticking her tongue at her baby brother.

Papa repeated what the men said. *"Now you're going to the bath-house, afterwards you will be sent to work."*

"What kind of work will I do, Papa? Schoolwork? Do they know I've never been to school except with Mrs. Corn blewit?"

"The work is probably for grownups," Papa said.

Holding his toy boat, Frammy asked, "Will I get to play with my boat in the bath house?"

"No, Frammy. It's probably a shower, and everyone is in a rush. You'll need to hold the boat tight, so you don't lose it."

More yelling by people in uniforms. "Form two lines! One for men only and the other for women and children! You'll go to the bathhouse separately, so two lines. Move! Fast! Talk again after the shower!"

Mama still held Bubbie's hand; they and Frammy joined the women's line. Frammy looked over his shoulder and saw two men talking to Papa; he left the men's line and went somewhere else. Maybe to get schoolbooks for the kids, Frammy thought.

The women's line snaked toward one building, and the men headed next door. "Am I dreaming?" Bubbie asked, "Or do I hear music?"

"I hear it," Frammy said.

Mama listened closely. "You're right. From the other side of the building."

"After people shower, they listen to music," Frammy said.

Mama, Bubbie and Frammy entered the building. Inside, soldiers with guns stood near the walls; other men, without uniforms, hovered in the middle of the room. Mama and Bubbie were told to sit on wooden stools, and the men started cutting their hair.

"I don't want my hair cut!" Mama said.

"You must. It helps the disinfecting. Typhus, stops lice," one of the barbers mumbled. He and the other barbers seemed strange. They cut so much hair off Mama, Bubbie and the other ladies that they looked like men. "It's good they're worried about disease, but cutting off our hair is ridiculous," one very unhappy mother said.

"Everyone get undressed!" a man announced. "For the shower. Fold your clothes and remember where you left them!"

Mama, Bubbie and lots of ladies were embarrassed to undress

in front of men, and Frammy looked away. Frammy got naked and carefully placed his toy boat on a long bench, on top of his clothes, but then worried someone may take it. He grabbed the boat and carried it with him. "Out those doors," a man pointed, "then follow the path to the bathhouse."

Frammy, a naked little boy clutching a toy boat close to his tummy, joined his Mama, Bubbie, and the parade of two thousand little children and moms walking through a narrow outdoor walkway bordered by a fence on each side. The crowd moved slowly, and two little girls were playing peek-a-boo as they walked with their mommy. Mama and Bubbie tried to cover themselves from the soldiers' eyes, and they headed toward a building with a big sign on it.

It was a nice-looking, one-story building, brightly painted. At the entrance sat pots with pretty flowers. Bubbie loved flowers. "Those are geraniums," she said.

"What does the sign say?" Frammy asked.

"Hackenholt Foundation. Bath and Inhalation Room," a woman near them answered.

A German in uniform stood in the walkway, smiling. "Everyone go into the building straight ahead for your shower. After that, you'll join the men."

He seemed nice, Frammy thought. "Will the water be hot?" Frammy asked.

"It will be perfect," the man said.

Mama, Frammy and Bubbie walked with the flock of naked moms and children into the building, past two soldiers, and into a big shower room. More and more people entered, each moving forward to make room for others. A big woman, smelling of sweat, pressed Frammy against Mama and against the shower room side wall. Children wailed, and even more people came in. Soldiers, with bayonets, ordered all to enter. Soon, each person butted against the next, a mass of bodies pushing and shoving for room, desperately seeking space for themselves and their kids. The claustrophobic screamed; some fainted. "Stop sending people in here!" Mama yelled.

The doors closed with a loud bang. Total darkness. Moms and kids screamed; pushing and pulling and crying. Outside the shower room, twenty-eight-year-old SS Sergeant Lorenz Hackenholt flipped a switch on an engine, piping in exhaust fumes and carbon monoxide gas.

Frammy cried, "Mama, why don't they turn on the light!"

"I don't know, Frammy. They'll probably come on." Mama's voice, calm for Frammy, comforted him.

Bubbie reached for Mama's hand. "Chana," she moaned, "it smells bad, like behind a truck."

"Mama, should I hold my breath?" Frammy asked. More shoving and wailing and pushing and Frammy's head began to spin. "I don't feel good, Mama!"

Bubbie fell to the floor.

Mama begged, "Please let us out!" Mothers frantically banged on the walls and shrieked in horror, "Help us!" A child pleaded in the blackness, "Mama, I promise to be good! Mama, help me!"

Mama's heart raced, and she drew quick, short gasps, unable to breathe; she thrashed wildly in the dark and vomited.

Terror.

Frammy dropped his toy boat and bravely struggled to drag his Mama toward the entrance. Maybe they could get out. But too many bodies pressing against them. Frammy's mouth was dry, his heart pounded in his little chest, and his legs and head felt so heavy. Petrified and nauseous, he couldn't move.

Frammy clung to Mama; she hugged him close, convulsing and moaning in agony. Tears streaking his face, Frammy tried to be a courageous and strong little boy and hold Mama up so she wouldn't fall on the floor like Bubbie.

But he couldn't. "Papa!" he faintly screamed.

Together, Frammy and Mama collapsed to the floor.

•••

Papa

When Frammy had glanced over his shoulder and seen two men talking to his Papa, they were saying in Jewish, "Come with us to the train. We have work for you."

"Will it take long?" Alexander had asked. "My family is in line, and I want to join them after the shower. And I need to shower–"

"No," one man said. The other silently waved for Alexander to follow them.

"Where you from, and how long have you been here?" Alexander asked as they walked toward the train.

"Lublin. Eight days," the talking man said.

"Where are the apartments?"

The men somberly shook their heads. "Enough questions. Help us, and then we'll show you other work." They climbed into a train car. These guys are strange, Alexander thought. Scary strange. But he silently helped them toss luggage and bags onto the ground, and other workers carried them away. "How will everyone find their things?" Alexander asked. He received only downcast eyes in reply, and Alexander felt uneasiness building within him. Were the Germans stealing their luggage?

When they finished emptying the cars, and without speaking, the Jews waved for Alexander to follow them to the back of the building marked "Hackenholt Foundation. Bath and Inhalation Room." Four Ukrainian soldiers stood outside its rear doors. Other Jewish men soon joined Alexander's group; they stood quietly, with heartsick faces. Alexander nodded, with no response. Odd sounds came from inside the building, but Alexander heard music and saw a small orchestra of six men playing a violin, accordion and flute a few yards behind him, in the open area behind the building. Nice music. One of the Jewish men saw Alexander's puzzled face. "They play while we work," he mumbled.

Alexander recognized the tune. "Everything passes, everything goes by." A nice song. The sun broke through the clouds and warmed the air. The men were sweating.

One of them handed Alexander a leather belt with a hook on the end. "The little ones, you can get by yourself, sometimes more than one at a time. The heavier ones may take two of us. We drag them there." The man turned and pointed to a huge pit behind the small orchestra.

"What? Drag what?"

The Ukrainian soldiers swung open the building's back doors and waved the Jews forward. The Jewish workers stepped inside, and one gestured for Alexander to follow.

Alexander stepped in and froze; a guard shoved him forward, and he tripped, falling face-first on top of a dead, naked mother and child. Bodies of women and children piled and twisted on top of each other. He immediately jumped to his feet, vomited from what he saw and smelled, reflexively yanked his hair and screamed "No! No!" A worker clutched Alexander's arm and showed how to hook the strap to a body and pull it out.

Alexander's arms and legs trembled, he looked at the man in open-mouthed disbelief and slowly shook his head. He heard the workers groaning as they tugged the dead bodies.

"Work or they'll shoot you," the Jew muttered.

Alexander stood motionless while other workers dragged bodies past him. A Ukrainian guard pointed his rifle at Alexander's head. "Work now, Jew! Work, or you're dead!" he screamed in Polish.

The Jewish men dragged more bodies past Alexander. On his left, Chana – an arm wrapped around Frammy – was sliding past his feet. Alexander crumpled to his knees, eyes bulging, hands on his head, anguish tearing his heart.

The Ukrainian shot him in the temple, and the Jews dragged Alexander's body with all others to the pit. They then soaked the shower room floor to clean it.

Frammy's boat floated on the water.

•••

KARL BECK

Karl made a long-distance call to his old friend Lorenz Hackenholt at Belzec. Karl and Lorenz had worked together disposing of handicapped Germans before the war, and Lorenz was the proud designer of Belzec's gassing mechanism. Karl was concerned – did the Krasau Jews arrive in the right frame of mind, or did they cause trouble for Lorenz and his team?

"How did things go today?" Karl asked.

"Very smoothly," Lorenz said. "No problems. Including your batch, we've disposed of about fifty thousand Jews since mid-March, and I expect to dispose of five hundred thousand by year's end."

"That's incredible. It's satisfying when hard work leads to good results. Send my love to Ilse."

"Will do."

Relieved, Karl called his Polish girlfriend. "Dinner tonight at your favorite restaurant!"

Good news called for a celebration.

PART FOUR

For Three Lines

APRIL 16, 1942
ANNA

Leah hugged Anna, cried and couldn't stop. Finally, Anna pulled away, her face empty and pale, Leah's caring hand lingering on the back of her neck. "Thank you," was all that Anna said.

Leah, Itzhak, Anna, Estie, and Benec were sitting on the floor in Jozef's and Leah's apartment. Jozef was standing. Also sitting were six representatives of other Jewish youth groups, from right wing to communist. All eyes downcast and full of gloom.

Jozef began. His voice was slow and solemn. "I just left an emergency meeting of the Jewish Council, where I explained the inexplicable. That five thousand of us, old and young, including from our own families, beloved teachers, rabbis, friends, Zionist leaders, children full of life – have been murdered. Along with countless Jews throughout Poland. That we're all scheduled for death. Next week, next month, in six months."

"What did they say?" Benec asked.

"Some said it's impossible; they'll ask the Germans for assurances it's not true. Two accused me of stirring up trouble. But most believed. They wrung their hands, moaned, 'Where is God?' Others said we must notify the world."

"Did anyone say we should fight?"

"I did. They asked, 'How? With what?' The Council is exhausted, defeated."

"What do you expect of old men!" someone said. "Our community leaders are worthless. They–"

"Stop, please," Anna muttered, barely louder than a whisper. "At Zakkai, we've worked so hard to maintain our high ideals, to behave considerately while others mock decency. The older folks, not blessed with our energy, have suffered three years of degradation. They live in black hopelessness, believing struggle is meaningless. We should feel compassion for them, not anger."

"It's up to us," Jozef said. "The youth groups and whoever wants to join us. We don't have children to look after, we're organized–"

"To do what? What are our options?" Leah asked.

"We can die, or we can fight and die," Benec said. "Those are our options." Benec's older brother, his wife and twin girls were on the train with Anna's family.

Antek, leader of a left-wing group, said, "Let's help as many as possible to escape. Aren't we 'our brothers' keepers?'"

Itzhak raised an eyebrow. "An avowed atheist quotes the Torah."

Antek shrugged. "I try not to, but it's in my blood."

"My contact in the Polish resistance," Itzhak said, "thinks he could get us a few pistols, some ammunition, maybe other small weapons. But nothing more. With those guns, we might rob police or soldiers to acquire other weapons."

"How many of the seventy-five thousand Jewish lives in Krasau would a few pistols save, even if we got them?" Estie asked.

"Maybe a few – or none. But with guns we can kill Germans – itself a very worthy goal," Itzhak said.

After a long discussion on the cost of weapons, lack of military training, the need for money, Jozef said, "We should stop. Jewish police may visit soon if they hear I suggested fighting. I don't know how the German extermination plans will affect them but don't want to take a chance. So I'll quickly summarize my thoughts, and we'll talk later. Hopefully, all youth groups will agree; Zakkai has seventy members; combined we have almost three hundred.

"I suggest we all try to get weapons, try to help our families and friends escape the ghetto or hide, advise everyone in the ghetto to do the same, and warn other Jewish communities. If we get guns, we must decide whether to resist in the ghetto, form Jewish units to fight on the Aryan side or in the forest, or individually join Polish resistance. Exactly what, how, who and when are for later."

"I have a question," Leah said. "I understand hiding and trying to escape. But can our young Zakkai members – who sing Shabbos prayers, talk about a future Jewish homeland and, as Anna put it, learn high ideals – transform themselves into fighters?"

"I'll answer that," Anna mumbled.

"I'm sorry," Jozef said. "We didn't hear you."

Anna stood and slowly turned her head, looking each person in the eyes. *"We won't let ourselves be led to the slaughter like a bunch of cattle. We'll defend ourselves, and our defense will be through offense. If we survive, it will be as a group, as a generation of avengers with weapons in our hands. For Jewish honor, we offer our lives willingly for our holy cause."*

She sat back down.

"And to that," Itzhak said, "we all say–"

"Amen!" the room erupted.

APRIL 18, 1942

Zakkai posted notices, written by Anna, throughout the ghetto.

DON'T TRUST THE GERMANS!
RESETTLEMENT IS DEATH.
THE TRAINS LEAD TO EXTERMINATION IN BELZEC.
ESCAPE! HIDE!
SPREAD THE WORD!

•••

APRIL 27, 1942
KARL BECK

Karl Beck met with the Jewish Council. "Someone is spreading terrible, crazy rumors that we're killing people in a diabolical murder factory. That we plan to murder everyone. I swear to you, with all my heart, that these are lies. Lies invented by someone insane. Don't believe them!"

Beck also spoke to factory workers. He stood with a Jewish man whose elderly parents had left on the first train. Beck asked the man to read a card the man held in his hand. "This is a postcard I received from my mother in Belzec," the man said. "We are fine. Everything here is nice. Love, Mama."

Beck emphatically hollered: "Don't believe the rumors! In two weeks, two trains will leave again to Belzec. We have room for two thousand five hundred people in each train. Fresh air, good working conditions, an apartment per family, and plentiful food. First come, first served! Bread and jam for everyone who goes.

"I've gone to great trouble to ease overcrowding. Don't fall for rumors!

"Thank you."

•••

APRIL 28, 1942

Leaflets written by Anna were distributed and notices posted throughout the ghetto.

DON'T TRUST THE GERMANS! KARL BECK IS A LIAR!
RESETTLEMENT IS DEATH.
THE TRAINS LEAD TO EXTERMINATION.
DON'T GO! ESCAPE! HIDE!
SPREAD THE WORD!

May 18, 1942
Benjamin

Benec informed everyone in Zakkai that he would forge Aryan documents for their families if they made plans to escape the ghetto. But their plans must include where on the Aryan side they'd live and how they'd obtain food for a long time – for which they needed Polish friends willing to risk their lives. Those sorts of friends didn't grow on trees – but they did hang from them.

Seventeen-year-old Benjamin Danzon, who had played football months before with Benec and Reuven, talked to his parents; they wanted to leave, and his father could ask good Polish friends for help. While his sister's two giggling, curly-haired little boys played on Benjamin's lap, he tried to convince her and her cautious husband to also go. "What if we're caught on the Aryan side – the penalty is death," his sister's husband worried. "Would you rather" – Benjamin gently placed his hands on his little nephews' heads – "see them tossed into a gas chamber?" They agreed to go.

Benjamin's father waited in line for one of the ghetto's few working telephones, called an old Polish friend and asked if he'd find an apartment for them on the Aryan side. Benjamin would leave the ghetto, go to the friend's house with rent money, and the friend would lease it for them. The friend hesitated, from fear, but agreed. Another friend said he'd help with food if the family could get out. The plans were set, and Benec forged documents for Benjamin.

Benjamin knew that some Jews snuck out of the ghetto by bribing guards, but he didn't like the risk. An athlete, he'd climb the wall at an isolated spot not likely to be watched.

Today was the day. Just after sunrise, Benjamin hugged his parents goodbye. "Please be careful," they prayed. He double-checked that he had the money for his father's friend, left his parents and went to the spot he'd chosen. No one was there, at least on the ghetto side. He removed his armband, climbed the wall, covered the razor wire with his jacket as best he could, and hopped down to the Aryan side. The wire cut his arms, but not too badly. He hurried from the wall, crossed the road, made his way through an alley, and turned onto a commercial street.

It was warm for an early morning in May, and a few people were already walking to work. Benjamin joined them on the sidewalk, pockets filled with his father's money, enough for three months' rent.

His jacket and clothes were baggy, and his hat pulled down to shade his dark eyes and narrow Jewish face.

He turned left at the first intersection. More tense than he'd expected, he couldn't shake a strange feeling that he was being followed. He took deep breaths to try to calm himself, wiped sweaty palms on his pants legs, walked one more block but turned again at the next corner and, for no particular reason, decided to head down Bogadowa Street. It was one of two routes he could take to his father's friend's neighborhood.

Benjamin looked down as he walked, occasionally glancing nervously at passersby. When he reached the next corner, he faced away from the other pedestrians but heard a woman's voice whisper something in Jewish. He looked up; a dark-haired woman motioned for him to follow her. He was afraid but thought from the tone of her voice that she might need help. The woman walked a short distance to the front of a business, not yet open. Benjamin followed her.

The woman smiled, and they talked as people passed. She shifted her purse from her left hand to her right. She said her name was Regina and offered to help him; he thanked her but said he was fine. The woman wished him well, and he left. Benjamin was puzzled by her, but his thoughts soon returned to his own concerns.

He was thankful that his father's friends would help with the apartment and food. Getting enough food would still be a problem, but they'd deal with that later. And how will his family escape to the Aryan side? They'd need to figure that out too. Benjamin wondered if his little nephews could stay quiet in the apartment, and he smiled when he pictured them.

He heard footsteps behind him but thought nothing of it. Many people were out and about. He didn't realize that the footsteps meant that he wouldn't need to worry about food or staying quiet in the apartment. Or how to help his parents or his sister's family.

Or that soon, he'd be on a train to Belzec's gas chambers.

He felt a hand on his shoulder. It belonged to Officer Peter Wojcik.

Peter's pockets were full, and Benjamin's empty, when Peter delivered him to the Germans.

May 19, 1942
Szymon

Five minutes before the clock tower struck 8:00 p.m., Szymon crossed the street, stopped momentarily outside a crystal gallery, and headed toward the Pulaski Café. He wore a dark suit, white shirt and black tie. Walking at his normal pace, he would arrive a minute ahead of schedule.

None of this was new to Szymon; he had been in the Polish underground for more than two years. Come September would be three years since his parents had disappeared. Szymon now worked full-time with the "AK," the Polish Home Army resistance group loyal to the Polish government in exile in London. Szymon headed a cell of fifteen people and reported to an officer commanding several cells.

When the clock tower struck 8:00, Szymon was standing outside the crowded café, folded newspaper in his left hand. A smiling, blue-eyed, young woman with blondish-brown hair approached.

"Hi – been waiting long?" she asked.

Szymon returned the wide smile. "No, just arrived. Would you like to get dessert?"

"No, I've done enough sitting today."

"Then let's go for a walk."

He offered his arm, which the young woman took, and they strolled past the stores lining the avenue, window shopping as they walked. They slowly made their way out of the commercial district, and Szymon talked about his favorite foods until they crossed into a quiet, dark residential neighborhood.

Still arm in arm, he said, "Itzhak speaks very highly of you."

"Thank you."

"I don't know anyone smarter than Itzhak. Or anyone whose recommendation holds as much weight. It's because of him that I agreed to meet."

Anna nodded. "I feel like we've met but don't know when." Szymon looked at her closely, narrowing his eyes, and shrugged.

They walked past tree-lined, modest homes on both left and right, turned up a walkway and into a house that looked like any other. Szymon led Anna into a kitchen badly in need of repainting. A young, dark-haired woman was sitting at a square, wooden table in the middle of the room. She stood – tall, solidly built with long, straight brown hair and a stern, serious face – and eyed Anna carefully. Her hands were stuffed inside the big pockets of a long gray coat.

"Kasia, this is Anna," Szymon said. "We're good."

Upon hearing the last two words, a smile spread across Kasia's suddenly pretty, round face, which brightened the room and put Anna at ease.

"Nice to meet you, Anna!" Kasia cheerfully hugged her; she then embraced Szymon and kissed his cheek. "I've made tea."

"Thanks – we'll be about two hours," Szymon said.

Kasia took Anna's hat and coat and laid them on the counter. "Then I'll say goodbye." Kasia reached out, squeezed Szymon's hand, smiled at Anna, and left.

Szymon gestured for Anna to sit, and he served her black tea without sugar. The room was cool despite closed windows, and the hot tea warmed Anna's throat.

"You can tell Itzhak you met my girlfriend," Szymon said.

"Ah... and I'll say she seems lovely."

"She is."

Anna smiled. She looked at this tall, handsome Polish man and had trouble picturing him with Itzhak. "I should have mentioned earlier," she said, "that Itzhak is also very complimentary of you. He said you're 'one of the good guys' – you know right from wrong and have the courage to do what's right."

"That's a little dramatic."

She tilted her head to the side. "He said you are old, good friends?"

"You seem surprised."

"Though I work closely with Itzhak, I still don't know him well. But I didn't imagine..."

"That he has good friends?" Szymon laughed. "If I needed proof you work with Itzhak, you just gave it to me." He chuckled again and looked at his watch. "My commander will get here in a few minutes. I'll first grab the items you came for." He walked to the kitchen door. "By the way, my name is Pawel."

"I'm Helena," Anna said.

Szymon returned minutes later and set a large canvas sack on the table. "Sorry I didn't wrap the gifts," he grinned. "Go ahead."

Anna reached into the bag, grasped something metallic and pulled it out. She set it on the table and cried, "Oh my God!" Burying her face in her hands, she muttered to herself, "If only we had..." Szymon said nothing until Anna took a deep breath, regained her composure, and emptied the rest of the sack onto the table.

"Two English-made Webley revolvers and twelve bullets," Szymon said. "At least forty years old, but in fine shape. Unfortunately, this is all I can give you. But I hope my commander will provide much more. Have you ever fired a pistol?"

Anna shook her head, and Szymon began to show her how to load, unload, cock and uncock the revolvers.

•••

When Szymon had crossed the street on the way to meet Anna, five minutes before the clock tower struck 8:00, he didn't notice a tall, large man window shopping at the crystal gallery. Possibly because several people were standing there, or because the man had cautiously turned his back when Szymon approached.

But Officer Peter Wojcik saw Szymon.

Peter had discreetly followed Szymon and admired how the young woman met him at their apparent rendezvous point so soon after Szymon arrived. Neither Szymon nor the young woman noticed Peter following them through the commercial district. Peter was too expert to allow that, especially with so many people around. They might have spotted him if he'd tailed them in the quiet residential area. But no need, Peter knew exactly where they were headed.

•••

Anna was practicing loading the pistol, at Szymon's direction, when they heard knocking on the door. Three knocks, followed by two knocks, followed by three more. Szymon stood. "Excuse me, but my commander is here. I'll talk with him in another room and then introduce you."

Anna placed the loaded pistol on the table and waited more than thirty minutes.

Finally, Szymon entered and introduced a nicely dressed man about forty-five, of average height, balding brown hair and a wide face garnished by a neatly trimmed mustache. A perfectly folded blue handkerchief in his front coat pocket stylishly accented his suit and tie. Stanislaw Nowak, formerly head of the Krasau passport office, now commanded eight cells of the Polish Home Army.

Nowak graciously offered his hand to Anna and, with a flourish, said, "I'm honored to meet you and apologize that we kept you waiting."

"The honor is mine, sir."

Nowak eyed the pistols and bullets resting on the table, and he gestured for everyone to sit. "Pawel told me he's giving you these weapons. Unfortunately – I'll save us all time – it's very unlikely you'll receive more."

"Why–" Anna began.

"I wish you well, of course," Nowak said. "But to be frank, I'm not pleased with the idea of giving guns to ... people not trained to use them. I appreciate–"

Three knocks on the door. Szymon tensed and stood. "I'm not expecting anyone." He pulled a pistol from inside his coat.

Nowak raised a hand. "I invited someone to join us." Szymon re-holstered the pistol.

Two knocks followed by three more. "He'll let himself in," Nowak said.

Moments later, a big, middle-aged man with a friendly face – Peter Wojcik – stepped into the room. He wore a navy-blue jacket, white dress shirt and dark slacks. Nowak and Peter hugged and kissed each other on the cheek, and Nowak introduced Peter as the "man who helps with our weapons supply and distribution."

Nowak turned to Peter. "Please meet Pawel, the extremely competent head of one of our cells, and Helena, who seeks weapons to fight Germans. But I apologize for bringing you here. I'd thought we might have a potential new cell, capable but needing weapons, so I invited you to discuss arming Helena's group. Unfortunately, I learned tonight that–" He looked at Peter and Szymon. "Let's the three of us talk in private."

Anna saw Szymon frown. "Please include me in the conversation," she said. "I can answer any questions–"

"Fine," Nowak said. "Let's talk. I was hoping to handle this differently, but we'll be candid with one another. The problem is that Helena and her group are Jews."

Turning to Anna, Nowak said, "You disguise yourself well – I mean that as a compliment."

Anna's face reddened. She noticed Peter flush briefly but maintain a poker face, and she felt his eyes assessing her. Or was she misreading base antisemitism as something nuanced?

"I'm willing to hear what you think," Nowak said to Peter. "I realize Jews are experiencing difficult times, but they won't fight, and I don't want to waste valuable weapons on them – regardless of what London may say."

"I met Helena tonight," Szymon said. "But I've known a guy in her group for many years. He's outstanding. And another was instrumental in repairing radios for me–"

"Repairing radios isn't fighting," Nowak said.

Peter looked at Anna. "Even if we got you weapons, we'd sell, not give 'em to you. You have thousands of zlotys to spend?"

"Money is not an issue," Anna lied. But she knew her answer would satisfy them. Antisemites believed all Jews stashed money in their cupboards even if they seemed poor.

"This could mean extra funds for your operations," Peter said to Nowak.

Nowak chuckled. "You know how this would play out if we sold guns to Jews? They'd haggle with us to lower the price and then try to sell them back for a profit." Peter laughed.

Nowak shook his head. "No. The extra cash would help, but we all know they'll drop the guns and run at the first sign of trouble, no matter how many radios they could fix." He looked at Anna. "I'm sorry, my dear, but the answer is no."

Anna calmly picked up the loaded pistol, stood back from the table, and pointed the barrel at Nowak's chest. Staring at him, she said, "The Germans murdered most of my family. My friends and I want weapons to kill Germans. But if anyone needs me to prove myself, I could do it now."

Nowak and Peter turned red but said nothing, and Szymon stifled a smile.

No one moved.

"Put it down before you accidentally shoot me!" Nowak ordered.

Anna cocked the pistol.

"Does anyone need proof?" Anna asked, her eyes glued on Nowak.

Silence.

"I like this girl!" Peter finally said. "Put the pistol down and we'll sell you some weapons – if everyone approves."

Nowak nodded. "Yeah – but only if we get a VERY good price."

"Agreed," Peter said. "Young lady, we can sell you between ten and fifteen pistols, ammunition, and several hand grenades for a high price, but one you can afford. We don't have rifles or submachine guns available." Peter glanced at Nowak.

Nowak nodded.

Szymon reached his hand toward Anna. She uncocked and placed the pistol in it.

"It will cost several thousand zlotys," Peter said. "I'll get you the exact figures later. You'll need–"

"His price is non-negotiable," Nowak said sternly. "Get us the cash and then we'll make the weapons available."

Anna sat down. "It's very risky for us to leave the ghetto. You don't realize–"

"Let's do it this way," Szymon interrupted and turned to Peter. "Get the weapons to me, I'll notify Helena's group, and we'll exchange them for the cash. All through me."

"Dandy," Peter said. "And I do know how tough it is for Jews outside the ghetto. I work with a cool-headed Jewish woman who helps Jews find places to stay, get food, other help. Spread the word. Not for your resistance group. I want to emphasize that. Only for the average Jew on the outside who needs help."

"I had no idea," Anna said, "that there is an organized–"

"We don't publicize it for obvious reasons. But if any Jew makes it outside the ghetto and needs help, the woman goes by the name Regina and often can be found in the morning near 24 Bogadowa Street."

"She must be an incredible person," Anna said.

"She is."

•••

The next day, surrounded by Jozef, Leah, Benec, Estie, Itzhak, and six others, Anna emptied a canvas bag onto the table in Jozef's and Leah's apartment. Potatoes that Anna had placed at the top of the bag tumbled out first. They had saved her life when a policeman hurriedly searched the bag. Then the pistols. Jozef gasped; everyone shouted with joy and, in turn, hugged Anna. None tighter than Itzhak.

Jozef lifted a pistol and caressed it as if he were holding a newborn baby. *"It is impossible to describe the ecstasy inspired by these weapons," he said. "The Germans' first act when they conquered Poland was to confiscate all weapons. Even buried revolvers were discovered, every bayonet was taken. Not even a single bullet could be concealed safely. None of us believed weapons would ever be found. What a joy it is to have some, knowing they will be used against the enemy!"*

May 21, 1942
Itzhak

Itzhak found white-haired Rabbi Leibman in the rundown apartment the rabbi shared with two families. He looked very thin; Itzhak was saddened by how old and frail his esteemed rabbi had become. In his tallis and tefillin, praying the morning service with three teenage boys facing southeast, Rabbi Leibman resembled an old scarecrow more than a person.

He nodded to Itzhak, who sat motionless watching the rabbi and boys rock back and forth while muttering the morning prayers. "Blessed is God who has given us the Torah... Honor your father and mother, do deeds of kindness... Visit the sick... Make peace... Lead us not into temptation... Keep us from evil..." Followed by the Shma and Amidah.

Itzhak watched them and thought about what resistance meant. Most ultra-religious Jews wouldn't fight because they believed whatever happened was part of God's plan. But because the Nazis had banned all public prayer services, they risked their lives praying in secret.

Itzhak sat patiently until the final prayers were uttered. The boys left the room; they apparently lived there, and Rabbi Leibman turned to Itzhak. They hadn't seen each other in months.

"Hi," Rabbi Leibman said with a wide grin. "How are your parents? Your health?"

"All fine under the circumstances, thank you. I'd like to talk about something. You've seen the leaflets about Belzec? You know they're murdering us?"

The grin vanished. "I know... If you ask me how God allows the slaughter of babies–"

"No. I have a different question. To ask your permission, perhaps."

"Questions." Rabbi Leibman deeply sighed. "I've told you some of the questions asked of me; they've become only more difficult. Many God-fearing people remain, after so much indignity. Yesterday, a young man asked: 'I know the Germans will murder me because I'm a Jew. What blessing do I say before my death?' What better exemplifies the chasm between us and them? They abandon God, and we seek to obey him until our dying breath."

Itzhak shook his head at the fatalism implicit in the question. "I belong to a resistance group. We want to kill Germans and save Jews.

For both, we need money. A lot of money. To buy weapons, to rent apartments, to bribe guards. We've asked for donations. Too little and too slow. We know of some wealthy Jews who will go on the trains when instructed. The Germans will take their jewelry, their cash. If we could get our hands on it... but the only way is to take it.

"My question is can we steal from doomed Jews to fight for Jewish honor and to save Jews?"

Rabbi Leibman's eyes narrowed. "Your question is can you steal from a fellow Jew who has suffered unimaginable torment? So that this Jew, on the brink of death, will languish helplessly as a fellow Jew degrades him further by theft or robbery?"

"Yes, but we would take only from those who plan to step onto the death trains."

"Don't you see what you're asking? To the Nazi, the individual is nothing. To create their master race, they enslave the weak and kill the useless. And since power is all that matters to them, their actions are logical: to strengthen society, they eliminate weak parts. But we say each person is made in God's image – including the feeble and the crippled."

Rabbi Leibman shook his head. "You want to act like them? You want to devalue some to benefit others?"

"For honor and to save lives. Isn't saving even one life–"

"No, I can't permit you to steal from them." Rabbi Leibman paused. "But I have a question: why do you ask? Don't you live according to humanistic notions of fairness, not God's commandments?"

Itzhak chose his words carefully. "I'm still a Jew, and the Torah guides me and others in my group. I've told my friends I would ask you. If you don't allow this, dissension may prevent us from accomplishing anything."

Rabbi Leibman raised his eyebrows but said nothing. Itzhak continued. "You taught me that God cares for the widow, the orphan, the downtrodden, and that Jews must imitate God by caring for them. No one is more downtrodden than the Jews. Doesn't God want us to help ourselves? Shouldn't you?"

"I still can't give you permission." He ran a hand along his white beard. "But these are horrible times. I'll think about it – come back in three days."

•••

That night, Rabbi Leibman sat quietly in the dank room he shared with four religious men and boys. Slowly rocking back and forth in a wooden rocking chair, he researched Jewish law with his eyes shut. He didn't open a book because he no longer owned one. All sold long ago to buy bread.

Ignoring his roommates' squabbles, Rabbi Leibman read – in his mind – extracts of holy books planted there decades earlier. Words written by ancient and medieval sages; words of genius, words from very different times.

Coloring them all was his vision from before the war: that a horrible calamity would befall the Jewish people in Europe. He had thought then, in a moment of hubris, that he'd received the message of doom so he could warn people. But his warnings proved useless. Jews had nowhere to run.

His vision had also included that a small remnant would survive.

A small remnant. Rabbi Leibman had no doubt that he and everyone he knew would soon be murdered. But might someone else, young or old, survive if Itzhak's resistance group acquired the means to act? If Rabbi Leibman's decision led to even one saved life, would his own life have been worth living? But at the cost of abusing the trampled innocent?

Was this task a blessing or a curse? Or had the vision come to him so that he might help save the remnant? Who knows what they – or their descendants – might accomplish. Was that why God placed him, seventy-four years ago, in his mother's womb?

Rabbi Leibman didn't know. But he continued to search his mind.

•••

Itzhak returned three days later. On the table rested an envelope with his name. In it, a letter with this cover note:

> I have spoken to a wealthy Jew on your behalf. If he does not contact you, the enclosed letter may be of use. As Joshua was told when he led our ancestors into the Promised Land,
>
> חזק ואמץ Be strong and courageous. God is with you.

Itzhak sat and read the letter.

> I have been asked a most unfortunate question. Resistance leaders need funds to buy weapons to fight Amalek and to save fellow Jews. A few rich individuals intend to bring their wealth onto the extermination trains due to their baseless trust in our

oppressors. I have been asked if it is permissible to take their money, by force or finesse, without permission.

I present the following sources. I cannot cite specific pages because I lack books and rely on my memory. Leviticus 19:16 establishes that one is forbidden from standing by as Amalek slaughters our Jewish brethren.

לא תלך רכיל בעמיך לא תעמד על דם רעך

"Do not deal basely with members of your people. Do not stand idly by the blood of your fellow."

As Chazal teaches, this verse is the source of the law that one must save another from drowning or being attacked by bandits even at significant expense. (Sanhedrin 73a). The Rambam writes that one must use time, money, and even one's body to save their fellow.

The Radbaz similarly argues that while one is not obligated to cut off one's own limb to save a life, he must incur significant expense to save a life. As the Rema notes on Orach Chaim 656 in the *Shulcḥan Arukh*, one is obligated to expend up to one fifth of his wealth to fulfill a commandment and all of one's wealth to not violate a negative commandment. This is a positive commandment as it requires active participation in the mitzvah.

Can Yehuda take Shimon's property without Shimon's permission to save a life? Rabbi Chaim Palagi argues that one must make his property available to save a life, and that this person has no claim upon another who takes the property by force for this purpose. It is well established that one may seize another's property to save one's own life but must compensate the property owner for any loss incurred. These authorities might support the following conclusion.

The Resistance may seize up to one fifth of the misers' property without repayment, as this helps them fulfill their obligation to save life. Any additional money taken must be repaid shortly thereafter and is considered a loan. Additionally, all seized assets must only be used for the direct purpose of saving a life in clear and present danger. Anything to help a Jew escape the Nazis clearly qualifies. Under current circumstances, one may purchase weapons as well. Of course, none of the seized assets may be used to compensate those engaging in this honorable fight.

JUNE 17, 1942
IRINA

Two months had passed since fifteen-year-old Irina had helped her family to the death train. At first, she and Anna continued to live in their family's apartment, but the pain of absence was too strong. They moved in with Jozef and Leah.

For weeks, Irina was detached, disinterested. How could the sun still shine? But she slowly noticed how her big sister seemed able to drown her grief in Zakkai. For the first time, Irina learned the extent of Anna's work: leaflets, weapons acquisition, courier, and Anna started teaching her about the Aryan side – how to act, to think, whom and how to watch. Irina listened carefully and learned. So that she could become a courier, like Anna.

One morning while sitting together in their leaders' kitchen, Anna said that she and Itzhak were planning to smuggle Irina out of the ghetto.

"My first mission?" Irina asked, with pangs of excitement and fear.

"No, to survive."

Irina narrowed her eyes. "What does that mean?"

"To live. Apart from us. On your own. To hopefully survive the war. Benec will forge papers, Itzhak's friends in the Polish resistance will find you a job – in Krasau or somewhere else – as a nanny or who knows what. We'll teach you the Christian prayers–"

"No!" Irina blurted, overcome by a different kind of fear. "I'm staying in the ghetto with you and Reuven. With everyone."

Anna gently grasped Irina's hand. "Within a few months, a year at most, every Jew in the ghetto will be dead. Most will be gassed at Belzec; others will die fighting the Germans. All Zakkai leaders, including me, have sworn to fight to the death. Every Zakkai member except you will be given the choice to join us."

Irina's eyes filled with angry tears. "Why–"

Anna squeezed Irina's hand tighter. "I talked to Benec about Reuven going with you, but he agrees it's impossible. Reuven is too Jewish looking. But you're not. Once you learn things, you could survive."

"No! You want me to abandon everyone – I won't do it."

"This isn't only about you! It's about Mama and Papa and Frammy and Bubbie. Can't you hear their blood crying out from the earth that at least one member of our family must survive? I've sworn to fight. You must live!"

Irina lowered her eyes. "I'm in love with Reuven. I won't leave. I'd rather die with him than live."

Anna sighed. "If Reuven is worth dying for, he'll insist you try to survive."

Irina's eyes burned as if she were about to respond, then her shoulders slumped, and she said nothing.

"We have two or three months," Anna said. "A lot for you to learn and us to organize. And then you'll escape this hell. So that thirty, forty years from now, when you're an old woman with your own children and grandchildren, you'll remember us. And you'll say there once walked on this earth people named Anna and Frammy and Reuven."

June 22, 1942
Heinrich Schmidt

Gestapo officer Heinrich Schmidt waited at his large desk for the heads of the Jewish Council he'd summoned. These Jews were as arrogant and wormy as the Jews he went to school with years earlier.

Schmidt was from the city of Danzig, the oldest of four children. His strict parents had expected him to take over their manufacturing business, for which one needed math and science skills. Skills Heinrich never possessed. He tried; it wasn't his fault that he lacked an aptitude for engineering. His specialty was analyzing people, not equations. Sure, his teachers had said that extra effort would help, but who were they to tell him what to do?

If he had competed only against well-rounded boys, like himself, he'd have received the good marks he deserved. But the Jews in his class didn't play fair. They knew things only cheaters would know. They probably had developed their sick math aptitude from generations counting money. Or they hid answers in their dark, curly hair.

It wasn't because of Heinrich's lack of effort or ability that he failed the university's engineering entrance exam. Or that his father chose an outsider to run the family business. When Jews cheat and lie to get ahead of you, the fault is theirs, not yours.

Schmidt stepped into the small bathroom next to his office, carefully combed his hair, straightened his tie, and listened until Karl Beck ushered the Jews into his office. Schmidt then waited two minutes, walked in, sat behind his desk, and motioned for Beck to sit. He opened a file and began to read, ignoring the elderly Jewish Council chairman and two other Jews standing in front of him, hats in their hands. Finally, he stopped reading and scowled.

"You're here to learn the results of your arrogance. Officer Beck has gone to great lengths to decrease Jew overcrowding, even providing transportation to your new homes. He arranged to resettle five thousand Jews last month, but only a few hundred accepted his benevolence. And why is that? Because the method of transport didn't meet your lofty Jew standards?"

"Herr Schmidt," a Jew began.

"Silence!" Schmidt's face burned red, and a vein bulged on his temple. "Resettlement is no longer voluntary. Herr Beck has urged me to be polite and kindhearted. I've had enough of that. You people started this war. If not for you, I'd be home in Danzig with my family. But your lust and greed, your disgust for everything virtuous, has brought death to Europe. And you sit back and mock us!

"We have too many Jews in Krasau. Beginning next week, the numbers will be reduced by thirty thousand. We require three thousand Jews each day for ten days at the train collection point by 2:00 p.m. – beginning next Monday – for resettlement the following morning. Everyone is subject to this order. The only exemptions are essential workers at German-owned factories. Each adult must bring their money, valuables, a small amount of luggage and food for one day.

"The Jewish Council is responsible for providing the thirty thousand Jews. If three thousand Jews fail to appear on any afternoon by 2:00, we will collect the Jews ourselves until the full thirty thousand have been resettled – beginning with Council members and their families. And we may reconsider the exemption for factory workers.

"Now get out of my office."

•••

That afternoon, the sixty-five-year-old chairman of the Jewish Council asked Jozef to prove that German resettlement meant death. Jozef and twenty-year-old Anna met with him, and Anna repeated what she'd learned in Zamosc. All color left the chairman's despondent face. At an emergency Council meeting the following day, he urged them to disobey the German order and warn all Jews to hide. His motion failed to receive a majority vote.

The Council vice-chairman said, "The Germans have assured us that the extermination rumors are lies! We've compiled a list of thirty thousand names, and the Jewish police should compel those people to go. Who knows what the Germans might do if we don't meet their demands. If resettlement means death, should everyone be put at risk? Cooperation is the best way to save lives."

His motion also failed to pass. No decision was made. The next evening, the chairman of the Jewish Council wrote in his diary, "*They demand from me to kill the children of my nation with my own hands. There is nothing left for me but to die.*" He died by suicide.

Jews frantically readied hiding places in attics, walls, under ground – in every conceivable place. The following Monday, only fifty Jews went to the train collection point. Late that night, German SS soldiers and Polish police swept into the ghetto and barricaded several blocks. They and unarmed Jewish police stormed inside each building, apartment by apartment, within the barricaded area. Some Jewish police refused and were shot; most helped as ordered. Thousands of Jews were dragged outside and forced into trucks. The Germans murdered, on the spot, all who refused, resisted, or moved too slowly. Men and women, elderly and babies.

The next morning, Itzhak and Benec hid behind a warehouse outside the barricaded area. Immediately across the street, within the doomed blocks, stood an empty house and, to the right, two other houses. Rabbi Leibman's apartment building was to the right of the third house. They watched soldiers entering that building but then heard screaming from the house directly across from them. They saw a German captain exit the house dragging by the arm a short, thin, crying Jewish boy – Leo, a fifteen-year-old Zakkai member.

The captain dragged Leo to the front of the house, shoved him against the gray brick facade, and ordered "Don't move!" Benec and Itzhak watched and listened helplessly to Leo's cries.

The German stepped back and unholstered his pistol but realized it had no bullets. He searched his pockets, found two bullets, placed them in the magazine, glanced at Leo and was about to insert the magazine into the pistol when a soldier came running and spoke urgently to the captain, who commanded Leo, "Stay here! I'll be back!" The captain ran with the soldier toward Rabbi Leibman's building.

Leo stayed. Against the house. Waiting, paralyzed with fear, for the captain to return. "Come here! Hurry!" Itzhak and Benec hollered from their hiding place across the street. But overcome by terror, Leo couldn't move. His feet felt as if they were embedded in concrete. "Come on, schmo! Don't stand there!" Benec yelled. But Leo stood, blank-faced, in shock.

Benec peered to his right, could see the captain and other Germans down the road, grimaced, raced across the street, hopped over a barricade, grabbed Leo and led him to Itzhak and then to Jozef's and Leah's house. Itzhak stayed and watched trucks pull up to the apartment building. He saw Rabbi Leibman, wearing his tallis and tefillin and carrying a prayer book, enter the back of a truck with his head held high, along with the boys from his apartment and others, all gaunt, dressed in worn, ragged clothes.

Several trucks drove toward the collection point, *loaded with Jews, sitting and standing, hugging sacks that contained whatever pitiful belongings they had managed to gather at the last moment. Some stared straight ahead vacantly, others mourned and wailed, wringing their hands.... Women tore their hair or clung to their children, who sat bewildered among the scattered bundles, gazing at the adults in silent fear.*

Running behind the last truck, a lone woman, arms outstretched, screamed:

"My child! Give back my child!"

In reply, a small voice called from the truck. "Mama! Mama!"

Itzhak *watched as though hypnotized. Panting with exhaustion, the mother continued to run after the truck... The cries of the pursuing mother became more desperate as the truck turned the corner. The cries of the deportees faded and became inaudible, only the cry of the agonized mother still pierced the air.*

"My child! Give back my child!"

Itzhak sat and wept.

September 4, 1942
Itzhak's Journal

Two months have passed since the Germans and their helpers forcibly deported thirty thousand innocents, ripping our hearts out, in the "aktion," as it is called. Including at least twenty-five Zakkai teens and their families.

Most of the remaining forty-five thousand Jews live in constant terror that death will arrive at any moment, without warning. Thousands hope their employment in German factories will save them and their children. Many even believe it. A small few have escaped to the Aryan side, but how long can they survive with no ration cards and danger at every turn?

All live with a dagger over our heads.

This includes my friends and our allies, whose single purpose is to exact revenge. And for that, we recently obtained money to buy weapons and fund our efforts! The question is where to fight: inside the ghetto or on the Aryan side? The answer is not easy.

Some, including Jozef and me, believe we should fight in small groups on the Aryan side and in the forests, where we could attack places of our choosing. Attack, disappear, and attack again somewhere else. But coordination would be difficult. Others think we should fight together within the ghetto, as a tiny Jewish army, and leave this world in a burst of flaming glory. Literally, because the Germans would burn the ghetto with us and everyone in it.

If we fight in the ghetto, the Germans will also murder the Jews working in German factories. We believe those Jews are marked for death anyway. But are we certain?

Weeks ago, the Germans changed the guards at the gates, rendering it very difficult to exit and enter the ghetto. We then feared that we'd have no choice but to make a last stand within the ghetto walls, and we began planning accordingly. But in a stroke of genius, twenty-year-old Benec explored the underground sewers, discovered an escape route under the streets through the smelly, rat-infested tunnels, and mapped them. Through the sewers, we and our fighters will move to the Aryan side.

Hallelujah!

SEPTEMBER 5, 1942
SZYMON'S JOURNAL

Germany controls almost all of Europe. Britain remains, but our hope for victory lies with Russia and America. The Germans, who attacked Russia in June of last year, have bogged down, especially at Stalingrad. We pray the Russians will turn the tide. Meanwhile, America joined the war last December! Their troops have not yet fought the Germans, but we know they will. Simply mouthing the word "America" gives us hope.

The Polish Home Army resistance group, or "AK," is gathering members and strength, perhaps numbering more than one hundred thousand across Poland. Widespread sabotage and other physical resistance should commence soon; we work toward an armed revolt to assist the Allied liberation of Poland.

But even in our wildest dreams, that is far off in the future.

September 8, 1942
Karl Beck

"Prost!" boomed Karl Beck. Beer mugs clinked together, and raucous, laughing men guzzled them. "To Karl Beck," a drunk Gestapo man lifted his glass and slobbered. "Our Jew disposer and social coordinator!"

Beck and Heinrich Schmidt sat in the Polna Bar at the end of a long table filled with Gestapo men. It was Tuesday night, and they were enjoying a new tradition that Karl had suggested. Camaraderie at one of the finest bars in Krasau. Already a popular hangout for German army officers, Gestapo men now met here monthly. Lively atmosphere, pretty waitresses, great beer.

Karl was always ready for a good time. He also liked learning things from liquor-lubricated Gestapo men. Like when they expected the bulk of Krasau's Jews to be deported for special handling. It wasn't up to them, but the Gestapo tended to know things. When it happens, Karl will be out of a job in Krasau, and he wanted to plan his next career move before some oaf transferred him somewhere unpleasant.

Karl liked to think big – why stay in Poland? Especially since almost all Polish Jews should be disposed of by the end of next year: more than a million and a half Polish Jews will be gassed by November 1943 at the Belzec, Sobibor and Treblinka carbon monoxide killing centers, and that didn't include Auschwitz, whose disposal capacity would dwarf each of the others. Karl heard Auschwitz was using a rat poison called Zyklon B in their gas chambers instead of carbon monoxide.

In terms of career advancement, Karl might try France or Holland. Or Hungary some day? Plenty of Jews there, for now. He'd need to say goodbye to his Polish girlfriend, which was too bad. But he was open to meeting someone new. He'd never dated a French girl and liked the idea. But Karl didn't want to annoy his bosses by suggesting a transfer before his Krasau job was done.

"Heinrich, I have a question," he said to Schmidt. "We had about eighty thousand Jews in the Krasau Jewish Quarter at its peak, including resettled Jews from surrounding villages. Thirty-five thousand have been deported for special treatment, and we're down to forty-five thousand. What do you think is the timing for the rest?"

"If it were up to me," Schmidt said, "we'd immediately send them all to the Belzec Promised Land. Five thousand a day until no more

Jews." He smacked his hands together. "But realistically? Next few months for most but perhaps a year for all. Hard to know. We must wait our turn because other ghettos in this part of Poland empty into Belzec, and German factory owners are squawking they need Krasau Jews to keep working. That's about fifteen thousand Jews. It may take time to deal with that. Poles are stupid, but they can be trained to take the Jews' place."

"Politics," Karl said. "Always politics. Other than that and hunting random Jews, what are you doing with your time?"

"Polish terrorists are becoming more active. In fact," Schmidt whispered, "I shouldn't tell you this, but we've uncovered a Polish Home Army cell in Krasau. We're tapping the phone of a dumb Pole who talks about someone named 'Pawel'; we think this Pawel character may command a cell. Hopefully, we'll soon get some interesting information."

Schmidt called over a pretty waitress, gave her a nice smack on the butt and ordered another round of beers for the table.

September 18, 1942
Jozef

A tall, thin, narrow-faced man in a dark coat and pants smuggled himself into the ghetto just before noon, slipped on a Jewish star armband and made his way to Jozef's and Leah's apartment. Tomazs Bakowski, an old Polish friend of Jozef's and a member of the resistance, had been communicating with Jozef through others but decided it was past time for a meeting. Jozef greeted Tomazs warmly and led him inside his first-floor apartment to a small table in the kitchen.

Friends since they were little boys, Jozef and Tomazs also shared the bond that comes from years of competing as close teammates. Starring together on the basketball courts in high school, they had drifted apart with adulthood, marriage, and Jozef's short-lived move to Palestine. But the German occupation and underground activities reunited them – until Jozef was forced with other Jews into the ghetto.

"You didn't reply to my last two messages," Tomazs said.

"Yeah, sorry, I–"

"It's time to go," Tomazs said firmly. "Everything is arranged. We've got an apartment for you and Leah on the outskirts of Krasau, far from the ghetto and this craziness." He cast his eyes at a narrow mattress leaning against the wall, a dripping faucet and the shabby, paint-chipped walls. "The place we found for you is suitable for humans."

Jozef sighed but didn't say anything.

"I know you're worried about Leah. It doesn't matter she looks Jewish. She'll stay in the apartment. You'll have a fake identity, ration cards, everything you need. No more ridiculous armband, you'll walk around like a man. Breathe again."

"I told you–"

"You'll have a job, papers so you don't get picked up for forced labor. And we'll work together in the resistance."

His elbows resting on the table, Jozef clasped his hands and leaned forward. "I've told you I can't go."

"That's why I'm here. To beat some sense into you. Every Jew in the ghetto will be dead soon – you know that. The Germans don't make exceptions for guys who get big rebounds at the buzzer."

"I have obligations. Can't do it."

Tomazs bolted from his chair, loomed over Jozef and forcefully grabbed his shoulders. "What the hell obligations are more important than living – and saving your wife? Has this place made you lose your mind!"

"My youth group."

"What! Are you–"

"Can't do it."

"Your youth – have you told Leah that–"

"Yeah. She agrees with me."

"So instead of escaping, you–"

Jozef stood and hugged his old friend. "I appreciate everything you've done... But you'll need to find a new rebounder."

•••

That night, seventeen-year-old Levi and other orphaned Zakkai teens huddled around Leah and Jozef, like puppies surrounding their mother. Their parents were dead – deported to Belzec's gas chambers, and each had a story like Levi's. He'd hidden in a secret closet, heard the Nazis seize his parents, and survived by reaching an attic, from there the roof, another roof and another. Or fifteen-year-old Rivka, who at the farm had giggled at Irina's misbuttoned blouse two years earlier. She watched, through a slit in a wall, as the Germans tore her little sisters from their mother and shot them dead. Her good friend, Miriam, who had laughed with Rivka at Irina's blouse, was among the many Zakkai kids gassed at Belzec.

And yet, God didn't send a flood to devour the earth.

Each night the past two months, almost every foot of Jozef's and Leah's apartment was covered with a blanket or thin mattress where teens slept. Six or seven to a mattress. Not because they couldn't return to their now empty apartments; here they had each other. During the day, each teen worked for Zakkai, the resistance group: gathering information, delivering messages, obtaining supplies.

They and the other remaining Zakkai members, all of whom except Irina had sworn to fight to the death, were meeting tonight to say goodbye. Jozef and Itzhak had decided they must soon leave the ghetto to avoid the next German aktion, which could occur any time, without warning.

As the teens mingled, Estie asked one of the younger guys about his best friend, David.

The forlorn boy looked down and sadly shook his head. "David's father is dead, and his mother didn't believe the stories about gas chambers. She begged David to go on the train and help with his two little brothers. He didn't want to, but..."

Estie hugged him.

Jozef and Leah called Anna, Benec, Estie, and Itzhak together in a small nook of their apartment. "Our plans are set," Jozef said. "Beginning tomorrow and continuing through mid-October, we'll leave the ghetto in independent fighting units. Six five-member cells to stay in apartments on the Aryan side and one fifteen-member group led by me in the forest. Once out, we'll intensify weapons training. Itzhak will stay at a Polish resistance safe house, and Anna will move from cell to cell. We'll then try to get others out.

"No cell will know the location of any other cell. Only Itzhak, Anna and I will know. This is for safety in case anyone is arrested and tortured. For now, only Anna and I will know where Itzhak will stay once he reaches the Aryan side.

"Itzhak and I have decided who is in each group based on weapons skills, relationships, physical strength and other factors. In a few minutes, we'll announce who is in which group. Almost everyone too Jewish looking will go with me to the forest."

"How ironic," Estie said darkly, "that even we decide a Jew's fate based on nose size and if the hair is brown and curly."

"You're right," Itzhak said. "It would be impossible for you, Leah, and the others in Jozef's group to stay in the city and fight. To circulate among Poles would lead to quick arrest. Only in the forest can you fight. After I reach the Polish safe house, I won't see daylight until the end of the war – or of me – whichever comes first."

"I get it," Estie said. "I'm not mad, at least not at you. Only at fate or God or the world that, like leprosy, my Jewish looks continue to plague me."

Leah hugged her, and they joined the group of forty around the table for their last Zakkai Shabbos dinner.

The small table was covered with a white cloth. On it rested bread and wine. *Hushed, they waited for the lighting of the candles that sent a sudden glow around the room. The girls were dressed in white blouses, and the boys in white shirts with collars open at the throat. First, a moment of silence, and then they greeted the Sabbath Bride in a swelling hymn of praise. Song followed song in a deluge of harmonies, each outburst binding them yet more tightly together.*

At the head of the table stood Jozef. He knew this was his last speech to Zakkai. "We leave the ghetto to fight. A youth group devoted to creating a just and peaceful society has transformed into warriors.

"But don't have false hopes. We can't force the Germans to stop exterminating our people like rodents. We fight for Jewish honor – to show that no matter how many lives their black boots stomp to the ground, they cannot make us all grovel.

"*We fight **for three lines** in the history books*. So that future generations – including, God willing, Jews living in a restored Jewish nation in Zion – might view us with pride and not merely pity.

"When you say goodbye tonight to those not in your cell, it is probably forever. And like you, each person you hug is a titan. For you have chosen not to try to survive the war but to fight for our people. *We're going out to face the angel of death, but we'll face him as bold idealists.*"

After Jozef's words came tears, hugs, slaps on the back, and kisses. Followed by more hours of singing, ending with Hatikvah. Finally, the teens slept on the blankets and narrow mattresses filling the apartment.

At dawn, with full but aching hearts, they parted.

Monday October 19, 1942
Benec

Twenty-year-old Benec could barely contain his excitement. Late morning, sitting quietly with his cell in an apartment on the Aryan side, he'd just received a call from Szymon's group. "The second meeting is on at the Polna Bar; 7:00 p.m. tomorrow," the monotone voice had said after confirming the password.

"Second meeting" was code for attack.

A month had passed since the final Zakkai Shabbos dinner, and all of Zakkai except Itzhak had left the ghetto. Benec's cell had been on the Aryan side for three weeks; he'd met twice with Szymon, who was planning a joint AK-Zakkai attack on the Germans. Benec had been waiting for the green light.

Benec snapped his fingers and gestured for everyone to sit with him on the floor: a sixteen-year-old boy, one seventeen and two twenty-one-year-old young men. And sixteen-year-old Irina, who looked twenty. She wasn't a cell member. Irina was staying with Reuven while the AK arranged for her to hide with a Polish family – though Irina hadn't yet agreed.

Silence was key to survival in the apartment. Six young people living together would arouse suspicion, so Anna and Benec had rented it as a married couple. Located miles from the ghetto, the guys and Irina had entered separately and stayed quiet inside. Only Benec went in and out though only Reuven looked obviously Jewish.

The guys, barefoot and shirtless in the airless room, formed a circle on the floor with Benec. Irina, barefoot and wearing shorts and a wrinkled white blouse, sat between Reuven and Levi.

"The Polna Bar is very popular with the Germans," Benec whispered. "Including the SS. Tomorrow night, we'll pay them a visit."

Benec unfolded a sheet of paper and placed it on the floor for everyone to see. "The AK prepared this drawing of the bar's interior. The place mostly serves drinks but looks like a restaurant, with tables throughout. Our group is assigned the right side of the bar, and the AK will take the larger left side because they'll have a submachine gun as well as pistols. With our pistols, we'll shoot dead every German on our side of the bar."

He looked at his sixteen-year-old brother, Reuven. Everyone knew Reuven was tough, daring, and reliable. "Except you, Reuven." Benec pointed at his diagram. "Most – if we're lucky, all – Germans will be unarmed. But three or four armed German soldiers may be sitting at a table in the back right. Bar security. You'll take them out with two hand grenades and dive behind one of these columns for cover." Benec again ran his finger on the drawing. "That's when we start shooting." Benec told everyone when they'd arrive and where they'd position themselves inside the bar.

"Will we come back here when it's over?" Levi asked.

"No," Benec said. "Too far away, and the AK will have cars waiting near the bar. I'll give you the details later. They'll take us to a safe house tomorrow night. Wednesday, we'll come back and Irina will give us a nice welcome home." Benec smiled at Irina.

"You'll make a nice dinner for us, Irina?" Levi asked.

"Of course," Irina said. "Tell me what you want, or I'll plan to make brisket, roast chicken, pickled herring, gefilte fish–"

"I'll take chicken soup, matzah balls and kreplach please," someone said. "And potato kugel."

"Perfect," Irina said. "If Reuven gets the ingredients, I'll have everything ready."

Irina twirled her finger in Reuven's dark, curly hair, wrapped an arm around his neck and kissed his dimpled cheek. "Don't you dare not come back to me," she whispered. "Don't worry," he smiled and kissed her. Never alone, they'd long ago dropped their inhibitions. The guys jealously watched and waited while they kissed until Benec said, "Reuven!"

Irina nudged Reuven away and fixed her hair.

"Irina, are you practicing how you'll greet all of us when we return?" Levi asked. Reuven slugged his arm hard.

"I thought it couldn't hurt to ask," Levi said, rubbing his arm.

Benec explained the attack plan and said, "I'll repeat everything tomorrow. Tonight, get good sleep." Then came a moment of serious silence, and Benec laid his hands on the shoulders of the boys to his left and right; everyone followed suit. "Tomorrow will be the first organized attack on Germans in Krasau," Benec said. "We'll kill the scum who specialize in massacring Jews. Whether we celebrate afterwards at a Polish safe house or die fighting at the Polna Bar, we'll have earned our place in Jewish history."

Quiet followed until Irina said to everyone, "You probably won't need this, but just in case, Anna said there's a woman named Regina who helps Jews on the Aryan side. Not thoroughly checked out, but if anyone gets separated and is desperate, you might find this Regina woman at 24 Bogadowa Street." The guys mouthed the address, committing it to memory.

That night
Heinrich Schmidt

Heinrich Schmidt sat moaning at his desk at 8:00 p.m., gently rubbing the sides of his head. Another terrible headache. They came so often now. Tension from work, he was sure.

His police job before the war had been stressful, but mostly decent hours. Then came all that work compiling lists of Polish intellectuals for the Germans to arrest after they invaded, his Gestapo promotion, keeping Polish police in line, controlling the Jews... Now, with an upcoming Jew aktion and orders from Berlin to crush the budding Polish resistance, he found himself working day and night. Never-ending aggravation.

He needed a break. On a lake somewhere. Sunshine, the outdoors. With friends, surrounded by others on holiday. Those were the nicest times, when everyone was in a good mood because they were away from work. He should focus on himself for a change. Plan something–

Knuckles rapping on his door.

"Come in!"

Gunter Kuntz, chief of the Gestapo's phone surveillance unit, entered with a wide grin. "I have some good news for you," he said.

"Tell me," Schmidt said, still rubbing his temples.

"The guy in a Home Army cell led by a man named Pawel. We tapped his phone weeks ago, and today he placed two very interesting calls. To each person, he said identical words: 'The second meeting is on at the Polna Bar. 7:00 p.m. tomorrow.'"

"They're meeting at a bar German officers go to?" Schmidt said. "That's ingenious. I've seen some Poles there. The kind who try to ingratiate themselves with us. It never occurred to me that Polish resistance would meet right under our noses – and they've apparently done it once before."

Schmidt paused. "These could be cell leaders... But even if not, we should finally meet the Pawel fellow who heads one cell. I'm sure he'd happily tell us who he reports to."

His headache fading, Schmidt rubbed his hands together in anticipation. "By coincidence, tomorrow night is our monthly Karl Beck soiree, so several Gestapo agents are already planning to be at the Polna Bar. I'll make sure they're armed. The Poles may be unarmed, but worst case, after they're seated we'll put our pistols to their heads and disarm them. To be careful, I'll make sure a few armed soldiers are present."

Schmidt dismissed Kuntz and leaned back in his chair. This was suddenly shaping up to be a very good week. Beck had arranged a Jew shipment to Belzec for Thursday and was coordinating an aktion to begin Friday to collect all Jews other than the fifteen thousand factory workers. That's thirty thousand Jews off to Belzec. And we might break Polish resistance tomorrow night.

Schmidt smiled. He may get that vacation.

TUESDAY OCTOBER 20, 1942
ANNA

Anna turned the key and slowly opened the door to the second story apartment on the outskirts of Krasau, five miles from the ghetto. Estie and the other three girls in Jozef's group of fifteen, except Leah, quietly greeted her. None had left the bare apartment since arriving two weeks earlier. Leah was staying with Jozef and the guys on the third floor.

The girls hugged Anna and gathered around her for news. "Your whole group leaves this Saturday morning. Our friends in the Polish resistance will drive you several hours to a forest, where you'll meet partisans and begin the next stage of your lives. Jozef will tell you more, but it will get very cold – whatever clothes you have, bring them."

After answering questions, Anna said, "Now I'll talk to Estie in private." Everyone knew that Estie, as a leader, heard things they didn't. She and Anna walked into an empty room; the girls' dirty clothes were strewn across the floor.

"The amount of space in this apartment is incredible, isn't it?" Estie said, running her hand through her hair. "For two weeks, no one has kicked me while I slept!"

"Good, because I'm staying here the next few nights. But don't get used to the luxury. In a few days, you'll be sleeping in the woods without a tent, in the cold. Soon, in the snow. You could open an ice cream stand."

"I know," Estie sighed.

Anna clasped her hands. "Here's what's happening. Tomorrow, Itzhak will leave the ghetto and move into an AK safe house. Thursday, I have a quick mission to a town near Krasau. Friday, I take Irina to Itzhak at the AK safe house. They've found a Polish family for her to live with in another city. On Friday or Saturday, I'll check out a woman who Polish resistance says helps Jews on the Aryan side, and I'll return to the ghetto to urge the other youth groups to leave before it's too late. Saturday, you go to the forest.

"And," Anna said, "something very exciting: one of our cells and a Polish cell will soon attack Germans, but I don't know who or when. Finally, we'll make the Germans bleed!"

"That's good," Estie nodded thoughtfully. "But what about you? After Friday, where will you stay – with Benec's group?"

"No – he still wants us to be more than friends–"

"Benec. Smart, funny, handsome. Remember when we argued over which Hollywood actor he looked like? With his perfectly chiseled jaw, his pretty eyes–"

"Yeah, I know..."

"Don't tell me that old fear has returned about not committing–"

"No, no, I'm going to ask to stay in the same house as Itzhak."

Estie's mouth fell open.

"Not only because it would make my work easier. I want to be close to him."

"Wow, I didn't know–"

"I didn't either," Anna smiled. "I still don't. I'm sure he doesn't. I don't think Itzhak knows I'm a girl."

"Oh, he knows. Just not what to do about it."

"Ha! – maybe. But I really like him, respect him. I think I may even love him if that's possible. And if you're wondering, I used to pray to keep Mordecai safe and to bring us together again." Anna sighed deeply. "But for the longest time, I've only prayed to keep him safe. With all my heart, I say that prayer. But I stopped praying for the impossible."

"I understand. Especially the word impossible. I have something to tell you that I'm very upset about. My parents–" Estie choked up.

"What?"

"When I told them I was leaving the ghetto, I didn't want to give them extra reason to worry. You know my mother. So I didn't say that we'll try to survive in a forest and attack Germans. My mother doesn't have enough on her mind that she should schvitz about me in a gunfight with soldiers?"

"OK..."

"So, I made things sound better. That we'll go somewhere safe. But I was so stupid! My father asked if they could come too." Tears filled Estie's eyes. "And I told him no. No room for them."

She sobbed, "I'd begged Jozef to let me bring them, but he said it's impossible – even Leah's parents are still in the ghetto, and we can't bring them either."

"Estie, you had to say no – you had no choice."

Estie raised her voice. "Do you understand what I did? You know I'm not so religious, Anna, but for God's sake – 'Honor thy father and mother?' I told my parents there's no room for them to live! I'm saving myself, and they'll go to the gas chambers!"

"You're not saving yourself. You left the ghetto to fight."

"I'm saving myself from the gas chambers. I was so surprised when my father asked me that I didn't think to say I'd begged Jozef to let them come too. All I said was, 'I'm sorry, there's no room.' What do my parents think of me, that I would abandon them?" She burst out crying.

Anna understood. Too well. "He never said it straight out, but my Papa blamed himself for not letting me go with Mordecai to Palestine."

Estie backed away and wiped her eyes.

"I knew he blamed himself, and I wanted to say 'Papa, it wasn't your fault!' It wasn't. Even if he'd said I could go, I probably would have been too scared."

"That's for sure."

"But I never told him. And I'm tortured with guilt because my Papa – whom I loved so much – went to his death thinking he'd caused mine and that I blamed him for it."

Estie sighed.

Anna couldn't bring herself to tell Estie about her other horrible guilt, already causing nightmares. That she could have returned earlier from Zamosc and saved her family. If only she'd accepted the ride offered by that nice doctor. She had told no one except Mordecai – a guy she no longer even knew – in a letter she wrote and threw away.

"When I return to the ghetto," Anna said, "I'll talk to your parents and explain. They're too Jewish looking to survive alone on the Aryan side, but I'll see if I can get them into hiding with that woman I'll check out."

"Oh my God, Anna, you're an angel of life! Thank you!"

"I'll do my best," Anna said solemnly. "You don't need to thank me. I'd do anything for them and for you." She paused and smiled. "I remember when I met your mother. We were in eighth grade, and you invited me over. She fed me so many cookies I almost exploded."

Estie laughed. "I remember. She kept saying how skinny you were... We've been friends a long, long time. Do you think we'll ever see each other again?"

"Probably not. It depends–"

"On which body part I ask?" Estie grinned. "Your brain says the Germans will shoot me in the forest and you'll be executed by firing squad, but your heart says–"

"You're right about my heart. It says let's hope and believe we'll see each other again."

"I'm not afraid to die. I'm really not," Estie said. "As long as it's not a meaningless death like the thousands rounded up and sent away. I want to die with a gun in my hand."

Anna nodded. "None of us *fear death itself, but we all dread the possibility of falling into the hands of the authorities for some trifling matter unrelated to the movement's work. We want to die with dignity, to go down fighting, not die a trivial death.* I pray I won't get caught and tossed onto a train to Belzec. Let them shoot me running free. Of that, I'm not afraid."

"Yeah," Estie said, "except one thing. I admit I feel sorry for myself for missing out on life. For God's sake, we're only twenty-one years old! All the things I never did and will never do."

Anna placed her hand on Estie's shoulder.

"I have a question that sounds silly and stupid but is very important to me," Estie said. "Please tell the truth, like a best friend should. If we had led normal lives, with no war, would I have found a boy who loved me? Or am I too plain? Would I have gotten married? And had children? I know it's foolish to think about–"

"Are you kidding? Of course you would have! The boys who wanted to talk to you but were too shy–"

"What boys?"

Anna blinked so that she wouldn't cry. "Here's what would have happened. Listen. A young man, cute and with a nice smile and a big heart, would have said to himself one day, 'I want to find the most beautiful, caring, smart, kindhearted girl in the world.' And God would have taken him by the hand and said, 'Well the top choice is Anna, but she's in Palestine and, anyway, she's taken, so you need to settle for the second-best girl in the whole world, but she IS the best choice in all of Europe. Her name is Estie.' And the guy would have asked, 'Does she make a good babka?' And God would have said, 'A good babka? No – she makes a great babka!'

"And you would have fallen in love with him, and gotten married, and I would have laughed and danced at your wedding, and you would have had lots and lots of children–"

"I always wanted four."

"That's how many you would have had! I would have laughed and cried tears of joy at your sons' brisses, and I would have laughed and danced and cried with you at your daughters' weddings, and you would have had too many grandchildren to count."

"Thank you, Anna."

"You don't need to thank me. I'm just saying what would have happened."

Somehow, Anna grinned instead of bursting into tears.

That night
Szymon

He stuffed the end of a Sten submachine gun in his belt, slipped on a dark-gray overcoat and left the house. The cold weather made his overcoat inconspicuous. A nice omen. He'd spent all day running the attack plan over in his head; he was worried, scared, and ready.

Szymon was now twenty-two years old. So much had changed the past few years. Before the war, he was set on becoming a priest, a man of compassion and peace. In half an hour, he'd lead a mission to kill as many human beings as possible. Hopefully, unarmed human beings to increase the chance that his and the Jewish fighters would escape. Was it murder to kill unarmed men? Not if they fought for evil, Szymon believed. And Germany was truly evil.

Evil. Before the war, that word had entered Szymon's mind only when he studied the Bible or discussed abstract thoughts. The Nazis had made it very real. He liked to think he'd have joined the resistance even if they hadn't murdered his parents. Because "religious" didn't mean only helping the weak. It also meant opposing evil.

Szymon still had hope for the distant future, after Poland was free of the Germans, but feared he might never see it. He could be dead within the hour.

He crossed Polna Street and headed toward the Polna Bar. This was a nice commercial area. The buildings, each butted against the next, were four or five stories tall with light blue, pink, yellow, or beige veneers. As Szymon passed a jewelry store, his cousin Filip, a member of his cell, pivoted from the window and walked with him.

The bar was about twenty yards ahead, on their left. It occupied the bottom floor of an ornate stone building with a huge arched doorway and three large windows, each window separated by stonework and topped with glass arches that matched the arch above the doorway. Above the center arched window was a nice balcony for the space above. The name "Polna Bar" was written on each window and on the door.

At 6:58 p.m., Szymon and Filip entered the bar. Szymon had scoped it out weeks before and prepared the diagram that Benec showed his cell. Szymon and Filip walked past a table of six men wearing dark suits, speaking German. Possibly Gestapo. Prime targets, Szymon thought. Beyond that table a young man stood and waved Szymon and Filip over. They exchanged hugs and kisses on the cheek and sat down.

Szymon glanced around the bar and saw uniformed German officers at several tables. Across the bar, Szymon saw Benec sitting with a young man whom Szymon assumed was part of Benec's cell. To Benec's left, several yards away, was a table of armed German soldiers. They were sitting where Szymon had expected. He saw a baby-faced, Jewish-looking, young man enter the bar and walk toward Benec.

Szymon glanced at his watch. 6:59. The attack would begin when Benec's group took out the armed soldiers with hand grenades.

•••

SCHMIDT

Heinrich Schmidt had been sitting with his men in the Polna Bar for about an hour. No alcohol yet, that would come later. Too bad Beck wasn't here. The minor excitement that Schmidt expected would be good for the paper-pusher Beck. But he was working late coordinating the upcoming Jew aktion.

Schmidt saw two young Polish men across the bar and then watched two others enter, walk past his table and join a man at a table behind his. Which group was Polish resistance? He may torture every Pole in here to learn who belonged to Polish resistance and who happened to pick the wrong night to visit a bar.

Schmidt sipped his water and noticed a young man standing near the bathroom. He might be waiting his turn at the toilet, Schmidt thought. He then saw two young guys enter the bar, but instead of heading to a table, they separated. One walked to the far side of the bar, where he stood motionless, and the other stayed near the front, where he disappeared behind a column. Both looked Polish. Odd, so many young Poles here tonight. Schmidt noticed a boy – Jew looking with both hands in his pockets – walking on the other side of the bar. Schmidt turned his head to the three Poles sitting behind him; the tall one still wore his overcoat, though seated, and was reaching inside his coat while looking across the bar.

Schmidt grabbed the pistol in his pocket and bolted from his chair.

•••

REUVEN

When Szymon had sat down, Benec gave Reuven the signal to throw the hand grenades at the armed German soldiers sitting near the back of the bar. Reuven dropped his hands into the pockets of his baggy pants, glanced at the column he'd run behind after throwing the grenades, and walked toward their table. Focused and determined.

He was about to pull the grenades from his pockets when a smiling, young Polish waitress approached the soldiers to take a drink order. Reuven froze. He was eager to kill Germans, and even their Polish girlfriends. But this waitress just worked here. She was innocent. He stood, watching, several steps from the soldiers' table.

The German ordering drinks laughed, waved his hand from right to left and said, "Look at this wonderful place where you work, and we must spend our days on the battlefield!" His eyes swept the bar, and he noticed Reuven standing motionless a few yards away. The soldier's smile disappeared when he locked eyes with Reuven.

•••

Szymon

Schmidt wheeled around and shot Filip in the chest. Szymon sprayed his submachine gun while pulling it from his belt in an arc directed at Schmidt, who ducked and dove onto the floor with the other Gestapo agents barely ten feet from Szymon. Horrible shrieks and panic.

Benec yelled, "Reuven! Now! Now!" and fired his pistol at the German soldiers Reuven should have eliminated with grenades. One of them shot Benec in the hip, dropping him to the floor. Terrified bartenders and waitresses ran screaming or hid with Germans behind tables as fighters and soldiers opened fire at each other. The deafening pop-pop-pop in his ears, Reuven's mind remained frozen on the Polish waitress, crouching petrified behind the soldiers. After an eternity of seconds, he pulled the grenades from his pockets, yanked the pins, threw the grenades at the table, and dove headfirst behind a column.

The Germans had killed three resistance fighters. Four other fighters exchanged fatal shots with Gestapo agents at point-blank range. The grenades exploded, with ear shattering blasts, killing the soldiers and the Polish waitress. Smoke, wails and groans filled the bar. Benec shot two SS officers hiding under a table, and Szymon killed a Gestapo man near him.

"Let's go! Let's go!" Szymon hollered, but of the fighters, only Benec and Reuven remained alive. Reuven rushed with Szymon toward the door, and Benec, who'd been shot in the hip, hobbled behind them. Schmidt had turned a marble-topped table on its side about twenty steps away, and using it as cover, shot at them, striking

Benec twice in the back. He staggered and collapsed to the floor; Reuven yelled, "Benec!" and lunged toward his dying brother. Szymon grabbed Reuven and pulled him behind a column near the entrance.

They crouched behind the column, and Szymon said, "We need–"

Szymon was knocked flat on his face by a huge, unarmed German soldier who had leapt from behind and pinned Szymon to the floor with Szymon's weapon beneath him. The soldier, lying full length on Szymon – whose arms were trapped under his body – grasped Szymon's throat from behind and started strangling him. Szymon, heart pounding and unable to breathe, tried with all his strength to break free, but couldn't. The German tightened his grip. Szymon's legs flailed helplessly.

Reuven frantically pulled the last grenade from his pocket and, using it as a rock, repeatedly bashed the German's head. Szymon crawled free and shot the soldier.

"Thanks – we need to go!" Szymon gasped. "Police will be here soon!"

"You go," Reuven said. "I'm getting the one who killed my brother." He pointed to where Schmidt hid behind an overturned table. "Then I'll go."

"OK. Come straight to Lesna Street, around the corner. A quick right, then left and left again – a truck – but they can't wait long."

Reuven nodded and, still holding the grenade, dashed across the bar toward Schmidt. Szymon fired multiple shots at Schmidt, forcing him to stay hidden behind the table, and rushed out the door. Reuven pulled the pin on his grenade, held the grenade until the last moment, threw it over Schmidt's table and dove behind a column. The grenade exploded inches above Schmidt's head, decapitating him.

His ears ringing badly, Reuven ran outside. Szymon was gone.

•••

REUVEN

Reuven was disoriented. Which direction was Lesna Street, where the AK truck was waiting, and did Szymon say to go right or left? Reuven turned left and hurried down the brightly lit sidewalk on Polna Street. No police or soldiers yet, but people flooded past him toward the bar; any of them might notice Reuven's curly, dark hair, his Jewish nose, and grab him until police arrived. He forced himself to walk, not run. Looking down, down, fearing eye contact.

Reuven thought someone called his name. He whipped around

and quickly scoured the people rushing by, recognizing no one. He paused. If anyone was calling him, the crowd noise drowned them out. He reached the corner, didn't recognize the cross street, and continued to the next intersection. Not Lesna.

Several minutes had passed – no way the truck would still be waiting even if he found the right place. Reuven realized he was alone. Totally alone, surrounded by Poles, any of whom might shout, "Get the Jew!" And he felt watched – too many streetlights and people on Polna. After another block, he turned into a dark, empty alley that smelled of urine. From behind, he heard sirens. He ran down the alley, away from the wailing and echoing sounds, but didn't know where it led.

The sirens soon blared from all directions, growing louder, coming closer. From the alley Reuven turned down another street, saw more people, and dashed into another alley. Sirens piercing the night, he crouched near a wall to think, head pounding, trying to catch his breath. The Gestapo will torture him. He checked his pockets; no weapon, even to kill himself.

Reuven's mind raced – he might hide inside a building. He ran to a back door and tried turning the knob. Locked. He rushed to another door. Also locked. He looked up. Through the darkness, he saw third floor apartments above the businesses. He could climb a fire escape, knock on a door, and plead for help. He might find a Polish patriot. But they may not open the door. Or they might hate Jews and call the police. He heard the sirens blaring closer.

He had no idea how to get to the apartment where Irina waited. He should go to the ghetto. Once there, he could climb the wall. He's about three miles away, but which direction?

He heard yelling, in German, from his left. He ran to the right, eyes wide, down the alley. His feet pounded the pavement, loud to his ears. He reached another street, turned left. No soldiers or police and few people. He crossed the street, walked a block, and sprinted into another alley, very long. With each step, his fear increased. He suddenly stopped – flashlights shining in front of him at the far end of the long alley. Slowly coming his way. He turned. From the street behind him, barking German voices. Voices of torture and death. Getting louder.

Trapped. Like a cornered animal.

Panic.

Filled with terror, he rushed in the darkness to a fire escape, tripped, and fell. But the Germans didn't hear. If he scampered up the fire stairs, and the people were good… Next to the fire escape was a large, metal garbage bin. He removed the lid, stuffed himself inside and placed the lid back on top. The putrid odor of rotting food made him gag.

A German voice yelled, and a more distant voice responded. Reuven remained completely still. He heard the soldiers come closer and thought his pounding heart might burst. He held his breath, overwhelmed with fear. Helpless.

Slowly, very slowly, the voices grew fainter and faded into the distance.

He heard the wind whistling down the alley. Then quiet. Petrified and contorted in the bin, he decided to stay the night.

Wednesday October 21, 1942
Reuven

Invisible hands posted leaflets throughout Aryan Krasau just after midnight.

POLISH RESISTANCE HAS STRUCK A MIGHTY BLOW!
THE BEASTS COWERED AT THE POLNA BAR.
THE MASTER RACE BLEEDS.
OUR FIRST STEP TO FREEDOM.
POLISH PATRIOTS – JOIN US!

•••

Reuven opened his eyes to total darkness. The stench and sharp pain in his back reminded him that he was crumpled in a tall garbage bin somewhere on the Aryan side. His back, arms, legs – his entire body – were aching. A few minutes of intermittent sleep. Scared and increasingly uncomfortable, had he been in here two hours or six? At some point, starving for air, he'd lifted the lid, saw darkness, closed it, and later fell asleep. For fifteen minutes? Or two hours?

Not wanting to crawl out in daylight, Reuven quietly raised the lid, saw that it was still night, stood upright with the lid in his hand, and suddenly heard movement behind him. Whirling around, he saw a snarling, ferocious dog held on a leash by its German master! Reuven tried to leap from the can, but it crashed onto the pavement with him half inside. Terrified, he scrambled to his feet and started to run, expecting the dog's sharp teeth to pierce his neck or thigh. He turned his head and saw a stray dog backing away. No leash and no soldier.

He sighed and shook his head. He was making himself crazy. He wiped moldy vegetables from his legs, returned to the garbage bin, swallowed a piece of rotten potato, walked down the alley and turned onto a dark street. He didn't recognize the name and still didn't know which direction to the ghetto. But the street was empty. He walked a block, didn't recognize the next street, ducked into another alley, sat with his legs crossed against a wall, rested his face in his hands and waited. Perhaps an hour. Or two.

At sunrise, Reuven left the alley; based on the sun, he walked east down a commercial street that he hoped led toward the ghetto. Block after block, eyes down. On and on he walked; hungry, thirsty and exhausted, the passing time brought more people onto the sidewalks and traffic on the streets. All watching, scrutinizing him, he was sure. He finally saw a sign that sounded familiar. Bogadowa Street. Bogadowa Street? Regina. The person Irina had said might help.

He made his way down Bogadowa Street to number 24 and saw a dark-haired woman standing in the doorway. Could that be her? Was he so lucky that his rescuer stood only yards away?

The woman smiled and walked to him. Reuven didn't notice a homeless man rifling through garbage across the street. Or the gusting wind or that the sky had turned from blue to gray.

"You look like you could use some help," Regina said. "You're Jewish?"

Reuven shrugged. Suddenly self-conscious of his filthy, smelly clothes, he stepped back as Regina looked him over. Like so many of them, his pants were too big, shoes scuffed and probably tattooed with holes on the soles. Too bad, because he's such a cute kid with his dimpled cheeks and tantalizing eyes. Would be handsome cleaned up, in another world.

She shifted her purse from her left hand to her right, and the homeless guy walked into a building. "A friend of mine will be here soon," Regina said. "He'll take you where it's safe. And clean. Lots to eat and drink."

"OK – wait – what's your name?"

"Regina."

Reuven felt a wave of relief sweep over him. He'd found someone he could trust. "I want to get to the ghetto, but I'm lost."

"You must be exhausted. The ghetto is only two blocks away, but you can't go there now. German soldiers, Ukrainians, police all over the place. Maybe starting another aktion." With the deportations to Belzec, more Jews had been escaping the ghetto, but lacking food, roamed the streets or returned to the ghetto. It had made for increased business for Peter and Regina on Bogadowa Street.

She and Reuven watched together as a Jewish women's labor group walked by. Regina took his hand and gently pulled him to the doorway. Smiling, she said, "Stay here a few minutes, and I'll watch for my friend."

Reuven obeyed. People walked by but didn't notice him, and Reuven thanked God for finding Regina. Minutes later, Regina said, "Here comes my friend. He'll help you."

Peter, no longer dressed as a homeless guy, approached them;

Regina waved and smiled. "Hello, this Jewish boy could use your help, and I said you have a good place to stay a day or two. His name is..."

"Reuven," Reuven said.

Peter nodded, turned and gestured for Reuven to follow him. "Let's go."

Reuven nervously ran a hand through his hair. "Aren't you coming too?" he pleaded to Regina.

She squeezed his hand with both of hers and said reassuringly, "No – but don't worry. You can trust him."

"Come on, it's this way." Peter started walking and Reuven went with him. Still nervous because of his Jewish looks, Reuven asked, "Is it OK to walk out here? Is the place close?"

"Yep," Peter grunted. The kid looked vaguely familiar, he thought. But so many Jews looked alike.

Peter had no interest in talking, and Reuven thought he should keep quiet, so they walked silently as pedestrians and cars passed by. They reached a corner, waited, crossed the street and kept walking. Two more blocks in complete silence. Reuven thought this big man looked familiar but didn't know why. The only non-Jews he ever saw were police and soldiers.

At the next corner, Peter pointed to his left, and Reuven turned with him. Two policemen were coming toward them on the sidewalk. Reuven's heart pounded; should he run before they grab him? He glanced at Peter's face and saw complete calm. Reuven looked down, and they and the policemen passed each other.

Peter was thinking this had to be his easiest catch in a while. One more block and he'd drop the kid at the jail. The boy may just walk right in there with him. Peter was ready for something easy, for a change. Never-ending hassles as a cop, and though he carefully hid the anti-Nazi work he did for Polish resistance, he knew bad luck could land him in a Gestapo torture cell.

They reached the corner and waited for a streetcar to pass. Reuven looked around and said quietly, "I see some police. Is it safe here?"

"Take it from someone who knows, kid, it's safe."

Reuven looked at Peter's face and gasped. "I thought I knew you! You used to watch me play football. You said I'd make it to the Olympics."

Peter studied Reuven's face. "You're..."

"I'm Reuven, but you told me to say my name was Roman, and I took your advice."

Peter paused and then remembered. Reuven had reminded Peter of himself, how he once played. "You were a great player – I remember you well! You were quick and smart. That was forever ago." Peter shook his head. He didn't want to turn in this kid. "Let's go a different way." Peter did an about-face and said, "Come on," nudging Reuven, who turned around with him; they took three steps and bumped into two uniformed Germans walking toward them. Peter knew them – they worked at the jail, and he sometimes handed them Jews for "processing."

"I–" Peter started.

"Good timing," one German said. "We'll take him; no need for you to come in. And we'll do the paperwork for you."

Dammit, Peter thought. "Great, thanks."

One German grabbed Reuven's right arm and the other his left, and they dragged him toward the jail. With bulging eyes, in shocked terror, Reuven managed a glance over his shoulder as Peter strolled away.

THURSDAY OCTOBER 22, 1942
ANNA

Wearing a dark coat on this cloudy, cold morning, Anna strolled – head up – through the open front doors of the central Krasau train station. The bench she and Mordecai had sat on when he left four years earlier was outside, in back.

Inside, pigeons loudly cooed from the rafters and swooped down to search the concrete floor for crumbs – near patrolling German soldiers and Polish police. As other travelers streamed by, Anna headed to a ticket counter, bought a ticket to the town of Wadowice, and saw that the train was an hour late. Fearful of train stations, she decided to go for a walk and come back in time for the train. Too many police, soldiers, and prying eyes of hidden Jew hunters.

The mission itself didn't worry Anna. She was taking money to Leah's cousin, named Rachel, who was hiding with her baby on the outskirts of Wadowice. Anna would return on the afternoon train.

Rachel was staying with her father's Polish friend. The saintly man didn't ask for help, but Rachel's father, still alive in the Krasau ghetto, asked Leah – who asked Anna – to bring all his money, more than a thousand zlotys, to his daughter. Too risky to put in her purse or an easily searched pocket, Anna had sewn the money into her garter belt.

Anna left the station and made her way on the busy sidewalk toward a nearby park.

"Read about the terrorist attack!" hollered a young newspaper vendor walking slowly near her. He held a paper close to his face, so that people could see the headline, and cradled a bundle in his other arm.

Anna read the headline, and her eyes widened momentarily. She bought a paper and began to read. "Eight terrorists were killed in their cowardly attack Tuesday night on the Polna Bar, where they murdered innocent Polish citizens." Anna glanced at a photo showing Levi's contorted, dead body.

Oh God! Levi was such a sweet, funny, loveable boy.

Stifling her emotions and folding the paper under her arm, Anna again headed toward the park. But she was suddenly worried about Irina – were Benec and Reuven also killed? Was Irina sitting alone in the apartment, mourning Reuven?

Should she go there now, and travel to Wadowice tomorrow? But the man is expecting her today. And she has her ticket. What if—

"Anna! Anna!" A woman's voice enthusiastically calling from behind.

Anna kept walking.

"Anna!" A hand on her shoulder. Anna turned. The smiling face of a woman about her age. Straight brown hair, a bit taller than Anna, casually dressed. Didn't look Jewish.

"It's me, Karolina, from seventh grade," the woman cheerfully said. "Or was it eighth grade? We had a class together in–"

"Sorry," Anna smiled. "I'm not ... Anna. My name is Helena." Anna did remember the girl. They weren't friends, and Anna wasn't sure they ever shared a class.

Karolina said, "sheyn veter" – "nice weather" – in Jewish.

"What?" Anna maintained a calm exterior, but her heart suddenly raced. There was no good reason for Karolina to speak Jewish to her.

"I said sheyn veter, Anna."

Anna looked annoyed. "Sorry, I don't speak German, and I told you – my name's not Anna."

"I'm really good with faces," Karolina said firmly. "I know who you are. You're pretending because you're Jewish. That's OK. I won't tell anyone."

"I'm not a Jew, and I don't like you accusing me of being one!" Anna turned to leave, but Karolina lightly clutched her arm.

"I understand – you're scared," Karolina said calmly. "I'd be scared too if I were a Jew." Karolina's eyes looked Anna over, head to toe. "But you look like you're doing well. Nice coat, nice shoes. I'm not doing as good. If you give me three hundred zlotys, I'll leave you alone."

Her mind spinning, Anna wanted to get rid of Karolina but not make her so mad that she'd call the police. "Listen," Anna gently said, "I don't know you, but if you need money, I could give you twenty zlotys." Anna unlatched her small brown purse.

Karolina's face turned cold, and she spat. "Twenty zlotys! I'm not a beggar, Jew bitch! If you don't have it on you, take me to your apartment and get me three hundred zlotys from your Jew stash. Or I'll turn you in!" She pointed behind Anna.

Anna glanced over her shoulder and saw an old Polish policeman walking their way. She dropped the newspaper, turned back to Karolina and screamed, "Get away from me!"

The policeman reached them, and Karolina said, "Arrest her! She's a Jew."

Anna slapped Karolina's face. "How dare you!" Anna pivoted to the policeman. "We can't even catch a train without lunatics accosting us!"

"Officer Zaborski, take my word for it," Karolina said. "Her name is Anna Allowitz." Anna's heart dropped when Karolina said the officer's name; they knew each other.

"I don't know if she's insane or a nice person who's just wrong," Anna said. "She says she knew me in seventh grade – she's confusing me with someone named Anna. My name is Helena Kowalska. Want to see my ID? My papers?"

Without waiting for a response, Anna opened her purse and handed her documents to the policeman. He looked them over.

"Her papers are in good order," he said to Karolina.

"I'm no idiot. She went to my school. We had a nickname for her and her fat, dark-haired Jewish friend, Esther. The two Jews, chocolate and vanilla, because this one has light hair. Take her to the Germans."

"Can I please have my papers back?" Anna said firmly. "I have a train to catch."

The policeman sighed. "No. Come with me." He gripped Anna's arm and led her toward the station. Karolina followed them.

"You don't need to hold me," Anna said. "I'm not a criminal. And I'd better not miss my train. It leaves in about forty minutes."

"If your story pans out, the Germans will let you go, and hopefully you'll make your train." He led her into the crowded station, past where she'd bought her ticket minutes earlier, and opened an inconspicuous door near the restrooms. They walked down a hall and into an office where two dark-suited, middle-aged German men were sitting at their desks. The police officer explained the situation to the bored-looking Germans and gave them Anna's papers.

One of the Germans glanced at Anna's ID and turned to Karolina. "Karolina, you sure she's a Jew?"

"Yeah. Positive. We went to school together."

"That's not true, sir" Anna said. "She says–"

"Shut up!" the German barked. His expression turned cruel. "Take her to be searched."

The other German roughly grabbed Anna's arm, led her down the hall and into a small, white-walled, windowless room with one chair and a small, oval table next to it.

"Wait here," he commanded and closed the door.

Minutes passed.

Anna paced, trying to remain calm. Germans are thorough. If they carefully search her...

The door opened, and Karolina ducked inside. Red-faced, she talked quickly and quietly. "Listen, I didn't mean to get you in serious trouble. I lost my temper! This door is unlocked. When I leave, count to ten, open it, turn right and then a quick right again and you'll be gone. Don't worry – it'll work. I'll be talking to the guys in their office."

Karolina turned to go.

"Thank you!" Anna whispered, hopeful but not fully trusting.

Karolina looked back. "You're welcome." She sheepishly glanced down and whispered, "I was serious out there about needing money, so if you have any to spare, I'd really appreciate it."

Anna opened her purse, which had eighty zlotys in it. She paused, took out fifty, and handed them to Karolina.

"Thanks." Karolina fished her fingers in Anna's open purse – still in Anna's hands – and grabbed the other thirty zlotys. "Can I have these too?"

Anna shrugged, and Karolina stuffed them in her pocket.

"Count to ten," Karolina said, and she quickly left.

Anna took two deep breaths, reminded herself to walk confidently, counted five more seconds and reached for the doorknob.

Locked.

Her hands trembled.

•••

A long time went by; Anna paced and finally sat in the chair.

The door opened, and she rose. In walked a tall, huge German policewoman with a scowling, pockmarked, blubbery face. Looked to Anna like an enormous witch in a dark uniform.

The policewoman waddled to the chair and sat. Anna stood silently in front of her. "Give me your purse," the woman muttered. She dumped its contents onto the small table, quickly sifted through them, took a knife from her pocket, cut open the insides of the purse and tossed it on the floor.

"Your coat."

"Excuse me?"

"Give me your coat!" she commanded.

Seated in the wooden chair, too small for her, the policewoman checked each pocket and started cutting open the seams in Anna's coat. Anna stood watching, sweating.

"You're destroying my only coat!" Anna said. "It's one thing to search me, but please don't destroy my clothes."

The policewoman grunted, stood, grabbed Anna's shoulders, pushed her backwards until they reached the wall, and pounded her fists into Anna's face. Open-mouthed, Anna bit her tongue when a fist hit her jaw. Only then did Anna realize she'd been screaming. The policewoman hit Anna again, knocking her to the floor. "Don't talk! Understand?"

Dazed, bleeding and in terrific pain, Anna lay sprawled on the floor, her neck and head bent against the wall. The German viciously kicked her in the stomach, almost flipping her over.

"Understand?"

Anna tried to answer, but no sound left her mouth.

The policewoman grabbed Anna, shrieking, by the hair, jerked her to her feet and shoved her against the wall. Pressing her face against Anna's, she growled, "Do you understand?"

"Yes," Anna managed, almost gagging on the foul-smelling breath.

The policewoman returned to the chair, finished cutting open Anna's coat, and threw what was left of it on top of the purse. "Come here!"

Anna staggered to her. The woman grabbed Anna's waist, pulled her close and said, "Don't move!"

Anna obeyed.

She stood meekly as the witch began cutting away, opening the seams in her blouse, nicking her skin. First the seams on her left side, then her right, her collar. Too terrified to speak, Anna tried to communicate by using her pathetic eyes and mouth, hoping to evoke pity, to reach something human.

Nothing.

The woman finished with the blouse and cut open the seams in Anna's skirt, leaving her clothes in tatters. She then grabbed Anna's naked thigh with a rough, sweaty hand; using the other hand she cut the seams of Anna's garter belt. The policewoman's scowl became a smirk, and she pulled out the hidden cash.

Anna looked down, despondent. The woman slapped her hard with an open palm and left the room. Anna buried her face in her hands.

The door soon opened, and the two German men entered. One was holding the money. "You're just a nice Polish girl, huh?"

"Sir, just because I try to keep my money safe–"

She stopped when the German waved one of the zloty bills, on which something in Jewish was handwritten in blue ink. He held it in front of her eyes. A note from Rachel's father to Rachel.

"Anna's hugs are from me. Stay safe."

The Same day
Reuven

Reuven sat trapped in the somber, cramped, windowless freight car as it rumbled to Belzec. Strangers pressing on all sides, he tried to block out the stink of the shared bucket and the loud clatter of wheels, crying babies and fussing parents. To figure out the impossible – how to save himself. He and three others had struggled to remove a slat of the car's wooden siding so they could jump from the moving train. But lacking tools, they failed.

The Germans had kept Reuven in jail overnight, tossed him with other forlorn Jews into the back of a truck, and driven them to the ghetto's train collection point. Four hours later, he was on this train. In the past two days, he'd eaten only a sliver of rotten potato and a crust of bread a kind woman gave him.

A few of his fellow passengers argued that everything would be fine. No one could be so deranged to take this car full of vibrant adults, lively children, and cute little babies, and snuff out their lives. Either the gas chambers were horrible fiction, or they'd be saved by a derailment or nice guards or an inexplicable change of fortune.

But most knew their fate. *They were images of dread and horror. Some tore their hair, some flung themselves about in despair, and some cursed with all their strength.* A young mom and dad, sitting next to Reuven against the side of the car, were each holding a little boy on their lap. The mom, her eyes wide with fear, wailing, "Where is God? Where is God?" and repeatedly squeezing and kissing her child. The dad, clutching his little boy, stared blankly into space. The boy asked, "Daddy, does it hurt to die?"

A middle-aged, bearded Hasidic man in a long black coat stood near the woman. "God controls all, and all is for good. We can't know what is in God's mind, but there is purpose and meaning, no matter what happens. And God will punish the murderers."

An old man answered. "God is crying. He's crying with us."

A woman, perhaps the young mom's sister, smirked, but the old man's wife nodded. "That means we're not alone."

Reuven tried to ignore the conversations and focus on his job. To escape. But he thought of nothing. After a while, one of the other guys who had tried to knock out the siding shoved his way to Reuven and sat. He was about Reuven's age, husky and pimple faced. "I've been thinking. We have only one chance. To hide in the train. When it leaves Belzec, we'll hop off."

"How can we hide in–"

"Not inside the car. Under it. We'll need to hold on tight, but we can do it. When we get to Belzec, if no one is watching you, drop down, roll under the car, and find something to climb or hold onto."

Reuven thought about it. "OK."

"And–" the guy noticed that the toddler sitting next to Reuven on his despondent mother's lap was staring at him. The guy said, "Hi!" filled his cheeks with air, stuck his thumbs into them and waved like a clown with his fingers. The little boy giggled and stuck a thumb into his mouth.

The guy turned back to Reuven. "But tell me if you have a better idea."

Reuven nodded, could think of nothing else, rested his head against the vibrating wall, and satisfied that he at least had a plan, drifted off to sleep. He awoke to the sound of gunfire. "We slowed – into a station, I guess," his new friend said, "and I heard Germans yelling and shooting. Listen!" The boy pointed to his left, and Reuven heard German voices shouting, followed by more gunshots. "Someone in another car must have broken out and jumped when the train slowed." The boy shrugged.

The shooting ceased, the train picked up speed and Reuven again leaned his head against the side of the car.

Three hours later, the train slowed to a stop, the doors slid open, and Germans yelled, "Out! Out! Leave your luggage!" The Jews roused themselves, stumbled over each other and climbed down. Reuven and the boy – he didn't think to ask his name – hopped down together, looked around, dropped to the ground, and rolled under the freight car. Each quickly scrambled atop horizontal metal bars near the wheels.

Heart pounding and sweat beading on his face, Reuven was terrified they'd been seen. But time passed. He could see nothing from his hiding place under the car, but he listened as the people were led away, and he heard a man's voice, in the distance, as if making a short speech. Then silence as he lay motionless under the still train. Reuven's thoughts raced. He's dead if the Germans look under here. It's quiet; maybe the guards all left with the Jews. Should he run away? Are other guards nearby? Should he stay – why would the Germans check under here? He should be OK – please God!

He heard footsteps and men talking. He shut his eyes and held his breath, terrified that he might make a sound that would alert the Germans. "Dear God, please get us out of here," his lips silently begged. He soon realized the men were speaking Jewish. It sounded like they were climbing into the cars and throwing bags and luggage onto the ground. He and the other boy didn't move, for perhaps twenty minutes, while the work crew emptied the cars. Then, again, quiet.

He waited silently, trying to control his anxious breathing, until finally the engine roared, and the train very slowly began to pull out. "Dear God, thank you," Reuven silently prayed. He craned his neck and stared; as the train slowly moved, he could see the ground passing beneath the car for several feet ahead. For a horrifying moment, his heart pounded desperately in his chest when he thought he glimpsed a soldier's boot and heard voices. But nothing, and the train kept slowly moving.

Flecks of dirt entered Reuven's eyes, which began to water. Legs appeared on each side of the tracks: uniforms and army boots. He heard German voices and reflexively jerked and clenched his teeth. *The men were shining flashlights under the wheels to see whether anyone was hiding beneath the cars.* Reuven's stomach churned in terror and his legs trembled. Panicked, he bit his cheek and tasted blood when a *German shouted "Halt!"*

The train stopped.

A light was shining a few feet from Reuven, and his friend *got a bullet before he could crawl out from under the car.* Reuven *was able to jump out and started running quick as lightning.* The Germans shot at him but missed; the future star of Poland's Olympic football team darted this way and that with blinding speed, desperately trying to escape. But there were too many soldiers and nowhere to go. A German grabbed him.

"I'm a great worker! I–"

The German started hitting his head as hard as he could with his rubber truncheon until he collapsed. Then a Ukrainian came up, turned his rifle upside down and with great force, as if chopping wood, hit Reuven *in the head with the rifle butt. Finally, they put a bullet in him. Then, at last, they left him alone. The train rolled out.*

THAT NIGHT
JOZEF

Jozef closed the door and left the apartment where sixteen-year-old Irina had been waiting for Reuven and his group to return. Jozef had held her and delivered the horrible news: that Reuven had been sent to Belzec, and Anna had been arrested.

Jozef said he'd talked to Szymon, whose contact at the jail tried early this morning to bribe a guard to free Reuven. The jailer refused but did allow Szymon's man to talk to him. Reuven wasn't tortured because the Germans didn't know he'd attacked the bar. They caught him as a Jew unlawfully outside the ghetto. Reuven said the woman on Bogadowa Street betrayed him. "Szymon will deal with her," Jozef had said.

Szymon later went to the jail himself to try to save Reuven and learned that he'd been sent to Belzec. When Szymon was leaving the jail, he saw a German bringing in Anna, her eyes down, face badly bruised. He didn't know anything more about her.

Jozef had been shocked at how calmly Irina initially took the news. Only after he'd finished talking did she lose control. "Oh my God!" Irina had shrieked. "I told Reuven to go to Bogadowa Street! Oh my God, I killed Reuven! And Anna!" Irina had cried and couldn't stop.

Jozef had hugged and tried to console her. He said Leah wanted so badly to hold her but couldn't risk traveling. Jozef had begged Irina to come to his group's apartment and talk with Leah and everyone else, or only with Leah, whatever Irina wanted. But she refused. He said this showed how important it was for her to go live with a Polish family, as Anna wanted.

Jozef hugged her and talked and hugged her more. She screamed and cried. He looked at her forged papers to make sure they were in order in case someone heard the screaming and questioned her.

She was still wailing when he left.

Friday October 23, 1942
Itzhak

Itzhak awoke at 1:15 in the morning, dressed and zipped shut the small pack he would place on his back and carry through the sewers. A wry smile crossed his face with the realization that the pack contained almost all his valuables: two shirts, underwear, socks, photographs of his parents and grandparents, and the certificate Anna had made for him.

His coat pockets held the rest. A flashlight, handwritten map of the sewers, and a loaded revolver. Itzhak had stuffed in a milk can his journal of Jewish life under the Nazis, sealed the can and buried it behind the apartment building.

He would soon say his final goodbye to his parents. As a special favor to his old friend, Szymon had arranged a Polish resistance safe house for Itzhak's parents, and Itzhak had planned to leave with them yesterday. But his mother refused to enter the sewers. Itzhak had pleaded, explaining that bribing guards at the gates wouldn't work because the Germans had added new soldiers; that the sewers, through which Zakkai teens had recently escaped, were the only choice; that a Belzec gas chamber was her alternative.

But his mother had a phobia of rats and snakes. She couldn't do it. As for the gas chambers, she believed, but then she didn't. Itzhak's father wouldn't abandon her, so Itzhak spent all day with them, reminiscing, delaying his exit by a day. Itzhak had then handed his father two cyanide capsules that a friendly Polish pharmacist had given the resistance.

His father had nodded thoughtfully and said thanks. Itzhak wondered if humanity could sink any lower. Death by cyanide was the antidote, for two healthy people in their forties, to avoid gas chambers built for them and millions of others. While the average person in half the civilized world worried about which blouse to wear and if their favorite sports team would win.

But Itzhak was not one to moan. He had never asked, "Why me!" when others could run and he couldn't, when he sat on the sidelines literally and emotionally. And he didn't join now with those Jews crying, "Why us!" Life or fate or simple bad luck places you in certain situations, and you must deal with them, however horrible they are.

He didn't dwell on death though it surrounded him. But Itzhak did look back on his life, which might end today. He had tried hard to educate himself on interesting subjects and felt satisfied with his efforts. He wished he'd made more friends, but realized he was partially at fault. And he wished he'd had a girlfriend. Whether he might have succeeded in that realm if he'd done something different, he didn't know. Some things you can't learn from books.

He had finally, in the hell-hole life under the Nazis, developed a crush and maybe even fallen in love – with Anna, that intriguing spark of life that flitted in and out before his eyes. And he believed she liked him too. Not as a love interest, of course. He wasn't a fool. But she respected him, and that invigorated his soul. He shook his head at the absurdity. He could face death but had never mustered the courage to tell Anna what he thought of her.

As for what next if he reached the Aryan side? Itzhak enormously respected Jozef and the Zakkai members, in their teens and early twenties, who had chosen to fight and die for Jewish honor – to avenge the innocent Jews murdered – instead of trying to hide and survive the war. But he also respected those who decided life was too precious to exchange for a death with honor, no matter how great the cause. Hopefully, at least some would survive.

His plan was different. His goal was to fight with his old friend, Szymon, for Polish independence. He knew that many Poles hated Jews, and he had once believed that Poland was irreversibly antisemitic. But Szymon had convinced him otherwise. He'd work with Polish resistance to establish a free Poland – the democratic Poland of his and Szymon's dreams.

He'd soon go into the night, a hunched over twenty-one-year-old Jew who walked like a man of seventy, hoping not to be spotted by policemen from whom his legs couldn't flee. He needed to walk about five blocks to the manhole. Once there, he'd enter the sewer and walk underground about two hours through twists and turns, forcing from his mind the rats, of which he also was not too fond, until he reached the rendezvous point where one of Szymon's men would lift a manhole cover at 5:00 a.m. and drive him to a safe house.

•••

KARL BECK

Karl Beck watched from his parked car as hundreds of German soldiers and their Ukrainian helpers swarmed the early morning darkness into the ghetto to collect Jews, load them onto trucks and dump them at the ghetto plaza, where a train would shuttle them to Belzec.

In response to the murders by Jewish and Polish terrorists, the Germans had arrested and would shoot more than a hundred Poles – men, women and children – as vengeance for the Germans killed. And the Germans would empty the ghetto. Under "Operation Heinrich," named in honor of Schmidt, every Jew in Krasau would be deported to Belzec within the next ten days.

German factory owners wouldn't be pleased, but everyone must accept some headaches in wartime. Including Beck, who must hurry his plans to find a position in France or somewhere else not too unpleasant.

Beck watched for a while as the soldiers poured into buildings, banging on doors. "Jews! Out!" As before, anyone who moved too slowly or resisted was murdered on the spot. Shrieks and pleading filled the air along with gunfire and barked orders.

Beck knew this would continue for many hours, and he had a long day ahead. He drove home and went to bed.

•••

Itzhak

Itzhak had walked three blocks when the distant roar of trucks froze him. Trucks in the early morning meant German soldiers, possibly a large aktion. He tried to quicken his steps past two warehouses. The Germans won't start here, but after he turns the corner, he'll enter a street full of apartments. The bastards will definitely go there if they're collecting Jews. At his fastest pace, seven or eight minutes to Sosna Avenue, and then the manhole.

He reached the corner and turned left. Street empty and dark. If only his legs could pump as quickly as his heart, Itzhak thought. Moments later, pop – pop – pop. Gunfire from streets behind and ahead. Distant shrieks and screams. Couldn't be more than a block or two away. If the Germans come here, he's dead.

But they hadn't, at least not yet. The gunfire was now all around him. Faraway orders barked in German were growing louder and coming closer, closer. As if especially for him.

But he must remain focused. Fear, terror, weakness served no useful purpose. He continued forward. No choice. He reached the end of the street, turned onto Sosna Avenue, and stepped from the sidewalk into the road. At the far end of the block, headlights of trucks vomiting silhouetted German soldiers. They ran into a building, pounded on doors, gunshots, blood-curdling screams of mothers for their children.

The soldiers will come this way. Itzhak, unseen, kept walking toward them, in darkness.

He reached the manhole.

But couldn't remove the lid.

Heart racing, he yanked the pistol from his coat. Using it as a crowbar, Itzhak pried off the manhole cover, stuffed the pistol back in his pocket, awkwardly stepped into the hole, gripped the cold metal ladder, and descended. He dragged the cover, scraping it against the concrete, closed the hole and dropped down three more steps. Pinching his nose to block the powerful smell of raw sewage, he remained still, on the ladder, while his head adjusted to the odor. He pulled the flashlight from his coat and flipped it on. Red rats. Several of them scurrying immediately beneath him on the concrete floor.

He shuddered, shined his light on the rats, and they scattered. He climbed down the last few steps to the floor and immediately felt cold dampness. Flashlight beaming, he looked around. He had entered a gray concrete and brick tunnel. The ceiling, at least in this section, was high enough to stand, and the water level was low, flowing slowly and silently down the center of the tunnel. The sides were wet and slippery but not submerged.

Itzhak heard muffled sounds of gunshots from the street above, pulled the handwritten sewer map from his pocket, found his bearings, and began to walk. Slowly and carefully to avoid slipping. After about ten yards, he heard voices. He shut off his flashlight, removed his pack and stood against the wall, heart thumping. German voices. In the sewer. The Germans must have learned that Jews escaped via the sewers. Itzhak silently cussed and removed the pistol from his coat.

He took a moment to determine which direction the voices were coming from. In front of him, he decided. Two voices? According to the map, the branch he was walking on continued about twenty yards and then teed into another branch. The soldiers must be on that other branch.

If he hurried, he could return to the ladder and might escape back to the street. But that would mean death. Or he could wait here, and when they turn onto this branch, shoot at the flashlight beams. But he didn't trust his aim so far away. Though he'd practiced endlessly with the pistol unloaded, he'd never shot a gun in his life.

Beams of light appeared about twenty yards in front of him. They were pointed downward, indicating that the Germans were shining the lights immediately in front of themselves instead of up ahead. He took a deep, pensive breath. He could wait until the Germans walked right next to him and fire at point-blank range. Unless they shine the lights far out in front... He cocked his pistol and waited as the two beams came closer.

He couldn't see the soldiers, but two lights meant two of them. Unless soldiers behind them weren't carrying flashlights. He'll learn that either from voices as they get closer, or from noise after he fires. Can't worry about it now.

He studied the beams carefully: were the soldiers carrying the flashlights in their right or left hands? That would affect whether he aimed to the right or left of each beam. He quickly decided that the German on the left was carrying the light with his right hand. But the other guy was swinging his flashlight, making it tougher to determine which hand was holding it.

The Germans were walking very slowly, and Itzhak still heard only two voices. He understood some German; they were joking and talking about girls. Their lack of focus gave him an advantage. Deciding that both soldiers were holding the lights in their right hands, he aimed slightly to the right of the light furthest from him, and when it was about six feet away, just before the beams reached his shoe, pulled the trigger twice. He instantly moved his hand to the right and pulled the trigger twice more. Both soldiers screamed, and their flashlights crashed to the floor.

Itzhak heard one soldier groaning and the other take quick steps and fall to the floor. Something clattered against the concrete. Itzhak lay flat on the floor and flipped on his flashlight. He saw one German lying still, face up, about ten feet away, eyes open and gasping. He held no weapon. Itzhak saw no one else, sat up and saw the other soldier a few steps away, face down. His rifle had fallen into the water. Itzhak heard distant yelling, too far away to recognize the language.

Itzhak pointed his gun at the soldier near him. The soldier clenched his eyes shut, probably expecting a bullet; Itzhak walked to him, bent down and took the man's pistol from his holster. He didn't shoot him. Not from compassion for the Jew killer; Itzhak didn't want to waste a bullet.

He turned off the Germans' flashlights and then his own. Standing in complete darkness, he heard the distant voices grow louder. Germans. Itzhak shined his light along the wall. Nowhere to hide. This time, when the soldiers turn onto this branch of the tunnel, they'll point their lights far ahead and see Itzhak. He'll lose the shootout and hit none of them.

Therefore, staying in the tunnel meant meaningless suicide. He might have a chance to do good on the surface, though he didn't know what. An infinitesimally small chance there was better than zero hope here.

With both pistols in his coat, he turned, walked back in total darkness to the ladder by rubbing his arm against the wall as he moved, climbed up, removed the manhole cover, stepped onto the cobblestone street and found himself amid a crowd of hundreds of Jews, sitting and standing aimlessly with packs and bags and suitcases. He restored the manhole cover and tried to walk away, but soon realized that the group was surrounded by soldiers.

The same day
Kasia

Twenty-four-year-old Kasia had been a member of Szymon's cell for two years and his girlfriend for one. Smart, reliable and dedicated. From a middle-class Catholic family, Kasia's parents had taught her to stand tall for what was right. She'd joined the resistance after the Germans abducted her older brother and younger sister and shipped them to Germany, where her sister worked as a maid and her brother in a factory.

Szymon was initially a bewildering paradox to Kasia. Handsome but humble, a self-styled introvert whose likability drew others to him. He commanded serious attention but was always ready to laugh; kindhearted with a short temper that quickly faded. Kasia had fallen deeply in love with him.

Kasia performed many tasks for Szymon's cell: organizer, baker – especially of Polish pastries – and assassin of traitors. Today would be her fifth. She loathed doing it, and Szymon hated asking her. But young women could more easily walk the streets without raising suspicion, and Kasia glided out of trouble with a flirty charm beyond a man's ability. And she was an excellent shot.

Szymon chose her targets with extreme care. The other four were Polish traitors responsible for the deaths of resistance members. Today's target was a Jewish woman who betrayed Jews. Szymon had never ordered the killing of a collaborating Jew because he believed that was best left to his Jewish friends. But this one had betrayed the boy who saved his life.

•••

Bleary-eyed, Kasia woke up earlier than usual, decided on an old, faded dress from among three choices, and tied her long, straight brown hair into a ponytail. She drank a cup of black coffee and listened again – and again – to Szymon's instructions while she attached the silencer barrel to her pistol. She slid her arms through the sleeves of a long gray overcoat, buried the pistol in the coat's inside pocket, hugged her cat and then Szymon goodbye, and left. She lit a cigarette to calm her nerves, walked in the cold morning air to a streetcar, rode two miles and walked three blocks to Bogadowa Street.

Horns honked, and a taxi stopped near her to unload a passenger. As she walked down the sidewalk, she repeated to herself Szymon's words. "Look for undercover police and abort if you see anyone suspicious. The woman is likely to be unarmed. Get her into the building, find a quiet place, finish quickly and leave."

Many people were out and about. A lone, young man passed Kasia on the sidewalk and smiled at her. She smiled back and walked past a dark-haired woman standing in the doorway of number 24. Kasia's eyes scoured both sides of the street for undercover cops. She saw no one concerning, walked to the corner, circled the block and again headed to number 24. This time, she approached the woman.

"Hello, are you Regina?"

The woman, dressed fashionably in a dark skirt and pink blouse with matching hat and purse, was smoking a cigarette. "Who are you? And why did you walk by a few minutes ago and come back?"

"Sorry," Kasia meekly shrugged. "I'm a little nervous."

Regina glared at her impatiently. "And...?"

"A friend told me you help Jews. I know some who need help. Um, I'd like to talk to you about it."

Regina eyed her suspiciously and asked in Jewish, "What's your name?"

"I'm not Jewish," Kasia said.

"How do you know Jews when they're all locked in the ghetto?"

"Can we go inside? Is there somewhere quiet we can talk?"

Regina took a final puff on her cigarette, dropped the butt on the sidewalk and squished it with the bottom of her shoe. "Answer my question."

Kasia frowned, quickly glanced to her left and right, leaned toward Regina and whispered, "My older sister's husband is a Jew. He and his family are staying with me. I didn't sign up for that. My sister was sent to Germany for labor, and–"

"How did you hear about me?"

"A man who brings food for my brother-in-law – can we go inside? I'd feel more comfortable if we did." Kasia pleaded with her eyes.

Regina paused, thinking. Peter should be here soon. No money for turning in this Pole, but we could get a pretty good bounty for the Jews. "How many Jews are staying with you?"

"Five."

"Alright, let's go inside and talk."

Regina entered the building, and Kasia followed. Kasia took deep, slow breaths to keep herself calm. They walked down a hall toward a stairway, and a man popped out of an office. Kasia tensed, but the guy simply went to the restroom.

"I see you're nervous," Regina said. "Don't worry, we're going to the fourth floor. No one works up there; it's quiet." Regina decided she'd lock the girl in a room upstairs where she sometimes trapped Jews. Peter can take it from there.

Kasia followed Regina up four flights in a narrow, steep stairway smelling of mold. The door to the fourth floor creaked when Regina pushed it open. She put her finger to her mouth, indicating that Kasia should keep quiet, and waved her toward an open door at the end of the hall. The entire floor seemed empty; the walls gouged and only partially painted.

Regina led her into a small, windowless room empty of furniture and badly needing paint.

"Sorry for bringing you into these luxurious surroundings," Regina said. "Now what–" Regina turned to face Kasia, who shot her twice in the chest and once in the head. The silencer muffled the shots, not audible beyond the empty fourth floor. Kasia returned the pistol to her coat, trembled for several seconds, took three deep breaths, left the room and hurried down the stairs.

THE SAME DAY
IRINA

Irina's exhausted mind had distilled what she must do. Tossing all night and convulsing emotionally, she had put on her coat early in the morning, left the apartment and walked toward the ghetto. With unbrushed hair and still wearing the blouse and skirt she'd worn the day before and slept in, Irina could have taken a streetcar and arrived much sooner, but the thought didn't occur to her. Straight ahead she stared, not noticing passersby. Twice, she was almost killed stepping into traffic. After more than an hour, she turned onto Bogadowa Street and walked to number 24.

Stone-faced, Irina entered the building as Kasia rushed down the stairs.

Irina waited at the landing as Kasia headed her way. "Are you Regina?" Irina asked in a flat, emotionless voice.

Kasia, her heart racing and still lightheaded from what she had done, saw in Irina a wild-eyed, terrified girl. Didn't look Jewish but could be. May have just escaped the ghetto. Kasia didn't have time for this, but the girl seemed to be in enormous pain.

"What?" Kasia stopped.

Legs shaking, Irina said, "Do you help Jews?"

"Maybe, but I'm in a big hurry. I'm sorry..." Kasia brushed past Irina and aimed for the door.

"Stop!" Irina screamed.

Kasia turned and Irina, gripping a pistol, shot her twice, hitting her in the stomach and leg. Kasia collapsed to the floor. Her ears ringing from the loud gunshots, Irina stood over Kasia, smoke from the barrel wafting up to Irina's face. Pointing the pistol at Kasia's chest, Irina announced, "In the name of Jewish resistance, I sentence you, Regina, to death."

"I'm not Regina!" Kasia moaned. "I just killed Regina upstairs. Please–"

Irina's mind didn't process Kasia's words until the gun had fired three more shots. Only after the third shot did Irina understand what Kasia had said. "Oh my God! Oh my God!" she wailed.

Two men rushed out of an office. Irina pointed the gun at them but didn't pull the trigger. The men darted back behind their door; Irina threw down her pistol, ran out the building and down the street.

•••

Peter

As Peter approached number 24, he saw a man frantically run outside hollering, "Police! Police!" Peter ran to him. "I'm a police officer."

"A woman was killed!" the man screamed. Peter hurried inside and saw Kasia's body on the floor. "What happened?"

"A girl. About twenty. She shot her and ran – a few minutes ago." He handed Peter Irina's gun. "She dropped this. And there's a dark-haired woman. Here all the time. Went upstairs with the dead girl, but I haven't seen her since."

The man stood over Peter's shoulder as Peter bent down next to Kasia's body. He growled, "Go back to whatever you were doing." As soon as the man had returned to his office, Peter rifled through Kasia's purse and coat and found the silencer pistol. It looked like what he furnished to Polish resistance. He thrust it into his pocket and rushed upstairs to the fourth floor.

Heart pounding, he walked quickly toward where Regina trapped Jews. She might have left when she heard gunshots, but probably would have waited for him. Peter entered the room and saw Regina's dead body.

"Dammit," he said aloud. He frowned and shook his head. There went his ticket to catching Jews and their money.

He turned and left.

•••

Irina

Irina fled down the street, tripped, and fell onto the sidewalk, badly scraping her hands and knees. Lurching to her feet, she turned the corner, ran into an alley, and her mind and heart racing uncontrollably, vomited onto her coat and the pavement. Consumed by anguish and pain, she held her face in her hands; agony drenched her soul, leaving no room for rational, coherent thought.

She left the alley and made her way toward the ghetto's west gate, two winding blocks away. Her mind clouded, she barely noticed three German soldiers walking toward her on the sidewalk. One smiled at the pretty Polish girl, and another asked, "Hey cutie, where you going?"

Irina passed them, not hearing, went another block, came to the west gate, and ignoring the guards, entered the ghetto. A soldier grabbed her arm. "What are you doing!" he yelled. "There's a roundup of Jews going on. Get out of here!" Staring blankly, Irina mumbled, "I'm a Jew."

The soldier threw her to the pavement. "Then go to the train!" he commanded, pointing to his left. Irina stood, numb to the physical pain, and headed that direction about a block. But instead of continuing straight to the train plaza, she turned right, toward her family's ghetto apartment, oblivious to the roaring trucks and shouted commands of German soldiers and police.

She walked several blocks to the apartment building, went upstairs and opened the unlocked door to her family's apartment. She entered, Bubbie pulled her in with a big hug and giant wet kiss, and Frammy, eyes bright, hollered, "Let's play, Irina is here!"

Irina wiped Bubbie's kiss off her face and bonked Frammy on the head with her open palm. "I've missed you so much, Frammy!" She pinched his nose; Frammy started giggling, couldn't stop, and Irina tickled his tummy. They fell to the floor laughing.

Mama peeked her head from the kitchen. "Irina, can you help me get dinner ready?" Irina walked into the bare kitchen, where she saw a pantry full of dishes and the ingredients for dinner spread all over the counter. Mama, smiling, was about to hand her the potato peeler when Irina felt a hand on her shoulder and whirled around. Papa, with a giant grin across his face. "We have Mama's passport! Soon, we'll start our new lives in Eretz Israel! But first, Anna's waiting for you in your room."

Irina walked into the bedroom and curled onto the bed next to Anna. "Irina, I want you to know I've thought about it a lot, and I really like Reuven. You're right – he's the coolest guy!"

"I know," Irina said. "Isn't he the best!"

Irina lay back with her hands folded behind her head and gazed up at the ceiling. A smile slowly crept across her face, and she gently bit her lower lip as a wonderful feeling of contentment, joy and warmth – of pure happiness – swept over her. She was again with her family, whom she loved and who loved her.

Irina was home.

•••

SZYMON

Szymon had checked his watch at 8:30 a.m. and started pacing. What if Kasia didn't spot a well-disguised undercover cop who might spring from behind, search her, find the gun, arrest and torture her? Kill her like they murdered his parents.

But Kasia was smart. She'd be careful; he was sure of that. The odds were very good in her favor. Szymon wouldn't have sent her if they weren't. Second guessing was stupid. Kasia would go in, do the job, get out and come home. Like always.

At 11:30 a.m., Szymon was again pacing. He had tried hard not to think about Kasia. To focus on work. But his mind kept tugging him back. She should have returned, but a hundred things might have delayed her. She'd come home soon, and he'd hug her tight while she shook and cried. Then he'd leave her be, she'd bathe and spend the rest of the day on her own.

At 2:00 p.m., Szymon had peered out the window with clenched fists. She must have feared she was being followed, took a roundabout way home and went on a long walk. Yeah, that's what happened.

"Why did I send her!" he'd suddenly yelled and pounded his fist into the wall, breaking a finger. "What was I thinking!" Szymon had cradled his aching hand and taken deep breaths. He should be rational – worrying did no good. He couldn't risk going to the scene. No choice but to stay and wait. They'd laugh together when he said he hurt his hand being stupid. She'd roll her eyes.

At 4:00 p.m., Szymon buried his face in his throbbing right hand.

•••

That night, Szymon's phone rang. His commander's voice. "I have details from the raid," Nowak said. "Even better than we had hoped. The local Gestapo commander, four other Gestapo men, two SS majors and an army captain – all dead, along with noncoms. What a fantastic success!"

"OK."

"I know you lost some men. That hurts, but we've struck such a blow! The impact on Polish morale is immeasurable."

"OK."

"I notified our government in exile in London of our great achievement. They're thrilled."

"OK."

"You should be proud. Good night."

Click.

SATURDAY OCTOBER 24, 1942
JOZEF

Jozef watched the fourteen members of his group hop from the truck onto the soft dirt at the edge of the Parczew Forest. Leah plus nine boys and four girls between the ages of sixteen and twenty-two. All dressed in long pants, heavy coats and hats. Leah, Estie and six boys concealed loaded pistols in their coats. Other than Jozef, the rest were unarmed.

A member of Szymon's AK cell had driven them, hidden under a canvas, several hours from Krasau to this spot to meet a guide. He was to take them deep into the forest to join an AK group that attacked and sabotaged Germans. Known for its dense woods, lakes and few roads, the Parczew Forest was a haven for partisans. Germans feared entering in small numbers.

Jozef's group sat in a small clearing and waited. The October air was cold, gray skies warned of rain, and wind-driven red, brown and yellow leaves scattered around them. After about an hour, two men emerged from the trees. Jozef walked over to greet them; as planned, the armed members of his group grasped their weapons and fanned out in case they'd been betrayed.

The two men identified themselves as "AK affiliated" partisans living in the forest. Jozef looked them over. Mid-twenties, clad in army-issued pants and leather jackets. One, almost as tall as Jozef, carried a rifle and the other, much shorter, fingered a submachine gun slung on his shoulder. The taller one asked, "How many fighters in your group?"

"Fifteen, including me."

"Good, we could use–" he stopped and eyed Leah, Estie and the others. The two Poles frowned and exchanged glances.

"Is there a problem?" Jozef asked.

"No problem," the taller one replied. "You have weapons?"

"Several pistols," Jozef answered.

"Pistols are no good against soldiers," the tall man said. "But they help get food from peasants. Let's get moving. We have about four hours in front of us, and I'd like to beat the rain. Tell your people no talking."

The two men turned into the woods and disappeared onto a trail invisible from the clearing. Jozef and Leah followed a few steps behind; the rest of the group single-file after them. All quiet. Almost immediately, their world darkened, light barely trickling through the dense trees as they meandered on what seemed an animal trail.

As they wound their way through the woods, only the sounds of their feet on the forest floor and occasional birds or conversation between the two Poles broke the silence. After about two hours, they came to a small clearing, and the Poles said they could rest. The guy toting the submachine gun asked Jozef to talk with him alone. They moved away from the others; the Pole leaned against a tree and Jozef stood next to him.

"How many of your group have military training?" the man asked.

"None."

The Pole frowned. "Any of you fluent in German?"

"One of the girls, Estie. She lived in Germany."

"Good. Do your people have skills that will help us if we take you in?"

Jozef paled at the word "if."

"I fix things. Radios, transmitters, guns. Anything electronic or mechanical."

"That's good too. Anything else?"

"Yeah, we'll fight. We're bringing you fifteen soldiers."

The Pole grunted. "We have almost forty in our group. Adding you would mean fifteen more mouths to feed. Fifteen Jewish mouths."

Jozef's eyes burned into the man, who kept talking. "Our commander and plenty of us don't mind Jews, but half our group does. Some would just as soon slit a Jew's throat as belch or scratch himself. They might accept you and the German girl a while to see if you're useful, but not the rest."

"But–"

"The woman you're walking with is your wife?"

"Yeah."

"None of us has a wife. She'd cause jealousy. A couple of the men would want to share her. Or, more likely, one of them would 'accidentally' shoot you and take her for himself."

"Are you–"

"What this means is that you, without your wife, and the German girl have a shot at joining us. No one else."

"We're not splitting up!" Jozef pressed his chest against the man, gripped his arm, and said in a hushed tone, "Why the hell did you agree to take us if you're going to dump us alone in the forest? We're not the helpless Jews you're used to pushing around." He tightened his grip and scowled down at the Pole. "I'll put a bullet in your head!"

"Relax. We're not going to abandon you. At least not here. But we didn't agree to anything. We were told fighters wanted to join us–"

"That's true."

"Not for Jews. I'm telling you the way things are, not how I want them to be. I'm fine with Jews, and so is my friend here. But what I said is true. If you come to our camp today, our commander will welcome you, and in a week the only Jews still breathing would be girls getting passed around. But you have other choices – let go of me."

Jozef released his hold on the man's arm and took a step back. What if this guy is lying? What if he's the antisemite, and the rest of his group would welcome us?

"The forest is very big," the man said. "At least four groups in this area. First is ours, loosely tied to the AK. About six miles east is a group of fascist, right-wing Poles. They fight Germans and also kill Jews on the spot. To the north about three miles are communists. They fight Polish fascists as often as they fight the Germans. And vice versa. The communists will accept you if you're communist or have military training."

"We're not communist."

"To the west is a small Jewish family camp. They don't fight; I don't think they even have weapons. They just hope to survive by hiding in the woods. About fifteen, last I saw. Been here a few months – escaped getting deported with other Jews in their town. Three families, with little ones, two of the men former Polish army. They live in holes dug in the ground, covered by brush, and they get water by filling buckets from a lake about a mile away. I don't know about food. Probably pay a farmer. Very risky because if he gets tired of it, he'll tell the Polish police. Or other farmers, whose produce is stolen by partisans, will call the police or Germans. The Jews are sitting ducks."

"How–"

"You should go there. Help each other. You have weapons, and they have experience in the forest. My commander might offer some protection if you furnish a German translator, can fix radios, and provide extra fighters when we need them."

"Why shouldn't we go to your camp, like we planned, and talk to your commander? See what he says?"

"You could, but I'm telling you it will turn out bad."

"Why should I trust you?"

The Pole looked around, leaned close to Jozef and whispered: "Adon olam asher malach b'terem kol..."

Jozef's mouth fell open. "How do you–"

"They don't know I'm a Jew. Not even my commander."

"But if they learn–"

"Not many happy choices. And what I said about my group is true for AK guys everywhere. Some will help Jews; others will kill them."

Jozef nodded. "Take us to the Jewish camp."

"Good. We'll get there in about an hour. I'll hopefully be back in a week with some equipment for you to fix."

"Stay with us. We could use you, your experience. Your submachine gun."

"I'll think about it. For later, after you settle in, if you settle in. For now, I can help you more by talking to my commander. Hopefully make an alliance. Make sure you do a good job fixing things when we ask. And keep my secret."

"I will."

They returned to the group, and the partisan glanced at Estie and the other girls. "If things go well and we all survive the winter, maybe I'll join you. I wouldn't mind meeting some nice Jewish girls."

Jozef smiled.

The sky erupted with thunder and poured down freezing rain as the two partisans led Jozef's group to the Jewish family camp.

THE SAME DAY
KARL BECK

Mid-morning, Karl Beck looked from the east at the Jews gathered on the concrete plaza immediately south of the railroad tracks. "About how many Jews are here?" he asked his assistant.

"Three thousand, give or take. We'll need to stuff them in today."

"And the train is arriving at 1:00 this afternoon?"

"It was. It's been delayed until 6:00 tonight."

Beck frowned. "That makes a longer day for us." He gazed at the gray sky. "Smells like rain," he muttered more to himself than to his assistant. "Have you told the Jews about the delay?"

His assistant smirked. "Do they really need to–"

"Yeah, they do. I know they're being sent to their deaths. You know they're being sent to their deaths. But many of them believe they're being resettled. We want calm decorum until the moment the train departs. Not a riot. Not mass executions and bedlam. Treat them as if they're off to nicer things. Consistent with that is to keep them updated on the train schedule."

"Yes, sir."

"I have things to do, including getting my rain jacket. I'll be back in an hour."

•••

ITZHAK

The dark skies thundered, the wind whipped, and a steady, cold rain fell on the miserable crowd. Like many, Itzhak tried to stay dry by sitting on the pavement, hat on his head, wrapped inside his heavy coat. His hands, each clutching a pistol, were buried in his coat pockets. In his left, the revolver with two remaining bullets, and in his right the fully loaded semi-automatic he took from the German soldier.

Itzhak saw that the plaza where he and thousands of Jews were sitting was rectangular, with the long sides running east-west. Immediately south of the plaza was a row of buildings butting against each other. German soldiers and Polish police lined the southern edge of the plaza, immediately north of those buildings. Just north of the plaza and parallel to it was the railroad track, extending to the west. North of the railroad track and parallel to it stood the ghetto wall. A gate for Germans only, manned by soldiers and police, was cut into the wall across the tracks from the northeast corner of the concrete plaza. Itzhak was sitting in the middle of the plaza, about a third of the way from the eastern edge.

He surveyed the entire area with his eyes, trying to decide who to kill as his last voluntary act on Earth. He saw soldiers and police walking through the crowd, and others manning the gate and stationed along the plaza perimeter. Some held German Shepherd dogs on short leashes. He then noticed two SS men enter through the gate, walk across the tracks just northeast of the plaza, and continue south. They were now due east of him, about fifty yards away. He'd like to get one of the SS men, or maybe both.

He would need to get very close to them. Logically and carefully, he sat there pelted by raindrops and tried to decide how to do it. His focused mind blocked out the murmur of the crowd, the sounds of children crying, parents soothing, the smells of dampness and fear. His eyes remained glued on the SS men as a man in a dark uniform, probably Gestapo, approached them. Itzhak squinted. The Gestapo man, holding an umbrella, laughed and patted the SS men on the back.

Karl Beck.

Itzhak was sure. He had met Beck when they discussed letting Zakkai kids go to the farm for a second year, and Itzhak had recently watched him give a speech encouraging Jews to "resettle" in Belzec. Itzhak gritted his teeth. He hated deceitful Beck even more than the average Nazi murderer. Because Beck had pretended he was human.

Ending Beck's life would be Itzhak's final act.

•••

Anna

Also sitting in the crowd, near the northeast edge of the plaza, was Anna – legs crossed at the ankles, elbows on her thighs, hands holding her swollen face. Soaked from the cold rain, Anna's empty stomach knotted as her mind replayed how she'd gotten here: the ghetto train plaza, where Jews went like sheep to the slaughter. The place she'd sworn never to set foot.

A few hours after the Germans had searched her, they brought Anna and two other prisoners from the train station to the jail. They threw her into a large, smelly cell with other women, mostly thieves and prostitutes, along with some Jews. Today, they tossed the Jews into a truck and dumped them here.

Anna's clothes were in shreds, her entire face and head hurt, and she hadn't eaten or drunk anything for more than a day. With her aching hunger came weakness, fatigue and the acceptance of fate.

•••

IRINA

Irina wandered slowly through the crowded plaza, searching for her family. Early this morning, she was lying asleep when soldiers ordered her downstairs and into the street. She had willingly obeyed because her family wasn't in the apartment. They were there yesterday. Where had they gone?

The Germans had marched her and other Jews, most dragging or carrying bags or luggage, to the train plaza. Perfect, Irina had thought. Her family was here when she saw them last, long ago. But didn't she see them yesterday, or was that a dream? Or did they leave the apartment while she slept and come here? She'd decided to look for them.

Irina had been meandering for at least two hours, tapping people on the shoulder and mumbling, "Have you seen Frammy? Frammy Allowitz? He's a really cute little boy. Or Bubbie?" No one had. Not yet. But she didn't give up. They must be here somewhere.

The rain came and soaked her, but Irina kept searching.

•••

ITZHAK

Itzhak's eyes hadn't left Karl Beck. Though Beck did some walking around the perimeter, his "command post," if that was a thing, seemed to be about fifteen yards east of the plaza and forty yards from where Itzhak now stood. Itzhak slowly hobbled through the crowd, from the center of the plaza toward the east, pack on his back and each hand clutching a pistol stuffed in a coat pocket. He must get within a few feet of Beck before pulling the trigger and wasn't sure yet how to do it.

The rain had let up, but most people still sat on the concrete. Itzhak made his way past a white-haired, elderly couple leaning against each other, and he tripped over their luggage. "Be careful!" the great-grandmother scolded him. Itzhak apologized, looked up and saw Irina walking slowly through the crowd about twenty yards south of him. His heart sank, and he momentarily buried his face in his hands. Not Irina!

"Irina!" he called, but she didn't hear. Itzhak headed toward her, around and through groups of people, as quickly as he could. Though she was looking his direction, she didn't see him. "Irina!" he yelled again, this time as loud as he could. She still didn't react.

•••

Anna

The voice burned two holes through Anna's heart. Itzhak. Calling Irina. Please God, grant that I have gone mad! Anna lifted her eyes and saw Itzhak. She heard him yell "Irina!" a second time, and her body shuddered in agony when she saw Irina on the other side of him.

Smothering the immense grief: their beautiful lives – her little sister and Itzhak – will be choked out today in a gas chamber, she stood and ran toward them, stepping around or over every person and thing in her path. First to Itzhak, whose back was to her.

Without calling his name, Anna wrapped her arms around Itzhak's back, almost knocking him down. Startled, he turned, and his eyes exploded in horror. They embraced, each moaning, "Why are you here!" until Anna looked up and saw Irina heading away. "I'll get Irina," Anna cried, and she ran toward her.

2:00 P.M.
ITZHAK, ANNA AND IRINA

Anna took Irina's hand and led her to Itzhak. He saw a blank emptiness in Irina's eyes and terror in Anna's. "Something is very wrong," Anna whispered.

"Hi Irina," Itzhak said.

"Hi."

"I see you found Anna."

"Uh huh." Irina shivered from the damp cold. "But have you seen my Mama and Papa?" she mumbled. "Or Frammy and Bubbie?"

Itzhak furrowed his brow and didn't answer.

"Maybe it's better this way," Anna sighed. "Where we're going, it's a blessing not to understand."

Itzhak didn't answer Anna either. Instead, standing among the thousands of doomed, he rested his chin on his clasped hands and stared into the sky, concentrating, struggling to remember if he'd once read something that might be helpful. He finally whispered to Anna, "She could be suffering a temporary psychotic state induced by stress. She needs peace and quiet." He looked around and frowned at the absurdity of his own comment. "We shouldn't encourage her delusions."

"I'm still not sure it's bad..."

Itzhak grasped Irina's hand and set her down with him on the pavement, still soaked though the rain had stopped. Anna sat on the other side of her. Itzhak circled his arms around Irina and gently pulled her close, one hand on her shoulder and the other behind her head. Irina rested her head on his left shoulder. "Close your eyes," he whispered, and she complied.

Itzhak started softly singing an old Jewish lullaby that Mama had sung to Anna and Irina when they were little. Tears came to Anna's eyes. How did Itzhak remember Anna saying that her mother sang that song? She'd told him only once! Anna watched Itzhak pour love onto Irina, and she realized how badly she wanted Itzhak to love her. She moved to the other side of him and rested her head on his right shoulder.

Itzhak soon felt Irina's slow, steady breathing. "She's sound asleep," he whispered.

Anna quietly asked, "The way Irina was acting, do you–"

"I think her mind could handle only so much pain. It rebelled. If it happened very recently, it may be temporary. If it's been going on for days, it's more likely to be permanent, I'm afraid."

Anna lifted her head off Itzhak's shoulder and stared at him open-mouthed. "Permanent? Did you forget where we are?"

He sighed. "Would it be bad or good if I had, for a moment?"

Anna nodded, and Irina began to snore. "Is her head heavy?" Anna asked.

"No, I like it. She's keeping my left side warm."

Anna again rested her head on Itzhak's right shoulder. "Am I also keeping you warm?"

"You've been keeping me warm for two years, Anna."

Anna flushed red, reached across Itzhak, gently cradled Irina's head in her hands, and slowly lowered it onto Itzhak's lap. Irina snored louder, and Anna and Itzhak grinned. Anna wrapped her arm around Itzhak's neck and whispered, "I love you too, Itzhak."

His bloodshot eyes lit up; he placed a hand on the back of Anna's head and stroked her hair.

"I don't remember the last time I washed my hair," Anna said.

Itzhak looked at her uncombed, wet, dirty hair, her black, blue and swollen cheek, and the dark rings under her eyes, and saw only Anna. "It's beautiful, and so are you."

"Fear of imminent death has benefits," she said, again resting her head on his shoulder.

They sat quietly, and he kept stroking her hair while Irina slept.

"You may not believe this," Itzhak said, breaking their silence, "but I've never kissed a girl."

Anna lifted her head, cupped his face in her hands, leaned in and kissed him on the mouth. She pulled back, they smiled and kissed again, longer and passionately.

Anna clung to him and caressed the back of his neck. "Anything else you've never done?"

Itzhak smiled, and Anna returned her head to his shoulder. "We swore we wouldn't go like sheep to the slaughter," she said. "But look at us. Sitting here, patiently waiting to be loaded onto a train and murdered. Before I saw you, I'd given up, but–"

"In my pockets are two pistols. A loaded semi-automatic and a revolver with two bullets. I intend to kill Germans here and never get on the train." He nodded toward a group of Germans standing southeast of them, about forty yards away. "The man in black is Karl Beck."

"Include me! When–"

"I was headed there when I saw Irina. You take the semiautomatic–"

"No, I only know how to work a revolver."

"OK. We need to move his direction. I haven't decided yet how to get near enough." Itzhak drew her close, unbuttoned and opened her coat so that it covered his right side, noticed for the first time that her coat was in tatters, and placed the revolver in a still intact pocket.

She rebuttoned her coat and looked at Beck. "They're about ten yards from the edge of the crowd. We'll go there, and I'll meekly walk toward him, calling his name and thanking him for all he's done. You'll follow after me, apologizing and trying to pull me back, but I'll keep wanting to thank him. I think he'll allow me near. Then we shoot him."

Itzhak slowly nodded. "I think that's a good idea."

Anna clasped Itzhak's hand. "The train won't be here for at least three hours if what the Germans said is true. Can we spend another few minutes holding each other?"

Itzhak again put his arm around Anna's shoulder, careful not to disturb Irina. "There is nothing I'd rather do for the rest of my life."

They sat quietly for a while, lost in thought.

"What are you thinking about?" Anna asked.

"I'm hoping my parents don't learn that I was killed today. And that they take the cyanide pills I gave my father."

A longer silence.

"What did you hope to accomplish with your life?" Anna asked. "People said you wanted to be a scientific miracle worker."

"When I was very little, I yearned to be a famous sports star," Itzhak chuckled. "That didn't last long. Then a famous doctor and then a famous scientist. A professor."

"Wanting fame was a common theme, I see."

"Almost every boy wants to do great things. Then age and the world intervene." He smiled.

"Did that happen to you – even before the Germans?"

"No, before the war, I'd set my sights on becoming a respected professor who through scientific research would help mankind."

"Did you want to marry and have a family?"

"I shared with every adolescent the desire to love and be loved. And now, at the wire, I've met both goals. You anointed me 'Professor,' and I helped you survive for a while – most certainly a benefit to mankind. And I'll live the rest of my life – the entire rest of my life! – knowing that I love a girl who loves me back." He squeezed Anna's shoulder. "And as gravy, we'll kill a Nazi murderer."

"That was romantic until the last part."

"Sorry." He paused. "I wish I'd traveled. Never saw Paris or Rome or even Warsaw. I never left Krasau my entire life, except when we went to the farm."

"Soon you'll travel – to a place far better than Paris or Rome."

Puzzled, Itzhak cocked his head.

"To heaven."

"Ah, the world to come. You'll be with me? We'll enter holding hands?"

"If they let me in."

"If? Really? God had you in mind when he made the place."

"Do you think–"

"And you, Anna? Your dreams?"

"I never–"

A screaming little boy ran by them, waking Irina. She blinked open her blue eyes, lifted her head from Itzhak's lap, looked at him as if through a fog and at Anna's head on his shoulder, and her bleary eyes narrowed. Finally, she gasped. "Am I crazy or did Itzhak die and go to heaven?"

"You're not crazy," Itzhak said.

Irina stretched and looked at Anna snuggling with Itzhak. A smile crossed Irina's face. "Good for you, Anna."

Anna scooted to Irina and kissed her cheek. "Have a nice sleep?"

"Yeah." Irina looked around, stood and saw all the people. Anna also rose and put an arm around Irina's shoulder. Irina saw the train tracks and began to tremble. "We're not getting on a train – we need to get out of here!" Anna squeezed her tight, and Irina mumbled, "How did we even get – why don't I remember..."

Itzhak slowly stood and took Irina's hand; Anna's arm was still wrapped around her shoulder. "We each arrived through our own independent misfortune," Itzhak calmly said. "I wasn't able to escape to the Aryan side because the Germans are patrolling the sewers." He paused. "And Anna–"

"Jozef told me about Anna," Irina said. "He–"

"Irina," Itzhak said, "you've suffered – you've suffered trauma and that's why you don't remember some things. Your mind is recovering. We can talk about this later."

"Later?" She pointed at the tracks. "I'm fine. When is the train coming?"

"We think in a couple hours," Anna said.

Irina shuddered and noticed the bruises on Anna's face. "Jozef told me you were arrested."

"Yeah," Anna sighed. "I wonder how Jozef knew–"

"The Polish resistance guy, Szymon, told him. Jozef also said, um," Irina's voice cracked, "that Reuven was sent to Belzec." She burst into tears.

"Oh no!" Anna moaned. "I'm so sorry, Irina." She hugged Irina tight and rocked her. "Irina, I'm so sorry, Irina." Anna pressed her face against Irina's and felt Irina's tears on her own cheek.

Irina finally withdrew from Anna's grasp and said Benec and his cell were also dead. She waved a sad hand at the tracks. "And now we're here?"

"We're not getting on the train," Itzhak said. "Anna and I each have a pistol. We're going to kill Karl Beck, the Gestapo man who–"

"Is he here?" Irina said.

"Yeah."

Irina looked down and muttered, "OK."

•••

KARL BECK

Karl Beck was walking the plaza perimeter, instructing the German officers to maintain peace and quiet. "Indiscriminate shooting is not peace and quiet," he said. "Be harsh to maintain order, but not otherwise."

"I don't agree," blurted the Gestapo agent promoted to replace Heinrich Schmidt. "I saw Heinrich's body – I'd line up every Jew here and machine gun them. Then grab other Jews to clean the mess."

Beck sighed. "We might enjoy it, but you'd make our job a lot tougher. We have another forty thousand Jews to round up the next few days, and the Jewish police have all been shot – so the job is entirely ours. Every Jew on this plaza will be dead in six hours. Don't add to our aggravation just to kill them a little sooner."

The Gestapo man frowned.

Standing south of the plaza, they looked over the crowd and noticed a group of about forty teenagers sitting in a circle singing. The Gestapo agent waved over a soldier and pointed at the kids. "Go shut them up."

"No!" Beck said. "I don't care if all three thousand of them sing, dance, or do cartwheels. If they're singing when they walk into the gas chamber, do you think the camp commandant will order them to stop? Hell no! He'll let them sing, gas them, and go on with his day. Let them be."

The Germans watched the teens, and then dozens of people on each side of them, stand and sing.

4:30 P.M.
ITZHAK, ANNA AND IRINA

Itzhak heard the singing and rolled from a sitting position to face-down on his elbows, lifted himself to a bent knee, and stood by pushing down with both hands against the top of his leg. Irina and Anna also rose to show respect for the words being sung: *"the hope of two thousand years, to be a free people in our own land..."*

Exhausted from thirst and hunger, they peered west, across the "huddled mass yearning to be free," at hundreds of people standing tall and singing Hatikvah, the Zionist anthem. Sorrowful pride moistened Anna's eyes as their hearts and voices joined others near them, old and young.

"Dammit! I see Beitar guys," Itzhak groaned. "They were set to leave the ghetto but were waiting for weapons." He bitterly dropped his face into his hands and shook his head. "The irony. We sing the Zionist anthem as a prelude to death. 'Hatikvah,' meaning 'The Hope,' now means 'The End.'"

"No, you have it backwards," Anna said. "It shows we're part of something eternal – we'll die today, but others will make our dream real."

Irina thoughtfully ran a hand through her hair. "Papa loved Hatikvah. And he never lost hope or quit trying to make things better."

"Until he sat here, I suppose," Itzhak said.

"No!" Irina said. "Papa stepped onto that train believing he was saving his family." She turned to Anna. "You killing Beck is good, but then they'll shoot you and send me to the gas chamber. Papa says – Papa would say we should try to live."

"Irina," Anna said softly, "we're surrounded by two hundred soldiers and police with guns. Even if Papa were here–"

Losing patience, Itzhak snapped, "Should we borrow shovels and dig under the wall? Or walk to the gate and say 'Pardon me, we'd rather not die today. Please let us out.'"

"Yeah," Irina said.

"Yeah?!"

"Yeah, ask permission."

Itzhak muttered to Anna, "I thought her psychosis had receded, but–"

"I'm not insane!" Irina said.

"Then accept that your idea is ridiculous – because it's impossible."

"When you have no choice, there's one thing worse than trying the impossible."

"What's that?" Itzhak asked, annoyed.

"Quitting."

Itzhak shook his head. "We're wasting our–"

"Attention!" bellowed a German with a bullhorn. "The train will arrive in thirty minutes. Form lines to the tracks!"

"Damn!" Itzhak said. "Getting Beck just got harder." Germans began strutting through the crowd, ordering everyone to quickly stand and get in line.

"Anna," Itzhak pointed toward Beck. "We need to go there and hope no one stops us."

"No!" cried Irina. "Anna, you know what Papa said. Some German soldiers are good. Maybe twenty of the two hundred or whatever soldiers here are good. Or maybe ten – or five. They know where the train goes. What if the good ones are guarding the gate?"

The other three thousand people on the plaza, some with families and others alone, young and old, were stirring, gathering their measly possessions and forming lines as ordered. A shriek stabbed the air – an irate soldier had clubbed an old, white-bearded man for moving too slowly. When he collapsed, the man's elderly wife bent over him and wailed; the soldier grabbed and threw her to the pavement. "Hurry!" he ordered.

"From these soldiers, you hope to find good men?" Itzhak asked.

Irina grasped Anna's left hand, and Itzhak her right. Both said, "Anna, come with me." Anna looked at Itzhak and then at Irina. She dropped Irina's hand, turned to Itzhak, and took both his hands in hers. "If I kill Beck with you, Irina will surely die. But if I go with Irina, perhaps – by a miracle, she'll live. I owe it to my parents to seek life for her. Come with us."

Itzhak quickly analyzed their options. If Anna came with him to kill Beck, Irina, alone, could still ask the soldiers to let her out. But Itzhak wanted Anna also to have a chance to live, no matter how absurdly small the possibility. As for himself, he wouldn't trade killing Beck for those ludicrous odds.

"No, go with Irina. I'll get Beck."

A German soldier, walking toward them with a nightstick in his hand, shouted "MOVE! NOW!" Itzhak quickly clutched Anna's and Irina's arms and guided them toward a line forming a few yards away.

"Let's talk as we go there – before he bludgeons us."

A teenage girl walking nearby with her family sobbed, "I don't want to die today, Mama!"

Above the din of crying children, people calling to each other, soldiers and police barking commands, Anna said, "Irina, I'm going with you. Itzhak will stay and kill Beck."

"Come with us, Itzhak!" Irina pleaded. "You should–"

"No." They took their place in line. Itzhak opened his arms to Irina, and they hugged.

Anna squeezed Itzhak's hand. "No time for a proper goodbye, I'm afraid," she said.

They embraced, tears in their eyes. "Thank you," he said.

"I love you," she answered.

"Next time, we'll say that a little earlier."

Anna forced herself away and grabbed Irina's hand. "Come on." She led Irina northeast through the crowd, as soldiers and police commanded Jews to "HURRY UP! GET IN LINE!"

Itzhak glanced at Beck, turned, and watched Anna and Irina. He noticed a German soldier following them as they left the crowded plaza and crossed the empty pavement toward the railroad tracks. Itzhak trailed the soldier to the corner of the plaza, where the soldier stopped. From there, the soldier's eyes followed Anna and Irina as they crossed the tracks and headed toward the gate.

About ten yards in front of them stood two sets of guards at the exit: three Polish police on the right and four German soldiers on the left. Anna said to Irina, "I'll do the talking," but they otherwise remained silent, hearts pounding, legs trembling, and holding hands very tight. After a few more steps, Irina said, "You were a great big sister." Anna, her eyes locked on the German soldiers' faces, said nothing, but she pumped Irina's hand twice.

The guards watched the two Jewish girls walking toward them, hand in hand. "What do we have here?" a German soldier asked the others.

"Good question," a soldier responded.

Anna and Irina *walked up to the group of German soldiers, and* Anna *said in German, "Lass uns durch!" – "Let us through!"*

They didn't shoot her. They looked at her with stunned expressions, remaining silent. A couple of soldiers left, two remained.

Anna *said in German, almost as if giving an order: "Retten sie zwei seelen" – "Save two souls!"*

One of them answered, "Aber schnell!" – "But be quick!"

And by that miracle, so hard to believe, they managed to get out of hell, rushed through the gate and into the Aryan side. The soldiers turned their backs to them and again faced the tracks and the Jew-filled plaza.

Ignoring shouted commands to get in line, Itzhak stood a couple feet behind the German soldier who had followed Anna and Irina to the corner of the plaza. The soldier saw them exit, immediately raised his right arm to point a finger and began to yell an alarm, but before a sound could leave his mouth, three shots from Itzhak permanently silenced him. Three German-made bullets from the German-made pistol into the German-made soldier. Itzhak pivoted, saw Karl Beck in the distance, aimed, and pulled the trigger twice, missing with both shots. Itzhak was then hit by multiple bullets.

"Shma Yisrael," he managed before his heart stopped beating.

And the man who would have cured cancer lay dead. Or was the person who would have cured cancer one of the other six million? Or their never-born descendants?

Anna and Irina, still hand-in-hand, ran down the street, turned a corner, and disappeared into the Aryan side.

EPILOGUE

Ashes and Dust

MAY 8, 1945

Germany surrenders to the Allies. The war in Europe is over.

•••

JULY 12, 1945
GMUND AUSTRIA
MORDECAI

A tall, thin-faced man about forty pushed a wheelbarrow full of soil to the front of his house. Under a bright mid-morning sun and clear blue sky, he dumped the dirt near pots of red geraniums he'd soon plant. Looking down his sloping yard toward the town of Gmund, nestled in a valley with its quaint, orange-roofed homes, tall church steeple and tree-filled hills in the background, he happily sighed. The beauty of Austria. He'd grown up in this modest country-house built on the side of a hill. It was nice to be home.

He grabbed a rake and began spreading the soil when a British army jeep rumbled up the narrow, winding road and stopped in front of his house. The British occupied this part of Austria two months after the war against Germany had ended. Two British soldiers exited the vehicle, and the driver remained seated behind the wheel.

"Hans Muller?" one of the soldiers called out. The man nodded, and the soldiers walked toward him. A major and a sergeant, the man saw from glancing at their uniforms.

"We're here to take you in for questioning," the major said in English.

The man, still holding his rake, shrugged his shoulders. "Sorry, I don't speak English," he said in German. The sergeant replied in German. "We're here to take you in for questioning. You've been accused of war crimes."

The man dismissively waved them away. "I've been questioned. Last week, and when they finished, they said they're done with me. Your information is wrong." He shook his head. "Typical British screwup."

"You don't get to decide that," the sergeant said. "Put the rake down and come with us. We don't have all day."

The man groaned, tossed the rake on the ground, took a step forward but then stopped. "The British officer who questioned me last week said very clearly that I'm free to live my life. The war is over, gentlemen."

"Not for you," the sergeant replied.

The man closely eyed the soldier's faces for the first time and felt sudden loathing and fear. "You're Jews! You're not British! Get off my land!"

The soldiers pulled Colt 45 pistols from their holsters and pointed them at the man's head.

"Take off your shirt and raise your left arm!" demanded the sergeant.

"No!"

The major jammed his pistol into the side of the man's head, forcing him to his knees.

"I never hurt a single Jew!" the man whined. "I swear it."

"Take off your shirt!"

"OK," he gasped. "I'll do it. But it doesn't mean anything."

The major took a step back, still aiming his pistol at the man's head. The Austrian stood upright, slowly unbuttoned his shirt, and raised his left arm, displaying the SS blood-type tattoo.

"To the jeep!" the sergeant ordered, pointing.

"No!" snarled the SS officer. He folded his arms against his chest and glanced around, hoping against all odds that a fellow Austrian might pass by. "I don't take orders from Jews."

The soldiers glanced at each other, and the major proclaimed in Jewish, "In the name of the Jewish people, I sentence you to death." He shot the Nazi between the eyes, and the sergeant added two more bullets.

They hurried down the slope to the jeep and hopped in. "What d-d-did you d-d-d-do!" cried their shocked driver.

"Drive, Mordecai! Go! We need to get out of here!"

Mordecai, wearing a Star of David patch on the shoulder of his British uniform, shoved the jeep into gear and barreled down the road and onto the highway. A two-hour drive lay in front of them to their army base. After about ten minutes, Mordecai asked, "What happened? Why d-d-did you kill–"

"He refused to go with us," Pinchus, wearing the major's uniform, said. "I knew he was guilty. He served in the SS in Riga, where the SS murdered tens of thousands of Jews. Children, old people, women."

"You can't – I wouldn't have driven you here if I'd known you'd k-k-kill him. The Nazi scum probably deserved to die, but without a trial? How do you know–"

"Spare me. That kind of Jewish thinking is what led to the gas chambers," Pinchus said.

Mordecai didn't answer. He'd known Pinchus for three years; there was no arguing with him. Mordecai would drop these guys at the base and continue alone on his mission. To find Anna and his parents.

Or learn what happened to them.

•••

Mordecai drove alone across Austria in a jeep and trailer that he'd "borrowed" with help from his British sergeant, Roger Smithson. "I don't believe the British army will miss these for a fortnight or two," Smithson had said. Patting Mordecai's back and wishing him luck, Smithson also helped secure a five-week leave for Mordecai from the British army.

Mordecai was a corporal in the British army's Jewish Brigade, finally formed in 1944. Like the other five thousand plus Palestinian Jews in the Brigade, he'd worn a Star of David sleeve patch on the shoulder of his British uniform when he fought the Germans in northern Italy in March and April 1945. Pinchus, who had killed the SS officer hours before, was also a corporal in the Brigade.

Driving through the Austrian countryside, Mordecai's mind turned to the four years since Sergeant Smithson had helped train him. He'd fought with the British against pro-German Vichy troops in Lebanon and had hoped the British would drop him and other Jewish commandos into Poland. But by the time the idea seemed feasible, most Polish Jews were dead. Mordecai did meet Jewish parachutists his age, including an amazing poet named Hannah. The British dropped her behind German lines in Yugoslavia, and she was captured, tortured and executed in Hungary in 1944. At twenty-three.

Instead of enlisting in the British army, Mordecai had considered joining the Irgun, the Jewish underground group seeking to expel the British from Palestine. Mordecai had long talks with their leader, a Jew from Poland named Menachem. How strange life is, Mordecai had thought. He joined the British army because that was the only way he could fight the Nazis, but his close second choice was to harass the British.

Mordecai had seen estimates that three million – 90% – of Poland's Jews were murdered. And millions of Jews from other countries. But some survived. Jews and others were flooding across borders into displaced persons camps run by the victorious Allies. A few members of Mordecai's Jewish Brigade, like Pinchus, were seeking vengeance, and some were working clandestinely to smuggle Jewish refugees past the British into Palestine. The British White Paper of 1939, which had blocked Anna and her family from Palestine, was still in effect even after the Nazi slaughters.

Mordecai's immediate goal was to find Anna and his parents. When he and Anna had last exchanged letters, she was barely eighteen and he was nineteen. Mordecai was now twenty-five, and Anna almost twenty-four – if still alive.

•••

With incredible luck, Mordecai met a Jewish Russian officer who helped him obtain an entry permit into Poland, now under communist Russian control. After a border hangup, he drove straight to Krasau, twelve hours without stopping. Much devastation along the way. When he arrived, Russian soldiers stole his trailer and everything in it. He barely escaped with the jeep and his life.

Wearing his British army uniform and Star of David patch, Mordecai drove to his family's apartment building. As he ascended the three flights of creaking stairs he'd walked a thousand times, his heart began to race. He entered the third-floor hallway and heard kids playing, speaking Polish, not Jewish. His feet instinctively led him to his family's apartment; he knocked, and a middle-aged Catholic woman, a small silver cross dangling from her neck, opened the door.

Mordecai introduced himself and said, "I grew up here."

The woman's eyes narrowed, she stood in the doorway and didn't budge. "This is our apartment. We've been here almost five years." Fear, quickly replaced by hostility, spread across her face.

"I just want to look around," Mordecai said. "I won't be b-b-back... For old times' sake."

She frowned, let Mordecai in and shadowed him through the rooms of his childhood, still filled with his family's furniture. The kitchen table and chairs – memories of his parents flooded his mind, and tears filled his eyes.

He walked into the small sitting room. The couch where he and

Anna had studied Hebrew and he'd first kissed her; the low table that had held warm cinnamon babka. He saw Anna and heard her voice, her laugh. "The furniture is all ours," the woman said. "We paid good money for it – more than it was worth."

"We had family photos on the walls and–"

"No, we don't have anything of yours. The place was empty, except the furniture."

Mordecai left. He knocked on doors in the apartment building and throughout the old Jewish neighborhood but recognized no one. He learned that the Germans had brutalized ordinary Poles; they murdered one of his Polish friends. He visited the only two of eighty synagogues not demolished by the Nazis – they'd used one as a horse stable and the other as a warehouse – and he saw signs in Jewish script above once Jewish shops. But no Jewish shop owners or customers.

"Where are the Jews?" he asked. "When I left, seventy thousand Jews lived here." He learned about the ghetto, the deportations to Belzec. "Only a few Jews in Krasau," he was told. "Try the Jewish Center on Broz Street – they have beds where people stay."

Mordecai talked to a man named Yankl, about thirty years old, who ran the Jewish Center with aid money from American Jews. "I survived Auschwitz, a death march, Belsen and returned to Lodz, where I grew up in a Jewish community of more than two hundred thousand.

"Lodz is gone," Yankl said in a gloomy monotone. "The streets, buildings, trees, they're still there. But my wife, children, parents, siblings, cousins, aunts, uncles are all dead. My friends are dead, everyone I played sports with is dead, the people who attended my synagogue are dead. No more Jewish stores, bakeries, schools. Nothing.

"I was so happy when the war ended because I thought I was going home, but home is gone. No one even to mourn with... I found this job in Krasau. Same story here."

Mordecai fought not to cry.

"You know," Yankl muttered. "I'm a Zionist from a family of Zionists. We almost moved to Palestine before the war. Like you." He looked down and shook his head. "My mother read in the paper that Arabs had murdered four Jews in Palestine, and then a week later another two Jews. Not safe there, my parents decided. So we stayed, and the Germans gassed them at Auschwitz."

"Arabs – it's the same as with Poles," Mordecai said. "Many don't like us. Why? Because we're d-d-different from them. Some people don't like anyone different. But Palestine – Zion, Jerusalem – is our home. We were there long before the Arabs, who will probably end up getting at least fifteen countries of their own across the Middle East. We'll do our b-b-best to get along, but I'm not running away from our homeland we've been praying to return to for two thousand years."

"Can I–"

"Come n-n-now. Join us."

"But the British–"

"Now. Help us restore our country."

•••

The Krasau Jewish Center was something of a transit stop, where Jews could stay while deciding where and how to rebuild their lives. People of all ages, but mostly young, many had no idea if anyone else in their family had survived. A bulletin board told the story, filled with handwritten notes such as "Isaac Symovitz looking for his parents Bluma and Yitzhak Symovitz, his brothers Mytek and Leo, and his sister Bascha." Or "Elsa Konigstein looking for her husband Dolek and her daughters Eva and Halina."

Mordecai did find a few Jews from Krasau, though he hadn't known them. One man said he knew of Anna and Irina in the ghetto. "Beautiful girls, both of them," he said. "Anna always dressed nicely. Both upbeat, full of life."

"What happened to them?" Mordecai asked, terrified of what he might hear.

The man shrugged. "Dunno. I heard rumors that the older sister was a courier for a Zionist youth group before the deportations in '42. But that was a long time ago."

A young woman, late twenties, with two long, dark, braided pigtails, was staying at the Center because she had no idea where to go. Her husband, parents, siblings and daughter were murdered. "Allowitz? I met an Allowitz girl. Light colored hair?"

"Yeah," Mordecai said.

"Long after the deportations. Maybe mid-1943, on a farm near here, but I don't remember exactly where. We hid in a barn with others, but I left. I remember her because she had a pistol, the only Jew I ever saw with a gun. She said it had saved her life – up to then...

"I don't know what happened to her. I do know, or at least I heard, that the Germans later shot the farmer and his family along with the Jews they were sheltering."

She bit her fingernails. "The Germans didn't leave here until February, five months ago. They knew they'd lost the war, but they kept chasing and murdering us. Including my baby girl." Her voice cracked, and she shook her head. "Hard to understand," she mumbled.

"Do you know the Allowitz g-g-girl's first name? Was it Anna? Irina? How old was she?"

The woman blew a deep breath. "Sorry, I don't remember. So many places, different people everywhere, the trauma... You should go to Krakow and Warsaw. You might learn something there."

•••

Mordecai did. He found nothing about Anna but was told that his parents had fled to Warsaw, where they were deported to the Treblinka gas chambers in 1942. He had known in his heart they were dead, but it didn't soften the blow. Was it partially his fault? Should he have pressed harder for them to move to Palestine with him? He struggled not to think about how they must have suffered.

He hoped they found a few random moments of happiness in their final months. That they didn't beg for food and watch each other deteriorate. He hoped they made a friend in Warsaw who gave them comfort. He hoped they still loved each other until the end, and that they didn't know the trains led to death. He hoped they smiled at each other when told to get into different lines for the "showers."

Mordecai mourned and then focused his mind on finding Anna. For almost a month, he searched in every city, town and village where he thought she might once have had relatives. And he tried to find Jozef, Leah and his other friends.

He learned from a young man what happened to his old coach – the guy who had taught him to fight when he was a teenager. "He died a hero."

"That's what I expected," Mordecai said, remembering his huge, powerful coach. "I can only imagine how m-m-many Germans he killed with his bare hands."

"No," the man said. "A different kind of hero. It was dead winter when the Germans sent the Jews in your coach's town to Treblinka's gas chambers. *He was a very big man physically, accustomed to winter and cold and rain. He had lived outside in the winter, and he could have escaped. He could have run off into the woods.*

"But he had in his arms a six-month-old baby – the youngest of his children. And he was together with his wife and other children. His wife said 'Get away, you will survive. What is the use of dying together?' But he said, 'No, I will not leave you.'

"This was an act of heroism: ***not*** *to escape."*

Mordecai realized that the millions who, under such horrendous strain and abuse and overwhelmed by fear, maintained their wits and kept their families alive until their final moments – they too were heroes.

•••

Every search ended the same – Mordecai found only ashes. In early August, Poles in Krakow rioted against the few surviving Jews. Against the Jews! As if they hadn't suffered enough.

Mordecai couldn't wrap his head around the contradictions that were Poland. He knew well of the antisemitism before the war; he now learned that many Poles during the war murdered Jews or happily turned them over to the Nazis. But he also heard of Poles who gave their lives and sacrificed their families to help Jews. Impossible to understand.

Dejected, Mordecai left Poland and returned to his base, only to find that his unit was moving from Italy to Belgium, and that within sixty days he would be returned to Palestine. But his commanding officer agreed that Mordecai could spend much of that time searching for Anna – a single straw of hay in a scorched Jewish haystack.

September 20, 1945
Jewish Brigade camp near Brussels, Belgium
Mordecai

"I have someone you need to meet," Mordecai's bunkmate, Jacob, said as he sauntered from their barracks door to Mordecai's bed at 10:00 p.m.

"OK," moaned Mordecai, shirtless, eyes bloodshot and head aching from lack of sleep. Without budging from his supine position, and with his bedsheet pulled over his legs and waist, he asked, "Who? Where? Outside?"

"A girl in a DP camp in Santa Maria di Bagni, a fishing village on the coast of southern Italy."

Mordecai sighed, lacking energy even to groan. He had exhausted himself for weeks chasing dead-end leads in Jewish Displaced Persons camps and taking care of his Brigade duties. Hours earlier, Mordecai had returned from Paris where he'd met with Jewish relief workers who had no information on anyone named Allowitz.

Running out of time, Mordecai was low on energy and hope.

"I talked to your buddy, Pinchus," Jacob said. "He and other Brigade guys gave a Jewish girl – in her early to mid-twenties – a ride to northern Italy. She was headed from there to a DP camp at Santa Maria di Bagni and hopefully on to Palestine. She's from Poland, had been a courier for a Zionist group, planned to teach kids at the DP camp."

Mordecai stared at him, suddenly listening very intently.

"You told me your girl was a courier–"

"Jacob, what's the g-g-girl's name, and is she from Krasau?"

"I asked. Pinchus couldn't remember. He just shrugged – you know Pinchus."

Mordecai frowned and shook his head. "Was he sober enough to notice the color of her hair?"

"He said it was cut very short." Jacob lowered his eyes and his voice. "Like the Germans did to people in concentration camps."

Mordecai grew pale.

"Pinchus said it was more than a month ago, and he doesn't know how long the girl planned to stay in southern Italy. He wanted to tell you sooner but got thrown in the brig after some altercation in Germany I was afraid to ask about. He just got back this morning, and you weren't around."

Mordecai sighed deeply, pulled off the sheets, twisted his body and planted his feet on the floor. "How long will it t-t-take me to get to southern Italy?"

"At least thirty-five hours of driving – wait until morning. Rest up first."

"You just said you don't know how long she'll be there. What if I miss her because I waited?" Mordecai rubbed his face, took a deep breath and blew it out slowly. Was he thirty-five hours away from finding Anna? "I need to g-g-go, and I need a jeep."

"I had a feeling you might say that." Jacob opened his hand. A jeep key dangled off his finger. "It's outside waiting for you, with maps. You need to get your own provisions."

Mordecai grabbed the key and left.

September 24, 1945
Santa Maria di-Bagni, Italy
Mordecai

She studied her reflection in the bathroom mirror.

And sighed.

Was it a man or woman staring back? Her hair, first shaved at Auschwitz in 1942 and at Neusalz only months ago, had grown mere inches. Of all the degradations, time would erase the de-womanizing head shaving. But what about her deeper wounds?

The young woman put on a gray skirt and white blouse, ate breakfast in the camp canteen and headed to the young girls for whom she served as teacher and counselor. All were orphans, ranging in age from six to eleven; the Germans and their collaborators had murdered their parents. Jewish Brigade and other Jewish groups recently smuggled the girls past the British to this fishing village. They would soon leave on a boat and, hopefully, sneak past the British again – this time to Palestine.

•••

She taught in a small classroom next to the kitchen; this morning, the smell of sardines permeated the air. The eight girls sat at four two-person school desks, and the young woman stood in front. She spoke Jewish to the girls, who came from eastern Europe. In another class they were learning Hebrew for when they'd reach Palestine.

"Who remembers what we were talking about at the end of class yesterday?"

A dimple-faced little girl with braided brown hair, wearing a polka-dotted, blue and white dress, raised her hand. "Oranges," she answered. "In Palestine, Jewish farmers grow lots and lots of oranges!"

"That's right!" the teacher grinned. "Who knows what an orange looks like?"

"They're square and blue," an unhappy eleven-year-old answered. The teacher ignored her.

"You said they're, um, round like a small ball, and, um, they're orange!" a seven-year-old said.

The teacher dramatically pulled an orange from her purse and held it above her head. The younger girls hopped from their desks and rushed to her. "Can I touch it! Can I smell it! Can we eat it?"

"Yes, yes, yes, we're going to share it. But first, everyone return to your desks."

As they sat down, the kids noticed Mordecai standing inside the classroom door. The teacher turned her head and looked at the handsome soldier in his Jewish Brigade uniform. Mordecai's eyes studied the teacher's face, and his shoulders drooped.

She wasn't Anna.

"Please come in," the teacher said. Mordecai walked to her, and she extended her hand. "Hi. My name is Bela Sztern. Are you looking for someone?"

"Yeah, I was looking f-f-for you." Deflated, his voice sounded weary. "Well, I'm looking for my old g-g-girlfriend, and I thought you might be her."

"Why did you think–"

"I was told you're from Poland, you were a courier for a Zionist youth group – so was my g-g-girlfriend."

"G-G-Girlfriend!" the eleven-year-old, sitting in back, mimicked to the girls sitting near her. "G-G-G–"

"Stop that, Wushka!" Bela scolded the girl, who countered with a defiant look.

Bela turned to Mordecai. "Was your girlfriend–"

"G-G-G" the girl loudly whispered to the ten-year-old sharing her desk. "G-G-G- k-k-k, d-d-d," she laughed.

"These are orphans?" Mordecai quietly asked Bela.

She nodded seriously.

Mordecai ran a hand through his hair, maneuvered past four kids to the eleven-year-old and gestured for her to get up. She made a face but stood. Wearing a patterned blue and gray skirt and blue sweater, she was tall and thin with long, uncombed, dark hair and bitter brown eyes.

"Your name is Wushka?" Mordecai asked.

The girl's wary eyes narrowed. "Yeah."

"I once knew a girl named Wushka."

The girl glanced around; everyone was staring at her.

"The Wushka I knew was so funny! Always saying clever things that m-m-made everyone laugh." He smiled and paused. "Are you like that?"

The girl shrugged.

Mordecai looked up at the ceiling and slowly rubbed his chin, as if deep in thought. "She also – the Wushka I knew – was a GREAT hugger. I mean the BEST hugger ever!"

Wushka fidgeted and bit her lip.

Mordecai, standing two steps from Wushka, smiled at her as all the girls and their teacher quietly watched. The only sound was faint whistling from a man in the kitchen next door.

"You know," Mordecai said seriously, "how some people, when you hug them, they hug around your neck... or they hug around your shoulders... Not Wushka."

Wushka stood quietly, looking up at Mordecai.

A giant smile made its way across his face. He spread his feet to lower himself to her height and enthusiastically but quietly said, "I bet you're a good hugger too. I can tell from looking at you... I'm right, aren't I?"

Wushka shrugged again, but her eyes slightly brightened. Mordecai opened his arms wide, they both stepped forward and Mordecai gathered Wushka in for a big hug and lifted her off the floor.

"You ARE a good hugger," he said, putting her down and stepping back. "You're a g-g-great hugger!"

"Thanks," Wushka grinned.

Mordecai leaned forward, whispered in her ear, "G-G-G," and smiled. Turning and scanning his eyes across the class, he announced, "Now, let's sniff that orange!"

•••

After class, Mordecai and Bela sat alone in the small desks and talked. She said she was a courier in Poland for Dror, a Zionist youth group, for two years, and was arrested on a train in 1942 while carrying a pistol. The Germans imprisoned, tortured and sent her to Auschwitz. But not as a Jew, which saved her life. They thought she was a Catholic member of the AK. With Polish Christian women, she suffered horribly in Auschwitz and endured a death march and other concentration camps under her fake Aryan name.

Mordecai noticed Bela blush heavily when she talked about the Germans shaving her head months earlier because she had violated a labor camp rule. "You are very pretty and will be b-b-beautiful when your hair grows back." Mordecai hoped she didn't take his comment the wrong way.

Bela blushed again and continued her story. "Finally, I was liberated by the Americans. What a day that was! I then traveled west and met members of the Jewish Brigade." She ran her fingers along the Star of David patch on Mordecai's shoulder. "You can't imagine my feelings when I met Jewish soldiers wearing the Star with pride instead of shame. The Brigade boys arranged for me to come here. I'll go with the orphans to Palestine – the British had better let us in!"

Mordecai told Bela his story. His training, fighting and discouraging searches for his family and his old girlfriend.

"You keep calling her your girlfriend. What's her name?"

"Anna Allowitz."

Bela wanly smiled and solemnly nodded. "I knew Anna. She was a beautiful, kindhearted soul. Very bright and a passionate Zionist." She looked down and shook her head. "And we were the same age. We talked about it. She was born July 28, 1921, and I was July 29 the same year."

Mordecai felt a lump in his throat. Bela was speaking of Anna in the past tense. She "knew" her. Anna "was" beautiful. He felt himself breathing rapidly and tried to calm down, rubbing his face with his hand. "You – you're talking in the p-p-p-past, as if you know–"

Bela dropped her hand onto Mordecai's arm and forced a smile. "No. I'm not saying that. I don't know for certain what happened to Anna."

"What do you know?"

"She went on many missions for Zakkai as a courier – once stayed in my apartment, on the Aryan side, in Grodno. Later, like me, the Germans arrested her and sent her to Auschwitz, thinking she was a member of Polish resistance. For months, we were together. Very hard work, always terribly hungry, freezing cold, depraved guards..."

For a moment, Bela stared silently at nothing – at least nothing visible to Mordecai. "In 1943, Anna, me and my best friend – another Jewish girl arrested as a Pole – all caught typhus, and they put us in the camp hospital. We were so sick; my best friend and Anna also got dysentery. My best friend died." Bela's eyes filled with tears and she looked down, silently, for a few moments. "When I gained my strength, they sent me to another camp. I never saw Anna again." She averted Mordecai's eyes.

"You think she d-d-died in the hospital?"

Bela shook her head thoughtfully. "I don't know. I don't know. Anna was very sick, but she was a strong girl. Young. Like my friend," she muttered. "Go to the American zone in Germany; DP camps there, I heard people say. Try near Frankfurt."

Mordecai stood. "I'm very sorry for m-m-making you talk about these things. You will love Palestine. We have much work to do, but the pride you'll feel rebuilding our homeland is enormous. Hopefully, we'll cross paths there."

"I'd like that," Bela said, standing. "Before you go – like your old friend, Wushka, I was once a good hugger." She looked into Mordecai's eyes, they hugged each other tight and cried for all who were gone.

September 26, 1945
Germany
Mordecai

It was almost noon when Mordecai crossed into Germany. Sunlight poured into his jeep in a contradiction his seething mind couldn't fathom. Germany should be black night for eternity. His loathing for everything German was so intense that he previously had avoided coming here. What if he couldn't control his hatred? But Germany was full of DP camps, and Bela had said to check near Frankfurt... Or so he told himself. But the truth was that like the curiosity that compels people to view a monster, Mordecai needed to step on German soil.

He drove through devastated, charred German cities. British and American bombers had destroyed them and killed hundreds of thousands of German civilians without distinction between Nazi supporter and opponent. But Mordecai felt no pity.

He drove to the outskirts of Nuremberg, an old hotbed of Nazism, parked in a quiet business area and watched Germans occasionally stroll by on the adjacent sidewalk. Mordecai imagined these same people proudly raising their arms in the Nazi salute and screaming "Heil Hitler." And smashing Jewish stores on Kristallnacht, volunteering for SS units that murdered Jewish babies and children.

His head pounded as he thought of his murdered friends and neighbors.

Of his parents, exterminated like rats.

Of his idealistic Zakkai friends longing to get to Palestine – murdered.

Of what the Germans did to Bela.

Of Anna, probably dead.

And of the other six million – each a human being – humiliated, hounded and murdered because they were Jews.

All by Germans – including those walking by. Resentment burned Mordecai's heart, and his pulse throbbed in his ears. So many helpless, unarmed people forced to grovel before the master race. But now, it was the Germans who were unarmed.

His teeth clenched; Mordecai remembered scolding Pinchus for killing the SS man in Austria. Pinchus had been right – the butcher deserved to die.

Mordecai noticed a group of five or six German men and women walking his way on the sidewalk. Two old people and the rest middle-aged, the men wore knee-length pants and suspenders like the Germans he'd seen in newsreels wildly cheering Hitler. Mordecai quickly exited the jeep and, pistol on the hip of his Jewish Brigade uniform, marched toward them. As they met, he tried to look into their eyes, but the Germans turned their heads and moved aside.

After they passed, Mordecai thought he heard someone mutter, "Jude" – "Jew." He immediately turned and thundered, "Halt!" They stopped about five steps away, turned and looked at him. He screamed in broken German, "I heard you! Who said that!"

An old man stepped forward, opened his hands and said in English, "Sir, we said nothing."

Mordecai replied in English, "I heard it!" He furiously pulled the pistol from his holster and pointed it at what he knew were Jew-hating Nazis. "The one who said 'Jew' when I walked by – step forward! Or I'll k-k-kill every one of you. Now!"

The old man translated quickly for his group and said to Mordecai, "None of us said that, sir. Please let us go on our way."

Mordecai's eyes narrowed, he marched to them and stuck his pistol in the old man's face. The man cowered, as did the others behind him.

"How many Jewish children did you mock!" Mordecai raged. "Which of your Jewish neighbors did you betray to the Gestapo!" Mordecai took a step to his right and pointed the pistol at the face of a younger man. "How many Jews did you murder!"

The Germans looked down and said nothing.

"I'll ask once m-m-more! Who said 'Jew' when I walked by!" Mordecai again pointed his pistol at the old man's face.

The man meekly shrugged and said, "We're good Germans. We didn't hurt Jewish people." Mordecai's hate-filled eyes burned into the Nazi, who clearly deserved to die; he aimed his gun directly at the man's forehead and desperately wanted to pull the trigger.

But he couldn't. He re-holstered the pistol, walked at the Germans, who skirted out of the way, returned to his jeep and drove into the center of old Nuremberg, totally devastated by British and American bombing. His hands shaking, Mordecai parked outside the rubble of an old church, crept into the back of his jeep, and slept for ten hours.

OCTOBER 1, 1945
FRANKFURT, GERMANY
MORDECAI

Late afternoon, Mordecai was sitting at a table in a small Jewish community bureau in Frankfurt sorting through handwritten index cards. On each card was written the name of a Jew who had somehow survived the war and was seeking a new home, and of the DP camp where the person currently lived. Though alphabetized, he'd learned from searching through hundreds of cards at other places that mistakes were made. So, at each of the four offices Mordecai had visited across Germany, he read every single card. Flipping one after another, after another and after another.

At a place he'd visited two days earlier, his heart had skipped a beat when he read the name "Anna Ullowitz." But the workers had confirmed Ullowitz was not a misspelling; the Anna on that card was ten years old.

The Frankfurt office contained thousands of cards and was run with help from an American Jewish organization trying to create a cumulative list of survivors. Mordecai had looked through every card with a name starting with "A." No Allowitz. Now, eyes glazed over, he was sifting through names starting with L. Lansky, Levi, Leavy, Lefkovicz, Leibkind, Lieberman, Allowitz. He blinked and reread the card. "Irina Allowitz." He cried out, "Irina Allowitz!" earning a startled look from the bespectacled, gray-mustached clerk sitting across the room.

Mordecai held his face in his hands and reread the card. "Irina Allowitz, Zeilsheim." He stared at the words, handprinted in pencil, and his eyes watered. Mordecai finally bolted from his chair, ran to the clerk and yelled, "Where is Zeilsheim! What is Zeilsheim?"

"It's a Jewish DP camp about twelve miles west of here," the clerk said. He gave Mordecai directions and Mordecai thanked him, shook his hand and thanked him again. Elated, he rushed out of the office, ran from the building and down several concrete steps, darted across a concrete pavement toward his jeep and slammed into a German businessman walking on the sidewalk, knocking him down.

The man, about forty and wearing a nice suit and tie, was sprawled across the cement walk. In his euphoria, Mordecai's hatred for everyone German momentarily receded; he took the man's hand, helped him up and quickly apologized. But Mordecai's loathing quickly reappeared; he wondered in what army or SS unit the man might have served.

Mordecai turned to go, but the German patted Mordecai's shoulder, pointed at his Star of David patch and said something in German. Mordecai clenched his fists but relaxed when he saw the friendly smile on the German's face.

"I d-d-don't speak German," Mordecai said.

The German switched to English. "I see your Palestine patch, and I wonder. I have an old, good friend, Hans Kernmann, went to Palestine in 1937. You know him?"

"No, sorry," Mordecai replied.

"Palestine is a small place," the German said. "If you ever meet him – Hans Kernmann – his old friend, Karl Beck, sends his greetings."

"OK." Mordecai ran to his jeep.

•••

Mordecai's jeep was almost out of gas. Near dark, he drove several blocks and found a petrol station, but it was closed. He could wait until morning or leave the jeep and walk twelve miles.

He couldn't wait.

He studied the map and started trotting. That his car needed gas was a blessing; he had plenty of time to decide what to say to Irina. He'd felt bad asking Bela about her horrible experiences. He wouldn't do that to Irina or immediately ask about Anna. He should keep the conversation upbeat as long as possible, and maybe talk about life in Palestine?

After about six miles, now in total darkness, he realized he was lost. Cussing in Polish, Hebrew and English, he turned back, found the road he was looking for, and again headed to Zeilsheim. He finally arrived at the DP camp's gate at about 9:00 p.m.

The American guard wouldn't let him in. "It's too late. Come back tomorrow."

Mordecai begged, pleaded, told the American his story, and begged some more; the guy could get in trouble if he let Mordecai in but felt sorry for him. He checked his master list of occupants. "You didn't hear it from me, but Irina Allowitz is in building 3, apartment 112. This isn't like the rudimentary DP camps – it's a bunch of apartments. Go to the third long building, and 112 is about halfway down. But she may not be in her room. There's a meeting going on right now for this whole place. Explaining rules and regulations. These people may be here weeks, months or years, waiting to find a country to let 'em in.

"And good luck, buddy," the American added.

Mordecai hurried in the dark past two gray buildings and came to number 3. He opened a heavy, metal door and walked down a long, narrow, empty hall smelling of fresh white paint. He checked the unit numbers, written in small letters next to each door, and found 112.

It was now almost 9:30, and the building was quiet. His pulse thumping in his ears, Mordecai rested his face against the brown door but didn't hear a sound from inside. He sniffed under his arm, made a face at the bad odor, took a deep breath and knocked.

Silence. She must be in that meeting the guard mentioned.

Tapping his foot, Mordecai waited impatiently. After a couple minutes, he started pacing, and a while later the door at the far end of the hall opened and people started entering the building. Most seemed in their twenties or thirties, and a few looked older. Mordecai heard noise behind him; men and women were now coming in from both ends of the long hallway. He kept turning his head, anxiously searching for a girl who might be Irina.

He returned to number 112 and watched as at least thirty men and women lingered in the hall talking in a variety of languages, entered apartments, or walked past. He then spotted two women, probably mid to late twenties, coming toward him. One had long, blondish-brown hair, the other dark hair. The light-haired woman was pretty but too old to be Irina, who would now be about eighteen. She was a young, pig-tailed kid when he last saw her. For the first time, it occurred to Mordecai that Europe might have more than one Irina Allowitz. His heart began to sink.

"You're at the wrong apartment," the dark-haired woman snapped in Jewish as the two women approached. "You're the third guy in uniform the past two days looking for Mendel Scheinman – he's next door, in 110. I don't know why you people can't get that straight." She dismissively pointed to her right.

Mordecai ignored her. Staring intently at the light-haired woman standing a few feet in front of him, he said, "Irina Allowitz?"

The woman silently stared back.

"Sorry for c-c-c-coming here so late," Mordecai said as he stepped nearer to her. "Are you Irina Allowitz from Krasau?" The closer he looked at her, the more–

"Mordecai!" the woman gasped, and her face lit up. "Oh my God! Yeah, I'm Irina! Have I changed that much!"

He spread his arms, they embraced, and Irina said, "Look at you! Oh my God! Oh my God! You're a soldier!"

"You can't imagine how happy this m-m-makes me," Mordecai said. "You've grown up, and you look wonderful!" He paused, and his head began to spin. "I've been looking–" His voice trailed off; he glanced down, rubbed his face and took a step back.

"Why don't we go inside?" the dark-haired woman said. "I'll get you some water." She waved Mordecai and Irina toward the apartment door, but they stood still, gazing at each other.

Mordecai took Irina's hand in his. He had told himself he'd wait to ask about Anna but couldn't do it. "D-D-Do you know what hap-p-pened t-t-to Anna?" he asked, barely getting the words out, his voice cracking.

Irina paused and pointed behind him, down the hall. Mordecai turned around; in the small crowd he saw a young woman, wearing a dark skirt and plain white blouse, walking toward them.

At about ten feet away, the woman noticed him – a dark-haired man in a British uniform – and she then saw his eyes, his mouth, his face. She managed a couple more steps, halted, stepped back, raised a hand to her forehead and stared, shocked, open-mouthed.

Mordecai stood frozen, his eyes absorbing the young woman's face, with its scarred cheek and short blondish hair – short like Auschwitz survivor Bela. No lavender eyeshadow or lipstick of a Hollywood actress or underground courier.

"I've been searching f-f-for you," he said tenderly, his vision blurred by tears.

Anna's eyes widened, she screamed "Mordecai!" and leapt into his outstretched arms.

HISTORICAL NOTES

This book is based largely on information contained in the following sources, in alphabetical order. Cites in the Notes are to authors' names.

Batalion, Judy. *The Light of Days.* HarperCollins Publishers, 2020.

Baumel-Schwartz, Judith-Tydor. *Perfect Heroes: World War Two Parachutists and the Making of Israeli Collective Memory.* The University of Wisconsin Press, 2010.

Berenbaum, Michael. *The World Must Know: The History of the Holocaust as Told in the United States Holocaust Memorial Museum* (2nd ed.). The Johns Hopkins University Press, 2006.

Berg, Mary. *The Diary of Mary Berg: Growing up in the Warsaw Ghetto, 75th Anniversary Edition.* Edited by Shneiderman, S.L., prepared by Pentlin, Susan; translated by Gutterman, Norbert and Glass, Sylvia. Oneworld Publications Limited, 1945, 2018.

Blum, Howard. *The Brigade.* Harper Collins Publishers, 2001.

Dawidowicz, Lucy. *The War Against the Jews, 1933-1945.* Bantam Books, 1975.

Draenger, Gusta Davidson. Pfefferkorn, Eli & Hirsch, David H. (eds.) *Justyna's Narrative.* Translated by Hirsch, Roslyn and David. The University of Massachusetts Press, 1996.

Friedlander, Henry. *The Origins of Nazi Genocide: From Euthanasia to the Final Solution.* The University of North Carolina Press, 1995.

Gilbert, Martin. *The Holocaust: A History of the Jews of Europe During the Second World War.* Henry Holt and Company, Inc., 1985.

Green, Arthur (Ed. and translator) & Rosenberg, Joel (translator). *Hasidic Spirituality for a New Era: the Religious Writings of Hillel Zeitlin.* Paulist Press, 2012.

Klee, Ernst; Dressen, Willi; Riess, Volker (Eds.) *The Good Old Days: The Holocaust as Seen by Its Perpetrators and Bystanders.* Translated by Burnstone, Deborah. Konecky & Konecky, 1988, 1991.

Kochanski, Halik. *The Eagle Unbowed.* Harvard University Press, 2012.

Oshry, Rabbi Ephraim. *Responsa from the Holocaust.* Judaica Press, 1983.

Pankiewicz, Tadeusz. *The Cracow Ghetto Pharmacy.* Translated by Tilles, Henry. Waldon Press, 1947, 1987.

Paulsson, Gunnar S. *Secret City: The Hidden Jews of Warsaw 1940-1945.* Yale University Press, 2002.

Person Katarzyna. *Warsaw Ghetto Police: The Jewish Order Service During the Nazi Occupation.* Translated by Nowak-Solinski, Zygmunt. Cornell University Press, 2021.

Polonsky, Antony. *The Jews in Poland and Russia, Volume III.* The Littman Library of Jewish Civilization in association with Liverpool University Press, 2019.

Sachar, Howard. *A History of Israel from the Rise of Zionism to our Time*. Alfred A. Knopf, 1996.

Shirer, William L. *The Rise and Fall of the Third Reich*. Simon & Schuster, 1960.

Sloan, Jacob (Ed. and translator). *Notes from the Warsaw Ghetto from the Journal of Emmanuel Ringelblum*. ibooks, inc., 2006.

Schiff, Ze'ev. *A History of the Israeli Army 1874 to the Present*. Macmillan Publishing Company, 1985.

Sykes, Christopher. *Orde Wingate*. The World Publishing Company, 1959.

The primary original sources for this novel are historian Emmanuel Ringelblum's *Notes From the Warsaw Ghetto, Justyna's Narrative,* eyewitness accounts quoted in the noted books, and miscellaneous recollections, including those preserved online of attendees of German schools, cited in the chapter notes.

Ringelblum's notes were part of an archive written and compiled by a group of Jews trapped in the Warsaw Ghetto and led by Emmanuel Ringelblum. Shortly before the ghetto's destruction, the archive was buried. Much, but not all, was discovered after the war, including Ringelblum's notes. He and most other contributors perished.

The character Anna was inspired by (but not closely based on) Gusta Draenger. A member of the Krakow Akiva youth group and passionate Zionist, she wrote while in German custody the story of Akiva's transformation from youth group to resistance group – *Justyna's Narrative*. Her personal story, including her work as a courier, turning herself in to the Germans so that she might stay with her already arrested husband, her daring escape, and other exploits are beyond admirable. The Germans killed her at age twenty-six.

The fictional Zakkai youth group is modeled after the Akiva group, active in Poland in the 1930s, of which Gusta Draenger was so proud. The character Jozef was very loosely based on Aharon Liebeskind. This novel aims to honor their memories with far more than three lines.

The character Karl Beck is a synthesis of Germans involved in Germany's program for the murder of handicapped Germans and the extermination of Europe's Jews.

Zygmunt Klukowski and Lorenz Hackenholt were historical figures. All other speaking characters are fictional, but many of their experiences are based on real events, as noted below.

PART ONE – Closing the Trap

MAY 8, 1938 ANNA

The term "Palestine" in this novel has the meaning understood at the relevant times: the geographical area also known as the "Holy Land," "Land of Israel," or the Israelites' biblical "Promised Land," where the modern nation of Israel and its disputed territories are located. From 1920 until May 1948, Britain governed it per a League of Nations "Mandate" for the establishment there of a "national home for the Jewish people." Not until later in the 20th century did the term Palestine refer to an aspired for or existent Arab political entity.

"Jewish script" refers to Yiddish (Jewish), written in Hebrew letters.

JULY 6, 1938 SZYMON

Yidl with a Fiddle was a Yiddish (Jewish) language movie released in Poland in 1936.

The mid-1930s saw a wave of anti-Jewish violence in Poland, especially in 1935-1937, primarily in small towns but also in larger cities. Polonsky at 85-86.

JULY 7, 1938 IRINA

The "World War," sometimes called the "Great War," refers to what is now called World War I.

One zloty was worth about 20 U.S. cents prewar. Berg at 3.

JULY 8, 1938 ESTIE

Zionist youth groups boomed in Poland in the 1930s, consisting of between 70,000 and 100,000 members. Polonsky at 94. Many members and leaders of Jewish resistance during the war came from these groups, such as Abba Kovner in Vilna and Mordecai Anielewicz, leader of the Jewish Fighting Organization during the Warsaw ghetto revolt, both from the socialist Zionist Hashomer Hatzair. Menachem Begin, active in the right-wing youth group Beitar, escaped Poland, later led the Irgun and became a prime minister of Israel.

Estie's experiences in Germany are entirely based on experiences of real people, per eyewitness accounts from German Christians and Jews. *See, e.g.:* https://spartacus-educational.com/Jewish_Children.htm These include when Estie's friends called her a dirty Jew, the comment by a German boy that the Jewish soldiers killed in World War I had died of fright, and others.

In many places in Germany before the war, Jews could not buy food because over the doors of bakeries, groceries, dairies, were signs "Jews not admitted." Some signs said "Jews strictly forbidden in this town" or "Jews enter this place at their own risk." Shirer at 233.

Nazi antisemitism was based on the idea that the Jews' alleged defects were passed biologically from one generation to the next. Unlike most earlier strands of antisemitism, which a Jew could escape via conversion, the Nazis saw conversion as Jewish pollution of the pure Aryan gene pool. Nazis thus came to believe the only possible solutions to the "Jewish problem" were emigration or extermination.

SEPTEMBER 30, 1938 ITZHAK AND SZYMON

Although many Polish Jews attended Jewish schools in the 1930s, the majority attended public schools. Polonsky at 132-133.

Violence against Jews, economic boycotts, limitations on entry to trade schools and universities, and Church encouraged anti-Jewish feelings plagued Polish Jews in the mid-1930s. Polonsky at 77-93.

After World War I, in addition to the British mandate in Palestine for the creation of a Jewish national home, the western powers and League of Nations established mandates or administrations for Lebanon, Syria, Transjordan and Iraq, which like Saudi Arabia, Egypt, and others were to become Arab countries. (Sachar at 116, *et. seq.)*.

The "violent rampage" Itzhak referred to was the Arab revolt of 1936 to 1939, in which more than two thousand Jews were killed. British concern that Arabs would support the Nazis and put British oil supplies at risk led to the British White Paper of May 1939. Sachar at 199-222.

The British limited Jewish immigration to Palestine even before the 1939 White Paper. Polonsky at 90.

The Americans who developed the polio vaccines, Jonas Salk and Albert Sabin, were Jews from eastern Europe. Salk's mother immigrated to the U.S., where Salk was born; Sabin was born in what became eastern Poland.

Albert Einstein said, "If my theory of relativity is proven correct, Germany will claim me as a German, and France will declare that I am a citizen of the world. Should my theory prove untrue, France will say that I am a German, and Germany will declare that I am a Jew."

Lists were prepared in Poland, apparently with input from ethnic Germans, of Polish "intelligentsia" prior to the German invasion and given to the Germans, who in "Aktion Intelligenz" during the first several months after the invasion, murdered or sent to concentration camps people listed. https://muzeum1939.pl/en/sonderfahndungsbuch-polen-special-book-wanted-poland-exhibition-fragment-msww/6305.html and https://polishnews.com/intelligenzaktion.

JANUARY 10, 1939 PAPA

Many officers and soldiers of Pilsudski's Polish legions who fought alongside the Austrians in World War I were of Jewish origin. Polonsky at 11-12.

For years, the question of citizenship of tens of thousands of Jewish residents of eastern Poland, from the former Russian Empire, was a matter of dispute between Jews and their opponents until resolved by Pilsudski in favor of citizenship. Polonsky at 74-75.

By the late 1930s, the Polish government's policy to solve its "Jewish problem" was to support mass emigration. Polonsky at 90-97.

FEBRUARY 6, 1939 RABBI LEIBMAN

Rabbi Leibman's vision was loosely modeled on a mid-1939 writing of Hillel Zeitlin, who predicted a tragedy to befall the Jews of Europe and wrote of the need for Jews to return to their mission of bringing justice to the world, caring for the downtrodden. Green at 28-31.

MAY 18, 1939 STANISLAW NOWAK

Issued to appease the Arabs to dissuade them from supporting Germany in the event of war (Sachar at 220), the British White Paper of May 1939 severely limited Jewish immigration to Palestine, prohibited the sale of land to Jews, and "sealed off Palestine as a haven for all but an insignificant fraction of Jewish refugees, and this at the moment when European Jewry faced a mortal threat to its continued physical survival." Sachar at 223. Winston Churchill castigated the British government for breaking its pledge to the Jews. Sachar at 224.

AUGUST 15, 1939 BERLIN, GERMANY KARL BECK

The origins, operations, and other aspects of the German euthanasia program for children and adults, the program's expansion into Poland upon the outbreak of war, and the evolution and application of gassing to murder Jews as described in this novel are historically accurate as detailed in Friedlander.

The facts stated regarding a boy named Erwin, his test results and sterilization are real. Friedlander at 32.

PART TWO – The Trap

SEPTEMBER 7, 1939 THE ALLOWITZS

Hundreds of thousands of Jews fled east when the Germans invaded Poland. Some continued to other countries not yet occupied by the Germans, many were arrested and shipped by the Soviets to the country's interior, including Siberia, ironically saving their lives. Others stayed and were murdered by the Germans when they invaded the Soviet Union in June 1941.

SEPTEMBER 14, 1939 ITZHAK

Among the many degradations mentioned in Ringelblum, Nazis forced a Jew to kneel and urinated on him. Ringelblum at 91.

OCTOBER 8, 1939 SZYMON

Poland was divided into three parts: the Soviet Union occupied eastern Poland, Germany annexed much of western Poland directly into Germany, and the rest was governed by Germany as a separate entity and given the name "General Government." Its area included Warsaw, Lublin, and Krakow.

As part of their subjugation of the Poles and to deprive them of leadership, the Germans rounded up and executed or sent to concentration camps tens of thousands of Polish intellectuals, lawyers, teachers, priests and former government officials. Polonsky at 365-368; https://www.ushmm.org/m/pdfs/2000926-Poles.pdf

FEBRUARY 20, 1940 ITZHAK AND SZYMON

The comments by Itzhak's mother that Jews were forced to move from towns and villages to larger urban areas mirrored the forced relocation of Jews ordered by Reinhard Heydrich on September 21, 1939. Polonsky at 374.

The mistreatment of Poles, including shutting down schools and forced labor roundups are per Polonsky at 364-370. The execution of university students for possessing a radio receiver is per Ringelblum at 10.

The Germans intentionally increased Polish-Jewish tension and encouraged Poles to rob or kill Jews and take their businesses. They portrayed Jews as responsible for disease, dirty. Polonsky at 402–404.

All the incidents of Nazi abuse of Jews listed by Itzhak are real, per Ringelblum.

APRIL 10, 1940 KARL BECK

The SS was the massive Nazi "political army" responsible, *inter alia,* for policing German racial laws and included combat troops, administration of the concentration and extermination camps, and the Gestapo.

APRIL 18, 1940 BUBBIE

Germans ordering Jews, including elderly, to perform calisthenics, including push-ups using paving stones or tiles as weights. Ringelblum at 86.

Ordering a Jew to lie in the mud. Ringelblum at 87.

Ordering Jewish women to use their underwear as rags. Berg at 17.

"You're not people. You're not even animals. You're Jews." Statement made to a rabbi in the Warsaw ghetto as recorded in Ringelblum at 24.

APRIL 25, 1940 ZAKKAI

Zionist training farms for Jewish youth, with German permission during the first years of the war, included the Kopilany farm near Krakow, one near Bedzin and a Warsaw farm at Grochow. Draenger at 35, et. seq., Batalion at 121; https://1943.pl/en/artykul/palestine-on-the-right-bank-of-the-vistula-river/.

JULY 14, 1940 IRINA

The italicized language is a rearranged description by Gusta Draenger of teens at the Zionist farm near Krakow. Draenger at 42. The description of the forest was based on Draenger at 35.

NOVEMBER 12, 1940 ITZHAK'S JOURNAL

The italicized language, slightly revised for context, was by eyewitness Toshia Bialer regarding one-third of Warsaw's population. Gilbert at 129.

The description of the Jewish police and their tasks are per Person at 40-44.

Some Jews thought the Germans put Jews in ghettos, concentrating them in major cities, in case of war with Russia so that the Germans would be "secure in the rear." Ringelblum at 124.

Many Christians brought bread for their Jewish friends on the first day after the Warsaw Ghetto was closed in; Ringelblum at 86. A Christian was killed for throwing a sack of bread over the wall; Ringelblum at 89.

JANUARY 7, 1941 PETER

The initial abolition and prompt reinstatement by the Germans of the Polish police is per Grabowski, Jan, *The Polish Police Collaboration in the Holocaust*, 2016, at https://www.ushmm.org/m/pdfs/20170502-Grabowski_OP.pdf

MARCH 25, 1941 ANNA

The Germans executed Jews for publishing unauthorized material. Ringelblum at 269-270.

The Nazis allowed Jews to emigrate from the General Government until the summer of 1940. Polonsky at 374.

The ways identified by Itzhak to leave and return to the ghetto are among those used by Jews in the Warsaw ghetto. Paulsson at 61-66.

APRIL 21, 1941 ANNA

Smuggling oneself out of the ghetto as a member of a work party is described in Paulsson at 65-66.

APRIL 21, 1941 PALESTINE MORDECAI

The Jezreel Valley was the site of several Biblical battles, including Deborah and Barak (Judges 5:19), of Gideon (Judges 7), and was where the Philistines defeated Saul (1 Samuel 28-31). British training of Jews there in 1941 near Kibbutz Mishmar Ha'Emek is per Schiff at 18.

Cooperation between the British intelligence services and Jews in Palestine, concerns about a German invasion, and initial efforts on dropping Jewish commandos into occupied Europe are discussed in Baumel-Schwartz at 5-9.

The italicized language as to why Smithson was sympathetic to the Jews was stated (with minor revisions for context) by Orde Wingate, the British officer who played an instrumental role training Jewish fighters in Palestine. Sykes at 110.

JULY 15, 1941 SZYMON'S JOURNAL

German treatment of Polish laborers in Germany, including compelling them to wear the letter "P," are per Ulrich, Herbert. *Hitler's Foreign Workers: Enforced Foreign Labor in Germany in the Third Reich.* ILWCH, 58, Fall 2000 at 194. By May 1940, more than a million Poles had been rounded up and forced to work in Germany. *Id*

NOVEMBER 4, 1941 FRAMMY

The school upstairs from the shoe repair shop and the shoe repairman's warning signal are based on Sam Weisberg's recollections of his secret school in the Krakow ghetto. See https://memoirs.azrielifoundation.org/exhibits/education-disrupted/ghettos/#9

NOVEMBER 5, 1941 ITZHAK'S JOURNAL

In October 1941, Hans Frank, head of the General Government, decreed that Jews who left their ghettos without authorization and Poles who assisted them were subject to the death penalty. Paulsson at 67.

The italicized language (paraphrased), examples of Jews executed for working on the Aryan side without a permit and shock at the executions are per Ringelblum at 236-237.

The ghetto riddle is real. Paulsson at 67.

Some Jews in the Warsaw Ghetto were Gestapo informants, but how many was unknown. Ringelblum at 281.

NOVEMBER 7, 1941 REUVEN AND BENEC

Jewish police involvement in rounding up Jews for forced labor, and policemen's widespread acceptance of bribes is discussed in Person at 62-63.

The sports field in the ghetto and Levi's statement were based on the Vilna ghetto where, even **after** thousands of Jews were murdered, the ghetto authorities organized sports and cultural activities. The head of the Jewish Council, Jacob Gens, said "We are passing through dark and difficult days. Our bodies are in the ghetto, but our spirit has not been enslaved... [It] was said that concerts should not be held in graveyards. True, ... but all of life is now a graveyard... We must be strong in body and soul." https://www.yadvashem.org/yv/pdf-drupal/en/education/sports-and-culture.pdf

A Warsaw Ghetto survivor said they "were always surrounded by terror, but... led normal lives right alongside it. Flirting went on in the ghetto, romances... The normal and the abnormal intertwined repeatedly." Berg at xxiii.

JANUARY 20, 1942

At this meeting, known to history as the Wannsee Conference, Reinhard Heydrich of the SS discussed with representatives of the relevant German government departments coordinating the deportation of Europe's Jews to "the east" and their murder – the "Final Solution." More than half of the fifteen men present held German university doctorates. No one objected. Berenbaum at 101-102.

APRIL 7, 1942 PAPA

Ringelblum at 194 records that people in the Warsaw ghetto became indifferent to death, walking by corpses.

The poem was inspired by Avramek Kapolowicz, eleven years old when forced with his family into the Lodz ghetto in 1940. He wrote poems in his "exercise book." Avramek was murdered in Auschwitz. Yad Vashem educational video at https://echoesandreflections.org/wp-content/uploads/2014/04/EchoesAndReflections_Lesson_Four_Poem-PoemByAvrahamKoplowicz.pdf

The Nazi offer to move elderly and young children to a "less uncomfortable place" as a ruse to murder them (and the Jews' joy at the opportunity) is based in part on the experience in Dvinsk as described by Maja Zarch, quoted in Gilbert at 179.

PART THREE – The Cauldron

APRIL 8, 1942 ANNA

The italicized language about a Jew's feelings on the Aryan side was written by courier Gusta Draenger. Draenger at 52–54.

Ringelblum, the Warsaw ghetto archivist, wrote as follows about young female couriers. "The heroic girls... Boldly, they travel back and forth through the cities and towns of Poland... They are in mortal danger every day... Without a murmur, without a second's hesitation, they accept and carry out the most dangerous missions... With what simplicity and modesty... The story of the Jewish woman will be a glorious page in the history of Jewry during the present war. And the [young couriers] will be the leading figures in this story." Ringelblum at 273–274.

APRIL 9, 1942 ANNA

The italicized language is quoted in Paulsson at 69.

REGINA

Gusta Draenger said that a ghetto Jew who takes off an armband must "regain [her] sense of human dignity" to pass as a "human being"; otherwise "you are nothing more than a Jew without an armband." Draenger at 52.

APRIL 13, 1942 ANNA

Dr. Zygmunt Klukowski was a physician and member of the Polish underground who documented life under the Nazis. The italicized language describing the April 11 German attack on Zamosc Jews was per the eyewitness account of David Mekler. Gilbert at 319-320.

Dr. Klukowski noted in his diary on April 12, 1942 the italicized language regarding the fate of Jews sent to Belzec. Gilbert at 316-317.

APRIL 14, 1942 BELZEC

The words *"Now you're going to the bath-house, afterwards you will be sent to work"* were spoken each day by SS officer Fritz Irrman to arriving transports of Jews according to Rudolf Reder, one of only two Jews to survive Belzec, where his work included pulling corpses with leather straps to the mass graves. The description of Belzec and the gassing process are based on Reder's writings. Gilbert at 413-417.

A German document notes that 434,508 Jews were killed at Belzec between March and December 1942. Berenbaum at 120-121. In total, as many as 600,000 Jews may have been gassed there. Gilbert at 502.

Given that Reder did not arrive at Belzec until August 1942, the layout of the camp would have differed somewhat in April (when Frammy and his family were murdered), as renovations took place that summer. Klee at 230.

The building description, including the geraniums, is per a German's eyewitness account in August 1942. Klee at 241.

Lorenz Hackenholt, who had been involved with killing German handicapped, operated the gassing mechanism at Belzec, and a sign on the building where the people were gassed read "Hackenholt Foundation" in his "honor." Klee at 241. He disappeared – likely escaping justice – after the war. Klee at 294.

Most of the German "euthanasia program's" personnel and some of its equipment were used in the extermination of Jews. Dawidowicz at 134.

The description of the orchestra and the reference to a song they played are per Reder's recollections. https://holocaustmusic.ort.org/places/camps/death-camps/belzec/

PART FOUR – For Three Lines

APRIL 16, 1942 ANNA

Anna's comment about older people is a paraphrase of words by Gusta Draenger, recorded in Draenger at 37 and 46.

The Jewish underground in most ghettos was led by young people trained in youth movements. Berenbaum at 175.

The italicized language about not being led like cattle to the slaughter is a modified quote of words by Gusta Draenger recorded in Draenger at 40 and 33.

MAY 18, 1942 BENJAMIN

Though the number of telephones was greatly reduced, some remained available in the Warsaw Ghetto as late as the April 1943 Jewish revolt. Paulsson at 77-78.

MAY 19, 1942 SZYMON

The italicized language about guns is paraphrased from Gusta Draenger's words in Draenger at 71-72.

MAY 21, 1942 ITZHAK

The Shma and Amidah are the two most important parts of the regular weekday morning prayer service.

"Orthodox Jews rarely participated in the rebellions" and "tended to accept the ghetto as God's will." Berenbaum at 176.

The Germans banned religious services in most ghettos, and for many religious Jews who opposed physical force, resistance was via organized prayer. https://encyclopedia.ushmm.org/content/en/article/spiritual-resistance-in-the-ghettos

The question "What blessing do I say before they kill me...?" was asked of Rabbi Ephraim Oshry in the Kovno, Lithuania ghetto. On "scraps of paper torn from concrete sacks," buried in cans and uncovered after liberation, Rabbi Oshry wrote this question, his answer, and numerous other questions asked of him during the war and his answers. Oshry at x-xii.

JUNE 17, 1942 IRINA

The chapter's last sentence is based on the comment by David Berger that he hoped somebody "would remember that someone named David Berger had once lived." A member of the Akiva Zionist youth movement, he wrote those words in a letter to his girlfriend, who had left Poland in 1938 for Palestine. The Germans murdered David in Lithuania in 1941. https://www.hmd.org.uk/wp-content/uploads/2014/04/Life-Story-David-Berger.pdf

JUNE 22, 1942 HEINRICH SCHMIDT

Schmidt blaming the Jews for the war is based on an essay to that effect by Joseph Goebbels, German Minister of Propaganda, in a November 1941 essay. https://research.calvin.edu/german-propaganda-archive/goeb1.htm

The instructions for what Jews were to bring for the deportation is based on July 1942 German instructions to Warsaw Jews, including to bring "all valuables such as gold, jewelry, money, etc." Paulsson at 73.

The italicized statement by the Jewish Council's head is from the diary of Adam Czerniakow, Chairman of the Warsaw Jewish Council, shortly before his suicide in July 1942 on the ninth of Av. Gilbert at 389–390; Berenbaum at 77.

In the Warsaw Ghetto, many Jewish policemen, under threat of punishment if they failed to meet their quota of deportees, diligently and viciously helped the Nazis round up Jews. Ringelblum at 329-336. Some helped Jews escape the roundups. Ringelblum at 311.

The German officer ordering a Jewish boy to stand against a wall and wait for the officer to return to execute him is based on a true story, recounted to the author by Leo Heim, later a congregational rabbi in the United States.

It has been reported that Hillel Zeitlin, the neo-Hasidic writer who predicted the calamity to befall Europe's Jews, wore his tallis and tefillin as he was sent to his death from Warsaw to the Treblinka extermination camp. Green at 32.

The italicized language about the mother chasing after the truck containing her baby was, with slight modifications, by eyewitness Alexander Donat, quoted in Gilbert at 393–394.

September 18, 1942 Jozef

The italicized words regarding the Sabbath, some reordered, are per Draenger at 126. Draenger noted that the members of the youth group, no matter where they were, "always greeted the Sabbath Bride with the same song." *Id.*

The reference to stomping lives to the ground is from a 1941 poem by Mordecai Gebertig of Kazimierz, the Jewish section of Krakow, murdered with his family in 1942. He wrote "I had a home. In the corner of poverty, I had a home, once upon a time... I had a home like any other man... Then came the enemy who destroyed my world. The meaning of my life stomped to the ground by his boots..."

"For three lines in the history books" is based on the comment by Akiva leader Aharon Liebeskind that they were fighting "for three lines in history."

The italicized words regarding the angel of death were spoken by Gusta Draenger. Draenger at 127-128.

Tuesday October 20, 1942 Anna

The italicized language about fear of a trivial death is a slightly revised quote from Gusta Draenger. Draenger at 55.

Tuesday October 20, 1942 Szymon

The bar attack is loosely based on the December 1942 attack in Krakow on the Cyganeria Café in which several German officers were killed. Draenger at 6-7, fn. 6.

Thursday October 22, 1942 Anna

The search by the huge German policewoman, the reference to her as a witch, and the cutting of seams in Anna's clothes are loosely based on the experience of Renia Kukielka described in Batalion at 314-315.

Thursday October 22, 1942 Reuven

The italicized language about the reactions of people on the death train is from the recollections of a twenty-two-year-old man named Aaron who, with five hundred others, was deported to Treblinka after the Germans tricked them to come out of hiding and register for a supposed prisoner swap because they had "relatives in Palestine." He and a few other young men escaped from the train; the rest were gassed. Gilbert at 511-512.

The reference to Germans shooting at Jews trying to escape from a moving train is based on a Nazi's description of his experience on a train to Belzec in September 1942. Klee at 232-235.

The italicized language about Reuven trying to hide under the train, his capture and the way he was killed are based on the eyewitness account by Jacob Krzepicki regarding an incident at Treblinka. Gilbert at 460-461.

FRIDAY OCTOBER 23, 1942
ITZHAK

Ringelblum's notes were placed in a milk can, buried, and discovered after the war. The Germans murdered Ringelblum and his family. Ringelblum at xxi.

KARL BECK

The name "Operation Heinrich," in honor of Heinrich Schmidt in the novel, is based on "Operation Reinhard," the German extermination of Polish Jews at Belzec, Sobibor and Treblinka named in honor of SS General Reinhard Heydrich, assassinated by Czech resistance fighters. Gilbert at 363.

SATURDAY OCTOBER 24, 1942 JOZEF

According to the United States Holocaust Museum, between 20,000 and 30,000 Jews fought in partisan groups in the forests of eastern Europe, including the Parczew Forest, an area "ideal" for partisan activity due to its forests, lakes, and few roads. https://encyclopedia.ushmm.org/content/en/article/partisan-groups-in-the-parczew-forests

THE SAME DAY AT 4:30 P.M. ITZHAK, ANNA AND IRINA

The reference to the Beitar boys honors an incident when more than a hundred young Zionist pioneers – "the cream of the young people" – were deported from Warsaw to the gas chambers. Ringelblum at 257.

Eyewitness accounts of Jews singing Hatikvah upon entering the gas chambers, sometimes along with their home country's anthem, include Greek Jews, Polish Jews, Czech Jews. Gilbert at 622, 636 and 658-659. Hatikvah became Israel's national anthem.

The words said and the Germans' reactions when Anna spoke at the ghetto gate are almost exactly as experienced by Michael Line when he and his family escaped deportation from the Warsaw Ghetto. Paulsson at 91-92.

EPILOGUE – Ashes and Dust

MAY 8, 1945

Poland did not become free when the war ended. Instead, it suffered under Soviet Russian domination and communist rule until 1989. Hopefully, Szymon, who might have fought in the Polish underground's 1944 Warsaw uprising, would have lived to see Polish democracy.

JULY 12, 1945 GMUND, AUSTRIA MORDECAI

The execution of the Nazi in Austria is based on Blum at 188-201.

"Hannah" was the famous poet, Hannah Senesch. The British operation in which she and other Jews parachuted behind German lines had been preceded by discussions about sending Jews into Poland, but Polish Jews had been exterminated by the time the idea had a chance to become operational. Baumel-Schwartz at 5-8.

"Menachem" was Menachem Begin. A Polish Jew, Begin had fled the Nazis, was imprisoned by the Russians and later joined the Polish "Anders' Army," which spent time in Palestine. With his Polish officer's encouragement, Begin stayed in Palestine when the Poles left, became the Irgun's leader and, many years later, prime minister of Israel. Begin's young wife managed to escape both Nazis and communists and get to Palestine, arrested twice along the way.

The Irgun called a truce with the British early in World War II and did not attack British institutions until 1944, when it was clear that Nazi Germany would be defeated.

The italicized language regarding the man who chose to die with his family is, revised for context, per Szymon Datner. Gilbert at 531-532.

Jews who tried to re-establish their lives in Poland encountered a wave of Polish anti-Jewish riots and murders in 1945-1946, resulting in more than half of Poland's surviving Jews fleeing Poland. Gilbert at 816–819. The number of Jews killed by Poles after the war was likely 1,500. Polonsky at 604. Yad Vashem would ultimately recognize more than seven thousand Polish "Righteous Gentiles" who risked or lost their lives saving Jews from the Nazis.

SEPTEMBER 24, 1945 SANTA MARIA DI-BAGNI ITALY

The character Bela Sztern is based partially on real-life experiences of Bela Hazan. https://jwa.org/encyclopedia/article/hazan-bela-yaari

Hair shaving as punishment in the Neusalz camp is based on Czarnecka, Barbara, *Women's Hair in Lager Narratives*. Acta Universitatis Lodziensis at 162. https://pdfs.semanticscholar.org/6cd4/72dd68945907e28373aace2e71a1ec87342e.pdf

Organized by Jewish underground groups in Palestine, thousands of Holocaust survivors attempted to sail from Europe to Palestine from 1945 until Israel's independence on May 14, 1948. The British intercepted the overwhelming majority and interned the passengers in Cyprus. Sachar at 267–270.

OCTOBER 1, 1945 FRANKFURT GERMANY MORDECAI

More than 250,000 Jews lived in displaced persons camps in the years following the war's end in 1945. Most remained in the camps for years, with nowhere to go. Ultimately most went to Israel, and many started new lives in the United States or other countries. https://encyclopedia.ushmm.org/content/en/article/displaced-persons

ACKNOWLEDGMENTS

I thank Chaim Mazo of Mazo Publishers for his untiring effort to bring my manuscript from draft to publication. And thanks again to Jim Frazier for his creativity and excellent front cover design and artwork.

Thank you to everyone who kindly read and commented on one or more of my drafts. Jeff Sokoloff, who read earlier versions more than once, and Hal Lerman, who focused on Part One. Thanks also to Elana Rubinstein for her early guidance.

Thanks to the Gratzes: my former student, Seth, who took the time, when he had very little, to comment on Part One, and my current student, Anna, who brought the perspective of an intelligent, well-read high school junior to the entire manuscript and then some. She offered innumerable helpful comments and suggestions.

Thanks again to each and all the Lefkowitz League: Beth, Kevin, Jessica, Allie and Johnny, each of whom read at least one full draft along the way, for their support, ideas, critiques, and suggestions. Thanks to Rabbi Kevin for writing most of the Rabbi Leibman letter and to Allie for multiple suggestions and edits. To Jessica for real-world accuracy and Dr. Jonathan for medical aspects. And to Beth for her endless support and for reading and commenting throughout the entire process.

ABOUT THE AUTHOR

Jeff Lefkowitz is the author of the *Window to Yesterday* Jewish history novels for middle schoolers. A writer, teacher and lawyer, he earned a history degree, *Phi Beta Kappa*, from the University of Texas.

Jeff explored Warsaw, Krakow, and elsewhere in Poland as part of his extensive research for this book. He is from Houston, Texas, where he and his wife Beth raised their four children.

www.ingramcontent.com/pod-product-compliance
Lightning Source LLC
Chambersburg PA
CBHW030935260626
47169CB00002B/482

* 9 7 8 1 9 5 6 3 8 1 9 7 9 *